Melissa Corliss DeLorenzo (signature)

The Mosquito Hours

A Novel

Melissa Corliss DeLorenzo

Thorncraft Publishing
Clarksville, Tennessee

ISBN-13: 978-0-9857947-2-9
ISBN-10: 0-9857947-2-0

Cover Design by MediaWorks in Clarksville, TN. Online at
http://www.mediaworksdesign.com/
Cover photograph, "Beach houses" by Melissa Corliss DeLorenzo.
"Mosquito" drawing by Melissa Corliss DeLorenzo.
No part of this book cover may be reproduced, by any means, without written permission from Thorncraft Publishing.

Library of Congress Control Number: 2013957635

Thorncraft Publishing
P.O. Box 31121
Clarksville, TN 37040
http://www.thorncraftpublishing.com
thorncraftpublishing@gmail.com

10 9 8 7 6 5 4 3 2 1

The Mosquito Hours is dedicated to my family and friends who have supported my writing and couldn't wait for this book to be published—your encouragement means so much more than you know. Many, many thanks to you.

ACKNOWLEDGMENTS

It occurred to me recently that I would not be a writer had it not been for the guidance of my teachers. My junior and senior high school English teachers: Al Caron, Armand Marchand, A.B. Walsh, George Charbonneau and Jim Mandly; my teachers at Naropa University, especially Keith Abbott, Bobbie Louise Hawkins and Reed Bye—thank you for helping me become a writer.

Diane Saarinen of Saima Agency—many thanks for your guidance and advice. (And fun conversation!)

Terri Giuliano Long—thank you for sharing your advice and experience. They have been a source of inspiration and motivation.

My gratitude to the editors who have provided the invaluable feedback and direction that has shaped this book for the better. Thank you Jackie Cangro, Kitty Madden and Beverly Fisher.

I am beyond grateful to those who have given their time and energy to read this book in its various drafts—especially since they happen to be moms with small kids. These wonderful friends include Denise Permatteo, McCormick Templeman and Sarah Markowski. I am fully aware of how precious that time and energy is at this point in your life and I am humbled by your attention, feedback and support. Thank you!

Special thanks must be extended to Nicole Daly. You not only graciously gave of your time, but your enthusiasm for the book is unparalleled and bolstered me through the tough times when writer's doubt crept in. Thanks for your friendship and encouragement!

To Shana Thornton a multitude of blessings! Working with you these past few years has helped me grow as a writer in so many ways. I am overjoyed to be embarking on this new literary adventure with you. My life is richer for calling you friend first and foremost.

I am lucky to have the most extraordinary sister. Rebecca Beck: thank you, thank you, thank you just for being you! And for all the support: literary, birthing, mothering, life. You also happen to be one of my most valued readers. Thank you for helping me work through some of the thornier details—in fiction and in life.

There cannot be enough thanks for my parents, Jeanne and Michael Corliss. Thank you for the unfailing support, encouragement and love you have graced me with my entire life. I am grateful everyday to have you as my guides. (And Mom, thanks for all the first sentences.)

Last, but most, Jim DeLorenzo. For everything. I love our little life. Thank you.

The Mosquito Hours

One's destiny is never a place but a new way of seeing things.
Henry Miller

Anyone who thinks they're too small to matter has never spent the night with a mosquito in their room.
Aunt Anne

MELISSA CORLISS DELORENZO

During summer they sit on the porch at the back of the house where the nearly ceaseless wind tempers the unruly heat. The porch, which opens out to the ocean, is pieced together with stones collected from the beach—stones smoothed by the coarse work of sand and the perpetual motion of water—then hand-fitted one at a time, many years ago. The house is old, but the stones are ageless. Here is where the women sit for a reprieve from the fever of summer.

But when the light begins to wane and the peak of the sky is a deep blue flecked with the first view of stars and the sun sinks into the roiling Atlantic, the harbingers of the dawning night arrive. Palms slap bare skin, hands flutter shooing motions around heads.

Behind the house, there is a small backyard—a short expanse of sandy beach grass—then the pure sand of the bare shore spreads out toward the water. Beach plum bushes, switchgrass, salt meadow hay and Indian grass, green ash tree, boisterous black-eyed susans and bright pink cone flowers—big, bawdy, audacious things—grow impossibly in the gritty soil. Lovely and bright. A flagstone path leads to a screen house. A black wrought-iron table, chairs and benches—the kind one would expect to see in

5

such a backyard at such a house—sit pertly in the midst of the beach grass. They sink with deep indentations into the ground stone beneath them inside the old twisted mesh and metal frame. Patched screens, rusting metal.

"It serves its purpose," Anne says by way of explanation.

"We need it once the mosquitoes get going," says Millie.

"It's ugly as sin, though, isn't it?" Anne titters.

"You would know, Anne!" Millie cackles, ends with a little snort. "You would know all about that!"

Their laughter burbles up and spills like the breakers. Pulls back like water flowing out over small stones.

"It serves its purpose," Millie agrees.

They say it's what's needed for the mosquito hours.

1

Vivian—Carry On

Waning Moon.

A solitary witch tonight.

Vivian stands before the ocean. She turns her face to the sky and searches out the moon, finds a delicate sliver. Two hurricane lamps swiveled into the sand contain white tapers; the flame holds steady inside each glass. A small empty cauldron squats between the lamps. Strong blessing incense burns. Its scent mingles with that of the ocean; the blending both calms and steadies her. Vivian can hear the sound of her own breath. She inhales and exhales evenly until she locates her center. She takes up the cauldron and holds it high above her in deference to the Goddess. She lowers it and breathes silently into its opaque black concavity. She conjures the negativity she wishes to expel. Her exhaled breath carries all of it. She closes her eyes. Then she swiftly turns the cauldron upside down.

"I come to you, Rhiannon, Lunar Goddess, Illuminated One. I give the contents of this vessel to the Earth, that it may receive my burdens, so I may move forward and become whole."

She makes an offering of milk and herbs. She watches the candles glimmer and flare. Vivian sits for a long time in the sand, unwilling to break the spell she has cast.

Finally, the late June air cools enough to bring her back to her body, and she shivers, stands and closes her Circle.

The waning moon is the time to let go.

Vivian will let go.

In the early mornings, Vivian sips herbal tea at the big table in her small kitchen.

She cherishes the early hours. Soon, the house will thrum with the energy of the others who live within it, but now there is only the slow streaming hum of a dawning day. A mild breeze flutters the curtains and carries into the kitchen the scent of the backyard flower beds. The morning birds repeat their ancient songs in the trees at the back of her yard.

From her robe pocket, she removes the letter sent by the mortgage lender. The creases and corners of the paper are soft and pulpy, unfolded and refolded as many times as this letter has been, and while the words penetrate, at the same time they seem a mismatched jumble. It is a matter of not wanting to believe that which the words come together to tell her. And yet this final notice of foreclosure is irrefutably believable and, moreover, she knew it was coming.

Ethan pads into the kitchen, his small feet slap lightly on the cool floor. He climbs onto her lap soundlessly, his body bed-warm and sweet-smelling—of sugar, of butter cookies. Vivian pulls him close and his honey-colored curls touch her, soft under her chin. She folds the letter once more and places it back in her pocket.

"Good morning," she says.

"Hello, Grammy."

"Mommy's still sleeping?"

He nods, the curls sweet on her neck. She smiles. "And your baby sisters, too?" He nods again, and she savors the movement of those curls once more.

She pours him some milk. Then they sit quietly and the peace of his small soul rolls unrestrained and she closes her eyes and breathes it in.

"Coffee..." Tania groans. She shuffles to the counter and stops in front of the cold and empty coffeemaker. "There's no coffee."

"Oh, I forgot to make it, honey," Vivian tells her daughter. "I've got my tea and Ethan's got his milk," Vivian says and shrugs. She watches her daughter pull the coffee can and filters out of the cabinet.

"You know what we should get?" Tania stops and turns to face her mother. "An espresso machine." She resumes scooping coffee grounds. She fills the machine with cold tap water. "Not big like the one at work. Do you know," she says, turning to face Vivian again, "those machines cost, like, ten thousand dollars? Refurbished!" She turns and flicks on the coffeemaker. "I mean a little one. Mr. Coffee. Maybe I'll look for a deal."

"Are you making coffee? If you are making coffee, I will love you forever," Guin says and keels into a chair. Her two babies follow close behind in rapid crawl. They reach her and pull themselves to standing at her legs. They jabber at her. She reaches down and pulls them both onto her lap.

"You love me no matter what," says Tania. "But I am making coffee."

Vivian breathes and squeezes Ethan. He squirms away and is off and running. He calls back, "I want cereal!"

Guin begins to stand. Vivian tells her daughter, "I'll get it." She touches Guin's long, curly hair as she passes by her. "I have to get up anyway. I need to get to the salon early today. I've got a color coming in at eight." She places the cereal and milk, Ethan's bowl and spoon on the table, then turns down the hallway to go get dressed.

Before she leaves out the kitchen door, she smiles and says, "You all have a blessed day, my loves!"

Vivian slides into her good old car. Her girl, Sally. It's the VW she bought when she was twenty-six. Her girls were kids. A mellow gold color, tan interior. Antiquated tape deck—she has a box of cassettes that she slides under the passenger seat. Frank is always trying to get her a new car, but old five-speed Sally is what Vivian still wants. She must keep replacing what goes but the essence of good Sally never changes even as her parts do. Vivian sits behind the wheel and, pressing the clutch firmly down to the floor the way Sally likes it, she turns the key. Stevie Nicks comes up through the speakers. Loud, her voice air, ethereal. Singing of stillness and possession and loss.

In 1977 when this song was new, Vivian was only six years old. She discovered Stevie for herself in the '80s. She was twelve years old in 1983—the year her father died. Stevie Nicks' *Wild Heart* was how she endured. She fell in love with Stevie on MTV. Stevie spinning in slow motion, chiffon billowing, singing, "If Anyone Falls," the unwavering strength in the song's passage. Stevie gesturing, *stand back*. There was no one quite like her. The scarves and long-skirted dresses, the bell sleeves. She was so pretty but so sure. So knowing and singular.

The gypsy.

Vivian, too, is a gypsy—she, like Stevie, leans toward flowing fabrics, empire waists, peasant skirts. Celtic lore and Goddess worship. All of it together draws a picture. She supposes there is some accuracy and truth in the depictions people sketch of one another. Everyone slips into a pattern, a recognizable shape, but the story behind that which embodies always breaks the mold into which one has been poured.

No one knows exactly what the heart of another carries.

Sally purrs and Stevie roars and Vivian breathes and shifts into first gear.

What was that thing Mark Twain said about the weather here? *If you don't like the weather in New England, just wait a few minutes.* Something like that, thinks Vivian as she cranes her neck to peer through Sally's windshield. Out one window charcoal gray clouds darken the sky and out the opposite, a clear blue spreads into the infinite. But the blackness out over the dunes and the harbor is moving in fast. Another storm. This weather has been odd so far this summer—a disconcerting season. Unexpected storms rush in, kick up a big fuss, and rush out. Then the sun returns to the rain-washed blue sky as though nothing out of the ordinary has just stomped through. There is nothing so unusual about these storms except for their recent frequency, their newborn ferocity. The winds are fierce and destructive; hail pelts the dune grasses. Everyone must rush through their houses to close the windows. It seems no one will leave home with open windows lately. The weather forecasters aren't even predicting these storms. Did she close the window in her bedroom? Well, no matter. Let the next owners worry about damage. They will probably put down new carpet in the room anyhow—it's old and worn. Something she was saving up to replace.

There is a little time before she must open the salon, so she goes out of her way and drives over the causeway and parks old Sally facing the open ocean. She waits as the water turns steely. The wind swirls. Whitecaps form, and the dune grass and beach roses bend close to the ground. Her hands grip the steering wheel as the rain first spatters and plinks on the windshield, the ocean, the land, and then drills ever faster, ever stronger. The wind pushes it all around. Sally rocks on her tires. It is loud. Vivian looks for seagulls—how do they fare in this?—and she can find none in her limited view. Maybe she simply can't see them in between the small spaces of insistent rain. Perhaps they hide in the places they know to go. Don't all creatures? (Here is Vivian safe inside Sally.)

The rain slows; the quiet descends in increments. And then there is an instant that feels as an in-between moment. The time between what was before the storm and what will come after. A suspended moment. The sounds and sights of the storm pass, the present restrained into quiet and stillness.

The sky blues, the sun ruptures the clouds, rays through rainbow drops of water on the windshield. The grasses sway in the usual light breeze, the gulls swoop and cry. When Vivian turns to look out her back window, the sky is as blue as that in front of her. And it is as though she imagined the storm—the whole of it. As if it never happened but for the tell-tale wetness it left in its wake. But it is drying fast and any moment there will be no evidence of it at all. Such turbulent and black moments as this give her pause to wonder their meaning and that which is unveiled in the brevity of the curtain's parting.

She inhales, listens for a moment to the sound of her breath, turns the key and drives to work.

Wet tires mark a fading path behind her.

Vivian unlocks The Hair Shop's door. She is almost always the first one to arrive. She turns on the lights and goes out back to start a pot of coffee for the other girls who will filter in soon. She heats some water in the microwave to brew a fortifying mug of tea for herself.

Although she likes her work and as much as it is a good and honest living, it nevertheless requires some bracing.

As she drinks her tea and tidies her rented booth, decorated with photos of her children and grandchildren and a framed adage—*Hello, You Beautiful Being of Light!*—embroidered in bright colors, the other stylists filter in. Most of these girls are in their twenties, nearly fresh out of beauty school. Lately Vivian feels older than the thirty-nine years that mark out the length of her life so far.

Becoming a hair stylist was not her original plan. When Vivian was seventeen and *only* seventeen and not seventeen *and* pregnant, she was a smart girl. She and Raine applied to colleges together—their teen-girl dreams aimed at Smith. They visited the campus in the fall of their senior year of high school. The foliage was at peak, the trees densely chromatic against a classic New England backdrop of old buildings and hilly green. It feels like a long time ago now, but there are moments when a certain slant of light illuminates the beach and Vivian feels as though her old friend could walk right through the cordgrass and sit down next to her in the sand as though no years have passed.

Raine, the product of real hippies. Raine who was granted freedom and trust far beyond that which Vivian knew. Raine who introduced Vivian to books she'd never read and ideas of which she'd never conceived.

"Don't feed the patriarchy, Vivian. Stop going to that misogynistic church. Come worship the Goddess with me."

"My mother will kill me."

"Do you really believe all that stuff?"

"No. But my mother doesn't need to know that because, I repeat, she will kill me. Or at least throw a hissy fit which will make me want to kill myself. She can be positively hysterical when she wants to be."

"I think she hates me."

Vivian's mother was convinced that Vivian was being dangerously influenced by Raine. This meant sex, drugs, alcohol, sex, boys, naughty words.

Sex.

"She doesn't hate you." More likely she was praying novenas or at least a rosary or two on Raine's behalf. "She's just old."

In part, her mother was right—Raine was influencing her. But what Vivian was soaking up from Raine was none of the things her mother feared—instead music and religion and books and woman-power, which neither Vivian nor her mother knew then were a lot more influential. Funny thing was, Raine needed Vivian in ways that Vivian needed no one. Vivian was only starting to realize that if one were influencing another, it was she having an effect on Raine. She was beginning to know her own strength of spirit and conviction and she found her mother's concern insulting. "And she doesn't think I have my own mind."

By the time Vivian received her acceptance letter, she was pregnant. She heard that Raine got hers, too. But by then Raine was no longer her friend and Vivian had no choice but to decline acceptance.

So now, more than twenty years later, she is a hair stylist and it is a good living. She likes the work and especially the people. Whether she sees her clients once a week or once every six weeks, she likes making them feel better about themselves. Her father used to say that even if your clothes were slightly out of fashion and your shoes were cheap, as long as your hair was freshly cut and styled, you could get away with anything.

Vivian places a CD in the player. Stevie sounded so good in the car and Vivian's musical cravings are seasonal, so *Wild Heart* fits her summer mood. She turns it up nice and loud and the lush guitar starts in with the muted thump of the drums. She closes her eyes since this is soul music. One of the younger women groans predictably.

"Does it need to be so loud?"

"Yes," says Vivian. "It does. Just listen and try to appreciate it."

Samantha picks up the CD box. "This is, like, twenty-five years old."

Vivian pauses at that. No, it can't be twenty-five years. Then she does the math. Oh, yes it can.

"So, what does that have to do with anything? Any Beatles record is much older than this one."

"But no one listens to The Beatles!" Samantha says.

"What?" says Vivian, "Of course they do! It's The Beatles."

"*Old* people."

Vivian laughs. "Oh, Sam!" And she spins around like Stevie in the "Gypsy" video, flicks her hair around her head. "Here's a deal—you listen to this now and I will listen to anything you like for the rest of the day. Okay?"

"Fine," Samantha relents.

Vivian remembers when things like this were acutely important—the music that was playing, the clothes she wore. She only doesn't remember the shift to not caring so much. When something heavier replaced those things.

She looks up when the bell on the door jingles and Frank ambles in wearing his gambeson. In one hand, he carries a piece of chain mail. It is part of his suit of armor.

"Hi, Frank," the young stylists chime.

"Hi, girls. How are you today?"

"Sam," he takes her hand. "That is a very pretty dress. Very summery." He smiles and speaks with a soft voice, his face close to hers, his hand on her arm. She giggles.

He moves along, from girl to girl, with his tall, lanky frame, his thinning hair, google glasses bugging his blue eyes. He dispenses long, tight hugs, conjures a compliment for each, circling his way around the room.

Girls of all ages adore Frank: young women, middle-aged, early retirees, the old ladies who come in for their blue rinses. None are insusceptible to his charm, capable of resisting his cloying but sincere flirtation.

Vivian watches from her station with a mixture of amusement and incredulity, her hands busy organizing her supplies for the day ahead. Amusement, because she would expect nothing else from Frank, and incredulity, because his effect on women never fails to amaze her. Frank carries the chain mail over to her. It is the coif that is worn under his helmet. "Good morning," he says smiling, and hugs her longest and tightest. "Can you take a look at this and fix the broken links?"

In college, Frank founded Wyvern Medieval Combat Society, a medieval role-playing league, to which he recruited Vivian. So, as a matter of necessity, she cultivated the skill of repairing and constructing chain mail over the last twenty-something years of friendship with Frank.

Frank owns a comic book store called Valinor. "*En hommage*," says Frank. Most often he tips from the waist in a bow and when he says this, flourishes his hand. Most people have no idea what it means, but the ones who do— the comic book connoisseurs and ornate ceramic dragon collectors, the Dungeons and Dragons players—swoon.

"Isn't it a little warm to be wearing that?" asks Vivian, eyeing the padded jacket normally worn under armor that Frank today wears over his tee shirt.

"Getting there," he says. "I'm meeting Bob about some armor he is selling. I might buy it if it fits." He leans in close, "Did you tell your girls yet?"

Vivian shakes her head slowly.

"You have to do it soon." He takes her hand.

"I know," she says softly.

"It'll be okay." He squeezes her hand. "Thanks for looking at my coif." He smiles and hugs her goodbye. The door jingles his departure.

Later in the morning, Alison, Frank's ex-wife, comes in for her monthly haircut. She is one of Vivian's long-time clients. Alison is one of those tiny women who has to shop for clothes in the petite section with short lengths and slim cuts, who always complains she can't find clothes that fit because she is so small and thin. She is a real estate agent and smiles pertly—hair perfectly smooth—on FOR SALE signs all over town.

Alison no longer blames Vivian for the demise of her marriage. She never blamed Vivian in full, but at least in part because she maintained prior and during—and does so still—that *Frank never loved nor will ever love anyone as much as he loves Vivian*. This is a melodramatic assessment and bears nothing on the fact that Alison is immovably difficult when she wants to be.

In spite of it, Vivian shares an odd but only occasionally uncomfortable relationship with Alison. They would most likely share nothing more than a stylist and client acquaintance if not for the complicated connection to Frank. Aside from him, they have nothing in common but motherhood. When Vivian can think of nothing to say to Alison, she resorts to asking about the kids, even though she already knows everything from Frank. It's something to say to soften the air when it gets tight.

For about a year after the divorce, Alison went to a different hairdresser. Then one day she showed up at The Hair Shop and announced, "I can't find anyone who cuts my hair as well as you, so I'm just coming back."

Vivian made no comment. She cleaned up the mess some other stylist had made of Alison's hair and cut it the way Alison liked it, the way she had been wearing it for more than twenty years—sleek, black, shiny, angled bob with bangs. Vivian asked, "So, how are the kids?" They picked up right where they'd left off.

"Hi, Vivian," Alison says today.

"Hey, Alison. Come sit in my chair. What are we doing today?"

"As if you need to ask. The Usual. Capital 'U.' I'm getting some grays, Vivian." And indeed there are a few bright white streaks, stark and showy amongst the opaque black.

"We can do a rinse, quick and easy," says Vivian.

Alison waves her hand dismissing the idea. "I guess I should give aging gracefully a try."

"I guess that's the admirable thing to do," says Vivian. "Not too many people are willing, I can tell you. I do a lot of colors." She whispers the last part.

Alison laughs. "Maybe I'll change my mind when it gets more obvious."

They are quiet for a moment while Vivian shampoos. As they walk from the sink over to Vivian's chair, Vivian says, "So, how are the kids?"

Vivian recalls a conversation she had with Frank shortly after his split from Alison.

"Vivian, did you think we'd make it?" he asked her.

"You and Alison? I don't know. I guess I hoped you would. It's just...you know..." she paused, searching, "two big personalities."

He'd been quiet. Then, "Why didn't you warn me?"

"Would you have listened."

"Maybe. Probably not."

"Of course you wouldn't have."

That was five years ago. Alison and Frank's kids are seven now—a set of twins, a boy and a girl. Tobias and Alexandra. They were conceived in a lab and placed inside Alison's chemically ready and waiting uterus. This was after eight years of trying. When Vivian's daughter, Guin, spontaneously and accidentally conceived twins (as Vivian had twenty years earlier) Alison, embittered by her body's failure to naturally reproduce, said, "It hardly seems fair how some of us go through physical and emotional hell to get kids and others just forget to take their pill, spread 'em for Pickle in the backseat of his car and, voilà, two babies!"

Vivian stopped, scissors and comb poised in the air, and spoke to Alison in the mirror. "Alison. That is my daughter you're talking so lovely about."

"Sorry. Oh, Vivian, I'm sorry. I'm still so mad about the whole thing."

Vivian sighed and went back to work on Alison's hair. "I know, I know. Feast or famine. Look at me."

"Feast or famine," Alison agreed.

She says today as she sits in Vivian's chair getting a Usual, "Frank was here earlier?"

"How did you know?" Vivian asks her.

Alison points to the chain mail. She sighs. "Frank," she says and rolls her eyes. Alison and Frank get along better as the years distance them more and more from their shattered marriage, but Vivian doubts they will ever like each other again.

"You never did get into the Society," Vivian says, her eyes on her hands, the gleaming black woven through her fingers, the silver of her scissors flashing.

"No—I always thought it was ridiculous. No offense." She pauses a beat. "Listen, Vivian, I'm so sorry about the house. I could kick myself for not stepping in when I heard you were going with Phil Cabral. I should have told you not to trust him. He'll do anything for a sale. I should have handled it myself." It goes unsaid that this was during the time Alison was not speaking to Vivian.

"I rolled the dice," said Vivian. Simple truths are the best she finds at times like now.

"Frank said you're thinking about moving in with your mom." Alison makes a face.

"I'll be okay." This is what Vivian can muster.

"What are you going to do next?"

Vivian laughs shortly. "With the credit I have now? I have no idea. I'll figure something out. I always do."

"That's true. You always make it through life's scrapes. I really admire that about you, Vivian."

She touches her hair and looks in the mirror.

Made perfect by Vivian once again.

Vivian gets home from work just after five o'clock. The late June sun is beginning its daily fade. Tania is in the kitchen. University is on summer break, otherwise Tania is hardly home, the kind of student she is.

"Hi, honey," Vivian says.

"Hi-ya, Mumma."

Tania stands at the counter, tan already, in cut-off jeans, the threads trailing down her thighs, and a tee shirt that reads *Feminism: the radical notion that women are people*. Vivian smiles when she sees the boxes of mac and cheese already on the counter, the big pot of water heating on the stove. Tania cuts up vegetables for a salad. A book lays on the counter held open on one side by a can of beans and on the other by a bottle of dish soap.

"Don't you think you're at risk for cutting your finger off when you try to read and chop at the same time?" Vivian asks her.

Tania's eyes remain on her book as she slowly slices a tomato. "I'm tops at multi-tasking."

"Do you know when Guin is going to be home?"

"She said by supper, so I would think any minute now. Enjoy the silence while it lasts," says Tania. She tips the cutting board over the salad bowl, dumping the chopped tomato on top of the lettuce without removing her eyes from her book. Tania's hands move to the boxes of mac and cheese and as she tears them open, there is a small pang deep in Vivian's belly.

Vivian is a terrible cook.

She is not one of those mothers who baked cookies and nutritious casseroles. She tried to remedy her deficiency over the years through the use of cookbooks, women's magazine recipes, Julia Child on PBS. She eventually resorted to a system of weekly scheduled cooking comprised of easy things she could manage well-enough. She has grown to love her system (even if her daughters have not) for its simplicity and the cessation of the necessity to plan yet one more aspect of her busy life. Mexican, which for Vivian means tacos or something rolled in a flour tortilla; macaroni and cheese (from the blue and yellow box—generic brand); Italian (box of spaghetti tossed with jar of sauce); fish and potatoes; pizza night (from Village Pizza). Saturday features everything left over from the week, which Vivian calls fridge supper. Random vegetables and salad are sprinkled through the week for the sake of good health.

On Sunday they go to her mother's house and eat a real Sunday dinner that Aunt Anne cooks. With little surprise, this is everyone's favorite.

Today is Tuesday, and there the yellow and blue boxes stand familiarly on the counter. Vivian notices the water has come to a boil and is glad to have something to do. She dumps the pasta into the pot. She stirs it and watches it spin around and she thinks she must tell the girls about the house and it has to be tonight. She is running out of time. She looks around the kitchen. She runs her hand along the counter.

Guin and the children blow in, obliterating the quiet.

Vivian takes a deep breath.

Vivian's split-level house was built in the 1970s. The original shag carpeting covers the floor—wood paneling overlays every wall. She could not afford to remove the paneling and replace it with sheetrock so she simply covered it over thickly with primer then paint with names she liked—flowing river, pearl moon, sunrise yellow. Frank said he would sheetrock it for her—"You can't just paint over it!"—but she knows that just because Frank doesn't know how to do something will not stop him from trying. She only laughed, waved her hand, "Oh, Frank! It'll be pretty!"

Vivian's house is not a perfect house, is not a dream house. But it is her house. And soon it will not be hers anymore. This is what it says on the paper they sent her— the one she keeps folded up in her pocket. The one she has read too many times, as if by reading it just one more time the action of running her eyes over the words will change their meaning. If she doesn't leave, they will come and remove her belongings and leave them on the lawn. Not her lawn. *The* lawn.

Once the loan adjusted, she fell too many payments behind, and the writing was on the painted-over wood paneling. But this house had been hers. Even for these few short years—hers. Now she is back to where she has always been which is nowhere with nothing to show but a lot of debt and trouble she can't juggle. She tries to think of this as an opportunity for growth. She performs another in a string of little candle spells to invoke positivity.

She takes a deep breath.

She leaves the kitchen and sits on the living room couch (still hers) and wonders what words she will use to tell her daughters. Then those she will combine to tell her mother. She imagines the shape her mother's features will take, the disappointment clear in her expression. She will have to go to her mother—there is no other choice right now. She has tried to think ten ways around it, but there is nothing else to do. She is so far behind that she can't even afford to rent a cheap place. If she goes back to her mom's, she can start over. She says a quick prayer to the Goddess for strength. She closes her eyes, imagines a bright white light around her.

"Mom! Supper's ready!"

She takes another deep breath and goes into the kitchen where her daughters and grandchildren sit at the table. She stands and watches them and her eyes fill even though she has promised herself she would not cry.

"Mom? What is it?" Guin says. Sweet Guin. Vivian's tears spill.

"You're freakin' me out, Mom," says Tania.

Vivian takes yet another deep breath.

She tells her girls the story of how the bank and the real estate broker told her—assured her—she would be able to refinance when the mortgage adjusted. She tells them that the house was not worth enough after the market tanked and neither was there enough equity to refinance. She tells them the bank refused to make any alterations to the interest rate. She tells them the bank is taking the house. She doesn't tell them that the bank will put it on the market at a fraction of what she owes, at a fraction of what she would have ended up paying them if only they could have given her a rate she could afford. She doesn't tell them that the bank will take a huge loss rather than throw her a small break. She doesn't tell them that she feels a little broken inside. She tells them it will be a new start and she smiles. She radiates white energy at her daughters. Her daughters are not children—Guin has three kids of her own, and Tania is almost finished with college. They are twenty-two. It's just that after so many missteps and years of struggle, she was finally offering them something besides trash. And now it is going away. She does not want to feel sorry for herself. And she won't. The

Universe gives you only what you can manage and the Universe does not make mistakes. She must have faith.

Guin cries, though she is trying not to, and Vivian knows it's not that she feels sorry for herself, but for Vivian. Guin, the sensitive one. She knows what this house means to Vivian. Tania is incensed at the injustice of the system; the preying upon of lower-income people, people who would be easily lured by the promise of the American Dream withheld from them so long. The promise at any cost. They duped the low people, is what Tania says. They preyed on their lack of knowledge. Vivian understands that Tania doesn't mean to imply that her mother is stupid. Her girls are good.

They both say, "Why didn't you tell us?" They say they would have helped.

"It's not your name on the mortgage," Vivian says, her voice gentle.

"Oh, Mom," Guin sighs. Tania, her face set, looks out straight ahead at what seems like nothing. (Although Vivian knows better.)

Because—what? Tania is going to quit college? And Guin is going to give up buying diapers and paying doctor co-payments and all the things the kids need just to give Vivian some of her meager waitressing money? Vivian knows a little something about being a single mother and she knows a little something about how far you get without going to college. *No*, that's what. *No*.

It is late June, just before summer solstice.

Everything is about to change.

Again.

At dawn on the summer solstice, Vivian gathers with her coven on the shore in the moments before sunrise. The dunes ascend behind them. They silently watch the sun rise until it floats on the surface of the waves that from

Vivian's vantage seem small ripples on the line of the horizon. The waves swell mightily, but from the sand and stone upon which she stands with the edge of the water at her toes, they appear small.

It is the longest day of the year.

Carol, the High Priestess, holds her athame—the witch's ceremonial blade, small and narrow—and walks slowly around in the sand, creating their Circle of sacred space. With an outstretched hand, Carol invites the women in.

"Daughter, how do you enter this Circle?" Carol asks each of them, one at a time.

"In perfect love and perfect trust, in the light and love of the Goddess," they respond.

Candles mark the quadrants—north, south, east and west—and one burns at the altar Carol has erected in the center. Vivian visualizes a ring of bright light etched into the sand, encircling them. The elements of earth, fire, air and water are called upon to watch over the rite. The Goddess and God are praised and beckoned. Vivian closes her eyes and warms as she is filled with the light she has grown to understand is joy—that this practice has granted her.

"The grand tribes have been gathering at midsummer since ancient times. The Goddess manifests as Mother Earth and the God as the Sun King," Carol intones as they stand in Circle.

They keep a sacred fire burning throughout the gathering as they welcome the rising sun at dawn. They dance around the fire. Together they eat the ceremonial cakes and drink the honeyed wine. Vivian makes a pledge to Mother Earth, to herself, *I will make no more mistakes I will fix this I will move ahead I will not go down I am good.*

After the rite, Carol closes the Circle.

"Thanks to you, great Goddess and God, and all good spirits who have gathered here with us this day! The

Sacred Circle is closed but unbroken." Carol extinguishes the candles that stand tall and bright in the clear glass hurricane lamps. "Merry meet, merry part and merry meet again. The rite is ended! Blessed be!" She lowers her outstretched arms and the women circle around each other, embracing one at a time.

When Carol embraces Vivian, she whispers, "Stay a moment after everyone leaves."

Vivian pulls back sharply but says only, "Okay."

Vivian helps Carol place their sacred objects into the big wooden chest on wheels that Carol's husband made for them. Once everyone has left the beach, Carol turns to Vivian and says, "Let's go sit by the shore." They walk down to the water. Carol sits heavily on the sand and Vivian sits down next to her. Somehow she knows instinctively to be gentle near Carol. The air, the energy that flows between them must be placid, must be soft.

"Vivian, I'm sick again."

"Oh, Carol." Vivian puts an arm around her. Carol is in her early seventies, the oldest of the group. One of the founding members, she has been practicing for over fifty years. Carol tells Vivian that her breast cancer has returned and metastasized in her lymph nodes and liver. She has decided to cease treatment. The doctors said treatment might prolong her life but she must consider its quality.

"I want to feel as well as possible for the rest of the time I have left. Oh, Vivian," Carol says because Vivian, who is trying to hold back, drops copious tears that commingle with the spray from the breakers. "It's a part of the circle of life."

"I know," she whispers. Truth is not necessarily a salve and Vivian must work to keep her face neutral. Carol has been an important mother figure for Vivian since she was eighteen years old. The kind of mother Vivian needed. She dries her tears because she knows she must. She bears herself up, she breathes in the light of the sun that has fully risen over the salted water of this generous ocean.

Vivian knows Carol hasn't been feeling well lately. She has been in remission for five years and everyone was hopeful. But. It is heartbreaking. Heartbreak is only a cliché idea when it is not happening to you. When she recalls the times she has had her heart broken, Vivian believes it to be one of the most appropriate descriptions she knows. It is as though the very center of you is cracked and tender and very fragile.

Carol takes Vivian's hand, the one that is closest to her own hands. "Look at me, Vivian." She turns and looks into Carol's clear blue eyes. "I'm hoping you will lead this coven once I'm gone."

Vivian instinctively rejects the idea. She thinks immediately, *Me?* "Oh, I don't know," Vivian laughs a little. "I don't know if I'm the leading type."

"Which is why you're perfect. This is not a position of power—it calls for selflessness and a sharp ability to determine what the members need."

Vivian knows she should be flattered by Carol's words, but she dismisses them. This isn't something of which she is capable. Her mind courses with the rapidly tumbling list of her missteps: teen pregnancy, university acceptance deferment, ongoing money struggles, home foreclosure. Personal failure, maternal disappointment. Her ongoing wonder: will I ever get it right?

Then she remembers her oath to the Goddess, a prayer uttered mere moments ago— *I will make no more mistakes I will fix this I will move ahead I will not go down I am good.*

I am good.

And she asks, "How do you know I'm the right one?" She wants to tell Carol she is afraid. She wants to put her head in Carol's lap and weep for the great loss she is going to have to endure in Carol's death.

As if reading her mind, Carol says, "You have nothing to fear. I wouldn't ask you to do anything I don't truly believe you can do. But neither will I ask anything that you're not willing to do."

Something shifts in Vivian and while she does not quite believe she is capable of this thing Carol asks of her, she is sure she wants to try.

"Okay." She smiles as much as she can in this moment.

"Good," she says. "Oh, Vivian, that is good." She turns her body to face Vivian and clasps her hands. Carol feels frail and breakable, and Vivian is not sure if it is because Carol actually is or if it is because Vivian has this new and terrible knowledge about her.

The relief and joy in Carol's voice makes Vivian feel she has given her a real gift. Vivian feels as though she has done something right.

After ceremonies, the members of Vivian's coven disperse into their own lives, their secret ritual names tucked away safely once again. They are sisters in the most sacred sense of sisterhood—a blessed bond. They have been sharing magic and ritual for more than twenty years together. They are mothers, wives, waitresses, lawyers, homemakers, hair stylists. They see each other weekly and for the Sabbats—the Holy Days—but mostly live separate lives and come from miles apart.

After their weekly Circle, the women caravan to a café up on Route 6. Something like coffee and doughnuts after Mass, Vivian has reflected more than once over the years. When the weather is nice, they sit on some benches outside.

This is where Vivian catches up with them after staying back with Carol on the beach.

"There she is!" one of them calls out. They don't ask why she stayed behind and she doesn't say.

It is still a little cool at this time of day in the mornings of early summer, and Vivian pulls her light cotton sweater closer to her body. It is a buttery yellow in deference to the newborn sun. She sips the tea one of them hands her.

"Vivian, when are you going to have to move?"

Vivian sighs, "Soon. I just told my girls. I haven't told my mother yet." She sips the tea as slowly as possible because this is sure to be a long, long day. How long can she nurse a cup of tea? She will see. Maybe she will have a second.

"Are you sure you can't rent a little place?"

Vivian shakes her head. "I'm so far behind," she says They all nod. "Go to your Mom's and dig out."

"Yeah," she says. She watches the cars zoom past on Route 6. Zing, zing in both directions. "Anyone want to get another cup?" But everyone has to go where they have to go. And Vivian knows she should get to the salon. There are perms and colors to administer and hair to be cut.

She says goodbye to the women. They embrace and say, *Blessed Be*, and she is alone in the parking lot standing next to good old Sally. She inhales some fine air, smiles up at the sun, slips inside her car.

At the end of the work day, more tired than usual, instead of heading home, Vivian turns Sally out onto the winding back roads that lead out to the ocean and her mother's house on the edge of the water. The house in which both she and her mother grew up. The house her mother now shares with her sister, Anne.

The house that survived a hurricane.

Vivian remembers the day Aunt Anne moved in. It was the moment when summer meets fall. Vivian's father was newly dead and she and her mother blew slowly through the house, leaves floating on water, never touching—the water, the shared pain.

Aunt Anne's big Cadillac, pearlescent pink body, oyster-colored interior, skidded to a stop on the crushed-shell driveway. Vivian watched from the kitchen window. Aunt Anne removed two humongous and two small flower-patterned suitcases from the trunk. Vivian scurried up to the safety of her room before Aunt Anne came in through the kitchen door. Vivian listened as Aunt Anne moved her suitcases up the stairs and into the room next to her own.

"Hello, Vivian," Aunt Anne said gently when she appeared in Vivian's bedroom doorway.

Vivian mumbled a greeting.

Aunt Anne had never married. She lived in Boston for years and years where she worked for the same lawyer. She could type almost one hundred words per minute. It was something to watch her do it. Aunt Anne's laugh was loud and when she visited, Vivian's mother laughed, too. And her mother's laughter, more abundant because of Aunt Anne, contained a completely different quality. Vivian listened to them, as she lay in bed awake far past her bedtime, her door cracked as their muted talking and frequent bursts of laughter drifted up the stairs to her room late into the night.

"Can I come in?"

Vivian mumbled again, which Aunt Anne took for acquiescence.

Aunt Anne sat on the bed. "How are you doing, honey? I know you must miss your daddy." It was nearly impossible for Vivian to talk about or even think about his absence. She instead recalled memories—concrete moments and also the way he smelled, the sound of his voice, the intangible feeling of his presence. Simple and full. Hearing the word *daddy*, a hot pain burned in her belly. "I hope to help you and your mom now that I'm here."

"Mom says you're staying for good," Vivian said.

"Yeah," she said, looking out at the blue ocean moving outside the window. "Be nice for me to be back in the old stone house on the beach." She smiled.

Vivian's mother was happier when Aunt Anne was around. Vivian wondered why she couldn't make her mother happy like that. She couldn't begin to unravel what she might be doing wrong—or how she could induce that kind of joy. But she could not deny the palpable relief of Aunt Anne's presence. It felt like a giant exhale when Vivian had not realized she'd been holding her breath.

"What about your job?" she asked.

"That old lawyer is going to retire soon. He won't be needing me much longer." She shrugged. "Seemed like it was time for a change."

The lightness Aunt Anne brought with her carried some air, and Vivian found she could breathe again. She noticed her mother could, too. And Aunt Anne was a wonderful cook. A lot better than Vivian's mother who never seemed to add enough salt, whose food was bland and gray, whose pies were soggy and over-sugared. Vivian's father had always been their cook—and even though she knew it wasn't possible for love to have a flavor, she swore she could taste it in his food. A cook in the Navy, he learned everything he knew from an old sailor who was the ship's mess cook when he was stationed in the Pacific during the war. From the stories her father told, he tolerated his wife's cooking for six months before he gently took over in the kitchen. He closed his hardware store at four o'clock every afternoon, drove home, washed his hands, rolled up his shirtsleeves, and tied a plain white apron across his waist and began preparing supper. And while the food simmered—a task her mother could manage to monitor—he and Vivian would take a walk.

After he died, her mother was forced back into the kitchen until Aunt Anne swept in and suddenly food exhibited color and possessed flavor once more. Her macaroni with three silky melted cheeses, the top crackling with crumbs browned by salty butter. Her pear and raspberry crumble, sweetly fragranced with spices sprinkled from the little glass jars she lined up on the windowsill. Their cabinets had known only salt, pepper and an antiquated bottle of cinnamon—none of which her mother used very often.

Aunt Anne has not lost her touch in the kitchen. Vivian often wonders how she and her mother would have survived each other without the buffering force that was—that is—Aunt Anne.

Now, as she gets closer and closer to the conversation she does not want to hold, Vivian hopes that Aunt Anne's magic will work yet again.

Vivian drives past the beach where she celebrated the new dawn within the safe Circle she and her friends raised. She holds on to that feeling. She will use it to fortify herself for what she must do, to what she must admit, for what she must ask.

Her daughters tease her about her religion now, but no matter. When they were little, they loved the Goddess. She thought she was raising two little witches. Maybe they would return. She hoped. All mothers with any faith bring their children into the fold and hope those children embrace it, too. But if they wander, you must let them. Vivian vows to this and allows them their path.

Vivian's mother is staunch Catholic, but fairly cheerful about it. Even at eighty-one years old, Millie still does works for her church. She refers to it as her "vocation." Parishioners think of her as sweet, old harmless Millie Crawford; rosary beads firmly clasped in her soft and wrinkled hands. But Vivian bears witness to that which she alone can summon: disappointment and shame along with the biting words her mother can conjure when she chooses. Although Millie exercises judiciousness in unleashing this thin strand in her personality, knowing it is there lurking is almost as bad as inducing it. Through her mother's vision, Vivian can see her screw-ups in sharp relief: getting pregnant at seventeen, the mistakes and fumbles with money and employment, the betrayal of the religion in which she wished to witness her daughter flourish. And now what her mother will think about this house foreclosure. Even if she manages to control her display of judgment, the unspoken will clang noisily in Vivian's perceptive ears. *Vivian, what have you done now?*

And she might not control herself... thinks Vivian.

Vivian is what the old ladies call "a change of life baby," born when her mother was forty-two.

"You could have knocked me over with a feather when I realized I was pregnant," she will say. "It was like when Sarah found out she was pregnant with Isaac after all those years of hope and disappointment."

Catholics of her mother's age never subscribed to the use of birth control. They utilized the rhythm method which follows the natural flow of a woman's menstrual cycle. It does not work very well, which is why Catholics of old had so many children and ended up with such individuals as "change of life babies" when they thought they were altogether done with childbearing. Vivian's mother is the kind of old Catholic who follows all the rules, hangs a picture of the current pope in the house and prays the rosary, performs the occasional novena. Aunt Anne drives her to Mass every morning (then promptly leaves to get a cup of coffee and read the paper until it's over), she walks the Stations of the Cross and works bingo every Friday night. She mends and alters the priests' vestments when needed. Vivian has watched as her mother holds those garments in her hands, her needle and thread weaving a part of herself into the holy things, imparting something blessed upon herself.

When the teenaged Vivian broke curfew, made questionable friends, started worshipping the Goddess and hid disturbing reading material between her mattress and box spring, her mother did not know what to do. So she prayed. She would have asked her friends for help had she not been too ashamed to name the sins. Instead she requested the intercession of the most immaculate of saints and especially the Virgin Mother. Vivian imagines her mother asking herself after each of Vivian's transgressions, *Why? What did I do wrong?*

Then Vivian had to relay the worst of all possible offenses for an unmarried Catholic girl—she was pregnant. Her mother simply shook her head and left the room. Vivian heard her mother go outside, and from the window watched her mother's figure recede down the beach, growing smaller and smaller. Vivian had expected hysterics. When her mother reacted with dismissal instead, Vivian realized she would have preferred hysteria.

Vivian stood on the back porch and stared down the shore where her mother had disappeared.

Aunt Anne's hand on her shoulder. "It'll be okay, honey. You'll see."

"She didn't even scream at me."

"It'll be okay," she repeated. "Give her time."

When she returned, her mother said, "Well, Vivian, now you have really done it. I hope you are proud of yourself. For the first time, I'm glad your father is dead." Vivian didn't say so, but she agreed. She could not imagine telling him this thing only to watch his sweet, soft face suffer with confusion and sadness. Or maybe he would have withheld judgment and loved her as much as ever. This idea made her grieve more than the former.

Aunt Anne inhaled sharply. "Millie, what a thing to say." She placed both hands on Vivian's shoulders. They stood in silence for a long time.

No matter what her mother thought, Vivian was not proud—she was scared.

Her mother tolerated her during the pregnancy. Vivian was pressured into the idea of adoption but could not do it. She embraced the Goddess—her comfort—to whom Raine had introduced her. She held on tightly yet tentatively to Raine—knowing there was good reason to expect imminent ruin.

Then she lost her, too.

Vivian parks next to the Cadillac in the crushed-shell driveway. The old ladies still toot around in that old whale. It is big and noisy, belches exhaust. The paint job has dulled. None of that matters to them. And Aunt Anne is not one of those old ladies who drives as slowly as she wants.

Vivian gets out of her car and gazes up at her mother's house, the stone foundation of which survived gales and continues to hold strong against the roiling Atlantic fifty feet from its footprint in the sand. Who builds a house in the sand? And yet, it stands. Millie and Anne's father, a doctor, built it before the Depression and the house has remained in the family all the ensuing years. The ruinous Hurricane of '38 could not trample or blow it away. Downstairs, the large parlor, formal dining room of gleaming dark wood and big kitchen have never seen a significant updating. There is a closeted powder room and a solarium off the kitchen. Upstairs, three modest bedrooms, one larger master and one full bathroom. As large as it seems, this house is unlike the McMansions built in the last twenty years—people took up less space when Vivian's grandfather built it here in this patch of sand, even as there was more space to be had.

Each room contains the original gas lamps, although the house has long been wired for electricity. The walls are covered with old paper that has gone out of style and now come back in. The woodwork is richly stained and still gleams even though so many hands have passed over it and perhaps that is part of why it shines so. The grand fireplace in the parlor is still functional, its mantel and the wall surrounding it made of hand-collected and hand-placed beach stones and shells. The stones are smooth and round like eggs. The shells are large quahog—cream, blue-white, topaz, butter, maize, violet.

As Vivian stands in her mother's driveway, she walks through the house in her mind. All its curious and old features—the dumbwaiter, the gas lamps, the stone fireplace—things that belong to an older era, that which were necessary once, that portray a time but leave behind few clues to shape the individuals. Thoughts, fears, loves, hates? Wrongs never reconciled? How easily we slide into the impression of a generation. How cheaply we write the spare stories.

Vivian crunches up the driveway. She walks into the kitchen and calls out hello to no answer. Vivian moves through the house toward the backyard. The wind is nearly constant here right at the shore. But during summer, it feels nicer. More like a steady breeze. In winter, a ceaseless cold smack to the face.

Vivian stops and watches the dune grass and beach rose bushes sway in the wind. She knows it is going to be her wind again. She steps out onto the porch and feels the waning sun and the breeze competing on her body. She looks out into the backyard and squints at the screen house. Her mother and Aunt Anne sit across from each other playing cards.

"Gin," says Aunt Anne, places her cards down on the table. Her mother protests loudly then laughs, snorts once.

"Hello," Vivian sings. She moves quickly through the door and into the screen house.

"Vivian!" Aunt Anne stands up to hug her. "Honey, how are you?"

Vivian leans in and gives her mother a kiss on the cheek. "Hello, dear," her mother says. She pats Vivian's arm. Her papery hand flutters there and Vivian thinks *bird*. "No work this evening?" her mother asks.

"No—I worked all day." Vivian sits in one of the wicker chairs, the flowered cushion slightly but perpetually damp. The cool ocean air chills her—Vivian's legs are goose-bumpy in her shorts.

On the wrought-iron table is her mother and aunt's supper. Several cans of cheap beer—empty—have been pushed to the side and a nine-by-thirteen aluminum pan of brownies, a third eaten, sits on the table between them, a knife resting in the empty side of the pan. By each woman stands a fresh cold beer.

Beer and brownies. Vivian shakes her head.

"How many brownies have you each had?" Vivian asks.

"I think the better question is how many beers," says Aunt Anne and tips back her head to laugh.

Vivian's mother snorts and laughs, slaps the table with the palm of her hand. "Oh, she's right!"

Vivian shakes her head and smiles. This is not the first time she has caught them having beer and brownies or something equally questionable for supper. "You could at least use plates," she teases.

"Do you want one, Vivian?" Aunt Anne says.

Her mother says, "Anne made them from scratch." Of course. No boxed mixes in this house.

"No, thanks. I haven't had supper yet," says Vivian. "Although clearly that doesn't matter around here." The two old women laugh. "I'll have a beer, though," says Vivian.

Her mother reaches down to the old, small, red cooler under the table, brings one out, sits up and hands it to Vivian. That cooler has been a fixture between these two women for as long as Vivian can remember. When did it make its first appearance? Vivian can't recall, but she would bet at the same time as Aunt Anne made hers.

The phone rings and Aunt Anne reaches over to answer it. "Hello? Oh, yes, Arthur. Hold on." She hands the phone over to Vivian's mother. "It's the prayer line."

She nods once and takes the phone. She pulls a small pad of paper and a pencil stub from her pocket. "Hello, Arthur. Go ahead, give it to me." She listens, jots furiously and nods her head. Mom's been on the prayer line for many years. She hangs up with Arthur, dials Jackie, the next person, Vivian knows, on the prayer line. A human prayer chain. Prayers come in through parishioners in the church, townspeople, local firefighters and harbor patrol officers, old guys who sit by their police radios in their garages. Vivian once scoffed at the prayer line, but over the years of her own meaningful worship has come to recognize it as not very different from the Circle casting and spell-making she conducts with the women of her coven. She has come to see little difference in any form of praying and any form of deity. It is all one grand and simple practice.

She and Aunt Anne chat quietly while her mother tells Jackie about the people who need prayers.

"What brings you out here, honey?" says Aunt Anne just as her mother presses the button on the cordless to end the call.

She can't think of any small talk although she would like to put off what she has to say.

Her mother's brow furrows. "Vivian, what is it?"

Is it on her face? In her expression? The shape of her body? She feels as though it is. So it must be. She sighs.

Her mother repeats in alarm, "Vivian, what is it? One of the girls?"

"No, no…"

"One of the babies? The twins?"

"Mom, no. It's…it's my house."

"Fire?" Aunt Anne breathes.

"Oh, my God! Oh, Blessed Virgin!" her mom wails.

Vivian thinks, *Fire. Now that's not a terrible idea.* But no. She hasn't the first idea how to commit arson and get away with it. "No! No. I'm afraid I have to move. I'm afraid…it's foreclosure," she exhales. "My house is going into foreclosure." Then she feels all that is solid in her— bones, cartilage, firm muscles—collapse and shrink. "I'm so far behind. We have nowhere to go," she says.

"Oh, Vivian! Now, how did this happen?" Her mother's tone is familiar.

"Millie," Anne says quietly. "Maybe there will be time for that later."

Vivian smiles at Aunt Anne then says, "It's complicated, Mom."

Her mother looks out toward the dark moving water, beginning to blend into the dark of the burgeoning night. She does not look at Vivian when she repeats herself. "How could you let this happen, Vivian? Again! Nothing ever changes. It's never the same with you, but it's always something…" She breaks off her words.

This certain tone to her mother's voice, this specific demeanor and particular shift and Vivian is twelve, is fifteen, is seventeen again, moving between fury and abject fear.

In Vivian's old room, there is a window seat. When she was a teenager, Vivian removed the top with the back of a hammer. She remembers glancing at her closed door with each tap and pull, worried she was making too much noise. Finally, she pried the square sheet of wood away from the frame. She peered down into a hollow space. She skipped over to the door, opened it quietly and listened. Satisfied her mother was nowhere near, she closed the door and unzipped her backpack. Carefully, she removed several squat votive candles, a box of sweet-smelling incense and small statues in the likenesses of the god Pan and the goddess Aphrodite. She hid the objects in the hollowed-out window seat, replaced the top and its flowered pillow.

And so began her quiet candle-lit worship.

Sometimes the fear of blasphemy crept in on cold feet, and with icy hands crawled up her body in the night and she trembled. But when the moon shone through the window, curved and white and pooling light on the ocean, the Goddess whispered Her safe, warm words and Vivian knew she had found her way.

One late night, the moon full and brimming with possibility, Vivian lit the candles and the incense and placed her statues on the window seat altar. She spoke the words—the prayers—that were new on her breath.

"Vivian?" A loud whisper from the hall. Her mother—who believed knocking to enter her own child's room was not only unnecessary but an insult—opened the door. "What is that smell?" Her eyes grew large. "What is this?"

But she knew. She had already found and thrown out one of Vivian's books.

Her mother blew out the candles and stomped to Vivian's wastebasket and with one full sweep of her arm, pushed it all in.

Furious, she bellowed, "Not in my house!" And left the room with the wastebasket tucked under her arm.

Vivian shivered in bed that night. She did not dare leave her bed for any reason. She cried soundlessly. Her mother never talked to her about it, but treated Vivian to a coldness that lasted for weeks.

"Vivian, how could you let this happen?" her mother says yet again.

Her mother's mouth is a straight line and her hands are firm in her lap.

Vivian remembers to exhale, and repeats, "Mom, it's complicated. We just need a little time. Tania will be graduating in a year and Guin...We can figure something out. We just need a little time."

"Well, it seems like the best thing would be for you and the girls and the kids to come stay here for a while until you get back on your feet," Aunt Anne says.

"Mom?" Vivian says quietly. She leans over and places her hand over her mother's. Flutter flutter flutter. Her mother nods her head.

"I don't suppose I can think of another solution."

"I can take the solarium. Tania can take my old room and Guin and the kids can take the biggest bedroom." These rooms Vivian knows are empty now.

Her mother shakes her head. "I'll take the solarium."

"This is my fault. I'll take it. You don't have to, Mom."

"No. My legs aren't working all those stairs as they once did." She pats Vivian's hand. "I'll take the solarium." Her lips turn up in a meager smile.

"Well," Aunt Anne says and stands. "Looks like the moon is out." Waxing back to fullness.

Her mother stands, too. "Time to head back on over to the porch." The mosquito hour is over.

Vivian helps them carry the beer cans, the pan of brownies, the deck of cards out to the back porch and as she says goodnight and walks away, she slogs in that old familiar gloom.

❖ ❖ ❖

Looking up to the sky, hoping for salvation.

The moon is big and white and round. A large warm white marble. Vivian is floored. She wishes she had the time to commune with the fairies tonight. But she doesn't and she is tired, so tired that her spirit droops.

She can see all the parts of the moon clearly. Craters, wrinkle ridges, capes (although no real sea, only plains early astrologers took for seas), channel-length grooves. They all have names. Names such as Brigitte, Litrow, Sumner, Yuri, Harker, Whiston, Mairan, Bode. Many more. Humans have identified and named it all. Claimed it.

The moon is directly overhead, her yard awash in shades of blue. The light is bright enough to cast shadows: the pots of flowers and herbs she grows, the tilted clothesline post, the trash and compost bins, their shadows stretch out across the grass which looks blue now in this moonlight, not green as she knows it is. The shadows of the secondhand Adirondack chairs she got cheap stretch long indigo on the grass. She painted right over the places where the wood was soft and rotten. Sealed it up—one a vibrant red, the other jeweled purple—and they have been fine that way for five summers, in spite of how Frank worried they would rot further.

She stands with her face upturned, thinking of the moon as another incarnation of the Mother. She says a little prayer. The salvation for which she hopes.

Artificial light casts beams into the yard, breaks the spell.

It is Frank with the U-Haul. He beeps twice.

"Hi, Frank," she says as he joins her in the backyard. She is never ashamed with Frank.

"Thanks for bringing the truck." He is the type to do this kind of thing—always goes out of his way. It's a thing for which she loves him sometimes and a thing that irritates the hell out of her other times. Dear, dear Frank who irritates the hell out of her sometimes, for going on twenty-five years now.

"No problem." He hugs her.

Tomorrow is moving day. Tonight they will get a jump on packing the truck. The house is lit up fully. She can see her girls inside, putting things in boxes. The children's room is the only dark window, where she knows they sleep, unaware of any of this. As it should be.

When they grow tired of the packing, when their spirits can take no more of it for this day, they drink a few beers in all that moonlight.

She can almost touch it.

Vivian has known Frank since 1985. They were both freshmen at Holy Family High School. He is tall—six feet four inches. His feet are enormous. She had never seen anyone as skinny as he was. Just tight muscle flush against bones. They wore uniforms—she a gray and blue plaid kick-pleat skirt and pastel oxford shirt and he gray pants, white oxford and a navy tie. His belt was notched as far as it would go and still his pants drooped. She could see the yellow and blue stripes on the elastic band of his underwear. He constantly hiked his pants, especially when he walked. As he walked, they would slip and sag and he'd hike. Slip, sag, hike. His glasses over his big blue eyes. The glasses themselves were huge discs, creating the illusion that his eyes bugged. And his eyelashes were long, like a doll's. The kind all girls wish they had themselves. Slip, sag, hike. Sitting behind him in homeroom, alphabetically, she *Crawford*, he *Cormier*, he talked to her nonstop. He talked to everyone nonstop. He seemed to have an inexplicable and bottomless well of words and confidence. Of the two of them, he was the really smart one. She was smart, but worked at her grades. He could coast right on through, understood everything as soon as it was explained. He never studied. He wrote fantastic papers in a draft or two. He, of course, took it all for granted.

Vivian walked home every day, down Main Street, over the bridge that spanned the bay, the cord grass swaying in the shallows and marshes, the gulls and cormorants perched on the large rocks that protruded out of the water during low tide. The fishing boats moved in and out of the harbor. Once she crossed the bridge, she walked down the road that flanked the shore, large dunes between the road and the shoreline. Her house on a small street surrounded on two sides by water.

Leaf.

By the middle of October, the foliage was at full peak, brilliant and perfect. It was Vivian's favorite time of year. There was calmness in her center that seemed to settle more and more as the year drew to a close. The colors of the trees against the blue of the sky was nothing less than astonishing. She could look at it forever. A deep peacefulness nestled in her. Main Street was lined with trees of all kinds, the colors combining in stunning and perfectly haphazard ways. The houses in this part of town were old, the original settlers' homes. They bore little placards furnished by the historical society. Green swaths of rolling meadow lay between the houses, turning all shades of yellow as autumn moved in slowly in its lush and magical way. The land near Vivian's house was covered in scrub pine, dune grasses and beach roses. Pretty, but not in the autumn way she loved.

The wood smoke combined with the freshness of the cool air and the smell of the dried and crunchy leaves scattered on the ground made Vivian linger on her walks home from September through November, after which the cold would set in and speed her up. The winter wind, fueled by the frigid Atlantic, was a thing into which a person had to be born to tolerate. Bright red nose and cheeks by the time she got home all winter long.

But in autumn, the sun was still close enough to the earth and soft rays warmed her skin. She lingered among all those trees, never felt rushed in any way. One day as she walked home, looking out ahead of her at the trees, she spied an especially tall one, its leaves that watercolor smear of green and orange, red and yellow. The leaves just beginning to fall from its branches in lovely swirls on the breeze. On an October day in her first year of high school, she walked to the edge of the meadow and lay down under the tree in the still soft, just slightly yellowed grass. She watched the leaves float down to the ground, slowly spinning, hovering in the air. The sky was an impossible shade of blue. The world felt cracked open and limitless. She believed deeply and without doubt that she could lie there forever and time would stop simply because this moment could not be surpassed. Sublime moments *must* be able to be frozen in time—this felt entirely possible to her in that instant.

"Hi, Vivian."

Frank stood over her, bent at the waist, looking down, his head framed by the blue of the sky. His eyes portals to that vast blueness beyond him.

"Francis," she said, sitting up. "You scared the shit out of me." She had only recently begun swearing and the words still felt like marbles on her tongue, foreign and strange.

"Call me Frank," he said. "What are you doing?"

She stood and brushed off her skirt. Stray leaves and dried grass drifted to the ground at her feet. "I just like looking at the leaves."

"I can walk you home if you want."

Vivian felt slightly panicked—she didn't want to give him the wrong idea. "You don't have to go so far out of your way." She began walking.

He followed. "My mom told me to stop at the fish market before coming home, so I have to go that way." He was apparently not the type to take a hint.

"But I live, like, at least ten minutes beyond the fish market."

"That's okay," he said.

Well, how does one argue with that?

In the short walk to her house, he expounded further on some of the facts of which she was already aware from his homeroom incursions. He was an avid (and serious) Dungeons and Dragons player, loved the Renaissance Faire which was running now—"Right now! Only thirty minutes away!"—and he collected comic books. Vivian was not aware of how much there was to know about comic books. Mint and near mint, acid-free backing boards, proper storage. With this new knowledge of Frank she could have pigeonholed him. Instead she thought he had more personality than anyone else she knew. He was so vibrant—she felt as though she had no interests or ideas of her own. He seemed so formed. So sure. She felt like a lump of bland dough.

And so it began.

She spent the next ten years reminding him they were just friends.

Fifteen years, twenty, going on twenty-five, Vivian and Frank still go to the Renaissance Faire together. She still listens to him rattle on about his comic books. So much has not changed and everything has.

Young Vivian was both horrified by and impressed with Frank. Horrified because he was so clearly strange and simply flaunted it out there as though there were nothing to hide. Impressed because, even though he must have known the things he liked and his general demeanor were outside the edge of acceptable teenage activities, likes, clothing and behavior, he didn't seem to care and made no apologies for who he was, what he liked and what he wore. Frank inspired bravery.

Vivian could talk to Frank about the boys she liked and Frank would talk to her about the girls he supposedly liked, but neither of them was fooled. They both knew she was the only one, but both pretended that the crushes and sexual longings and aspirations he purported were sincere. He even went so far in the consensual ruse as to assist her in her efforts to get together with this boy or that. Occasionally it would all bubble up, on some scale that was internal to Frank, the repressed emotion would hit the saturation point and boil over. An evening out would begin fairly normally, but as it progressed, Frank would become more and more subdued, more quiet and sulky. She would find herself sitting parked somewhere alone with him in his mother's car as he tearfully implored her to love him.

"Please, Vivian. Please just give me one chance," he begged. He cried real tears on her lap. "*One*. If it doesn't work I will understand. *Please*." She always refused him. She was as kind as she could possibly be.

"But, Frank, I don't want to mess up our friendship." Which sounded like a canned answer but she was too young to know about canned answers yet and meant it most sincerely. What *would* she do without Frank? "Why can't you just accept me?" She meant this, too. She felt as though she loved him for exactly who he was, but his love for her hinged on something more she couldn't give him. Would he stop loving her if she continued to refuse him? She was sure he considered his love for her more pure than hers for him, but she thought it just the opposite because she required nothing more of him.

"I do, Vivian." He tearfully paused. "I just wish I could have one chance." His head was now off her lap and he faced forward behind the steering wheel resignedly. He drove her home slowly and wouldn't hug her goodnight;

faced forward hands firmly on the steering wheel, wouldn't turn his head.

"Night, Frank." Nothing. "I'll call you." Nothing. "I'm sorry, Frank." Nothing. "Ok, Frank. Bye." She sighed, stepped away from the car and watched him drive away.

In a day or two it would blow over. Every now and then she would have to get a little angry and then they might not talk for a week or two. Inevitably, one or the other would start calling and coming around again.

It took a long time for it to stop altogether, but finally it has. In a way she misses it—the validation of her worth to someone. But she knows it is far better not to cause Frank pain. Does he still carry the torch for her? She doesn't know to what extent he might but she prefers to think he does as strong as ever. Although, she would never tell him that.

Love in any form fortifies us.

After fifteen years, twenty, going on twenty-five, are explanations and apologies really necessary anymore?

You simply carry on.

Dear, dear Frank sits in one of the painted-over Adirondack chairs. Vivian can see where his leg presses into the rotted wood. He shifts. She guesses he is trying to protect what remains of the integrity of the chair. He knows how Vivian must make things stretch.

They drink ice cold beers under the wash of blue moonlight and Vivian wonders how much is planned and how much is random. Must it be one or the other? Neither? A little of both?

Sitting in the chair she painted, under the moon she adores with her best friend, Vivian wonders if we choose those with whom we share our memories, with whom we build our lives, with those who comprise our stories, or if it is a part of some greater scheme.

The screen house smells of eucalyptus and garlic. Eucalyptus, because Millie swears by it and garlic because Anne says it's the only thing that works.

Vivian maintains that nothing works and across the years she has tried every trick.

There are unguents to slather on the skin. Spritzes of aromatic liquids. Poisons. There are candles to burn. Electrocution by purple lights. Certain frequencies of sound are said to put them off. There are preventions: eliminate pools of standing water, plant marigolds which give off a scent that is repugnant to them, keep chickens, ducks or bats which are natural mosquito predators. Alleged to be effective in staving off the pests are oils of: citronella, lemon, eucalyptus, cinnamon, castor, rosemary, lemongrass, cedar, peppermint, clove, geranium, verbena, pennyroyal, lavender, pine, cajeput, basil, thyme, allspice.

They have tried many of these remedies.

What it amounts to, though, is mosquitoes either want to bite you or they don't. And no one knows why or why not.

The simplicity of the screen, the effectiveness of that tiny mesh wall, is a thing of pure human capability of dominance over beast. It is a place of refuge.

They huddle inside until the mosquito hour passes, the sun fully sets, the moon rises on the nights it does, or hides on the nights it does not, and then they move back onto the stone porch. Their view unobstructed. Their gaze released from the tiny mesh boxes.

2

Guin—Bad Days

It is evening after a long day at The Grille and Creamery. Guin worked through breakfast and lunch on this busy day. It still amazes her how many people come in and out of The Grille and Creamery, where she's worked since she was sixteen. It was more fun when she didn't think of it as her life. Out on errands, she wears her waitress clothes which at one time she never would have been caught wearing in public. But now she is just quick-stopping at Kmart for diapers and butt wipes and it doesn't really seem to matter much anymore.

It is a warm evening in late June. Not hot yet, only a lovely early summer warmth. She tries to think about anything but their lost home, but it keeps creeping back, making her feel blue. She is sad, not for herself but for her mom. She is sad because her mom scraped away for so many years only to end back scraping up from the ground. Lately Guin isn't sure where exactly she belongs. She is simply floating along, waiting to land. But she knows where her mom belongs and it is in that house for which she worked so hard.

She sighs, the blues skulk deeper. A long day behind her, her dress stained with ketchup and chocolate sauce, she must now fetch more diapers.

(It seems that she always needs more diapers.)

The parking spots at Kmart are angled—she always drives up the wrong way in these kinds of parking lots. She hates Kmart but it's the cheapest place for the diapers and she must save a little wherever she can. She feels like someday she will have made it in life when she can walk into any store and just pay whatever they are asking for toilet paper, diapers, tampons—no thought to the price tags whatsoever.

She angles into a spot and the space forward of it is empty so she pulls through. She won't have to back out when she leaves and this is a small thing that usually makes her happy, like when the leftovers just fit into the Tupperware. But she is distracted tonight and simply parks the car and heads inside, walks straight back to the baby section. She usually spends a minute or two looking at the Martha Stewart home stuff. She imagines what she would choose for her own home. Even though that Martha Stewart Kmart stuff is pretty inexpensive, it still looks really nice and classy. Clean and sophisticated, which is how she would furnish her own place. But waitressing at The Grille and Creamery isn't exactly a cash windfall every week and Pickle can't manage to hold down a job for very long. When he does have one, he's good about giving her some child support, but a small percentage of a small paycheck is not much. When he's unemployed (which is often), a small percentage of nothing is nothing. Pickle is a dreamer. She loves him for that. How long can you love a dreamer? She has loved him since they were fifteen.

She grabs the generic diapers and wipes (why people pay extra money for brand loyalty to a product that is peed and pooped in is beyond her understanding) and she carries them to the register, where she is affronted by more reasons she hates Kmart. They never have enough cashiers and the lines are always long and it seems that most of the people who shop here always have some problem with the transaction that slows things down. While she waits Guin reads the headlines on all the trashy magazines, which are depressing in their lowness. Some celebrity's cellulite up close, *Whose thighs are these?* She kind of wants to open the magazine and find out, but it's just too mean and she can't bring herself to participate. Meanwhile this celebrity probably looks a hundred times better in a bathing suit than what she witnesses every time she goes to the beach.

Finally she reaches the front of the line and as the cashier begins to scan her diapers, the woman who was just in front of her comes stalking back, pushes in front of Guin and says, "You rang this up wrong." Her tone is nasty. The cashier shows her that she did not and politely clears the confusion. The woman says, "Oh," and leaves. The cashier was a lot nicer than that woman deserved. Guin smiles at her and makes small talk and tries to be extra nice to make up for the rude woman in some small way.

Guin walks to her car and the nasty woman is parked right next to her, getting ready to back up. Guin is waiting for her to pull out since their cars are pretty close together, enough that it will be easier to get in once the woman is gone, but not close enough that she noticed it earlier when she first got out. She smiles at the woman. It is a fake kind of turning up of the mouth that Guin is accustomed to wearing, but still it is something and *not* nasty.

The woman fake smiles back and leans out her window and says, "Hope you didn't hit my car when you parked so close to me."

Guin's fake smile broadens, "I didn't hit your car."

"Well, you parked close enough."

Guin looks down. "That's because you're parked over the line."

"There were plenty of other spots."

"Have a nice day," Guin sings.

"You, too," the woman sings back.

The woman backs out slowly, slowly—no one needs to drive this slowly. "Take your time now," Guin says. She is still waiting to get into her own car.

"Oh, I will."

Guin's face and head are hot and her vision has gone dark around the edges. *How dare she!* Guin did not intentionally park closely. She was not out to get this woman. She feels wronged and falsely accused and angry. This will bother her all night. She will have to breathe it away when she never possessed negative intentions in the first place. She only needed diapers for the twins.

The woman is backed all the way out and Guin reaches for her door handle when, instead, she calls out, "Wait!" and walks briskly to the woman's window.

"What?" the woman's face is darkly screwed up.

"Just wait," Guin says. She stops in front of the woman. "Hi, I'm Guin. What's your name?" she says softly. She is scared and not exactly sure why. Yes, this woman seems tough, but it is more than simply that.

The woman looks at Guin, her brow furrowed. Then her face softens a little. "Darlene. Why?"

Guin says, "Because I have bad days, too."

"What is that noise?" Tania moves the curtain and looks out the window.

Guin sighs. She closes her eyes for a moment, opens them before Tania sees the look on her face. "It's Pickle. In his new RV."

It is moving day.

Tania turns her head toward Guin. She is smirking. "Pickle has an RV?" She says it *AAAHH-VEEEE*. "Since when?"

"Since he decided to make a 'Patriots tailgating machine.' That's what he plans to work on this summer. He wants to get it done before football season. I think it's a nice idea." She thinks to add this last statement. She hopes it sounds sincere.

"Will he also be 'working on' gainful employment this summer?" Tania says.

"He got a really good deal on the RV—it cost him practically nothing."

"That's good since that's what he usually takes home…"

"Tania."

"*Sorry*, Guinevere!" Tania sings in a fake English accent. "But even at 'practically nothing,' where the hell did Pickle get the money to buy it?" She lets the curtain fall back over the window, then touches the fabric, holds it lightly in her hand. "Oh, we've got to pack these." They begin to remove the curtains from the windows.

Guin darts her a barbed look because she knows what Tania is really saying—if Pickle has the cash for a stupid RV, why isn't he using it to buy diapers, wipes, groceries, clothes, doctor visit co-payments, laundry soap, baby lotion, etcetera etcetera. ETCETERA. Tania acts as though she thinks Pickle is an idiot. A firefly in a jar is brighter than he, in Tania's opinion. And compared to Tania, who is the smartest person Guin knows, Pickle *is* dim. Tania and Pickle have an adversarial relationship. Guin calls it "love slash hate." But, really, Tania simply gets a kick out of making Pickle look stupid. That's the hate part. The love part is that she does it in a way so Pickle never realizes what just happened. That's one of the ways Tania is so smart and also how it proves she loves Pickle in some way even if she swears to the border of Rhode Island and back that she does not. Pickle gets mad at Tania sometimes but always lets it go. That is another good thing about Pickle; he does not hold grudges.

But then there are many good things about Pickle.

"He's here to help us move," Guin says. "I need a screwdriver to take these curtain rod thingies down—what are these called?"

"Brackets," says Tania.

"Oh, yeah, right. I need a Phillips head."

"See if Pickle has one on that rig of his. Ours are packed already," Tania says.

Guin goes to the window and calls out, "Pickle, if you have a Phillips head in there, can you bring it in, please?"

Soon, Pickle struts in, by which his gait can only be referred. Pickle—short and slight, with skin as smooth and blemish-free as a baby's. His soft straight dirty-blond hair always looks a little overgrown as though it's perpetually at the point just before it needs a trim. It feathers a bit on the sides, the back just touches the collars of his tee shirts. When he walks (struts), he periodically flips his hair back with a quick toss of his head. "Flippy," Tania calls him sometimes, though not to his face. (As if he needs another ridiculous name.) His jeans are on the tight side but because he's slim, he pulls it off—501s he's worn soft since high school.

Guin still thinks he's hot. He still turns her on. She supposes the twins are the most recent evidence of that sentiment.

"RV, huh?" Tania says to him. "I hear you got a mad plan for it."

"Yeah! She's gonna be wicked cool all football season! A portable grill, a little working refrigerator. Hook her up for electricity—radio, a little TV. Even a place to take a piss!"

"Oooh, piss! Where are you going to tailgate?"

He shrugs. "I don't know. Around. I don't know."
Now he looks uncomfortable because he knows Tania
knows something he doesn't or she's going to zing him
somehow. He knows Tania's way of leading a
conversation like this. He never possesses the faintest idea
where it's going. Guin watches him, knowing exactly what
is going on in his head.

"Tania," Guin warns.

Pickle turns toward her with his arms out *stop* and
says, "Let her talk, Guin." Guin puts up her hands in an
expression of surrender. Pickle hates it when she tries to
protect him. "I'm not a baby, Guin. I'm not stupid," is
what he usually says.

Tania rolls her eyes. "Jesus, it's no big deal, Pickle.
And Guin. I was just observing that most tailgating goes
on at the game. At the stadium. In the parking lot. By
people who hold actual tickets. Made from actual paper
from actual trees, you get the idea. Ergo, my curiosity
about your tailgating plans." Her arms are crossed over her
chest.

"Well...I just..." he flips his hair back, then blows it
off his forehead with a puff from his bottom lip. "I just
thought it would be cool. Who cares if I don't have it all
figured out yet."

"I see," says Tania.

"We should, um..." says Guin.

"Take some boxes out?" offers Tania.

"Yes," says Guin. "Boxes."

They all go outside, carrying boxes to load up.

From the limited knowledge Guin possesses
regarding RVs this one may have been manufactured in
the 1980s. Maybe—when she looks more closely—the
'70s.

"How *old* is this thing?" Tania says.

"I don't know, thirty years, but you'd never know it.
Come inside." He opens the door with a loud creak—it

sounds as though it will come unhinged any time from the accumulated rust rotting down, flaking onto the ground. Then the smell hits Guin. She sees Tania's face contort and Guin catches her eye, sending her a mental message, *Don't mention the smell. Please pretend you don't notice the smell.* Tania rolls her eyes at her. Guin would like to be able to identify the smell herself, but it's likely a combination of horrific unmentionable things. Many unmentionable things over many years.

"What do you think, babe?" he asks her.

"It's nice, Pickle. It's really nice," Guin says.

Unidentifiable blotches of stain-colored patches cover every upholstered seat, bench and sleeping surface. The carpet underfoot is dun-colored from all the stuff that has been mashed down into it. The tables and counters are stained, marred with gouges and small burns from cigarettes or cigars. The curtains are torn and faded. They remind Guin of the curtains Maria in *The Sound of Music* used to sew play clothes for the von Trapp children.

"I haven't cleaned it yet," he says.

"No?" says Tania.

"No," he says. "But I will. I have to do some redecorating, too. Guin, you can help me with that— women like to do that. Picking out colors and curtains and stuff."

"Sure," she says.

"I'm gonna cover the exterior with gray primer then paint her sparkling white with the Patriots logo on both sides. Above the windshield, 'PATRIOTS #1' and on the back," he pauses, grinning. "'DYNASTY.' Huge letters. HUGE. I think I'll call it the Patsmobile."

They stand in silence for a few moments looking around, then start moving boxes into the RV.

They wait for Mom and Frank to return from the first trip with the U-Haul so they can load up the last of it.

When everything is out of the house, they stand on the front lawn, Mom in the middle and Guin and Tania on either side of her, looking at the house. Pickle and Frank have floated away somewhere, thoughtfully leaving the women alone.

"We've lived in a lot of shit holes, haven't we?" Mom says. They agree.

"But this wasn't one of them," Tania says.

"This was nice, Mom. Really, *really* nice," says Guin. Her eyes fill with tears. "I'm really sorry."

"Yeah, Mom. Me, too."

"Well, don't be. I should have known better." She apologizes for losing the house and for their having to move in with their grandmother and for dragging them down.

"No, Mom."

"Mom, stop. We're adults, for God's sake," says Tania.

"Goddess," says Guin.

"I just wanted a good thing for us. A good thing that lasted."

"We have that," Guin says to their mother. They hold each other for a few minutes then turn away from the really nice house that is no longer theirs.

They move boxes and furniture all day long. It is hot work.

"We need a break," Tania says to Guin. "Let's make a coffee run." Guin is quick to agree and they take orders and jump in Tania's car, blasting the air conditioning as they drive. They sink into the cool air. They don't speak in their usual, easy manner and Guin wonders if Tania is feeling the same sadness that requires a kind of quiet to endure.

Guin is at times amazed and at other times horrified by her twin sister.

She watches Tania—vocal and belligerent when she must be—stand firm and unapologetic in her beliefs and demands while Guin stands mute, a smile on her face. Guin is the nice one.

There seems to be nothing she can do about it.

She has begun to wonder if this being good is not such a good thing. It is beginning to feel intolerable. Her skin crawls with every forged and fraudulent smile. A fairy tale. (Not the good sort.)

Guin doesn't mean to be such a good girl. Sometimes being so good goes against every instinct she possesses. Which is not to say being good is not good. Oh, what *does* she mean? Being good when it means swallowing the bitterness instead of spitting it; when it means smiling while inside you seethe; when it means grinding your teeth in order not to upset anyone; then good is not good.

And Guin is a good girl.

Where did it come from? No one ever expected this of her. Her mother never demanded this kind of acquiescence. It is as if she is the polarity of Tania's defiance. The balance.

"You don't always have to be so good, Guin," Tania tells her. "Just get pissed off."

"I'm not pissed off."

"You must be sometimes."

"I don't know. I don't *feel* pissed off."

"Bullshit."

Is that tightening in her chest, is that constricting of her throat, is that inability to draw full breath and expand her lungs, is that anger being squelched by an ideal of goodness?

Is "pissed off" a volcano—a dormant, slumbering mass of boiling fire—lodged inside the goodness?

Lately the good girl veneer feels thin and insubstantial. Guin is not sure how long it can hold. She is one part curious to see what will happen and one part terrified.

The air inside Dunkin Donuts is almost frigid. Guin's skin feels chilled—the sweatiness dries right up. They wait for the cups of iced coffee and carry the trays out to Tania's car, next to which is a sedan, running, no one inside. Tania looks around furtively.

"Let's go," Tania says.

Guin looks around and hisses, "Do we have to?"

"Just be the look-out."

"Oh, Tania!" But Guin's words are swallowed by the closing of the sedan's door. Tania quickly looks around and backs out. Moves the car to a spot several spaces over. She hops out, leaves the sedan running, trots back over to her own car. This is a stunt she has been pulling since she received her driver's license.

"Why would you leave your car running while you get your coffee?" she has asked repeatedly over the years.

"So your car stays cool in the summer or warm in the winter," Guin always replies.

"Does it not occur to these morons that someone could simply come along and drive away with their car?"

"You can't always assume the worst of people, Tania. And this is a pretty small town—people know each other."

"You are too trusting."

So Tania began moving running cars. "Just to screw with 'em." Only a space or two over so when they come back out, they might wonder.

People always ask what it's like to be a twin. Which is difficult for Guin to answer because it's not as though she's spent any time *not* being a twin. It's like asking a whale what it's like to be a whale. Or a flower a flower. She usually smiles and says, "It's nice—I'm very close with my sister."

"People are so fucking stupid," Tania says.

"They're just curious," Guin says.

"It's not like we're world record holders for the longest fingernails or something. Or bizarre like that tree man."

"Tree man?" says Guin.

"You haven't seen that tree man? He's from, like, Indonesia. He has what looks like bark growing on his skin. He looks like a tree. His hands literally look like parts of a tree. You haven't heard about him?"

"No. I'm kind of glad I didn't know, but now I do, so thanks for that," says Guin.

"It's gross."

"I can imagine."

"We can Google it," says Tania.

"No, my mental images are bad enough, thanks."

"All I'm saying is that it's not like twins are all that uncommon," says Tania. "Geez, it's not like we're freaks."

"Well, I'm not," says Guin.

"Har har," says Tania. "Explain Pickle then."

The year they turned thirteen, their mother moved them into a three bedroom apartment. It was more expensive than the two bedroom places they had rented until then and, Guin now realizes, it must have meant a lot more work and worry for her mother. Before this move, Guin and Tania always shared a bedroom. And lamented it and whined about it and fought and slammed doors—no one can, with more precision and exquisite perfection, anger a girl more thoroughly or efficiently than her sister. Both Guin and Tania were elated to learn they would have their own room. This was a step toward self-reliance. Toward separation.

In the new apartment, their bedrooms were across the hall from each other.

Both girls spent days decorating their rooms. They scoured thrift shops for linens and decor that would define them. Guin felt as though she were establishing something fundamental. She pored over home magazines and catalogs. She especially liked the feel of old beach cottage—something out of *Coastal Living*. She chose pure whites and shades of blue. Extra pillows on the bed. She spent every cent of babysitting money she had saved until the room was just how she envisioned it.

Tania went with black overall.

"Dismal," Guin said when she walked into Tania's finished room.

Tania walked across the hall to Guin's. "Fluffy. And so *puuuur*-it-ty."

"Enough," their mother trilled from her own room.

The first night was too quiet. The second night was intolerably quiet. The third night, Tania showed up at her door. Guin showed up at Tania's the next night. From there on out, they slept nights in each other's room, curled together, cats, in each other's beds—as always.

"Well, I sure am glad we got the bigger apartment!" their mother said. But she said it with a smile.

They were simply attached and they discovered that neither one wanted it to be any different.

It was like when they had a friend over for an afternoon or an overnight. Even though it was fun, they were relieved when the friend left because they could go back to being just them. Just them alone together.

That's part of how it feels to be a twin.

If she had to explain, being a twin is having a person who understands you implicitly. Who can make sense of you when you are not able to do so yourself. It is having someone who knows the intricate history of you and is wound, roots to roots, trunk to trunk, branches curled, leaf by leaf to you. For good or ill. But there it is. It is something deeper than friends. Something wider, of greater depth and breadth. It is numinous and untouchable.

She and Tania are fraternal twins, although everyone insists on drawing the comparison: Guin is a twin who gave birth to twins. But her babies are identical which makes it apples and oranges. She simply smiles and grins, *Yes, how about that? I am a twin and I had twins! Wow!* There is absolutely no biological connection between the two incidences, but she has grown tired of explaining it, so she simply doesn't bother anymore.

Guin was twenty-one weeks pregnant when an ultrasound revealed what she was hoping was Ethan's baby brother was, in actuality, his two baby sisters.

"Two heartbeats," the technician said. "Twins."

Guin could not speak. She laughed a little at first, cried a little, then went numb. She settled into a feeling of being nowhere as if she had been cleared clean away to a place of nothingness. Nothing was expected of her and she could cease to exist as a defined thing—she could simply be.

Pickle sat in a seat by her side with Ethan, still a baby, on his lap. Pickle was wiggling and jumping in his seat, excited and laughing quietly.

"Guin," he kept saying. "Can you believe it, Guin!"

"Oh, Pickle," she sighed in the car afterward.

"Guin? Aren't you happy? Two babies! Can you believe it? Two little girls—it's amazing!"

She rested her head on his shoulder and he put his arm around her. "It's amazing," she said. She could not say all the things she was thinking and all the things that were worrying her because these were, after all, her babies. Pickle just didn't get it. Even if she told him everything that was going through her mind, he would dismiss it; he only ever believed in the best. She was the doomsayer—Pickle just wasn't wired that way.

When the shit hit the fan, as she knew it would, it would be she who would have to clean it up with her ever-present mop and bucket anyhow.

And yet, something in her could not suppress the joy of knowing her daughters would have that greatest of gifts: a sister.

When she found out their house was no longer their house, Guin asked herself: *Would now be the time to move out on my own?*

She wishes her mother had told her about the money problems. She also knows there would have been little she could have done. But it is still nice to think she could have helped in some way, even if it wouldn't have changed a thing.

What do we think when we think of ourselves? Guin wonders.

Guin is twenty-two. As a waitress at The Grille and Creamery, she is required to don a green checkered polyester dress with puffy short sleeves and a white ruffled apron. She wears the kind of shoes nurses wear—white and clunky. Orthopedic-looking, though her feet are just fine. She would prefer to wear sneakers, but her manager, Mr. Whiting, thinks sneakers are sloppy. Mr. Whiting has been the manager at The Grille and Creamery for twenty years. Yes, twenty. Since he was twenty-five years old and he will say proudly, *I have been the manager of The Grille and Creamery for twenty years since I was twenty-five years old. I started as a busboy when I was fifteen and worked my way up.* The age-old started-as-a-busboy story. Guin feels sorry for him. Or maybe she only feels sorry for herself.

This is why she lives with her mother. She has not made anything of herself. The age-old started-as-a-waitress-and...there is no *and*. She has no education beyond high school. The path of her life has been mired in tall weeds, and she has stumbled upon avenues she couldn't see until they were under her feet. Motherhood, her job, her stalled-out high school relationship with Pickle. He lives with his family, she with hers. It as though the idea of marriage has occurred to neither of them. It is only lately that she has begun to think of it all as peculiar.

When Guin was fifteen, she fell in love with the cutest boy she had ever seen. He was dark-eyed, long-lashed, with perfectly silky light brown hair, soft as a kitten. She passed him in the halls at school and she agonized over every detail of her being, every nuance of her movement. In her preoccupation, her face flared pink, her muscles stiffened, she was only able to stare straight ahead. She only ever saw him peripherally.

He was Pickle Fournier.

It was so real. Ardor, desire, passion pure and sharp. Peering back into her history, it occurs to her that realness gets forgotten. Rawness gets grown over—paper-thin layers grow waxy and rubbery with age. Thick scar tissue. When people grow up, they laugh at that depth, that kind of feeling and emotion; laugh at how seriously the kids take themselves. Assume those feelings are neither real nor possible in one so young. They forget how real it is. They forget that vulnerability—a willingness to let everything in—all of it. Feel it full-force. Also, the naiveté that does not yet know the consequences of such hazard, such openness, such susceptibility.

One of the worst things about growing up is realizing you're not the only one. The only one to love with such depth that your soul is exposed. That your heart is unveiled. But when you are fifteen, you are the only one. Everything is magnified, brilliant.

But experience is shared. It is repeated.

This is another heartbreak—this surprise. This astonishment. Experience recurs. And then it recurs for someone else. Is it good to learn this? Dimming the lights, softening the edges—is that good? Does diminishing the pain attenuate the joy?

She still loves Pickle. She likes to think back to being in those high school halls, just hoping to see him. A glimpse. That time was like Christmas Eve—bursting with hope and anticipation. She takes an old photo out of her wallet. He barely had facial hair then. He was soft as a baby. The first time she touched him she marveled at the softness of his skin.

Their children are named Ethan, Megan and Laura. She chose really normal names for them. Her name is Guinevere (King Arthur's) and Tania's entire name—which she never, ever admits unless forced for some reason—is Titania, after Queen Titania, Queen of the Faeries (*A Midsummer Night's Dream*). And then there is Pickle, and that's just too many odd names in one family.

Since Pickle is not as regular as she would like regarding child support, she is, in essence, a single mother. He is a good father in many ways. The children adore him. He's a lot like a big, grown-up playmate. He will do anything she asks. Except hold a job. Sometimes she tires of having to figure out what to ask. He is the high school boyfriend with whom the relationship never evolved. She and Pickle go on dates, have sex in the car (now the RV, which, she supposes, is a step up). But they are twenty-two and have three kids. She simply loves Pickle and he loves her and they are stuck in their little rut. Now that she has kids, there is only time to work and take care of them and keep life going. There is no time to think.

Sometimes it is a good excuse for not having the time to sort it all out.

Pickle's mother watches the children so she can work. If it weren't for Mrs. Fournier, Guin does not know what she would do. But even with the help of Pickle's mom and her own, being a mother to three really small children is like being stuck perpetually on a hamster wheel of work.

The kind of work that never ends—after the laundry is done, there is the laundry to do and after you eat the food and clean the dishes, there is a meal to cook and serve and dishes to be cleaned and then, again, the laundry.

She is always hunting for things: socks, pacifiers, toys, the other shoe. She is always tripping over things underfoot or kicking them across the room by accident: socks, pacifiers, toys, the other shoe. She only ever finds the other shoe when she doesn't need it anymore and she trips on it underfoot by accident.

And here is what she thinks too often: what if the best I can do for these children is survive them?

There are times when her children stay in the same diapers for hours. She doesn't mean for this to happen. Time goes in a flicker and she cannot remember the last time she changed diapers. She is relieved Ethan recently potty-trained—now there are only two whose diapers she will be too busy to change.

The other day, Ethan spilled some juice on a blanket and she got upset because it was two jobs he just created on top of all the things she already had to do. Actually—three jobs: clean the spill, clean the blanket, find a clean blanket. She rambled on about it and told him how much work she had to do and couldn't he be more careful. He wordlessly watched her clean and then he hugged her and said, "I just love you." And she held him tight and said *I'm sorry* a hundred times.

Moments such as these are when she wonders if she is failing them.

This sort of bright hysterical feeling has seized her. Teetering somewhere between sobbing and laughing; joy and crushing despair. It is strange yet familiar.

She has taken to bribing Ethan with Lifesavers. All the experts and books and parents' magazines say this should never be done, but what they fail to mention is that it works. Like a charm. What is so wrong with it? But she worries: how will he be damaged by the things she does simply to make him get out of the car and climb the stairs into the house?

She knows she must love them more than she needs to throw something through the window. This is harder than it seems—harder than she ever imagined a thing could be. Not the loving them part, but the *not* throwing things through the window part.

She remembers when the girls were smaller and she sometimes relied on the baby swing to get one of them to sleep for nap. She would look at the one in the swing going back and forth and back and forth, tiny hands curled, little head turned to the side, eyes closed and face peaceful and what she would feel was gut-wrenching guilt. Maybe the baby was thinking, *Wow, this swing is great*, but Guin imagined the baby was thinking that Guin had abandoned her. Did they seem defeated? She was sure she saw it in their small faces. The twins required so much time and attention, and that left her wondering if she was giving enough to Ethan. She didn't color with him or do craft projects—the mommies on the mommy blogs had it all figured out. She couldn't seem to keep up. Shouldn't she be doing more to help him learn things? Flashcards, workbooks, sensory tubs…what else?

She wonders what she is doing that will result in catastrophic ends. What is she missing that would make all the difference. She worries that she will screw them up without even knowing why or meaning to because of her shortcomings.

But then suddenly she remembers to spend a little extra time with them instead of doing what needs to be done—laundry or paying bills—and she remembers to hug a little more and she remembers to play with them and she remembers to be kind. She remembers to give and to open her heart wide, wide, wide.

For those moments, she is sure. She knows she is doing good by them.

And even though her life has been more a series of stumbles than a planned design, there is more than enough love to steady her feet through the weeds.

"Pickle, what if we slept in the RV tonight? Would your mom watch the kids until morning?"

It took most of the day, but all the boxes and furniture sit firmly in the rooms in the old stone house that are now to bear them. Guin stands outside in the dark of the evening. The Milky Way winds its iridescent way through the night sky. The breakers crash behind the house. She holds her arms around her in the chill. Pickle comes up to her and wraps his warmth across her skin. He leads her to the RV.

Guin has never been away from her kids all night, but she could use a break from their constant and powerful need of her. Just for one night. Guilt courses through her equally with her need to be away. If she were to go and get them, she would long deeply for solitude; if she does not go and get them, she will worry that they need her. But she takes a little leap and decides to let them stay with Pickle's mom.

She tells Pickle she isn't quite ready for the move. For a new bed. A new nighttime quiet. This move is jarring her. Thoughts she didn't realize she had, questions of which she was not aware are now blowing through some veil she did not know was there.

She and Pickle park the RV out by the beach. They sit on the boulders that flank the road and separate it from the shoreline and watch the water move in and out. They lean into each other and she is glad to have him.

This is a very familiar scene. A lovely lush full tableau.

She holds on to what she knows. She is acutely and painfully aware that she has no clear vision of where she is going. She is also aware that this has never mattered before.

She is scared because all of a sudden it does seem to matter.

She leans in closer to Pickle and he tightens his arm around her, nuzzles his nose into her long curly hair. The wind kicks up and a few drops of rain touch their skin. "Looks like one of them storms," Pickle says, and they move into the RV.

It does not feel as though it is an accident that she is with Pickle. Their kids are not accidents, either, even if not planned. Nothing feels exactly haphazard with Pickle—it all feels set in their comfortable way. She is not bored nor does she want another person. What does strike her occasionally is that maybe she *should* want things to be different. She is fully aware that people must think this whole arrangement is odd. Or that they just need to grow up. At times, she is compelled to make excuses and give explanations, especially to people she doesn't know well. She is ashamed of these feelings and she cuddles up closer to Pickle on the blanket he has spread across the bed that spans the full width of the RV. She closes her eyes to the possibility that she would want anything to change. She is afraid and she doesn't know why.

Rain begins to beat against the metal roof.

She needs to shake her feelings, so she speaks. "Pickle, I almost got in a fight with this woman at Kmart yesterday," she says.

"A fight?" he says. Guin is not the type to fight.

"Well, not a *fight* fight, just an argument." And she tells him about it and that she's not sure what made her stop Darlene from driving away, but she's glad she did.

"I mean, don't you just get weary from all the crap sometimes? The way things can happen when you didn't even mean for them to?" She begins to cry. He says nothing but holds her close.

"It'll all be okay, Guin," he says softly. "Don't cry."

The wind howls and rocks the RV. Lightning illuminates their faces, their bodies in the dark. Thunder cracks directly overhead, loud and angry, booms and shakes.

She closes her eyes and rubs his hands which never fails to calm her. Ground her. She takes deep breaths of good ocean air.

Pickle asks her if she is okay. She says "yes" and smiles up at him. This dear Pickle.

He begins to kiss her and she lets the world fall away as she gets caught up in the desire he never fails to raise. She runs her hands up under his shirt and over his smooth hairless belly and chest. He is so slim and she can feel his taut muscles under his soft, thin skin. His smooth palms roll over her belly down the waistband of her shorts and into her panties. She breathes in his scent, whispers *Pickle* as he touches her until she is begging for him. He lifts her onto his lap and she slides over him and sighs with the sound of the ocean, the storm. They move slowly together and he fills her with a warmth spreading like melting, like light. Thunder claps, then moves away. The rain slows to a patter. The sound of the ocean, the ferocity and calming of the storm, consume their cries.

The screen house leaks rain.

Just a little, mostly along the edges. A little from the roof, which is canvas. The fissures are not wide enough for the mosquitoes, but water will not be denied—water will always find its way.

If the rain is falling steadily enough, the mosquitoes are kept at bay, but a light rain will not thwart them. Mostly a moot point, as when it rains, the women most often stay indoors.

Except during a heat spell when it is too hot to stay inside if it can be avoided.

Sometimes during such a heat spell, virulent, swift storms come through on the face of a cold front. They usher in blessedly cool air and sweep away the humidity. Then, depending on whether lightning is in evidence, the women sit in the screen house, the cooled air swirling around them. One or two might be found standing out in the yard, face upturned, the rain slicking down the body, pooling at the (usually) bare feet. Then when the storm has glided, torn or waltzed through, depending on its particular temperament, the sinking sun breaks free of the clouds and the blue of the sky materializes from the gray flying fast out of town, and they emerge from the screen house, dry. Or shake themselves of the wet. And they get back to whatever it was they had been doing.

They carry on.

3

Tania—One Sure Thing

Tania and Guin leave the grocery store with a cart full of food. "It never fails to amaze me how much it costs to feed this family," Tania says.

Guin pushes the cart of filled canvas bags, the ones Tania makes sure they always use. "It will only get worse as the kids grow," she says.

As they exit the building, they are surrounded by bouncy, bright teenaged girls.

"Would you like to contribute to the high school cheerleading fund?" they say in near-perfect unison.

"Oh, no," Guin says.

Tania stops abruptly.

Guin tugs at her shirt and says, "Come *on*, Tania."

Tania ignores Guin. "No, *honey*, I will not give you a donation." She intends *honey* with irony, although she suspects it is lost on these effervescent girls. "And here's why..."

"Tania, please. Let's just go," says Guin.

Tania holds a finger up to silence her sister. "Clearly you have not begun to recognize the sexist cultural subtext of your little hobby. The subservient, secondary role you play in the scheme of high school hegemonies and the larger schema of gender roles. And you show off your panties every time you jump or kick!"

"They're shorts!" says one of the girls.

Tania continues. "While some females strive for equality, others," she pauses and stares pointedly, "deliberately set themselves out for exploitation while standing as subordinates of the real status of power—the male athletes. It is a position of female to male servitude: supporter to the athlete and sex object to the voyeuristic male audience. You are spectacle. You are a fetish. Do you know that there are pornography websites devoted to the cheerleader?"

"Oh, Tania!" says Guin.

"Hey!" a mother comes barreling over.

Tania watches as Guin sighs and shrinks, but she stands firm.

"Don't you talk to my daughter that way!" the woman says.

Tania says to the woman, "I didn't say anything untrue. I did not use profanity." She turns back to the girls. "Here's a question for you girls: Why is it you only cheer for the boys' teams? What about your fellow females who play sports?"

"That would be *weird*," says one of the cheerleaders and makes a face.

Tania narrows her eyes, "Would it?"

Another mother comes over. "How dare you? Cheerleading is a positive, enriching activity," she says.

"Women are NOT decoration!" Tania shouts. She turns and strides away. She hears Guin apologizing.

"Guinevere!" she barks. "We have nothing for which to feel sorry!" she says in her favorite lofty English accent. "That was exhilarating."

"We could have given them a buck..." Guin says.

"Oh, please, like I ever would. Anyway, this stuff costs so much, we have nothing left."

"Why must you embarrass me?"

Tania tosses an arm around her sister. "You love me! You love me so much, Guinevere!"

"I do, Titania."

"Don't call me that."

Tania wanders through the big stone house, lingering in her memories of it. She longs to feel the grounding of home—a grounding of any sort—but worries she will remain untethered. Which is a feeling she cannot shake lately. She makes her way outside, basks in the sky and the sun, inhales the salty breeze.

She finds Aunt Anne out front. She is inspecting one of the beach rose bushes. Another storm blew through yesterday late afternoon and Aunt Anne is checking for damage.

"This is not good for the flora," she says. She gently parts the green branches and peers in toward the trunk. "Your grandmother came home from bingo the other night and tells me some of the old biddies are saying this is all a sign from God. 'He's trying to tell us something with all this wild weather!' they say. I say enough with the storms—just tell us!"

"God works in mysterious ways."

Aunt Anne turns and looks at Tania squarely. "You don't believe in any of that bunk, do you?"

"No. I was raised on Goddess." Tania says, although she isn't sure what she believes anymore.

Aunt Anne turns back to the bush, "Well, no one thinks She's got much pull around here anymore."

Tania shakes her head slowly. "Well, except for my mom."

"I would think Goddess would have a lot more to be pissed off about than this God that's been foisted on us."

Tania is inclined to agree.

There is a crunching on the crushed-shell driveway. The car halts and Shea unfolds himself from the confines of his car—he's come over to help Tania move boxes into the house.

Shea is twenty-five, a graduate student and the program manager for the university radio station.

They met three years ago at a rally on campus. It was Earth Day, one of the first spring days carrying a warm breeze that no longer held a remnant of winter. The kind of new spring day that makes you feel giddy and that all things are possible. No limits. This is how Tania felt that day.

She was managing a table with information about vegetarianism, the impact of the meat industry on the environment, global hunger and agriculture, the inhumanity and dangers of the factory farm. He was doing some recording, roving live while a disc jockey back at the station played music, patching Shea in between songs.

He approached her. "Can I put you on the radio?" he asked.

His eyes were like melting chocolate. His eyelashes were so long they tangled up in each other. Of course, she agreed to whatever he said.

After he interviewed her, he asked if she would have a drink with him later.

"I'm not old enough to drink," she said.

He grinned at her and she caught her breath. "Is that no, then?"

She smiled genuinely, deeply. Of course, it wasn't.

The form of Shea is simply lovely. He is a fixture on campus and for months she watched his long, lithe figure move around the grounds. From a top floor of the library, as she sat curled in one of the upholstered chairs with a book, she'd watched him through the high wide windows as he crossed the grassy parts of campus. His black hair is longish on top, like a floppy, uncombed pompadour, brushed back on the sides, a little curly all over. Longer sideburns than most of these boys around here. Lean, his muscles small and taut and right beneath his smooth skin. Tight jeans and a staple black or white printed tee shirt, laundry-worn thin and soft.

But there's more. He smells and tastes of cigarettes and coffee or beer, depending. Some women would undoubtedly be turned-off by this detail, but not Tania. The whole thing put together intoxicates her. The whole thing simply makes her weak. Makes her ache. She wants to eat him, drink him, smoke him, envelop him, swallow him. Consume him.

The sex with Shea is stunning. Startling. The way she wants him is like pain. It contains an urgency that she is powerless to control. They are unable to keep their hands off each other. Their mouths and hands seem to be propelled on by a thing outside themselves. When she is with Shea, she possesses no inhibitions and there is nothing to stop her from feeling everything and reacting to it naturally. She leaves her head completely and melds with his body. It is like changing from flesh into hot liquid. It is like being entirely and perfectly filled. It is good in the way that makes the knees weak and the belly fluttery. Just thinking about him sends waves of heat through her. She loves the way he feels in her hands; she loves the way she feels in his. She knows he shares the same feelings for her.

But none of this is certainly and decisively all there is to Shea.

Shea himself is simply extraordinary.

He is the boy who will carry her books or run across campus with an umbrella on a rainy day because he knows she always forgets hers. He remembers her favorite drink and will bring it to her from the campus coffee shop to soothe her on a bad day or celebrate a good one.

He is devoted to her.

She sends him into the house with boxes marked "books" and "toys" and "kids' winter clothes."

He returns and finds her in the garage, bent over a stack of boxes. She feels big warm hands on her hips, his groin pressed against her backside.

"I like you at this angle."

She wiggles her hips.

"You are some *good* help." She turns and presses close. "I think everything that needs to go in is in."

He kisses her. "Want to show me your new room?"

"*No.* My grammy is right downstairs."

"I just want to see it," he says with boyish innocence. He holds her against his body. Oh, he is lovely. A warmth that originates in her thighs rises up. She runs her hands along his ribs and her fingers bump along the muscles, the smooth grooves, under his soft, washer-worn tee shirt.

She smiles. "All right, come on." She points at his feet. "Take off your shoes."

They sneak upstairs, barefoot, tread on their toes.

Once in her room, the door clicked shut, the little door knob lock turned, she unbuckles his belt. He pulls her shorts down and she kicks them aside. She pulls his shirt over his head, rumples his hair, and runs her hands along his firm stomach. Smooth skin. She unzips his pants and slips her hand inside his pants. He groans and she tells him to shush. So he slides his hand into her panties and rubs her gently the way she loves. It becomes a contest of who can be most quiet.

She pushes him on the bed, pulls off his jeans and drops his boxers to the floor. She takes off the rest of her clothes slowly but won't allow him to touch her. Naked, she crawls over him and swivels against him. She leans over and grazes his lips with a nipple. He pops it into his mouth and moves his tongue in a slow circle. She inhales and glides him inside of her. Every time it feels as good as the first time. She is filled up and her vision breaks apart in shards of broken light. She moves over him and over him until the movement is all she knows. It becomes her entire awareness. Their fingers braid. She never wants it to end. It must. She puts her mouth on his and they come together in quiet intermingled breath.

Afterwards, "I love you," he says. "Sorry to be trite."

"I love your lack of originality," she says.

She curls up near him and watches as he drifts off to sleep. He always falls asleep almost immediately after sex. It is a joke between them. She gazes at his face. His beautiful face. She feels intense love and consuming fear. She rests her head on his chest and listens to his heart beating and she doesn't let go. She doesn't let go. She does not let go until the holding on is the only thing she knows.

After Shea leaves, Tania heads back out to the garage to be sure she has brought all her things upstairs.

All that remains is the stuff for storage—duplicate items that a lived-in house would already possess, like all the things that belong in a kitchen. Or curtains and bath towels. Someday her mom will need these again, but for now they will sit in storage, waiting, much like Tania imagines her mom will be. Since Tania feels as though her own life hasn't really begun yet, she is in a strange place of simply being where she is wherever that may be. She is waiting in a different way—the kind of waiting that involves work toward an end.

"What's this?" She finds a stack of composition notebooks—the kind with the black and white speckled covers—behind a pile of boxes that have been left sitting on her grandmother's front lawn. They are the kind of notebooks Harriet the Spy used. There are eighteen of them in one neat stack which is tied together with twine, like ribbon on a present. No one heard her ask about them and now she looks around furtively.

On this first day at Grammy's, Tania requires some distraction.

They've moved around a bit—Tania and Guin and their mother. Not so much that upheaval is a thing that defines her, but enough so that it wasn't a novel occurrence. Tania recalls packing up her room quite a few times. They never moved far. Once it was as close as three houses down the street. The difference was floor three to floor one and a hundred bucks cheaper on the rent.

"And the landlord is a nicer guy," their mom told them. A few times it was a hurried affair—Mom short on rent money and needing to start fresh with a new landlord. Tania had no idea how her mom made the money work out. Somehow she did.

Only once they were outright evicted. Their mother never would have told them. Tania found the notice by accident. She never said a word about it. Not even to Guin.

Of her family, she cares the least about this move to her grandmother's. She is certainly affected the least, and all she feels is anger on her mother's behalf. She knows how much her mom loved that house; she knows how hard she worked for it. She is furious at the injustice of a system that can so readily break people. But for herself, there is nothing. It's almost as though her ability to form an opinion has seeped away. The beliefs and convictions she always held dear have become a bit colorless. They droop. They were replete and substantial as to be nearly personified. Now it feels as though they have turned their backs on her. She must work now to defend them, most of all to herself.

But she is tired.

And she feels flat.

She is like a heat wave that shimmers up from the road. Waves that dissipate into air. Flaring hot into nothingness. What amounts to a mirage.

She sits down on the rock ledge that flanks the walkway. It leads to the porch that wraps around the house. She unties the twine, flips open one of the notebooks and her mother's loopy script fills the dated pages with words top to bottom. The notebook, the one from the top of the stack, begins in 1981, when Mom was ten, and the final entry in the last notebook on the bottom is from 1989, just before she and Guin were born. Tania hears the door creak open and drops the notebooks quickly into the box at her feet. Mom walks toward her.

It is late morning, the sun warm on her back. Mom kisses her goodbye and gets into her car and heads off to work.

Tania is on summer break. She is going to be a senior in the fall. She commutes in her little junk car—the university is close by, so if she breaks down, there is usually someone to come get her. She double majors in English literature and women's studies and works part time at the same local supermarket she has worked at since high school. Guin had been smart—being a waitress is a lot more profitable and Guin could get a better job than The Grille and Creamery someday and make really good tips. Tania is always encouraging her to quit but for some reason Guin just won't do it. Tania has been at George's Supermarket for long enough now that it slides on like a comfy old shitty shoe. She barely needs to think when she's there. Which is not to say she doesn't do a good job. She does—her best. The owners are flexible with her schedule and, for a student, that is a good find. She is grateful to them for their kindness and generosity. She will never be accused of having a rotten attitude. She can't tolerate kids like that. Tania is adored by her managers because no matter what task she is asked to do, no matter how lowly it may be considered by the masses, she takes it all very seriously. She not only follows protocols, she makes up her own and enforces them. She is neat and organized, she is reliable, she is always on time, she is the cleanest worker for which any boss could hope. But she is set apart because she is neither a spoiled kid nor a retail-lifer. She is on the outside of things—even though it's never broached, she knows that someday she's moving on and so do the lifers. She likes everyone, she simply is not one of them. She doesn't fit.

Sometimes she thinks she doesn't fit anywhere.

There is something fastened on Tania—she cannot escape its weight. She is consumed with an urgency to *do* better, *be* better. Than other people? Than herself? She cannot pin an answer down, but there will be some mighty and enduring collapse if she fails.

To shake the leaden feeling, she distracts herself.

She had no idea her mother once kept diaries. But here they are. If she takes them, will her mother notice they are missing? She suspects her mother has bigger worries right now. She knows she should ask her mother for permission to read them, but she doesn't want to. She doesn't want her mother to know she knows about them at all. Besides, if she asks, she risks a "no."

Tania is an honest person. She considers it a defining aspect of her being. It goes beyond other people thinking her to be honest—more important is that *she* knows she is honest. Honesty is a very cut-and-dried thing. One decides simply and cleanly to be honest, and then simply and cleanly is honest. So when confronted with a temptation to be dishonest, one simply and cleanly disregards the conflict. Actually there is no conflict because dishonesty is not a thing in which she participates. The conflict disappears because in all circumstances, she will choose to be honest. It is a choice.

She carefully places the diaries tied together with their twine into the empty box and she carries them up to her small bedroom. Tania has been given the tiny room at the back corner of the house, but that is fine because even though it is the smallest room, it overlooks the ocean. She listens to the waves breaking as she falls asleep. She wakes to the same sound mixed with the morning calls of gulls. This used to be her mother's room when she was growing up here. She gazes out the window. To her right the long shoreline extends out and to her left is the causeway that leads to a very small island. Straight ahead is the open ocean and it might as well be forever because it looks and feels like forever. A surety that cannot be denied.

She closes the door with a quiet click. Fixes her mind on this one sure thing.

Puzzle.

Aunt Anne and Grammy like to piece together ornate jigsaw puzzles. The kind that take up an entire rickety old folding card table. They keep the table in a corner of the sun porch under one of the big windows.

Apparently they enjoy being perplexed. Or perhaps they like to figure things out.

Tania wanders over to the table. The older women examine the puzzle on the old card table. Their gazes probe. They have constructed the entire outer edge, because that is how they always begin. Sort out those straight-edged pieces. Empty cans of beer sit in amongst the cold ones in the little red cooler.

Aunt Anne tests a piece. "Nope." Places it back in the appropriate color pile. They sort the pieces by general color and the texture of the pictures they can decipher, only vaguely in some instances.

Grammy laughs and snorts lightly. "You have no patience, Anne."

"Oh, you keep quiet."

Their reading glasses perch on the ends of their noses.

Tania picks up a book out of the basket on the floor beside the sofa. This one is about the Hurricane of 1938—the Great Hurricane. Old sepia pictures—a house being washed away in the churning water, collapsed cottages tipped on their sides. One is flipped onto its roof. Houses thrown off their foundations and dropped to entirely different places. In some photos, there are no houses, but only possessions that remain on the beach: bed frames with the linens in a wet heap, a wooden chair, a large soup pot. Intact things. Tania remembers hearing about a tornado out in the Midwest. It leveled houses and buildings and ruined most of an entire town. One of the houses was flattened, but a single wall of kitchen cabinets was left standing. Inside the cabinets, rows of glasses remained in the same position as before the tornado came through. Tania imagines they might still have been warm from the dishwasher.

She has no homework, no papers, no reading she must do, so time moves languidly. She can pore over this book about the Great Hurricane. Houses floating in the ocean. Footprints of vacant foundations in the sand. There is a photo of an empty beach which would simply be a photo of a stretch of shoreline except for the caption that tells her that a row of cottages once lined up in this sand but were washed away. An empty beach unless you knew better. People picking through the ruins, salvaging what they could. That which once comprised homes floating in the water-filled streets.

Flooding. Driving rain. Storm surge.

The following day was sunny and calm.

"You know this house survived the Great Hurricane," her grandmother says, peering up from under her glasses at Tania.

"Were you here during the storm?" she asks.

Her grandmother nods her head. "We both were. I was nine and she was seven. We went to school that day." She nods toward Aunt Anne. "It was a perfectly lovely September morning."

"You stayed in this house?" Tania asks.

"Oh, yes. For some of it, anyway. Well, we didn't quite know it was coming in the ways we know nowadays. There was no twenty-four-hours-a-day news and they didn't have computers to tell us what to expect."

"The seamen knew."

Grammy nods in agreement. "They knew something was coming. That was back in the days when we counted on intuition; when we looked back at what we knew in order to look forward to what we might expect. We could still feel things in our bones then."

"But still no one quite expected that storm. Not like that. It was a moon tide," said Aunt Anne. "A new moon."

Tania's grandmother moves some puzzle pieces around with the tip of her index finger. The pieces are about three quarters of an inch square. About the size of the wrapped butterscotch candies they keep in a glass dish on the wide windowsill. The ones they suck on regularly as they work their puzzle, the golden cellophane wrappers accumulating on the edge of the table.

"Of course, now they make the weather out to be like the second coming of Christ every time a storm is about to hit!" says her grandmother.

"Then we get four measly inches of snow!" caws Aunt Anne.

From Tania's experience working at the grocery store, she knows what they are talking about. Every time a big storm is forecast—a Nor'easter, a blizzard, the remnants of some hurricane, a dusting of snow for crying out loud—the residents flood George's and buy up all the jugs of water, matches, batteries, candles, canned goods and can openers. They clear the shelves, including the beer and wine. Because who could sustain a storm without that? Fiona, George's daughter who now runs the store, loves it when a big one is forecast, while all her employees steel themselves for the onslaught.

Then, almost always, all the hype amounts to nothing. Just more fuel for the general anxiety of the masses. She thinks back to last September when a hurricane was forecast to make landfall over the South Coast and the islands. As she drove to work, she witnessed the storm preparations: crisscrossed masking tape over exposed glass, plywood covering the big windows, people packing up cars full of kids and dogs to drive to inland relatives. And then the jammed parking lot of George's. The mania and fear. The *better-to-be-safe-than-sorry* sentiment, the endless speculation of potential damage. The parroting of meteorological jargon and doom. The attempt to gain control and the satisfaction of having achieved it.

Then the high pressure system sitting north of New England moved off allowing the remnants of the hurricane to veer east out over the northern Atlantic. Hardly a cloud in the sky and not one drop of rain. The leaves in the trees barely rustled in their branches. The grocery store was blessedly quiet the day after. Their very own eye of the storm. There was nothing left for anyone to buy. Tania suspected they were all at the mall.

"Everyone gets so worked up today," says her grandmother. "We just buckled down and rode it out."

"As soon as the power went out at the school, they put us on the bus and tried to drive us home. But trees had already fallen and were blocking the roads. So the bus driver just opened the door and we all got out and walked home."

"The wind was fierce! And by the time we got home we were soaked."

"To the bone!"

"We were laughing like loons because we kept getting blown into the trees and phone poles!"

"We thought it was hilarious!"

"The bus driver just dropped you off?" says Tania.

"Yes—can you believe that! Today they bubble-wrap the kids, but in those days you had to get home and you got home the way you could, whatever that might happen to be."

"In a hurricane, it was avoid flying objects and wipe the rain out of your eyes!" Her grandmother snorts with laughter.

"Then when we got home, Mother dried us off and got us in warm clothes and Father packed us all in the car and we drove over to the big stone house. Lots of others were there, too. It wasn't planned—it just seemed like the logical thing to do and everyone had the same idea. It saved our lives."

"Where was the big stone house?"

"Over across from the Point, honey. It's still there."

Tania turns back to the pictures of the houses being washed away, blown out to sea, flipped over in the sand. "You were pretty lucky," she says.

"Oh, yes, we were."

"What happened to this house?" asks Tania.

"When we got home, it was rather a shock. The entire landscape had changed. All the cottages that used to line the beach—*gone*. And our house, *this* house, well..."

"It was pretty beat down."

"But we rebuilt. The weather was just beautiful that fall. Remember, Millie?"

"I do. It was a help, a blessing. There was no power for about two weeks. But we just rebuilt. We were among the lucky few."

"Give me a hurricane over a blizzard any time. At least hurricane season is warm and sunny. Try fixing your house in half a foot of snow, with the wind blowing a gale off the water. At least September is one of the prettiest, gentlest months."

"Oh, yes, I agree. But no matter what, you just rebuild."

"Oh, sure. What else can you do?"

Tania gets up and takes the book outside. It is a quiet, sunny morning and the low tide water laps at the rocky shore. The horizon is clear and the ocean as still as it ever gets. The quiet strikes her—the ocean's roar brought down to a gentle burbling over stones. It is a captivating sound.

As she reads about the hurricane, she is struck by the forces that gathered to culminate in calamity. A collision of random circumstance. The storm moved northward up the coast from Cape Verde, sparing Florida, the Carolinas and the Mid-Atlantic, never making landfall, preserving its speed and strength out over the warm waters of the southern and middle Atlantic. A high pressure system north of Bermuda prevented the hurricane from turning eastward out to sea. Devastating storm surge was the result of a high moon tide. A new moon, a high tide on September 21, 1938. The sun lined up with the moon and the earth and this acted to amplify the tidal forces, drawing the tides even higher. A Neap tide.

A people accustomed to the idea of no warning.

She gets up suddenly, remembering, and strides over to the far side of the porch, where her great grandfather had written a message in wet cement:

Part of this porch and house remained in survival of the Great Hurricane of September 1938.

She looks down the beach that stretches westward. It was once filled with cottages, now gone. It is a state reservation now—a public beach. An entirely new landscape was carved out in a matter of hours. How tenuous.

Tania turns again to the image of the house submerged in water.

She studies and studies it. How can an entire house—that solid mass—float out into the ocean?

How delicate, she thinks. How flimsy and illusory are that in which we place so much trust.

Tania started working at George's Supermarket after she went to city hall at age fifteen with her mother and got herself a work permit. The clientele is seasonal—the summer people (which also means the rich people, who are thought of as summer people even though some live here year-round) shop the gourmet and organic sections, buy the imported and local artisan cheeses, the wines from the regional vineyards, the lattés from the espresso machine at four bucks a cup. The summer people live in the huge houses down by the shore. The houses are very tall even though all the others around them are much lower to the ground.

The regular people, the ones who live here year-round in the old run-down houses that have been in their families for generations—the people who have always been here and keep the town going by pumping the gas, fixing the cars, running the cash registers, cleaning the houses of the summer people—those regular people shop at the other end of the store in the aisles with rice and potatoes and carrots in the can. Regular food. Some of them hit the food pantry in the dead of winter every now and then if they have to, in the bad years, to take home the canned goods the summer people donated after their last sweep of the kitchen cabinets on Labor Day weekend.

George's is small compared to the big box supermarkets—only seven cash lines which are almost never open at the same time, except the predictable big holidays: Fourth of July, Labor Day weekend, Thanksgiving, Christmas. Tania started out as a bagger, then moved up to cashier and now holds the coveted spot in the coffee bar. There are only three people assigned to work in the coffee bar, which is called George's Café. It is *the* position in the store because not only is it sort of a cakewalk, but it's fun to work the espresso machine and blender.

"Miss? Can I get a large decaf iced mocha—extra shot of decaf, two and a half pumps of mocha?"

She cocks her head and smiles at the tanned man standing next to a woman so thin and tan Tania knows managing her weight and melanin must be her singular vocation.

"Anything for you, ma'am?" Tania asks.

"Large skim, decaf iced Americano. Sugar-free vanilla, three pumps." They barely look at her as they toss out their orders.

She thinks of Guin saying to Ethan, "Can you think of a better way to ask?" To which he automatically responds, "Pleeeeease." She longs to ask this couple that very question, but turns to the espresso machine and pulls the shots of coffee for their elaborate drinks. She makes the drinks to the customers' specifications and hands them over with a smile which they do not return. Tania thinks people getting fancy drinks should automatically be happy. They don't make eye contact with her, just walk away to the registers to pay for their drinks along with the bottle of wine, expensive wedge of cheese and fresh baguette that sticks out of their basket in its brown paper wrapping.

The store is a split personality. The dichotomy is disquieting to Tania. There is a convenience store across the street from George's and even though they have the coffee bar right here, most of the employees walk across to get their dollar cups of burnt-tasting drip coffee rather than pay three times as much right here in the store at which they are employed. Because it costs too much and what they can afford to drink is burnt-tasting dollar cups of coffee from the convenience store.

How do we all get to where we get, she wonders. How much say does one have? She wants to believe there must be some; and until recently, she had been certain. Isn't that what college is for—to make everything certain? Maybe it's all a loosely veiled joke. The planning and thinking and intensity, when maybe none of it does any good—meets no specific and assured end.

Tania's tuition is covered by academic scholarship. She lives at home because the scholarship is strictly for courses and fees and does not cover room and board. This is fine with her. Being on campus so much, she has witnessed the silliness of the dormitories. The foolish giggling of girls chasing after boys and the relentless judgment of those boys' gazes on the girls' bodies and faces. The beer and puking in the bushes. The hooking-up and walks of shame. The pregnancy pee sticks and the tears when as far as Tania can see, they should have known better.

School holds gravity. School is a heavy orb resting firmly in her cupped palm. Solid and very real and she must be sure to move slowly and precisely and steadily forward so as not to drop it.

Do not drop it.

She carries it.

Along the way, she has picked up more so her load grows and becomes heavier. Environmentalism, gay rights, anti-poverty, equality in healthcare, anti-war movement, feminism, global poverty, clean energy, race rights and equality, urban sprawl, pollution. Toxins in the food, the water, the shampoo and mascaras, body lotions, diapers, vaccines—everywhere. She abhors graffiti. There is a lot of information circulating and she absorbs all of it into her mind, still young, still spongy, still malleable. The information seeps into her body, her limbs, solar plexus, third eye, her legs that aren't able to stay still.

"Excuse me?"

Tania looks up with a start. "Yes?"

"I've asked you three times for an iced tea."

"Sure. Sorry. Anything in that?" *Besides my saliva?* she would like to add. Not that she ever would, but some days she imagines doing it. It is baffling to her the way rude people remain blissfully unaware of the vulnerability of their food and drink.

The evening moves along and Tania sweeps the floor of the café. It is almost closing time and she has the place just about cleaned up.

"Hey, sweetie. How's your night going?"

It is Sue, a lifer. She has worked at George's Supermarket since she graduated high school and is a fixture in the deli. Tania thinks she's in her fifties, but isn't sure.

"Good, Sue. Pretty quiet. You?"

"Same over in the deli. Monday night—what can you expect? You clean your machine yet, honey?"

"Not yet. What do you need?"

Sue pulls out a scrap of paper. Tania recognizes it as a slip from a roll of register tape. "I'm buying a little something for everyone—I hit for a hundred bucks on a scratchy."

Tania moves behind the counter. Hits the steam wand on the machine and listens to it hiss. "Nice! Give me the list."

Sue hands it to her and she gets busy making the drinks. "You seeing that adorable boyfriend of yours tonight?"

Tania smiles. "You betcha."

"Oh, what I wouldn't give for that young love feeling again! But I get to go home to Ronnie. How's your new place?"

"Not too bad. Settling in."

They shoot the breeze a little more as Tania rings up the drinks, and then someone at the customer service desk is making the five-minutes-to-closing announcement. She cleans the espresso machine, washes the floors and takes out the trash. She says goodnight to everyone. *See you tomorrows* all around.

As she walks out the door, her cell rings. It is Thom. She ignores the call and deletes it from her call log as she slips into Shea's car and his embrace.

"Hi, babe," he says.

"Hi, babe yourself," she says. He is the flavor of cigarettes and coffee and it is delicious.

He is beautiful.

She knows how lucky she is to have him. Love like this can be fragile. Will she hold it with care, or handle it recklessly? She wonders as an outside observer might.

In early morning, the sun rises just beyond the causeway, seemingly out of the barrier of beach roses that hides the sandy shore, and Tania squints into all that light as her feet pound the tarred road that flanks the shoreline.

She runs back to the house, up the outside stone steps and onto the sun porch where Grammy and Aunt Anne sit in their chairs.

"Do you ever move at a moderate pace, Tania?" says Grammy, but not unkindly.

Tania laughs. "I don't think so."

Tania runs everyday at dawn. She craves the solitude and the air flowing past her when the world is quiet and unmoving. She cuts fast through all that stillness. She absorbs nothing. The nothingness fills her, quelling and quieting the cacophony in her bones.

"I think it's great, honey," says Aunt Anne. "You should move like that as long as you are able." Aunt Anne herself ventures out alone down the beach everyday. Slowly but steadily. She is seventy-nine. This age is unfathomable to Tania. She witnesses it right in front of her eyes, but can conjure no image of herself at that distant age. It is beyond her to believe she will ever be that old.

Tania is five years older than her mother was when Tania was born. Tania knows that she and her sister were unexpected. It was, undoubtedly, an *uh-oh* moment for her mom. Seventeen is seventeen, after all. Seventeen is seventeen unless it was medieval times when seventeen was actually pretty old to have a kid and you were lucky if you were not dead by forty. But Tania was born in 1989 just as the hair bands were about to die their imminent death by grunge. She does not think she was unwanted. Mom always said they were her fairy girls—women of the Goddess.

Guin and Tania are Crawfords, like their mother.

"In the Goddess' time, before the patriarchy took over," their mother has always told them, "lineage was drawn through the mother. A child's paternity couldn't be surely known, but its maternity was certain."

There are stories Mom is hesitant to tell.

Tania resembles her mother very little. Guin does. Guin inherited their mother's fair, freckled skin, the strawberry blond curls, the petite frame and fine bones. Neither their mother nor Guin can break an A-cup bra.

Tania does. Solid Ds which she laments and Guin covets.

"I'm nursing twins and I'm barely a B!"

"You just think you want them because you don't have them."

"No, I want them."

"Guin, you'd tip over or develop scoliosis. You'd, at the very least, require a great deal of chiropractic attention."

Tania is five foot seven. Coppery-brown hair, olive-toned skin. Curves. She hides them as much as she is able. "I don't want to be evaluated by the size of my breasts and the curve of my hips. I don't want to be figured out that way."

"You're pretty. You'd look amazing in a bikini," Guin will say.

"Never."

"I know, I know," Guin sighs.

Strangers express disbelief in their twin-ness. "You look so different!" they say, as if this were an original sentiment.

"That's because we have our own separate DNA, dumbass," is what Tania would like to say. With a smile. It's what she does say to Guin. No smile.

"We're just a fascination to them," says Guin. "Twins always are. I know, believe me."

"Whatever."

Tania suspects she resembles her father, about whom she and Guin know little. A high school fling, a broken condom, a boy who ran away. No love lost. Just a knocked-up girl left with the remains of fumbling teen sexual exploration.

Tania maintains that if he does not want to know her and Guin, then she doesn't want to know him. If he entertains the notion that she will come looking for him, he'll have a long wait on his hands.

"Are you angry?" Guin asked her once.

"No. I just don't care."

"Me neither." Guin, in her sweetness and unveiled sincerity, spoke true.

Family is Mom, Frank, Grammy and Aunt Anne. Guin's kids. Pickle and Shea. Tania has no use for someone who does not want her.

Tania climbs upstairs. It is her day off—she wants to finish unpacking. Everyone is out—the house will be quiet today. No one talking to her, no kid running wild, no babies fussing.

Once her room is put in order and the boxes collapsed into the recycling bin, she contemplates the stack of composition notebooks. Tania explores the room for a good spot to stash them. This house is old—it must have a nook somewhere. This was her mother's bedroom when she was a kid. Where would her mother have hidden something she needed to hide? Tania is willing to bet there must have been a thing or two her mother would have wanted to hide.

Tania gets down on the floor, peeks under the bed, pokes around in the closet. A secret door? That would be awfully cheesy. She crawls the perimeter of the small room on her hands and knees, her eyes creep along the floor and molding. Nothing unusual. She sits up on her knees, looks around. There are two dormer windows in the room—the windows that face the ocean. One is open straight down to the floor, creating an open squared space. The other has a built-in window seat. A big flowery cushion sits squarely and perfectly inside. It is the perfect place to curl up with a warm mug and a book. She is sure her grandmother or maybe even her great-grandmother made the cushion because it fits exactly so. The flowery pattern is old and does not appeal to Tania so she has wrapped an old tapestry around it, folding the excess on the underside of the pillow nice and taut over it. Now she pulls the tapestry-covered pillow to the floor and knocks on the surface of the window seat—hollow, of course. She pushes around on it and it wobbles a little. She rocks it back and forth until two opposite corners angle up and down. She grabs the upended corner and carefully lifts the flat piece of finished wood off the fitted edges of the window seat. A big empty space. She places the diaries safely inside, replaces the wood and the pillow.

She sits wearily on the window seat and stares out at the ocean. Her body is heavy and it is as though her insides have hollowed out and filled with thick liquid. The sun warms her. She feels as though she will never move from this spot—will never be able to move her limbs. A cloud covers the sun and she feels just a bit cooler and the shift of the sun and the cool air on her skin makes her shiver and her body resumes its normal heft and shape.

She leaps up off the window seat and removes the top. She lifts out a notebook from the stack of her mother's diaries, cracks it open.

She sits in the window seat facing the everlasting sea and opens the notebook up to the date September 8, 1987: the Tuesday after Labor Day, the first day of a new school year, the day all academically-minded people think of as the first real day of the year.

A salted breeze circulates through the old stone porch.

Aunt Anne sits at the table chopping green olives with pimentos, mixing the chopped bits into softened cream cheese. The silver wrapper is pushed off to the side. This she and Grammy will spread lasciviously over saltines. Like every year. It is summer fare, cream cheese and olives on saltines.

Grammy sits at the table, too, reading one of her trashy papers, waiting for Aunt Anne to finish with the olives. The gossip magazine is spread colorfully across the big table, next to the cream cheese and olives and saltines and in front of the bottle of bourbon. Tania wonders at her grandmother's penchant for celebrity dirty laundry—it seems completely incongruent with her devout godliness. Grammy has told her before, "I confess it. I do my penance every week." She buys them religiously with the weekly groceries. Aunt Anne says everyone must have a vice.

"Tania, I need a bowl for this. One of the pretty ones." Tania moves into the dining room, reaches into the cupboard and removes a small lilac-tinted glass bowl. Its surface is bumpy with an elaborate design of winding leaves and bunches of grapes.

"How's this one?" Tania asks.

Aunt Anne picks it up and looks it over. "Oh, yes. That's a nice one." She places it back on the table and continues chopping olives. All the while their hands move and move, so do their mouths in conversation or laughter. The bottle of bourbon sits squarely in the middle of the table. They drink it with ice cubes and water from heavy-bottomed, clear glass cups of simple clean lines which are only unusual because everything else in the house is so ornate.

"The glasses belonged to Father," Aunt Anne says.

"Everything else was Mother's," says Grammy.

Then the cream cheese and olives are ready.

"Who wants one?" says Aunt Anne.

"It looks a little..." Tania trails.

"Oh, try it," says her grandmother.

"Here, have a little sip. It's real good with this," says Aunt Anne, and pours her three fingers of bourbon, a splash of water, and two ice cubes.

Tania takes a cracker loaded with the spread, bites it in half, washes it down with the icy bourbon. "That is good." She is genuinely surprised.

"Would you like one, Vivian?" Aunt Anne asks.

Tania's mother shakes her head at the whole ritual. "Just give me one of those." She points to the bourbon. "I'll take it without the cracker chaser."

Aunt Anne makes delicious things—not fancy, like the food Julia Child made on channel two back when, but really good. It is all the butter. All that butter because they started cooking in a time before they knew how bad butter was. Maybe Aunt Anne knows now, but that doesn't stop her.

"Anne, hand me that other newspaper there," says her grandmother.

Aunt Anne moves the bottle of bourbon, shifts the cream cheese and olives and they spread the tabloid out flat on the table.

Grammy titters, "Oh, look what he's up to!" she snorts. "How many wives has he had now?"

Aunt Anne flips the page. They stop at a spread in the middle of the paper. "What has she gone and done now?" asks Grammy.

Aunt Anne gazes down at the paper through the bottoms of her bifocals. "Oh, isn't she just a sneaker full of shit."

"Oh, Anne!" Grammy exhales in her best shock and scandal voice, titters and snorts.

"Mom, did you see the doctor today?" Tania's mother asks Grammy.

"Don't worry about me, Vivian." Grammy brushes off the question.

"But, Mom, you've been so tired lately." She peers at Grammy's legs. "And I don't like the way your ankles look all swollen."

She tucks her feet further under the table. "Vivian, I am *fine*."

"Well, there was that heart attack at bingo a while back, Millie," Aunt Anne says.

"Anne, you know full-well that was not my heart."

Anne just laughs.

"What's she talking about, Grammy?" Tania asks.

"Oh, it's just silly," she waves her hand impatiently. "I was at bingo keeping track of the numbers and suddenly there was a hand pressing down with all its might on my chest. A big hand. The hand of God, I thought. I still think so. And I am thinking *I am ready Lord; take me home!* But then I had to help with the bake table since Connie Arruda failed to show her face and without calling and not for the first time. She always has some excuse, of course after the fact, once everything has been taken care of by someone else. That's just the way she is, as long as I have known her and I know her from way back since the old days when we were all in grade school." She stops and returns to her bourbon and slathered crackers.

"Millie, the story," says Aunt Anne.

"And there I am waiting to die and so happy to be doing the Lord's work while I am dying and not something unimportant, but I have the bake table to contend with on account of Connie Arruda. So there I am having my heart attack and trying to die, and cleaning up hermit bars and walnut tarts and whatnot. These are not things many of these people should be eating, let me tell you. So many are f-a-t!" She whispers f-a-t. "And the diabetes and the gout and the high blood pressure. But I can't make their choices for them."

"So what happened, Grammy?"

"I did what had to be done with the bake table and then got a ride home from Angie. I went to bed and waited some more to die. I was disappointed that it hadn't happened at bingo. The next day I was still dying but all I was doing was going to get my hair done since it was Saturday. I didn't really want to die at the beauty parlor, but you get what you get. Then Anne got up to have her breakfast and drive us there and looked at me and said,

'Millie! You look terrible!' and took me to the hospital. Turns out I wasn't dying at all. Just indigestion. I have never eaten one of Jeanette's walnut tarts ever again. I try to avoid the bake table altogether. But some of it is so tempting. I hope when I do die, it's at Mass. Bingo would be okay, but really, Mass would be best." She pauses largely. "Who knows where Anne will die, since she neither goes to Mass nor does the Lord's work at bingo."

Aunt Anne glares. "Not this again, Millie. Please."

Grammy's palms and fanned fingers face Aunt Anne, "I am just saying, Anne. I am just saying."

"Mmm-hmmnn." Hands busy spreading more cream cheese and olives on saltines. A little more bourbon.

When Guin gets home from working and picking up the kids from Pickle's mom, Tania inhales largely and says to her, "Mmmmm. You smell like French fries and warm ketchup."

Guin sits heavily and stares up at the ceiling. "Thank you, Titania. College has made you more observant than ever."

"Oh, Guinevere," she says. The thing Guin doesn't know and at which she would probably laugh and assert disbelief, is that Tania likes the smell simply because it is one of Guin's.

Guin looks around and says, "How will I ever baby-proof this place?" The twins crawl around her legs. They are not walking yet, but they will be soon enough. She lifts one to her lap and the other beside her and nuzzles each. They giggle and touch her face. She pretends to eat their hands. "Yumyumyum," she says. "Yummmmm," they echo.

"They are either going to kill themselves or tear the place up. Or, with my luck, tear the place up then kill themselves. Which of this stuff is expensive? Aren't old things worth a lot of money?" Guin asks.

Tania shrugs, "It depends, I guess."

"Well, I don't really want to take a chance."

Aunt Anne says, "Don't worry about any of it." She makes a dismissive motion with one of her hands. "Come on, Tania. Come help me make supper."

"I don't know how to cook," Tania says.

"You have to learn sometime," says Aunt Anne.

She doesn't really care to learn how to cook, but she follows Aunt Anne into the old kitchen and to the big white gas stove with six burners. "This is the original stove. She can be a little cranky sometimes, but if you treat her well enough, you can usually figure out how to soothe her."

"Is this the original fridge?"

"Oh, no—that would have been an old icebox. That old dinosaur is down in the basement. We store cannings in there. But this fridge is pretty old, too," says Aunt Anne.

"We should get a new energy-efficient one."

"Probably we should. Where the money for that comes from is another topic altogether." She removes ingredients from the cabinets and refrigerator.

"Okay," she says. "How much do you know?"

Tania says, "I can boil water and make anything from a box with clear instructions printed on it. And toast. I can operate a coffeemaker and a can opener."

"Square one, then. Okay," she says brightly. "A simple macaroni and cheese. Not from a box. Not bright orange."

Shred cheese, boil pasta, grate a little onion and sauté it in some butter. Then cook up a thick béchamel sauce. Combine it all in the big old stainless steel bowl.

"Add lots of black pepper and you have to crack it fresh. That already ground stuff in the little plastic bottles—God knows when that was ground. That junk is flavorless. The little details in cooking make for a big difference, honey. The little things—you remember that. And fragrance matters as much as the flavor—they work together. Some grate in a little nutmeg, but I like my little bit of onion. You could do both, I suppose. But I just stick with the onion myself."

Tania grinds the pepper.

Turn it into a baking dish, sprinkle with breadcrumbs (*yes, fresh—canned food is canned food, you know*) and dot with some salted butter.

"There," says Aunt Anne. "We'll be eating within the hour."

"The box is done in about twelve minutes," says Tania, grinning.

"Well, twelve minutes of effort is gonna get you twelve minutes of result. Know what I mean, jelly bean? Now, something green to go with it." And they make a salad from good ingredients Aunt Anne collected at the farmer's market that morning. "Fresh matters. From the ground. We have all forgotten the source. Some of us never even knew it to begin with."

They return to the porch and watch the ocean move while the casserole bakes.

"Aunt Anne, why didn't you teach Mom to cook?" Tania asks. "Do you know what we have been eating our whole lives?" She means this as a joke. There is a long and weighty silence. Everyone pretends not to notice. Vivian keeps her eyes on the water.

Aunt Anne breaks the silence. "Vivian had so many other interests. You couldn't keep her in the kitchen for long, except to grab an apple or a muffin, then she would run right out the door. She had bigger fish to fry."

"Hmmmn," says Grammy. "I tried to teach her, but she always had something else to do. Vivian was never that interested in domesticity. She never learned knitting or any of those things, either."

"Well, neither did I, Millie. She's like me; would rather read a book or wander off and see what's to see."

It is a lovely evening. They set the big table out on the porch. Then they carry the food out and sit and eat together gathered around the big table.

Aunt Anne announces, "Tania cooked supper."

"Well," says Tania, "Aunt Anne helped. She taught me."

Tania's mother takes a bite, "Really good. Almost as good as from the box." And she smiles.

"Oh, blasphemy, Vivian," says Aunt Anne. Tania can't help but think of the other ways in which her grandmother probably thinks of her mother as a blasphemer. There is silence around the table and just at the moment it is getting a little uncomfortable, Ethan shrieks.

"There's *something black* in my mac and cheese! I think it's *pepper*!" He stares down into his bowl, his eyes wide.

Guin's face freezes in resignation. Ethan is a notoriously difficult eater. Supper is their battleground. She begins to open her mouth to speak.

"Oh, no," says Aunt Anne, with utter calmness and composure. She doesn't even look up from her plate. "That's not pepper, honey. It's dirt."

He closes his mouth, snaps it shut. "Oh," he says, sits back down and begins to eat. And he cleans his plate empty.

❖ ❖ ❖

Ordinary stories—not what she craves for herself. And yet, they're all she's got. Ambivalence for an absent father. Muddled and buried disdain for the pregnant teen who was her mother. The bitterness is trite. She wonders why women choose the men they do and then she wonders why they don't have enough sense to avoid getting pregnant.

She is more ordinary than she hoped.

She thinks about her immovable pronouncements. Her mother, her sister. Women who should know better.

Maybe she was too hasty in her judgments. Maybe she is not smarter than other women as she had smugly assumed; all these women upon whom she has passed judgment, whom she has categorized, reduced to fools. Isn't she a feminist, after all? Whose side is she on anyway? Maybe it's just a little more complicated and a little less black and white. Individualistic and thorny.

Or maybe she is right about all of it and just a fool, too.

She pulls her knees to her chest and wraps her arms around them in the window seat and stares out at the farthest point she can see on the small island. She has discovered that when she focuses the entirety of her senses on a point, she can be there—she is there, as though she's been carried. She is a dissolved part of the endless whole. When she turns her face to the sky, she is free. That is all it takes. That is all there is.

She can't control where her mind flows and she is cast back to the dying month of November and she remembers: one day, she was hoping would be the day to bleed. A week late and she was never late. The triteness of the situation was embarrassing enough to sustain a level of pain. It was, on the other hand, almost funny. She had not yet done a test because she kept hoping to see the telling red in her underpants and then be able to breathe freely. She had not yet done a test because the longer she put it off, the longer she could be hopeful that this was not happening. Once she took the test and it proved positive, she could no longer live on the line of *maybe*. And although *no* was better than *yes*, *maybe* was also better when you were fairly sure of the answer.

Tania has felt closed-in on herself since winter. Stuck in the cold and ice, she thought the spring would release this thing in her that is dragging, shrinking her slowly.

Making her feel as though her insides are slowly ossifying. She is drawn to solitude, yet worries she is somehow slipping away from those she loves. She is filled with contradictions. She is disappearing in some way and is not sure whether it is terrifying or welcoming. She is also filled with self-doubt—is that the stultifying substance?— and everything at which she thought she excelled and in which she believed about herself is ebbing away, dripping away through the tips of her fingers and toes. She cannot escape these feelings no matter what she does. They follow her—she can hear their footsteps lightly tapping behind her. When she runs, they run, too.

And she has no idea where she is running.

Sometimes you can't think about something. You simply cannot allow it to enter your mind. And if it does— as that which is avoided will inevitably arise again and again—you must run to be free of it. Even when you know you can't outrun it—that such a thing is not possible—you try anyway.

She leaps from the window seat, in which she has slumped too long—leaps and hits the floor with her solid feet, a thud of bone, skin, muscle on smooth lacquered wood.

She runs down the stairs and out of the house, the screen door slams shut behind her, but she is already gone, already on her way, already gone, gone, gone. The slamming comes from far behind her. And still she runs. She runs across the causeway, her feet hit the sand, the coarse grit grinds against the smooth skin on the bottoms of her feet. She runs onto the sand path lined with beach plum bushes, until she breaks free to the shore, until her bare feet are in the water lapping to her ankles and collecting around her shins, her knees, her thighs. She keeps running until the depth of the water makes it impossible to run any farther. The muscles in her legs simply cannot drag themselves any farther forward. She raises her hands above her head and dives under a breaking wave. When she surfaces, she swims out deeper, her arms pumping, tearing through water. Once she is out past the breakers, she flips onto her back. Her breathing is fast, her heart beats rapidly. She works to slow all of it, knowing part of it is simply waiting. She points her face to the sky. All that blue and a few small white puffy clouds and the long flat line of the horizon reduce her size down, down, down to a manageable speck. She feels small and insignificant in her body. The smallness makes her life sustainable; the insignificance makes her free. The ocean opens up on either side of her and the wind flows around her body and the sun spills its warmth upon her. She feels it on her head and through her hair, on her shoulders, running down through her hands.

Feels it in the whorls of her fingertips.

"They don't make screen houses like this anymore,"
says Millie.

"We've looked, believe me," says Anne.

"This one is still good," says Tania. Everyone agrees.

"You have made it so lovely, Tania," says Millie.

*Tania took their strings of Christmas lights out of the
storage boxes and lined the joints and seams of the screen
house. Now the inside stars twinkle as the tea tree oil wafts
in the light evening breeze. A pot of hot fragrant tea is
shared and some shortbread Anne baked this afternoon
crumbles on the plate.*

*They share the quiet of the dusky twilight hour, each
thinking her own thoughts while they wait for night to
arrive and the light of the genuine stars to fall to earth.*

4

Vivian—Every Petal

Mosquitoes mottle the air at dusk. A thriving nasty mass of buzzing. It was a wet spring and the mosquitoes are sure to be intolerable this summer. These terrible mosquitoes. Every spring, as snow melts and rain muddily accumulates, the puddles provide the perfect habitat for the reproductive efforts of mosquitoes. The larvae will die if the water dries up, but this year the puddles persisted because of all the rain. Vivian knows from a lifetime of experience that this year they will not be rid of the horrible creatures anytime soon. And it is never soon enough, even if the disappearance of mosquitoes means the same of summer.

Vivian hates mosquitoes. Everyone hates mosquitoes, but she does more than most, or at least imagines so. No one could possibly despise them more than she does.

When Vivian was a child, she was not allowed to spend dusk outdoors. If she ventured out during that twilight time of day, she'd end up with a ring of mosquito bites—the welts a crown around her forehead and into her hairline. While she was stuck inside, the other kids in the neighborhood played out there in that glorious waning light as the hot summer air cooled into mild evening. Then, after dusk passed into darkness and the mosquitoes quieted, her mother would say it was too late to go out. And Vivian was a child who craved the outdoors—loved to be in all that open air, all that endless sky and ocean and meadow and tall trees, wide sprawling bushes. The sublime perfection of flowers and leaves and small things that made her slow down, look closely, to shrink and yet expand. She grew to hate those mosquitoes—they buzzed in and flew away with her freedom. She would have rather they took her blood.

"Vivian, they carry diseases that can kill you! And even if you don't get a disease, I don't want you becoming anemic."

None of this meant anything to her, of course—she knew nothing of disease. Having only ever endured a cold and a little flu here and there, she could not conceive of something worse. Neither did she have any sense of her own mortality and so she spent dusk forlornly pressing her forehead to the door screen, experiencing only injustice.

Every summer they tried sprays, ointments, clothing from head to toe, anything anyone had ever heard of that worked for someone somewhere. But nothing worked for Vivian. She was stuck inside, face against the mesh of the screen. Instead of mosquito bites around her head, only tiny squares pressed into her soft flesh.

Vivian's religion prescribes love for all creatures, but she cannot muster it for the mosquitoes. The best she can do is acknowledge their place in the ecosystem which must be significant considering how many of them exist and she tries to honor that. But she doesn't hesitate to slap them dead if she finds one sucking her blood. If they are biting, fair is fair.

When she was ten, her father gave her a book about mosquitoes.

"Better to understand them, honey," he said.

She vowed silently that she would always despise them, but she read the book. She discovered, if not a beauty in their complexity, a respect for it.

It is a mystery why mosquitoes choose whose blood to suck. Only the females bite—they need blood to develop fertile eggs. Mosquitoes consume plant nectar, fruit juices and fluids from plants to provide energy for flying. Mosquitoes find their target from the path left behind by exhaled carbon dioxide. A winding, puffing, spreading path. They can smell it from thirty miles away. They seek warmth. The fragrances in body care products such as hairspray, gel, perfume, lotion can mask the natural odors that attract mosquitoes, but then some can enhance attractiveness. It seems that only the mosquito knows exactly why one person is more attractive than another. And they're not telling—Vivian couldn't blame them for that.

A mosquito's entire adult life span lasts about two weeks. Most of their lives end by being eaten by birds, dragonflies or spiders, or they're done in by wind, rain or drought. They don't live very long, but they are capable of great damage during their short life spans. Vivian's mother was right: mosquitoes are capable of carrying a multitude of diseases. Most of the diseases Vivian read about were far from her part of the world, but every year birds and horses died of West Nile or Triple E right there in her town and even sometimes, though not often, people.

Malaria captivated the young Vivian's attention. She was ten and the world was only beginning to expand in her mind. Widespread in its part of the globe, and fatal, malaria killed between one and three million people every year, mostly young children.

She never knew this kind of thing went on.

"One million children, at least. Sometimes more. Every year! Because they are poor!" she told her father.

He looked at her a little sadly and seemed to have some regret in his expression. He pulled her into a hug. He was a big man, comfy and soft, his scent uniquely his own—Old Spice, metal, coffee. She could try to pull the elements apart but left it alone. Left it his mystery.

"Oh, honey. Bad things happen. It's just the way of the world."

"There's nothing we can do?" Vivian thought until that very moment that something could be done for anything that needed to be done.

"There is not always an easy answer," he said. This was the first time this truth was applied to a thing about which she was thinking. And it was the first time she consciously felt powerless.

"There must be something." Her voice was very quiet.

Winter arrived in her twelfth year—several months before the spring that her father was taken from her—and she and her father were out on one of their walks. It was early on a Sunday morning before Mass. The air was more still than usual for a winter day. The sky was a brilliant blue, as blue as the sky could be, and the sun bright white. With the wind quieted, she could feel the sun's warmth on her skin and she turned her face toward it and closed her eyes against its brilliance. Her hand in its warm mitten was encased in her father's own gloved hand. They passed the meadow, yellowed and spotted with thin patches of snow.

Vivian won an honorable mention in the seventh grade science fair for her project examining the mosquito. She received a white ribbon with *Honorable Mention* printed in red.

"It's really like fourth place, so maybe they should just call it that," she said.

He laughed his wonderful, distinctive laugh—a sound that came partway through his throat and partway through his nose. Then he squeezed her hand. "Yeah, I suppose you're right. It's just tradition to have three winners and at least one person who came very, very close. You did a really good job on that project, honey."

She glowed in his pride.

Vivian's father was forty-seven when Vivian was born, which was pretty old for a man to become a father in 1971, the year she arrived. It was not so long after the summer of love—in which her parents had not participated, but only *tsked* at news footage on the television. He had served in World War II, and he and his wife, a very young bride, had produced their age-of-love baby many years after they wed. Vivian was not expected and they were not sure what to do with her.

It was difficult. They were older than all the other parents of small children and Vivian seemed to have more energy and original ideas than any child they had ever encountered. Her mother was exhausted every day when her father came home from the store so he took Vivian out for a walk so her mother could have some peace and quiet. *Peace and quiet* was a big thing for her mother. He took Vivian outside hand in hand, and they walked for a while. Longer and longer as she grew. In summer, her mother called out, "The mosquitoes, Tommy! Watch her with the mosquitoes! Make sure they don't eat her alive! She is very vulnerable!" He squirreled Vivian out the door and sometimes they would cross the causeway and go for a swim before supper. Rinse off all the sweat from the hot day and languor in the glorious cool water. In autumn they crunched through the leaves in the flower meadow. Spring in the meadow, too, they were careful not to crush the new shoots. In winter they bundled up tightly in layers of wool against the howling wind off the water and they set out down the quiet road that flanked the shore. Sometimes they talked and sometimes they were quiet. She was happy simply to be by his side. She felt safe and loved and none of this she could have expressed as more than a powerful and filling feeling.

When they got home, her dad would roll up his sleeves and he, her mom and Vivian would prepare supper together. Then the three of them sat and quietly ate. There were times Vivian was acutely aware that her family was different and it made her feel outside of things—unsure of where she fit. But not at this time; not at supper with the food they made and after her daily walk with her father. It was a quiet life and sometimes lonely for a young girl, but there was love.

"I keep thinking about kids and malaria. I still don't understand why no one can do anything about it." It seemed it should be of utmost importance to the people of the world who figured things out. "Why can't they fix it?"

"Not everything can be fixed, honey. Some things take a long time and a lot of work to figure out. Not all problems get solved quickly."

"But why not?"

He didn't answer. Vivian supposed there was nothing to say and she supposed she knew, or at least was starting to understand. The ocean pounded at their side and when they reached the part of the road that curved away from the ocean, they turned around and started back toward their house. It would be time to get in the car and head to church soon. Mom did not like being late for Mass. She preferred to be early. *As if Mass is not long enough,* Vivian thought. She wanted to ask her father something that had started to cross her mind soon after she learned about malaria killing the children. She was a little afraid because she had the feeling it was not a good thing to ask. Not a thing that should be thought. But she asked anyhow because she could not help herself.

"Daddy?"

"Yes?" he said. She paused and he said, "What is it, honey?"

She looked straight ahead and said quietly and quickly, "Why does God let it happen to those little kids? Why does He let them get sick and die?"

He didn't say anything at first, just stared ahead. She watched his face closely and it was very serious and firm and not giving away much. Then he said, "I don't think God is like that. I don't think it works that way. God is just an idea we have, Vivian. I don't think it's real in the ways they sometimes say."

She was shocked. "So..." she wasn't sure what he was telling her. "So, what they tell us at school and in church about God up in heaven and Jesus and everything? What is that?"

He stopped and sat on a large rock. She sat next to him, snuggled close. He was nice and warm. "It's just one way of trying to explain the world."

That answer seemed strange to Vivian since so little of it made sense to her. Sometimes it made no sense at all. "But I don't really understand." Mom always said that which happened was God's way and mustn't be questioned. God always knew what was best. Her mother grew angry with Vivian when she dared to show any sign of challenging the faith. Vivian never meant any harm. She only wanted to know why.

"I'll tell you the truth, Vivian." She waited. She watched his face. He seemed to want to say something and not say it at the same time. Then he looked up, right into her eyes. "I'm not sure I believe any of it."

"But why do you go to Mass?"

"Well, I go for your mother. And for you—it's the choice your mom and I made for you and I stick by it. But, honestly, I'm just not sure."

Vivian didn't know whether she was angry or proud that her father would entrust her with this knowledge, this honesty.

"So all those kids die for no reason? They get malaria and it's for no reason at all? It's not God's will, like Mom says?"

"Do you want to believe in a God like that?"

She shook her head. She did not want to believe in a God like that. She didn't realize she'd had a choice all along.

"I think there is something like God, but I think everyone has to figure out what that is," he said.

Although Vivian didn't fully understand, some small bell inside chimed distantly. A small sound that she could barely hear. A whisper. The sound of sand flowing over sand when the wind blows lightly.

"All the bad things that happen?" she asked.

"Maybe for no reason. Sometimes it is what it is."

Simple as that.

"Does Mom know this?"

"What? What I think?" He shook his head no. "Some things you just keep to yourself. Unless you have a kindred spirit."

"What's that?"

"Someone who thinks like you do. A person who understands you because they feel the same way about things."

"Oh," and she smiled.

They got up and started to walk home. She knew they would go to Mass and she knew she would never tell her mother about this. About what her father believed and what maybe she did, too.

Later as she knelt in church, she thought about how maybe it wasn't God's fault that the children died. No one caused it and no one stopped it and no one was responsible either way. In one way this was a relief and in another she had never felt so alone, so bereft of meaning and direction. What were the rules then, if not these she had heard all her life? The *only* rules, she had been told.

She looked around at all the bowed heads. Her mother's eyes were closed, her rosary beads wrapped in her folded hands. Her mouth moved, her lips making the silent shapes of words. Prayers. Who was listening? Vivian felt untethered, but not afraid. Sort of free. But it was a freedom she could only share in intimate conversations with her father. Their secret knowledge bestowed the gift that it was acceptable to question everything, even this. Even God. What was bigger than that? Vivian was free to find out. The world opened out and up and wide.

Then came the day, when some men, two of them, and one waiting in a running car, whose names and identities were never discovered, wanted to steal the money from the register at his hardware store. But it was less than they wanted and they got angry. A witness said her father gave the money to them without a fight, tried to speak reasonably with them, tried to make sure no one got hurt. They shot him point blank in the chest. They wore masks over their faces and gloves over their hands. No one could tell the police anything descriptive about them. No one recognized their voices or their car. They shot Vivian's father not for the money—though they did take what there was to be taken—but because there wasn't enough.

When her father died, Vivian couldn't believe in anything. Nothing made any sense. Until Raine introduced her to Goddess. She has always wondered what might have been different if he hadn't died. How would the path have wound and the story have been written.

The task to which Vivian is being called is that of teacher and leader. Mother. It is service. She must see to the spiritual needs of the women and the community they have created. Counseling, mentoring, marriage, birth and death. Leading the weekly rites and the holidays. Carol explains everything to Vivian, and although she already possesses a sense of it from her years of practice, all the elements begin to come together in her mind. Vivian must initiate and guard all healing work, keep the coven in balance, lead and guide their ceremonies and rites of passage. She must teach and preserve the wisdom of their traditions. She must envision the future, commune with the Goddess deeply and learn Her secrets. As high priestess she must continue on her own path while listening attentively for the whispers of Goddess and carrying out Her duties.

She begins to understand that it is not a role of power but a responsibility to do what is best for the coven and the individual hearts who comprise it.

She and Carol meet weekly and suddenly none of this seems unmanageable to Vivian. It's not as scary as in the wide-awake moments of the middle of the night, when everything always feels at its worst.

Some days they practice the rites and Carol coaches Vivian on some of her own ideas for ritual. Sometimes they discuss theory and theology. Other times Carol begins to hand off the tools.

Doubt occasionally seeps through Vivian and her fingers grow cold and her palms wet with perspiration. To say her confidence is low right now, how foolish she feels and how she must work to shake off her most recent failing and hold her head high, is the least of it. It has taken many years to build herself up, to shed fear—she has peeled the layers and layers painfully away. Some were thin onionskin; some dense husks. There is also the shame in the haphazardness that has proven and formed the trajectory of her life. She must continuously fight to keep her perspective from shifting from pride in her ability to rise to her challenges back to regret for a life lacking in a purposefulness that comes from laying out logical steps.

But it was not always this way. Once, there were plans.

I can't wait to get out of here!! Raine wrote in one of the daily notes they passed in the school hallways. The two girls could hardly stand being separated by the grind of their classes—gym, study periods, French or calculus.

It will be so different once we're in college—you'll see, darlingest Vivian! We will get an apartment off-campus. We will study diligently and earnestly and earn nothing but 4.0 grade point averages and eat nothing but delectable vegetarian cuisine and our apartment will be fitted with the finest accoutrement the thrift store can provide.

Raine's tight and quirky handwriting, the blue ink pressed hard into the pulpy notebook paper. Pulled from the spiral binding, frilly left edge.

This forged future changed abruptly when Vivian found herself caught in that surreal moment when, lifted above her physical body, she peered down and witnessed her hand holding a positive pregnancy test. *This cannot be happening.* The girl down there says to herself. *This cannot be happening to me.* But in the moment before those words formed in her mind, right after she looked at the lines on the test, the ones that told her everything, there was a blissful moment of sheer nothingness in which her body was separated entirely from the essence of Vivian. And in that moment nothing was happening: not a teen pregnancy, not *not* a teen pregnancy. Nothing. Nothing at all. When she crashed into it—her essence crashed into her physical body—the knowledge of the thing slammed into her consciousness, and she knew with complete certainty that it was all over. Everything.

"You can have an abortion," said Raine.

"I can't. I just can't do that."

"Why not?"

"I just...can't."

"You're not Catholic anymore, Viv."

Just because you say you're not and think you're not, and don't want to be, doesn't mean the fear does not still cling with a ferocity and determinedness. She shook her head. "I can't."

"You've got to get this guy who knocked you up to help."

She shook her head again.

"You can't let him off the hook. He needs to step up."

"No."

"I'll call him for you. I'll run him up and down for you. Who is he?"

"No. It's...just let me think." Raine took Vivian's hand in her own.

"It'll be okay, Vivian."

Oh, what a mess she'd made. What an undoing. And try as she did to hold on as tightly as possible, she could do nothing but stand by and watch the unraveling.

Now, with two grown daughters woven into her life, if given the choice she would not willingly choose a different path. To do so would be to unwrite Guin and Tania. And Ethan and Laura and Megan.

She waited as long as she could to tell Frank about the pregnancy. She had discovered that the telling of such things is nearly as difficult as living them. She had no specific time in mind—more of a series of times during which she thought she might, but then lost courage.

The day she told him was ordinary. Frank was drinking a bottle of soda and eating a bag of chips, bright orange. He had a habit of licking the orange powder from his fingers after each chip. Every time he ate them in her presence Vivian suggested, "Eat them all then find a sink with soap and water to actually wash your hands. You're like a cat. A really gross cat. Who I don't want to watch doing its endless licking." They were sitting on the curb outside the convenience store after school. The words were right there, the thing she needed to tell him. It was early fall and the trees rustled above them, the leaves colorful but still velvet. There was softness and life left in them.

She merely shook her head at him.

"Look the other way," he said. He licked the orange lasciviously off the fingers of his right hand. Slurped the soda.

"Along with being totally gross, it's also really germy."

"It's not like we ever swap spit. What're you worried about?"

Vivian said nothing. She nibbled on her candy. The colorful fruity buttons she'd loved since she was a little girl.

Frank could be a difficult person with whom to talk about sensitive topics. She was trying to avoid rubble. It seemed each time she shared the knowledge of this thing, the more wreckage piled up in her wake. Breakage and rupture and debris scattered. Fragments. Frank fixed problems zealously, passionately, with an impressive single-mindedness and application of effort. His exertion was exhausting to watch.

Or maybe he would be angry and wouldn't want to be her friend anymore and this possibility she could only contemplate from some safe peripheral distance.

She heard the ding of the gas bell from inside the store. She stared at Frank while he ate.

"What?" he said. "Quit gawking at me. If I am so revolting, look somewhere else."

"Fine!" Then she said, never taking her eyes off of him, "Frank, I'm pregnant."

His mouth fell open, the orange corners of his mouth sticky.

"How?" he said.

"How do you think?"

"Who?"

She looked down. "It doesn't matter. He's not around."

"What? He has to take responsibility! Did you tell him?"

"I can't."

"You *can't*? Vivian, you call him up and…"

"Frank, just take my word for it that I can't."

Frank could not just take her word for it, which she expected.

"You have to."

He sat down right next to her and took her hand in his. She rested her head on his shoulder.

She sighed and looked up through the leaves of the oak tree shading them. The sky was a pretty blue and clear clear. The colors of the leaves were captivating against it. "Frank, if I tell you, you have to promise not to tell. Anyone. Ever."

"I promise."

She inhaled deeply and told him the biggest secret of her life. A thing she couldn't imagine anything surpassing in its necessity to be hidden.

Secrets concealed and bared.

Today she and Carol bake a batch of the ritual cakes to be shared during rites—Carol's own secret recipe.

"You'll have to add something to it to make it your very own, though. Some secret ingredient that you tell no one. I have left mine out of the recipe." She tells Vivian this with a glint in her eye and won't tell Vivian what it is even when Vivian begs. Then they laugh about it. Vivian thinks about her secret ingredient and knows it will not be found in a blue box of macaroni dinner.

"The most important thing to remember is to think of rain falling," says Carol and she looks up toward the sky, although it is a clean slate of blue, not one cloud. They sit on the beach, a cooler between them. Carol wants their meetings to be fun, not too serious. "Nothing like school. We've all been through enough learning like *that*," she said before the training began.

"Rain?" says Vivian.

"Yes, rain falling gently but decisively from you. Flowing off your body. Whenever they come to you with their personal and spiritual needs, open your heart, but don't be a sponge. Think of their words as if they were rain flowing from you. It touches your skin, rests there for a moment then flows away. You must care sincerely, but you can't take it all in. You can't internalize it, Vivian. This is very important. You can learn the rites in time, and you can flub them in the beginning, and it will be okay. But you must learn to balance out their needs and your self-protection."

When Carol says this, Vivian realizes she's been worrying about all the wrong things. She's been worried that the other women will envy her this honor. Question her abilities. But those concerns are the least of her worries. She has been friends with most of these women for nearly twenty years—it is only insecurity that leads her to believe they would reject or resent her.

"What are you afraid of, Vivian?" Carol asks.

Vivian inhales. She finds it difficult to put into words. "I think I'm afraid they won't think I can do it. That I'm not smart enough or strong enough," she pauses as her throat constricts. "That I'm not worthy." She has to fight not to cry.

"Oh, Vivian." She takes Vivian's hand in her own. "That's what *you* think. You have to let all that go. It does not serve you."

"But what if it's true?"

"It's a self-fulfilling prophecy; it's true if you believe it is. And what you believe is what will come to pass. Let it go. There is nothing truthful about it."

Vivian wants to believe in her strength. She knows she must find it to be able to serve these women. She marvels at Carol's wisdom and dreads the impending loss of this insightful woman, this lovely spirit.

"Rain," Vivian says. Maybe that is the way to let go of all that you must.

Carol cuts a nectarine and carves the flesh away from the stone, hands a slice to Vivian. They share the fruit in silence as they look out at the endlessly moving water.

"It's good," Carol says.

Vivian is not sure to what Carol refers: the ocean, the nectarine, the idea of rain.

"Yes," Vivian says. "It really is."

In her best moments, Vivian is able to see herself with a crystalline clarity and her pure essence shines forth, shimmers through. Other times it can be difficult to let go of the old feelings that drag on her. Those enduring roots that took hold with a depth and strength that are difficult to sever. She wonders if she might spend her life learning to let go just in time to die. She wants only to live fully, completely immersed in the beliefs she has adopted. But the old ones linger. That is the only devil she knows. The only one in which she does believe.

It is a quiet day at the salon. Vivian has long breaks between clients. She uses the time to clean her station. As she sorts the curling rods she uses for permanents, Frank comes in with a roll of foam tucked under his arm.

"Hi, Frank," she says. She nods her head at the roll of foam. "Building a new sword?"

"No. Well, yes. But I might not be needing it in the long run—I have some exciting news. Gary is leaving the Society."

"But he's the king."

"He's moving to Connecticut. His job was transferred." He pauses and leans closer to her, lowers his voice. "Vivian, when this gets out as common knowledge, there will be a lot of political posturing. I need to get out in the lead as soon as possible."

"You want to be king." A statement of long-standing fact.

"Of course. And you, m'lady, will be queen." He takes her hand and then bows from the waist.

Frank no longer flirts with Vivian as he does with other women. He is as affectionate as ever. But she has exerted a great deal of energy putting him off, and it has finally stuck.

It took many years.

The first time Vivian went to his house, they were fourteen—a Friday night.

"It's not a date, though," said Vivian.

"I know!" he said. "Geez, how many times are you going to say it?"

"I'm just saying."

"I know. Stop saying it."

"Fine."

He brought her to his large bedroom.

"You have a TV in your room?" she said.

He shrugged. "I'm spoiled. What can I say?"

"Wow," she said. His bed was double size, which was also strange to Vivian. Every kid she had ever known had a narrow twin bed, just like the one in her own bedroom.

He showed her his comic book collection. She tried to seem impressed. There were a lot of them, that she could see. She had never given any thought to comic books whatsoever.

"I don't mean to sound like a jerk, but isn't this something little kids read?"

He looked at her like she was nuts. "No! Lots of adults read them. Serious collectors, like me. Look. No! Don't just *touch* it. Let me show you the right way to do it. Lie down on the bed."

She gave him a look. "Just do it. I'm not going to try anything—I'm not going to attack you. Unless you want me to…okay! I'm kidding! Okay, just do it. Trust me. I can control myself."

She lay down and, per his instructions, turned on her side. He placed one of the books gently on the smoothed-out surface of the comforter.

"See? That way your hands have minimal exposure on the paper. Hands are filthy—even clean ones. This way the least amount of surface area is handled, thereby decreasing the incidence of skin oils finding their way onto the pages or covers. Open the comic gently. Since it's resting on the bed, the spine won't be broken, or even creased. You want a minimum of pressure on the spine."

She said, "Seriously?"

"Deadly."

He kept double copies of most of the comic books: one he immediately put in storage and one he read extremely carefully and then immediately put in storage. The one he read carefully and immediately put in storage could be taken out at other times to be reread or referenced or shown to another human being (a very careful human being whom he trusted deeply), but must be treated as carefully every time as it had been the first time.

"That way one copy will always be classified in mint condition and the other copy as near mint or, worst case scenario, very fine. I wouldn't even really bother keeping any comic book that was anything less than very fine or fine at the very worst. Unless it was a really rare classic, then I would decide on a case-by-case basis. I usually wash my hands before I read, but I won't make you do that if you think your hands are clean. Are they clean?"

"I don't have to touch it. I can just watch you."

"Oh, no, I want you to touch it. I'm kidding! God, stop giving me that look. Fine, I can just show you. You know, some people wear gloves when they read their comic books."

"That seems a little extreme."

"Oh, it isn't," he said.

Each comic was in a plastic bag with a backing board. "Everything is acid free. That's what can totally fuck up your collection—acidic paper. The backing boards are essential as they provide support and prevent spine stress and protect the pages from wear. These bags are Mylar and the backing boards are virgin, alkali-buffered paper. In theory, I will never have to change them. Cool, huh?"

She raised her eyebrows and nodded.

His comic books were ordered; organized by title and number, the titles alphabetized.

"Another trick is in the storage. They have to be stored in a cool, dry and dark location, where the humidity and temperature are relatively constant." He kept his in his closet. "I knew a guy—totally crazy—kept his collection in his basement. Not only is that a bad idea because basements are so damp, but a pipe burst, flooded the whole place and they were completely ruined. I personally don't think he was very serious about collecting even though he said he was. I have to say he did seem genuinely upset when it happened. Moisture is the number two enemy of comic books."

"What's number one?"

"Fire."

She nodded slowly.

"But even though I keep mine in my closet, which I believe is relatively free of dampness, I still check them religiously. If you notice *any* mildew, you need to *immediately* remove the books and air dry them. This has never happened to me—thank God—but I know a guy who had some real trouble with mildew. He air-dried, checked them after a few weeks. They *still* stunk of mildew. He had no choice but to amputate—he had to destroy them to save the remainder of his collection. Mildew is mold—it is a living thing that will grow and spread and infect everything. And if you were trying to sell your collection, forget it. If a prospective buyer detects the slightest whiff of mildew, he'll be out the door so fast you won't have even seen him leave."

In their youthful days, Frank vacillated between undying love of Vivian and forays into earnest flirtations with other girls.

That was how she met Raine.

She was, at first, just a new girl on the bus. Neither Vivian nor Frank would have admitted it to anyone besides each other, but they really loved the bus. The other kids, jaded, were waiting to earn their driver's licenses or for friends to earn theirs. Anything to get off the bus. Vivian and Frank were appropriately aloof. (Secretly and discreetly delighted.)

This was their junior year and they were new public school students. And, as such, new to the public school bus system.

On a morning the previous June, Vivian walked to school on the path that wound along the beach from her house. She carried her shoes, navy knee socks stuffed inside them, backpack heavy over her right shoulder. The scrub pine and beach rose bushes grew on both sides and scented the path she walked to school. The sound of the ocean floated over the green, over the sand under her bare feet. She couldn't see it over the bushes and pine. She could smell the water and the mineral warm scent of the sand. She could almost forget where she was going. She was so solidly *here*.

Then Frank. "Holy Family is closing." Frank, winded and puffing. He ran right up to meet with her as she walked. The end of their sophomore year was closing in.

"Did you *run* here? From your *house*?"

"Yes," he gulped at the air. He was sweating and pink. "Did you hear what I said?"

"Yes. The school is closing."

"Did you know already?"

"No."

"You're not upset?"

"God, no. I am ecstatic, actually." Inside, her heart was beating feverishly. She felt unfastened, burst open. The world was cracking wide. A huge terrifying, breathtaking and brilliant change. What would happen? What could? Anything, anything. Everything.

"Vivian! We're going to have to go to the public high school."

"You say that like it's a bad thing."

"It is a bad thing!"

"Why?" That shut him up. Which was a rare and very quiet thing.

Although not for long. "It just is!"

"Very convincing argument," she said, deepening her voice.

"Do you know how many kids go to that school?"

"No, but I'm sure you do."

"Over three thousand!"

"So? Doesn't Holy Family make you feel a little claustrophobic at times?"

"No!" The problem was, Vivian knew, that Frank was a big fish at HFHS. She suspected he was not keen on being a teeny minnow at South Coast Regional High

School. But Vivian, with every step closer to school that morning, was increasingly energized, exuberant about this thing that made Frank breathless with anxiety and her breathless with possibility. This was the first time she saw his confidence crumble—he was not entirely unshakeable after all.

She stopped and so did he. "But Frank, don't you know what this means? No more stupid uniforms, no more nuns talking about hell all the time. There are so many more classes we can take. We can escape from this same group of kids we've been shackled to for the last, like, ten years! Frank, I think you don't understand what an opportunity this is."

"No. I really don't, Vivian. All those people, the school is huge, I mean *humongous*. I've been in there. Corridors everywhere. Hundreds of doors. It echoes."

"Calm down. You sound so panicky."

He walked for a bit, then said, "It's just too much. I talk a good game but...it's just too much. What's going to happen?"

"Anything, Frank. That's the best part—anything can happen."

It was as though the life that she assumed was prearranged simply was not. On the path she unwillingly walked, there appeared a sudden and unexpected fork.

Then September arrived. Cooled air, skies of impossibly saturated blue and Vivian was filled with all of it, almost intolerably wondrous.

She had spent the summer babysitting the children of summer families to earn as much money as possible. She took any job she was offered. Not because she liked children—she didn't really—but the money was good and she needed all the cash she could get her hands on for the wardrobe she was building in her mind.

Frank spent the summer stuck in his worried place. The only person who worried more was Vivian's mother.

She and Frank sat out on the porch overlooking the beach, their gazes set on the breakers, their worried vocabulary washing up over each other like salve. Vivian, to whom no one paid attention during these troubled conversations, rolled her eyes and made plans in her notebook or paged through a magazine. Vivian's mother adored Frank. Vivian would leave for a babysitting job with the two rocking on the porch sipping iced tea and come back hours later to find them on the porch sipping hot tea in the chill of a late summer evening.

"Oh brother," she'd mutter and slip upstairs to avoid them.

Occasional morbid curiosity getting the better of her, she would eavesdrop from the stairs where she could not be seen. Frank worried about the size of the school and fitting in and having as significant a place in the drama group and keeping up good grades. And the pressure. Vivian's mother worried about sex and boys and drugs and boys and sex and the lack of religious instruction and embodied examples of Christ and the Virgin Mary. And sex. She never said "sex" explicitly in front of Frank. She spoke in veiled euphemisms. *Sinning*, a word that encompasses a colorful array of wickedness and mischief, meant, when her mother said it, *sex*. And not simply coitus—not merely going that far into the black depths. She meant any kind of touching, kissing, stroking, caressing, skin-on-skin (or even clothed closeness) contact between a boy and a girl. She feared bad influences. Vivian suspected her mother had not fully defined, had not given definite shape, to what this might include. It was simply and definitively bad.

"And you won't even pray every day! They don't let you do that in the public schools anymore!" Frank nodded solemnly. Vivian knew he only nodded to please her; to make her think he actually cared about that. Frank had a side to him that aimed to please adults. With kids, he would say anything and do anything he wanted. He pandered to adults. They took it for respect, Vivian imagined. She rolled her eyes again.

"It's such a shame," said Vivian's mother.

"It is." The sadness in his voice was nearly palpable, almost a physically soft and overly warm, damp thing. Vivian made a face. "It was such a nice school with nice people." *Really?* thought Vivian. She refused to talk about it anymore with Frank, and she tried her best to avoid it with her mother, knowing that outright refusal was an impossibility.

Vivian stood in front of the bathroom mirror on the first day of school. It was early, the sun just reaching out over the ocean. She could hear her mother, a notoriously early riser, clattering around in the kitchen. She knew when she went downstairs they would struggle to speak of things that would not cause dissonance. They sought harmony, to ring out sweet sounds to fill their kitchen, not by locating common ground but by avoiding the themes that brought forth the discordant notes.

In the mirror, Vivian saw a girl who was bloomy with anticipation, who believed within her reach, at her fingertips, was the whole of the world.

Frank adjusted to the new school and found his flirtatious place in the sea of girls. Then the new girl appeared on the bus and Frank was love-struck. "I am besotted," he murmured.

"She seems to have a boyfriend." The girl and the boy seemed at all times to be touching. Hands, feet, heads together. Lips.

"Yeah, but how serious can they be?" said Frank.

Vivian raised her eyebrows and cocked her head, "Looks pretty serious."

"What do you know?"

"What do *you* know?"

One morning, the girl was alone on the bus. Frank hissed in Vivian's ear, "Where's the famous boyfriend now?"

"Missed the bus? Sick? Dog ate his homework? Who knows."

"Or they broke up." This being the exact kind of conclusion Frank typically reached. He grinned, his blue eyes large inside his fluffy light eyelashes behind the lenses of his glasses. "I'm going to go talk to her."

"Frank..." Vivian warned.

"You can't always be careful."

"Oh, words of wisdom from the guy who was scared to leave the nuns."

"They're *NICE*!"

"When?"

He ignored her and moved down the aisle of the bus.

"Si'down, kid," the bus driver yelled back immediately, his eyes locked on Frank's in the rearview mirror.

Frank dropped his skinny frame on the edge of a seat already filled by two kids. Their heads turned toward him with surprise, their faces awash with disgust.

At the next stop, he jumped out of the seat and trotted up the aisle, dodging kids who'd just climbed onto the bus, and pushed his way onto the girl's seat. She looked up in surprise from the book she was reading. Vivian, at the back, could only watch. It didn't look, from her vantage point, as if it were going particularly well from the expressions flowing in torrid waves across the girl's face and the way her hands moved in the air inches from Frank.

Once they arrived at school, Frank waited for Vivian outside the bus.

She stepped down and stood in front of Frank. She raised her eyebrows. "So, shall I be expecting an invitation to your wedding sometime soon?"

"Har har."

"She still has that boyfriend? Or does she simply find you unattractive?"

"Both, I think. But," he pointed his index finger in a forward gesture, "things can change."

"What's her name?" Vivian asked.

"Raine. With an e on the end."

They both watched her walk off the bus and through the school doors.

Frank learned (squirreled the information) that the boyfriend, whose name was Dave, attended track practice most mornings.

"He runs cross-country. That's long distance."

"No kidding, Frank. By the way, I care?"

This meant Raine was alone on the bus for the morning ride. This meant every morning, once track season began, there was Frank.

Vivian hung back behind them. One day Frank was sick and Vivian boarded the bus alone. As she passed by Raine's seat, Raine said, "Where's your friend?"

Vivian stopped. "You mean Frank?"

"Yeah," said Raine. "Sit with me." Vivian sat next to her. "You're so quiet back there every day."

"Well, if you hadn't already noticed, Frank kind of never stops talking."

"I hadn't already noticed," said Raine. Vivian smiled. "How long have you been friends with him?"

"Since freshman year. We started at Holy Family."

"Yeah, he told me about Holy Family. He was pretty bummed about that place closing."

"Well, someone had to be…"

"Is he always so persistent?"

"Yes. You haven't actually experienced him at his most determined." This certainly was not the first time a person had, in essence, asked Vivian why she and Frank were friends. She had been asked, simply with no adornment, "Why are you friends with him?" They said this with a sincerity that clearly expressed their genuine bafflement. As though being friends with Frank were truly a burden or a mark of insanity. While plenty of people liked Frank, plenty more didn't understand him in the least.

"He doesn't give up easily," said Raine.

"I hadn't noticed," said Vivian.

Frank was out sick for three days. By the time he returned, Vivian had taken his place in the seat by Raine. He perched on the edges near them. His passion for Raine dwindled as her annoyance with him bloomed out until what remained for the rest of high school was a tolerance of each other punctuated occasionally with bald hostility. The common link: Vivian.

Those early moments on the bus precipitated an infatuation and passion the likes of which Vivian had never known before.

Now as she sorts the colorful curlers, she reflects on the roots and tendrils of history. That which shapes a life.

"I think my time has come, Vivian," says Frank. "I am finally going to be crowned King of the Society."

The Society—Wyvern Medieval Combat Society—is the role playing organization Frank founded with several other Tolkein enthusiasts when he was in college. He has never attained its highest position. Not for lack of trying. There have only been two turnovers in the highest rule in the years the Society has been in existence. Several overthrows have been failingly attempted.

"Frank, you've tried this before..." Vivian says. She wants to be gentle. Frank does not respond well to this tired old tactic of hers, which never works but which she instinctively undertakes each time she thinks Frank needs to be handed a dose of reality.

"Don't go getting all negative and *realistic,* Vivian. This time, I'm going to be strategic about it."

Ah, strategy, Vivian thinks. She sighs.

"Don't sigh. Look, I have been planning on this for a long time."

"You knew Gary was going to be transferred?"

"No. But I knew that someday this kind of opportunity would arise. Call it fate, kismet, destiny—it was bound to happen. No one can be king forever."

"Except actual kings."

"Even *they* die," says Frank.

"I'm relieved you don't have to kill Gary."

Frank has gathered a contingent in support of his potential sovereignty. To which she extends her allegiance. He gives her a look (but knows she is sincere). Gary has no direct lineage to claim the throne, so Frank knows this is bound to turn into a political battle. But it is different from Frank's previous campaigns because he is backed by a multitude of allies.

"They have sworn fealty," he proclaims.

Vivian imagines this oath being undertaken in Frank's comic book shop under the influence of many Styrofoam cups of coffee from Dunkin Donuts. They drink it extra sugar, extra light. Except for Frank who drinks it black.

"By the time we start meeting again in the fall, I will be king. And you, queen."

Vivian sits with Carol in her garden and drinks the tea that Carol's husband, Richard, has brewed for them. Vivian sees that Richard is trying not to be fearful; trying not to treat Carol like a delicate piece of glass because he knows as well as Vivian does that Carol does not want to be thought of as fragile and insubstantial. Carol envisions herself as a she-wolf. It was difficult to see at first, a vision that almost brought Vivian to laughter. Mild and quiet Carol as a she-wolf. It took time, but now she does see it. She recognizes it more now than she did when Carol was not sick. Slight and powerful, noble and lovely. Romulus and Remus were fed the mother's milk of the she-wolf. She nurtured a nation. Wolves win battles with bears. Carol is not territorial, not easily threatened, but fiercely protective in her own quiet, definitive way. Vivian is certain that Carol is a she-wolf in ways known only to her and kept to herself. Only *she* knows the precise tenor of her own howl and the heart of it.

"Richard is sweet."

"He's scared," says Carol. She leans her head back in her chair, closes her eyes. Vivian wants to look at Carol closely, scrutinize her, but she does not because she suspects Carol would not want her to. Vivian wants to reassure herself in any way she can of Carol's continued existence, be it a rosiness of Carol's skin or the amount of fat over her muscles or maybe the very shape of her bones. But she does not. Instead, she willfully turns her face, too, toward the warmth of the late day sun.

"He can't sleep at night. He hasn't told me that, but I'm not sleeping very well either. I wake in the night and he's unsettled. He isn't tossing around, but I can sense that he's awake. Sometimes he's reading with a little book light. I don't even know when he bought that thing! I don't let him know I'm awake. I have a feeling it would worry him. So I stay nice and still and keep my breathing steady." She pauses, her eyes are still closed. "I never let him know that I'm awake."

Carol is not in the least maudlin when she speaks of such things. For Vivian, this time she is spending with Carol is a gift. Not just the Wicca, but more so sharing in the essence of Carol herself. Vivian is left filled with a nostalgia for a thing that is not yet departed. The sensation is visceral—waves flowing through her from her crown through her belly and thighs and down and down. It makes it so she needs to catch her breath. It makes her realize she is not breathing. It makes her gasp.

Carol says, "He'll be okay. Maybe not right away because I don't think he remembers *himself* without *me*. I know I don't remember myself without him. Eventually he'll be okay. I think if it were me, if I were in his place, the waiting for the inevitable would feel worse than the end itself. I don't know why I think that, but I do. I really do."

"Like you're holding your breath," says Vivian. That is what she imagines it might feel like to Richard. It is how *she* feels.

Carol nods. Her eyes are closed. She tells Vivian she is feeling pretty well right now. A little tired overall, which she hates and rails against. It is a terrible thing to have your very force seeping away, a slow wet leak.

After Circle this week, she told the others about the return of her illness, but not about the plans for Vivian. Carol told Vivian she would wait to see what manifested. "See what emerges from our small family of women." Carol believes that the tide most often flows where it needs, and how it goes is its very nature and cannot, therefore, be flawed. It is the very sign of nature. She wants to see how they begin to buzz. Vivian wishes she could be as sure and comfortable as Carol, that she possessed the capacity to wait with ease and a still heart.

Even when Vivian's worries about her abilities wane, she sometimes feels uncertain she wants the responsibility at all. She does not say this explicitly to Carol, but Carol intuits it from her hesitancy and assures her these feelings are not only natural but expected. Vivian will be, in essence, mother of this family.

"You know more than you think you do. We all do, Vivian. Our task is to unknot the snarls of the years. The stuff that gets in the way."

Unknot, Vivian thinks. And she imagines herself with nimble and clever fingers. Untying, untying, untying.

Vivian, in all her earthy witchiness, is a devoted and passionate gardener and so the abandonment of her garden is a small heartache.

Her father taught her to grow things. The soil around the stone house on the beach is sandy, only good for growing scrub pine and beach rose bushes. Cordgrass. One of the local farmers rented him a parcel of land every spring and he grew a small lush and fertile kitchen garden. Before he opened his hardware store every morning, her father had his hands in that soil at sunrise. In the center were his vegetables: tomatoes and zucchini, cucumbers, all matter of summer fare and herbs—*What will we do with all this basil?* her mother would ask when he delivered the bounty—fall harvest of winter squash, more greens, potatoes. A pumpkin vine winding. He planted flowers just because they were pretty—a cutting garden—in a circle around the food. Attracted the right kind of helpful insects. Her mother loved vases and small cups of flowers around their house all summer, even if she lamented the copious heap of zucchini. Although, no woman who lived during the Depression ever genuinely grieved over large amounts of food.

He began taking Vivian with him to his garden, and she loved it, as she loved everything she did with her father. He taught her to grow things—how and why. After his death, she continued the garden every summer. She struggled without him; the garden was smaller initially, but more glorious every year.

At her own house, Vivian planted a lush and abundant kitchen garden every year and flower beds all around the property. Hidden gardens, fairy gardens, herbs. Her own family compost enriched the soil, rendered it luxuriant and moist. To think of her lost garden is a kick to the stomach. Then a lingering ache in her chest.

Several weeks have passed since their move. She cannot help herself from driving by the house occasionally. She does so slowly. She never gets out. Who would stop her? No one, but she simply doesn't. Seeing it close-up might be a little too painful. It's better to drive by slowly and take it all in one long, slow blur.

The weeds are winding, her plants are choked and dry. No one is there to water them. She knows it is pointless to wonder but she does wonder why it is better that no one live there, paying nothing to the bank, than she live there paying something, even if it's not as much as they think they are entitled.

Vivian's loss is not merely her house or her garden. It is so much deeper. It is the smell of things growing in the rich earth she cultivated. Crusted dirty fingernails and soil worked lovingly into the very whorls of her fingertips. Peace and serenity and loss of the awareness of the movement of time except by where the sun falls on her back.

When she drives by, she exhales slowly over the ache, trying to expel it. Knowing, though, that there are aches that can be, at best, only expected to subside to dullness.

The weeds are boisterous and determined. She itches to get out and pluck them, knowing their roots are delving and digging deeper and more and more firmly into her precious, lovingly worked soil. The grass is overgrown, not having been mowed in weeks.

The house looks so empty.

It is.

At the far edge of the property, she cranes her neck to look into the backyard, trying to catch a glimpse of her vegetable garden. Even though she knows it must be burnt up and foraged by the rabbits and deer who live in the woods behind the house. Her tomatoes bent over and rotting—she had to move before they were tall enough to stake—and now they must be overgrown and too heavy to stand without support. She tries to see it, but she can't, and she thinks it's probably for the best.

She knows she must stop these drives. They only keep her gripping the past. They don't allow her to move forward. She must let go.

So today will be the last time. This is some of what Carol says to let go. This is part of what she means when she tells Vivian *let go*.

As she gets closer to the property line, she slows Sally to a crawl, as slowly as she can go without stalling. She embraces the house with her eyes, she takes it in deeply. She scans every inch of grass and every flower she once planted. She tries to rest her eyes on every tiny detail, if only for a moment. The white trellis wound with blue clematis, the old gliding swing where she used to rock with her family in the afternoon. Even the shutter that never closed properly—it was not perfect, it was *hers*. She takes it in deeply, so it will plant itself inside her. She is trying to cultivate a memory—a vivid and lasting one. And she knows that the living that went on here is the basis of the memory. The remembrance of flowers, the work of her hands, will remain even after every petal fades and falls.

Vivian carries terra cotta pots—small, medium, large—into the screen house. She wears her green and pink gardening smock. It is covered in pockets in which she keeps her gardening tools, packets of seeds, notecards, permanent markers. She places the pots in the sand. She leaves and returns with a big bag of moist and rich potting soil. There is no fertile soil here, only sand, so she must use the pots.

It is late in the season to think of planting, but this year it is the best she can do.

She fills each—all dozen of them—with the soil. With her fingers, she pokes narrow, deep holes, makes trenches of soil and drops tiny seeds into the divots. Coriander, parsley, zinnias, daisies and more.

You do what you can.

You try to do it joyfully.

Guin and the children join her.

"Guin, can you close the door? The mosquitoes are starting up," Vivian says.

Ethan sees what she is doing and asks, "Can I help, Grammy?"

Vivian takes his small hand and shows him how to prepare the soil for the seeds. She tells him to put his face close to the brown dirt and smell.

"Good, right?" she says.

He nods. There is a smudge of earth on his nose. Vivian rubs it gently away.

"When will they grow?" he asks. "When will they be done?"

She explains that they are living things and must take their time—as long as they need. They won't ever be done, just alive. "Like you and me," she says.

She shows him how to water them gently, careful not to use too much, or too little. They touch the soil after they drop the water in—rain falling from the old green metal watering can. "See?" she says. "That's exactly how it should feel. Not too much, not too little."

Balance.

They light the tea tree oil candles. They sit and wait for the mosquitoes to pass on by.

5

Guin—Hold On Tight

Guin is exhausted.

Ethan is only three and the twins just ten months and Guin is so tired all the time, as if she floats a half inch above the ground, while at the same time she feels a profound and deep heaviness. She must continue moving because when she stops, the exhaustion spreads through her like warm honey and it is all she can do to keep from curling up and giving in to the sleepiness. Sleepiness sounds so nice and sweet—the better word is weariness. Weariness right down into the center of her bones.

Now that she has moved to her grandmother's, she is more aware than ever of the clutter her children scatter throughout the house. Every floor of every room. Shoes and books, snapping blocks and dolls and trucks. Abandoned cups. Books, toy cars, pacifiers. She is perpetually bent over and collecting.

Lately she is acutely aware of a tension coursing through her. It is a terrible current that holds her up in spite of the fatigue. A running stream of electricity on which her slack muscles and bones jumble in the limp bag made of her skin. The electric current and the limp bag in sharp contrast, she is pulled along wildly. What she wants most is to walk into a quiet meadow with no one around and sit with her back up against a solid tree and stare out with a soft gaze at nothing and everything and be still. She thinks maybe then the humming and buzzing might stop. Or at least slow to a tolerable pace.

This morning, she drops the children off with Pickle's mom, whose name is Evelyn and whom she has always called Mrs. Fournier. She feels foolish calling her Mrs. Fournier after so many years and after all, she has three children with her son, but she can't bring herself to call her Evelyn, and she's not married to Pickle so she can't very well call her mom. So she avoids saying her name at all and when she must, she tries to do it somehow through the children so she can refer to Pickle's mom as "Memèré." This whole thing is awkward and ridiculous. Another level of absurdity.

"Hello," she calls out as she herds them in, the twins, who have just begun to walk, tripping all over each other, Ethan barreling in ahead of them. "Ethan! Be more careful—don't knock your sisters over."

"Sorry," he calls back in a rote manner. Guin rolls her eyes. At least he says sorry. The next step is getting him to mean it. The step after that is getting him not to do it in the first place. It's an endless process—another spoke in the hamster wheel of her life.

"Hi, Guinevere!" calls Pickle's mother. She loves Guin's name. "It's so romantic, so beautiful. So full of history and magical-ness!" she'd said when Pickle first brought Guin to meet his family. "Your mother must be a very smart woman." Guin had smiled and nodded, and remembered to say, "Thank you, Mrs. Fournier." She hates her name as much as Tania hates hers. Sure her mother reads a lot and she is a witch, but this was not necessarily anything Guin wanted out there as common knowledge when she was fifteen years old.

Mrs. Fournier always calls her Guinevere, never Guin.

"How are my loves today?" she says now to the children. Guin puts food and sippy cups of watered-down juice into the fridge. She unpacks snacks and little sandwiches. She brings the food which she says is not to trouble Mrs. Fournier or put her to any added expense, but it's really because she doesn't trust what Mrs. Fournier would feed them. Guin reads about nutrition and what kids should and should not eat and she knows Pickle's mother does not know these things. And if Guin told her what to feed them, she suspects Mrs. Fournier would laugh at Guin and reference the five children she managed to raise without any fancy diet. "And they're just fine." She can hear it. So she takes the low road and keeps her mouth shut on her opinions.

"Where's Pickle?" says Guin.

"Oh! He got some work with Freddy at the garage. Maybe it will turn into something full time." She shrugs, her eyes roll upward. "Let's keep our fingers crossed," she says, leaning in toward Guin, whispering the last part. Chuffs out her smoker's laugh.

Guin smiles and nods and tries not to immediately squelch the small flame of hope this news ignites—it's not as though it's the first time Pickle has started a new job, but just like all the other times, she needs to give him a chance. Even though all the chances have chipped away at her ability to easily dole them out. She kisses her children goodbye and is off to The Grille and Creamery to sling fries and burgers and fried clam strip plates with tartar sauce, scoop sundaes into those old fashioned clear glass bowls with the little stands at the bottom.

She thinks about Darlene from the Kmart parking lot throughout her shift and wonders if she has the courage to actually call her. She has Darlene's number tucked in her pocketbook—they said they should get coffee sometime, but it all feels like a bit of a dream now.

Guin can't exactly explain her preoccupation with Darlene. It's not so much about Darlene as the encounter itself. Something shifted in Guin upon which she can't quite rest a finger. Simply an overwhelming sense that something must change.

And yet, of course, she is terrified of change.

She's never liked it. She doesn't like it when things feel different. Does that make sense to anyone besides her? It's a state of mind thing, a sensibility of space and time. She craves the comfort of her usual grooves. Lately, she can't seem to abide even the smallest changes in routine. They undo her—she feels somewhere between a little afraid and completely panicked. Her regular grooves ensure her footing. They are loose roots, but roots nonetheless. They hold her, tether her down some.

Guin is afraid of odd things. She has always been afraid of odd things but lately the things seem more odd. Old fears have crept back in, those which she thought had been put to rest a long time ago.

She remembers lying in bed at night when she was a child trembling with fear. The house dark and silent, dread settled on her thickly. What was she afraid of? Some unknown thing—dark and creeping up on her when she was powerless against it.

What she did to combat it was to maintain a nightly ritual. It was a ritual to ensure safety. She reasoned that on the nights when she performed it nothing bad happened, so nothing bad would happen any night as long as she kept it up. It was a great comfort. Anything that assuaged her fear was a salve she held onto fiercely.

Tania called them her "systems."

Tania expressed impatience with the systems but she tolerated them and never told their mother. Somehow, without articulating—or even understanding why—both girls felt it was a thing to keep between them.

Most nights, the girls ended up sleeping in the same bed—neither liked sleeping alone. Sometimes Tania simply wanted to go to sleep, but Guin would be awake running through her ritual, the last part of which was to turn out the light.

"Hurry up, Guin! I'm tired!" Tania whined.

"I am, I am! Don't make me mess up." If she made a mistake, she would have to begin again.

She started in the back hall, checking the door to be sure it was locked. She pushed on the door to make sure it was clicked shut, then ran the index and middle fingers of her right hand over the lock twice and then pushed on the door again. She walked through the kitchen and touched certain cabinets as she passed. She went to the bathroom and progressed through the normal bedtime routine of hand-and-face washing, teeth-brushing and last pee. All in a certain and same order, with particular use of toothpaste and towel hanging. Then to her room to set certain objects in a particular order. Finally lights out. Everything the same exact way every night. It had to be the same exact way. Nothing, nothing, nothing could be altered or shortened in even the slightest manner. It was exhausting. It didn't matter how tired she was—that was irrelevant. The components of the ritual grew until it took her over half an hour to complete it.

Her mother never knew it was going on.

Guin was convinced that if she didn't do it, the bad thing would happen. A haunting night, the worst, was when she was unable, for some reason, to run through the ritual. She hardly slept, trembling uncontrollably as though she were freezing, cowering into Tania's body, the only comfort. Even if nothing happened on those nights (and, of course, nothing did happen), it was not enough to convince her that the ritual was unnecessary. She only felt that somehow she had merely lucked out. She was compelled to keep doing it. She could not conceive of not doing it.

Tania never mocked her about it except to exhibit that small amount of impatience when she was tired. Guin knew, could sense without Tania ever saying so, that Tania felt sorry for her. They were young, but Tania felt sad that Guin had to do this.

Sometime, she can't remember when or why, she just knew she had to quit. But she was afraid. She devised an end: she removed one act of the ritual every night until the entire thing was undone. If she took one thing away and still remained safe that night, then it was okay to let that piece go. She accomplished it and she was okay for quite a long time after that. The fear did subside but it grew more tolerable.

She was twelve. She realizes now what a brave thing it was and she tells that twelve-year-old incarnation of herself how proud she is of her courage. How impressed she is by twelve-year-old Guin. She wishes that now, at twenty-two, she could tap into the bravery she once possessed. That act of letting go of the fear freed her from it to a great degree. Why can't she do that again? She can't recall the knowledge of how to do it even though she has done it before.

Once again she is steeped in dread and doom. The fear is powerful and colors her existence, shrouds her joy.

Lately the intimacy of the fear has returned to consume her.

Sometimes, for no apparent reason, a terrible feeling descends upon her and she needs to leave wherever she is—immediately. If she does not move without delay, she will be unable to breathe. Suddenly, breathing is a thing she must consciously maintain. It used to be a task her body simply performed, but now *she* must do it and she's afraid sometimes that she will forget. She gets to the bottom of a breath and worries that she won't recall how to inhale. And she must do it again and again and again. The best times are the times when the task returns to her body and for a while she forgets about breathing. It is a great relief. But then the fear always comes creeping back.

This happens in line at the store, at red lights, at work—any place she feels she can't leave, just leave and be free right away. There is a band around her chest, the air confined to the very tops of her lungs. She cannot simply expand her chest and bask in the rushing comfort of a full breath and the release of a giant exhale. A cinder block is lodged in the middle of her torso. Her stomach feels jumpy, a hot ball swirling right in her center. It keeps her from falling asleep at night.

She went to the library and logged on to one of the computers. She looked around at what Google had to say about this and it turns out there's a whole name and set of symptoms. There are more than one hundred symptoms she found on one website and it was like a light had gone on *yes yes yes*! She may be crazy, but she is not alone and her crazy has been documented.

...heart feels as though it is beating too hard...floor feels like it is shifting down or up...fear of what people think of you...fear of losing control...obsession with hoping the feelings will just go away...

She wonders how long has this been going on—the idea of it, the definition and lists and people who feel it. It feels embarrassingly self-absorbed. Is this what happens when all the real dangers are eliminated? No one is being eaten by saber-toothed cats anymore. The planet (at least where she lives) is not ravaged by disease. Most people can assume their children will reach adulthood. It was not so long ago that children died all the time. She remembers reading stories from as recently as the Depression of children dying as a matter of course. Now, everyone feels the lives of their children are their right—as if life itself is a right. As if simply because you want something you are entitled to it.

The funny thing about this fear that swirls through her daily, is that even though she is embarrassed by her self-indulgence, it's a little deflating to learn that nothing she is feeling is hers alone. All of it is on the Internet. A small comfort, yet she feels more isolated than she did before she read the list.

The list tells her what everyone is feeling but provides no explanation. Why is everyone so afraid?

Pickle comes by after work.

Guin is out front with the kids. The babies play with the crushed shells of the driveway—they make little piles. They move the piles around. There seems to be no end to the game or their interest in it. Guin sits in the sand with them. They decorate her hands with small shells and rocks.

"So pretty," she says. She can't get enough of their soft skin. She gently rubs their arms and kisses their hands.

Ethan relays endless facts about Tyrannosaurus Rex which he has learned from the dinosaur book they checked out of the library. He carries the book around with him all day. Falls asleep with it in his bed.

"His teeth were as big as bananas!" he tells Guin.

Guin stands. "Bananas!" she says. "You're bananas!" And she chases him around the yard until she catches him and tickles him until he collapses. He crawls into her lap and opens the book and she reads about Pterosaurs and Iguanodons. She bends her head to sniff the sweet scent of his neck and kiss her favorite spot, the plush flesh beneath his jaw.

"Mommy! Read."

"Okay, okay," she says but gives him one more kiss.

The RV rumbles into the driveway, coughs and sputters, stalls to a stop.

"It's Daddy's house car!" Ethan yells and barrels toward Pickle who has just stepped out onto the driveway.

"Buddy!" he picks Ethan up and tosses him high. Guin tries not to wince. He tosses the kids so high that their backs curve and Guin always imagines their little spines snapping with a sickening crunch. Her grandmother watches these antics, horrified.

"More than one has crippled their child that way," she always says to Guin.

Guin doubts this but must try not to wince nevertheless. Rather than watch, she goes inside to get beers for Pickle and herself.

When she comes back out, Pickle trots over and kisses her, takes the beer. "Thanks, hon," he says.

"How was work?" she asks.

"Oh, you know, good."

"Getting the hang of it?"

"I think so," he says. He doesn't look at her and she tries not to read too much into that fact. "How about you? How was your day?"

"Oh, you know, boring. I'm just..." she doesn't know what.

"What?" he says.

"I don't know." She begins to cry.

"Aw, Guin." He puts his arm around her. He hates it when she cries. He has absolutely no idea what to do. So he just holds her, and without knowing it, it is exactly the right thing to do. Except no man will ever accept that truth. They want to fix it. But Pickle being Pickle, he just doesn't know, so he shuts up and holds on tight.

She stops and sniffs. "I have been a nervous wreck lately, Pickle. I'm so anxious all the time."

"Why?"

She shakes her head slowly. "I have no idea."

She wants to describe it to him. Wants to tell him about the collapse of her lungs, the tightness in her chest, the need to flee at any cost. But she can only cry some more and bury herself in his arm still encircling her shoulders. There is no way the meager words will be expansive enough to capture the whole of it.

"It's okay, Guin. It'll be okay. Listen," he says. "You stay here and relax. I'll take the kids down to the beach to play for a little while? Okay? Give you a break."

She smiles. This dear Pickle. "Okay," she says.

She watches the RV rumble down East Beach Road. She knows he'll park over on the rocks of the city beach and take the kids down to the sand where they'll run and collect pretty rocks and discover periwinkles stuck to the big boulders that protrude from the sand at low tide.

Guin tips her head back and basks in the late afternoon sun. She closes her eyes and breathes deeply. Her lungs expand in her relaxed chest. It feels so good just to breathe. She opens her eyes when she hears a car pull into the driveway. She waves at Tania as she walks over, sits down.

"Hard day at George's?" Guin asks.

Tania shakes her head. "Long, long quiet one. Can I have one of those?"

"They're in the fridge. Grab me another, would you please?"

Then the sound of their mother's car.

"Hi, Mom. Tania," she calls inside. "Bring one out for Mom, too."

Vivian sits down on the stone wall beside Guin and takes a deep breath. Lets it out slowly.

"Long day?" Guin asks.

"Oh, the usual. Frank is going to make a go at becoming king."

"What happened to Gary?" Guin asks.

"Gary is moving."

"Does Frank have a shot?"

Vivian shrugs, "I don't know. His coups have always ended in disaster. He's being politically strategic this time."

Tania returns and gives each of them a cold bottle of beer. They twist the tops. Her mother says, "He wants me to be queen."

"What is Frank up to?" asks Tania.

"Gary's moving. Frank wants the crown," says Guin.

"I see. Do you want to be queen?" asks Tania. Guin is impressed with Tania's seriousness about this—usually she can't help but make fun of the Society at any opportunity.

"Well, sure. I just don't want Frank to get his hopes up."

"Stop being scared, Mom. Go for it," says Tania.

As they continue to discuss the goings-on of the Society, Guin longs to tell them about this terrible fear that threatens to devour her. Smother her. But she can't bring herself to say the words. As if to give them form somehow solidifies this unnameable thing that terrifies her. She swallows her beer and brings her attention back to Tania and Mom.

"If Frank does become king and I become queen, I will have so much work to do sewing the appropriate garb. Queen Aine." She tests this out. Aine is her Society name. She was a Celtic queen of the fairies. It means *radiance*. Frank's Society name is Earnan, which means *one of knowledge*.

"I hope you become queen, Mom," Guin says.

"Yeah, me, too, Mom," says Tania.

"Thanks, girls."

Her mom is quiet, but Guin can tell she has more to say. She touches her mother's arm and says, "What is it, Mom?"

Mom inhales and says, "Carol is sick again."

"Oh, no," Tania says.

"She wants to train me to take her place."

Guin hugs her tightly. "Mom! That's wonderful! I mean, not about Carol..."

"I know what you meant, honey," she pauses and takes Guin's hand. "What if I'm not up to it?"

"You?" says Tania. "Of course you are! You raised two kids on your own. You solve all the problems. You can handle anything. Mom, you can do this."

Her eyes fill. "I don't know."

"Oh, Mom. Yes, you can. You can," says Guin.

They drink their beers in silence as the sun begins to waver and the air begins to cool. Guin wishes again she could speak, but can't because she doesn't know the right words. The words that will lend sense to this. She will be quiet and wait for the words to form from the depths of her where she hopes the fear cannot go.

Guin's car is an early '90s model Subaru hatchback. She bought it after she turned seventeen, the week she received her driver's license. It is rust colored, which is good because the actual rust blends right in. The engine will not die and mostly she is fall-on-your-knees grateful but every now and then Guin wishes it would crap out so she would be forced to figure out a way to get a new car. Strange unexplainable things happen—things the mechanics can't quite figure out or fix. One of the weirdest is that the horn beeps whenever she makes a left turn. She doesn't want anyone to think she is beeping at them out of impatience or anger so she waves enthusiastically. She thinks then everyone will assume she is saying hello to someone she knows and no one will realize she doesn't actually know any of them. She makes passengers in her car wave as well. Usually that means Tania, who, of course, thinks the whole thing is ridiculous and always threatens to stick out her middle finger rather than wave.

The car has a tape deck which recently refused to relinquish the last tape Guin happened to pop in, which is *Journey's Greatest Hits*. For the last three months, she has listened only to *Journey's Greatest Hits* while in her car. Or nothing. Or her kids. Or *Journey's Greatest Hits* turned up loud over the din of her kids.

The thing about a car with an engine that won't die is that everything around the engine begins to seize up or fall apart. Sometimes on the highway it loses parts in locations from where they can't be recovered. Sometimes right in her driveway. Pickle has been saying to get a new car for a while now. She wants to holler, "With what money, Pickle?" Instead she says something like, "Oh, it's fine, Pickle." Everything is always fine.

When her car emits sounds that makes her feel uneasy, she turns the music up a little louder.

It is Tuesday and very slow at The Grille and Creamery and she leaves after only five hours. They have more than enough staff and even though she shouldn't leave early—she needs the money—she volunteers to leave when Mr. Whiting asks if anyone wants to go home.

But she doesn't go home. She tries to run a few errands before picking up the kids. It is so much easier to run errands without them in tow. It literally takes a third of the time when she is alone. Maybe a quarter of the time. She goes to the supermarket and fills up the cart with things they need. She hates being in stores since this anxiety has risen in her.

She gets to the register and loads her stuff on the belt. This is the worst part. She wants to bolt out the door when she gets to this part. She feels trapped as if under glass and she wants to be anywhere but here. Any moment she will feel as though a bag has been thrown over her head and she will not be able to breathe or see or move. Her palms sweat. She digs her fingernails into them and the sensation of pain alleviates the anxiety just enough to get through this—pay for this stuff and go. She can hardly concentrate as she runs her card through the little machine. And when she is done with that, she must wait for the kid to finish bagging her stuff and it takes so long. Then she is pushing the carriage out the exit and placing the bags into her car and getting in and starting the engine and driving away and only then she begins to breathe freely again.

She does not drive to Mrs. Fournier's and it's okay because it's still early. She drives to the hospital and parks in the back part of the lot near the emergency room. She has been doing this lately because she feels safe there. If there really is something wrong with her—even though everything she reads assures her there is not and even though she almost believes it—if she is right there at the hospital, they can help her if suddenly her heart bursts or her lungs refuse to accept air. She could simply stagger into the emergency room and someone would take her to a bed and give her something to feel better. And she could stay in that bed for a good while and just look at the wall which she imagines to be a soothing, muted green color.

Although her body is a thing she can no longer trust, she feels safe in the hospital parking lot. She can breathe here.

Days like this when she has a little spare time, before she goes to pick up the kids, she gets a tea from the Dunkin Donuts drive-through and then she drives to the hospital. She drinks her tea and feels very calm and sometimes she listens to the Journey tape stuck inside her tape deck and sometimes she sits in silence.

There is a tree in an island in the middle of the parking lot. It's not one of those enormous trees, but not small, either. It is a nice green, round-shaped dome of a lovely tree. Usually when she is in the parking lot, it is around four o'clock, soon after her shift ends. Around four-fifteen—and she has checked this time and again—a flock of birds flies into the tree seemingly from out of nowhere. Hundreds of small birds. They fly in, perch and commence chatting noisily. She imagines what they tell each other.

How was your day?

Oh, it was okay. How about yours?

Oh, it was quite good. Found a lot of bugs in a boggy little field. I'm quite full, thank you.

Every day at the same time. Then, about thirty minutes later, they all fly out as fast as they flew in.

It's something to see.

She drinks her tea and breathes and feels a little bit grateful to witness these birds.

She breathes deeply into the bottoms of her lungs until the birds fly off and it is time to collect her children and go home.

She sits in the emergency room parking lot of the hospital more and more often. Sometimes for just five or ten minutes after work. Longer if she can. She tries to park in different spots so that anyone who is supposed to be at the hospital as much as she seems to be will be less likely to notice the crying woman in The Grille and Creamery uniform in the old shitbox car.

Today she is tearless, though. She is tired of crying. She has an hour and a half before Mrs. Fournier will be expecting her. She opens up her cell phone, roots around in her purse for the slip of Kmart receipt she knows is in there somewhere. She finds it and calls the number. Darlene answers on the fourth ring.

"Hello, Darlene? This is Guin—we met at Kmart the other day. Yeah, hi. Listen, do you want to get a cup of coffee? Yeah, now, if you can, I know it's short notice...oh! Great. Okay—Dunkin' Donuts on Ashley Boulevard, ten minutes. See you."

She starts her car and drives over to the coffee shop. She has no idea what has gotten into her lately. She is curious to find out.

They sit in Dunkin Donuts and Guin drinks a boiling hot cup of decaffeinated tea with sugar, and she says to Darlene, "I feel like something is slipping. I feel so thin, like papery—that paper that's sort of tissue-y. You know what I mean?"

Darlene nods and drinks her coffee. She did not order decaf. She looks as tired as Guin knows she herself looks.

Darlene is twenty-five and she has two children. Two girls who are four and two. She understands. She is married. "He's not very hands-on with the kids. He's not a bad guy, just not very helpful. I work, so it's not like I have tons of time on my hands. It's just, well, men, you know. He got fired a few months ago and says he can't find a job. I'd be happy if he just did a load or two of laundry."

Guin agrees. When it comes to Pickle she has an at-odds feeling. She loves him but sometimes she despises him a little because she has to do just about everything. He can't hold up his end of the bargain. She tries hard to get him to understand her and she tries so hard to understand him and sometimes she wonders if he understands anything about her at all. Even after all the years. They are too young, but old somehow. Older than their years because they have done these things that maybe should not have been done until they were older. They had no platform to do this—to have these kids and accelerate their lives before they were ready. The problem is you don't know these things ahead of time.

Darlene looks into her cup of coffee. "I'm thinking of leaving him."

Guin is immediately compelled to talk Darlene out of it, but stays quiet. She keeps her Pollyanna streak at bay.

Guin and Darlene talk for an hour before they both have to go. They talk in the parking lot near their cars for fifteen minutes more until they are both running late.

"I still don't really get it why you stopped me that day at Kmart," says Darlene.

Guin thinks a minute, "I just knew as I was getting ready to open my car door that I would be mad at you—a person I didn't even know—for hours, maybe even the next day. I knew I would have thought about it and thought about it. And I would have done that thing we all do when you relive it in your head over and over thinking of better and smarter things you could have said and should have said. And we would have gone off thinking the other was a bitch. We would have thought we had the other pegged. That seemed too simple to me all of a sudden. To do that, which everyone does all the time." She pauses and looks out at the trees at the back of the parking lot. "I don't know. I didn't want to feel that way just because I thought I was more right than you were and I thought maybe if I decided to be nice instead, maybe you wouldn't feel all those things, either. Does that make sense?"

Darlene smiles, "Yeah. It makes me really sorry I was such a bitch."

Guin laughs, "I was, too. But I'm not most of the time and I don't think you are, either."

She nods. "I was having a lousy day."

They promise to talk again soon and they each drive off to the lives that they hold together as best they can.

Guin hears the RV from down the road. How can it be louder than the ocean?

"Daddy's here, guys!" Guin calls out to the kids.

Ethan comes clomping down the wooden stairs.

"Careful now," she says automatically. She herds the twins out the door and helps them down the steps of the front porch.

"Daddy!" Ethan catapults into Pickle's arms.

"Hi, buddy!" Guin watches as they climb into the RV. Ethan, of course, thinks the RV is the most amazing thing he has ever seen. Guin is sure that it is, to his eyes.

She tries to look at it with the same fresh perspective.

"It has beds, Mommy! And a little table and chairs built in!" He opens the lavatory door. It creaks loudly and Ethan shouts, "A toilet! It has a toilet!"

"Look up, bud," Pickle points to the shower head. "It's a shower in here, too."

"You can pee and wash at the same time?"

"Yup!"

Ethan wants to try it right then—she is not certain if he means the peeing or the showering—but Guin says, "Another time, Ethan. It's supper time now."

Pickle's name is not actually Pickle. He was named for his father, so he is actually Walter Allen Fournier, Jr. But his mother thought *Junior* was too common and Walter an awful name, though she never shares that sentiment with her husband who was immovable about the naming of his son. She told Guin under the greatest secrecy. She called Pickle *Babyboo* or just *Boo* until he was a little boy and then she called him Pickle because he loved to drink pickle juice. He loved to drink pickle juice and milk together—in separate cups, though. She thought it was revolting, but who was she to say so? As with most nicknames, *Pickle* just stuck.

A few years ago, when he was in high school, Pickle tried to demand being called Walter, but everyone said that was his father's name. He tried Walt, but no one bought that, either. Nothing stuck, except Pickle.

"It's kind of a stupid baby name, Guin," he said at the time, downtrodden.

"I know, Pickle. I mean...Walt...er..." she said. Even she couldn't do it and she was trying so hard.

"You can't say it, can you."

"You're just," she put her hand on his cheek. "Pickle." When she said *Pickle*, what she really meant was *good*.

His name may be silly, but he is not. He is not a caricature, though Guin fears some perceive him to be. Almost anyone can be seen as a cardboard cut-out if the time is not taken to peer a little deeper. Understand that which lies beneath and before. Guin supposes almost anyone could be accused of that.

Pickle is not silly.

She and Pickle buckle the kids in and motor over to the drive-in seafood stand down near the beach. They eat fried clams, French fries and ketchup. The kids nibble on fried haddock. They do this out in the late-day sunshine. It smells of ocean and frying oil. It smells of summer. Pickle wipes the babies' faces with wipes from a canister of wet naps he gets from the galley in the RV. He gently swabs their ketchupy mouths, their sticky, greasy hands. He leans over and kisses Guin on the mouth and the sensation is familiar and loved. He and Ethan chase seagulls on the sandy shore. Guin watches the girls explore, pulls rocks from their chubby hands when they put them to their mouths and they squeal in outrage—*how dare she*?

They go back to her grandmother's house and he helps her bathe the kids and get them to bed and when they are asleep, she and Pickle slip into the RV. He takes her hand and their fingers intertwine slowly—she relishes the softness of his skin. He pulls her close and kisses her softly then deeply. She puts one hand on his cheek and the other on the small of his back. They lie on the bed and make love slowly. She remembers when it was frantic which was good, then. But now is better, every movement nuanced, familiar yet fulgent. They move together in complete understanding one body of the other, until she begins to cry out and he follows her, waiting for that moment. He always waits, he always follows her down.

Afterward, they lie coiled together. His breath in one ear, the sound of the movement of the ocean in the other.

"I'd better get inside in case one of the kids wakes up and needs me," she says.

They dress and embrace. He kisses her forehead near her hairline. He loves the feel and smell of her hair, she knows. He kisses the spot between her jaw and earlobe, his favorite spot.

She is not tired of Pickle—she can't imagine growing tired of him. But some restless thing moves beneath the skin. It is not him, it is this life of theirs. Nothing scares her more than the thought that she could possibly cease to love him. She harbors a secret fear that he might not be able to change. And if she keeps the thing at bay, she can live with the hope that everything can be different. If she confronts it straight-on, openly, then it might become apparent that it never will be different.

She would rather live in hope.

She stands out in the cool chill of the summer night, wraps her arms around her ribs and watches the RV roll away. She turns and goes inside to her bed alone.

"Pickle got a job," Guin tells Tania. They are out shopping together at the bulk store for multitudes of toilet paper and huge boxes of maxi pads and mammoth boxes of cereal. Their mother was going to go but they talked her into watching the kids so they could go together. Vivian adores the grandchildren and can easily be wrapped into watching them.

"Go, girls. I'd rather play with them than drive a half hour to the bulk store anyhow."

They got into Guin's car and cleared out. Guin loves these times because it is a little break when her attention can just wander, when she doesn't have to be alert in the way that she must be when with her kids or even Pickle. Tania is an extension of herself. She is easy to be around.

"He did? Doing what?"

"Car repair."

"He knows how to fix cars?"

"Not that I know of. I think it's sort of like an apprentice type of thing."

Tania nods. "How do you think it will pan out?"

Guin moves her head back and forth slowly. "Wish I could say."

"His track record…"

Guin cuts her off. "I prefer to stay positive. Let's hope for the best."

"Why, Guin? How, Guin?"

"Because it is a finer thing to live in hope than despair."

"You found that in a fortune cookie? No, you hate Chinese food…"

"No, I hate Chinese food," they say simultaneously. She stops and heaves up a massive bag of rice, looks it over. "It was a tea bag tag."

"Oh Guinny, why? Why Pickle? Why?"

She shrugs, "I love him. And he's the kids' dad. What can I do?"

"Jesus, this place is always freakin' freezing. It's not even that hot out today," Tania says.

"Can we go look at the books?"

"Sure. You know what's good about coming here?"

"Enormous tampon boxes that provide a lifetime supply?" Guin answers.

"Yes, that and we can pay for this stuff instead of Mom insisting on it herself. Do you ever think we should just clear out of her hair?"

"You're asking the wrong chick. I'm more stuck right now than you are."

They get everything on the list, check out and head to the car.

A beautiful man stops in front of Tania. "Hello, Tania," he says.

"Hi, Professor Clarkson." She stops unnaturally. He looks at Guin. "Oh," says Tania. "This is my sister, Guin. Guin, this is Professor Clarkson. I took one of his classes this spring."

The man is tall and his body is lean and defined under his tee shirt and jeans which fit his form perfectly. His honey-colored hair catches the setting rays of the sun amongst the little dreadlocks. His face is almost too perfect. He looks down at Tania and grins. He stares at her in a familiar and smoky way. "Good to see you, Tania. Have a nice summer." He walks toward the store.

Guin looks at Tania closely; her brow furrows. Her mouth is slightly agape. "Are you screwing him, Tania?"

Tania spins toward her. Her mouth is open. "Why would you *say* that?"

"Are you?"

"Oh my God!" She stops and just stares at Guin. She whispers, "How did you *know* that?"

Guin starts walking fast toward the car. "I cannot believe you, Tania! What about Shea?" She stops and faces her sister. "Tania! What about Shea? He's the most wonderful boyfriend you've ever had! I think he's the most wonderful boyfriend I've ever heard of! How could you do this?"

"Did you see that guy?"

"Well, yes. But..."

"Did you *see* him?" Tania says slowly.

"Stop trying to be funny!" Guin walks faster. "I am so aggravated with you right now."

They reach the car, load up and head home. Guin can think of nothing to say. She wants to understand this. Tania is the most honest person she knows—honest to a fault, honest to a level of obnoxiousness. She cannot understand this. She feels incensed and somehow wounded by this transgression, as if Tania has done the thing to her and not Shea. She knows this woman—this is not a thing Tania does.

And so she says, "This is not a thing you do, Tania. I don't get it."

Tania sighs and slumps in her seat, "I know. I know!" She covers her face with her hands. "I don't know what I am doing! I love Shea! And the sex is great. We have great sex. No, amazing, earth-shattering sex. I don't need any other sex! He would break up with me in a second if he knew."

"Oh, Tania, please stop." She looks over at Tania, "Please stop." Guin feels panicked. It is so important that Tania stop this.

Tania begins to cry. "I don't know what I'm doing. I don't know."

Guin reaches over and holds Tania's hand. She holds it all the way home as Tania weeps.

She picks up the kids at Pickle's mother's house after another long day. She takes the long way, which is only maybe five minutes longer, but little things are big to a woman with three children under four years old. She takes what she can get and she finds that although it would not have been sufficient before she had kids, she realizes she can get by on a lot less than she ever would have thought.

"Mommy, why is red *stop* and green *go*?" asks Ethan.

"Um, because red makes you feel like stopping and green makes you feel like going."

"Oh. Mommy?"

"Yes?"

"Memèré says there's a pot of gold at the end of the rainbow."

"Oh yeah? Did you guys see a rainbow today?"

"After the storm," he says.

Another storm came roaring through. Hail the size of peas in the parking lot of The Grille and Creamery. She was too busy to have noticed a rainbow. Yet there had been one right above her head.

"Mommy?"

"Yes, honey?"

"Mommy, if I find the pot of gold at the end of the rainbow, can I buy a dinosaur?"

"Sure," says Guin.

"Yay!" he cheers.

There are times when one of them retreats to the screen house long after the mosquito hour has passed. There is something comforting in those mesh walls—just a little something to hold it all in. To hold a person together. There are times when they need to know that there is something that will keep them from falling apart.

Guin sits out there at night sometimes after the children are asleep. She clutches the cordless baby monitor. When the babies turn over in their sleep it sounds like a jet taking off, but she has become accustomed to the sound. Her grandmother has asked her if simply hearing them cry through the open window wouldn't suffice. But the monitor makes it possible for her to relax and let go. Besides, the sound of the ocean masks almost any other sound out here.

She sits curled in a chair, her arms wrapped around her knees. She breathes.

There are times when Tania joins her and they sit in perfect silence. And Tania breathes, too.

The rest of the world—at least their world—sleeps and they sit and they breathe, and the sound of their breath is absorbed by the bigger breathing of the ocean and this is a comfort, to be reduced safely and soundly.

And the old screen house contains them.

6

Tania—We Are All Liars

Tania is absorbed.

She hides in her room and devours her mother's words. She is starving and her mother's words are rich cream. She laps at the words ravenously.

Tania glosses over the first composition books, filled with the rambling scrawl of a young girl. Mean girls, pre-teen rants, the real heartache of the death of a father. But none of that is what Tania seeks. Once high school started, her mother's diaries turned into this wonderful mosaic of her thoughts and dreams, pasted-in letters from friends, drawings and notes passed back and forth during shared classes.

Tania cannot stop reading. The diary seems explicit in detail, but some of the time it is difficult to tell what is going on in the notes from her friends—it's half of an ongoing conversation into which she is stepping. But a picture is coming together like the pieces of a puzzle falling into a cohesive pattern. All the colors and sharp edges coalescing into the loveliest of murals, lengthy and spacious.

There is one friend, a girl named Raine, whom Mom wrote about a lot and there are dozens and dozens of notes from her. It is clear they were very close. They seemed to do everything together and their correspondence was full of innuendo and humor and most notably a natural and unadorned affection. They shared classes, mostly Advanced Placement, with which, as a smart girl herself, Tania is intimately familiar. Their handwriting is so distinctly different and Tania is trying to figure out what that says about each girl. Raine's is messy. Like a third grader's, but she is very clever. Her mother's handwriting back then, different from how it is now, slanted backwards and was loopy and large. Now her mother's handwriting is smaller, more defined and controlled in a way Tania cannot exactly peg.

Vivian: *Well, I'm bored silly, how about you?*
Raine: *No, I'm bored to tears.*
Vivian: *I fell asleep in the chair by the living room window after school yesterday and I had a dream I was driving and I fell asleep at the wheel. So I pulled over and could not open my eyes! It was so weird! Then I was like half awake and half asleep and I really could not move my body—any part of it! It was like I was dragging myself out of sleep. I couldn't move my neck or arm or anything. I guess it's true that when you dream you really are paralyzed.*
Raine: *I guess so! HONK if you are sleeping at the wheel! Beam me up, Lord!*
Vivian: *HONK if you take A.P.!*
Raine: *HONK if you think this is bullshit! I am really not impressed by this at all. Pink is not Mr. J's best color. Sorry, Viv.*
Vivian: *I still think he's F-I-N-E. It's not every A.P. History teacher who can pull off a pink button-down with such aplomb.*
Raine: *That is such an A.P. word!*

Vivian: *GIVE FULL ATTENTION!!*

Raine: *I want a new job! Waitressing sucks!*

Vivian: *You can work at the supermarket with me. Hahahahahahahaha!*

Raine: *Maybe I will get a yucky cashier job...Maybe you should look for a new job for the summer. But the supermarket pays well...OH, DARN!*

Vivian: *I want a new job! Where's Hellish Pest today? She was absent yesterday, too.*

Raine: *Visiting with friends in Southern hell!*

Vivian: *English next! Ack-ack-ack! (That is my cat-horking-up-fur-ball impersonation.) God save us! God save the Queen! Off with her head! That class had BETTER go fast today. Are you going to take the A.P. test?*

Raine: *Yes, probably, as long as they're paying for it. It's kind of a waste of a day, but I am encouraged by all my 4's, 5's and A's lately. I'm soooo smart.*

Vivian: *You must cease this modesty immediately. HONK if you know everything!*

Tania has never heard her mother speak of Raine—and she would remember such a name. Raine's parents must have been baby boomer hippies. The ages are exactly right for such a deduction.

There are many more of these notes—not all of them are dated, but they seem to be in order, tucked into the pages of the diary which is dated, so the notes might be chronological. It appears her mother kept everything—since some of it is irrelevant drivel, it would indicate that her mother did indeed keep all the notes exchanged between herself and some of her friends. Which is not like her mom at all—not the mother she knows. The mother with whom she is familiar is always cleaning things out. She says clutter is bad for the soul. It bogs you down spiritually, impedes growth. So these things that her mother kept mean something.

Tania wonders what will be mined here. She takes it all in.

One of the many things she has learned from her mother is that what we keep matters.

September 30, 1987

I met a new girl on the bus today. Well, Frank met her and bothered her for a few weeks, but then he was sick today and she came over and sat and talked with me. She's really smart and totally into cool things. She has a boyfriend and they've been together for a really long time—more than a year. She's totally in love with him. Her name is Raine.

This intrusive unearthing of her mother's past is wrong. It is as if she is prying open her mother's mind and heart and soul and digging around with no compunction for delicacy.

But the theft of the diaries is merely symptomatic.

Honesty is supposed to be black-and-white, but lately hues of gray have seeped in. The muted colors soften the firm edges of her convictions, which she once held as absolute. Are there shades of gray? She is lately seeing not only gray but a prismatic array of all colors.

Lao Tzu wrote: "Be honest to those who are honest, and be also honest to those who are not honest. Thus honesty is attained." She used to pride herself on the idea of being honest, even—and especially—when no one would ever know of the honesty. This is the highest form, the purest form, of honesty.

She has read that honesty comes from deep within the self. She looks deep within but it is all muddied. Her inner voice is supposed to be clear. She digs down to her bones.

There she will find something assured, something undeniable.

But no. She doesn't find it.

When these nebulous feelings arise and threaten to take over, practicality demands the use of intellect. But Tania cannot trust her head now. She relies on passion, desire, impetuousness, impulsiveness. All her emotional experiences have risen to the surface and have begun defining her life. Defining *her*. She cannot get her heart and her mind in balance. They cannot seem to coexist in her body.

She wonders at the lengths she will go, the distances she will traverse, to defend her stories and her illusions. How far will she be willing to go? How desperate will she become? How desperate is she already? There are elements that line up in nice little rows that must be furiously defended. Carefully constructed. She is bound by them, their sticky web.

Sticky tangle.

It occurs to her that from the moment of birth and throughout the span of humanity, during the possession of one body, each is educated, influenced and catechized to *be* something other than what they truly *are*.

We are all liars.

Our little white lies and half truths, our spin. Fibs. The sugarcoating. There are untruths and how's that for a twist on an idea? Invention, misrepresentation, tale, whopper. Fiction, hyperbole, withholdings. Myth. Subterfuge.

Lying is so ubiquitous as to fool even oneself which is why many will take offense at an accusation of dishonesty, at a lie big or small. Because no one believes they are lying.

But how can she be honest when truth may be indecipherable? Malleable? Subjective?

She is a snake that has tied itself into a knot.

Tania has two boyfriends. This is shocking to admit, even to herself.

Only Guin knows she has two boyfriends. And the married boyfriend knows about Shea.

Like the theft of her mother's diaries, she realizes now that the other boyfriend is merely symptomatic.

When this started, it was both terrifying and exhilarating. She couldn't say she felt free exactly, but she felt loose. Slightly lightheaded and giddy. Drunk on sweet alcohol—warm and uncontrolled.

Now all she can say is she's numb. She would not normally approve of or engage in this behavior. She remembers her values, still supports the idea of them, but in an abstract and detached way.

The boyfriend who is married is not really a boyfriend. He is someone with whom she is having an affair. Her motivation for keeping it secret runs toward the obvious: hiding it from his wife and Shea. But her secret reason is embarrassment. Not because of what he looks like or who he is personally, or, she is slightly ashamed to say, because she is doing an immoral thing (if she had any morals right now, which, clearly, she does not) but because it is one of the most clichéd affairs in which one can participate: he is her professor.

There was a day after class when he complimented her work. Tania has always been told she is smart, and that attribute is paramount in defining herself. She wants to feel smart and she wants others to think she is smart. She may be afraid others think she is stupid. Or that she fears she is stupid—at the least not as smart as she would like to be. Probably it is some combination of both.

He said her papers were perceptive and thoughtful— that kind of talk is her Achilles' heel and her aphrodisiac.

Some eat oysters, bittersweet chocolate, figs—but feed her lines about her alleged intelligence, drop those kinds of morsels at her feet, and see where that gets you.

And she knows the very condition of being impressed by that which comprises this man only adds to the cliché.

His wife is a potter and textile artist. She teaches at the university, too. She is beautiful. Her hair is long and braided and usually tied up in a colorful scarf that matches the colors of her clothes. The garments grace her neck with length and an undeniable elegance. She is tall and lissome. Her skin is smooth like caramel. Tania knows who she is because she went to the arts campus to see what she looks like. She was compelled not by jealousy, but extreme curiosity. Then when she saw her, Tania could not understand why the professor was sleeping with *her* when he had this woman at home. But there is always more to any situation than aesthetics.

His name is Thom, with an "h." Thom is pretentious, but well-read. And very attractive. He says she is the first woman with whom he has had an affair and never before with a student, even prior to his marriage. She doesn't say so, but she finds this difficult to believe. Then again, because it is such an improbable thing to proffer, it may be the truth. She can't really understand why he chose her, but knows the reason doesn't really matter except to coddle her ego and she would never embarrass herself by asking him to articulate it.

After their first time in bed, he said, "Titania, your mother made interesting choices in the naming of her children."

She was puzzled at first, "Oh, my name. It's so embarrassing. I try never to let anyone know, but schools and government offices always require the real deal."

"Queen of the Fairies."

She felt slightly unnerved by his disparagement of her mother. Her instinct was defense, but instead she said, "Medieval Period enthusiast—more than enthusiast. Whatever word means 'greater than is considered normally enthusiastic.' Wiccan practitioner." She paused, then asked, "Want to know my sister's name?"

His soft curls moved up and down on her chest where he rested his head. "Guinevere. Yes, *that* Guinevere. The original." He opened his mouth wide and laughed in earnest. She remained quiet and still.

They meet at an apartment off campus. She is not sure to whom it belongs but it might be that of another professor. Once, she asked him, "Whose place is this?" All he said was, "A friend's." Someone with whom he is in cahoots, which leads her to believe it must be another man. She wonders what Thom provides this other man in return. What secrets of his of which he is the keeper. She wants to feel contempt for this arrangement of theirs, but knows she is in some murky waters herself, and that she, too, is a keeper of secrets.

The apartment where she meets Thom is in the city next to the university, in one of the old mills downtown that have been turned into loft-style units. The windows range from floor to ceiling which makes them seem narrow. They are dressed with long and wide swathes of what looks and feels like sailcloth. It is heavy and thickly woven, a creamy white. The place is bare, and Tania imagines the general idea is minimalism. She understands that her estimation of the apartment as sophisticated may indicate that she is not. Of course she says none of what she is thinking. Art on the walls, not reproduction prints, but actual paint on canvas. Loaded bookshelves, *de rigueur*. From the window, there is a view of the harbor where all the commercial fishing boats are docked.

She is inclined to think that the sex with him is good. It is difficult to tell since she is stuck in her head so much—conscious about technique, how her body and face look, the sounds she makes. Is she good enough? Thom seems happy enough to keep doing it, but that is no great reassurance. She finds herself concentrating on the experience more than experiencing it. She has had two lovers prior to the two she has now, though the first two did not overlap—they were one at a time and only high school boys. They didn't matter at all except to gain experience—to dismiss virginity. Not that it wasn't enjoyable. It was, in a backseat-of-the-car or a blanket-at-the-beach sort of way.

This affair started six months ago and now it is late June. She stands by the window and he comes up behind her and kisses the back of her neck. His lips are like warm pillows and she feels the sensation of those lips way down in her belly. She turns to face him. She reaches up to put her mouth on his and he bends down toward her. He leads her to the bed and undresses her deftly, touches her skillfully. His body is sculpted and she can't help but think of his wife's hands on her clay, shaping it, running her palms and fingers over it. His skin is the color of coffee with extra cream. Touching him is like touching marble. His face with its perfect lines chiseled out; his eyes yellow-hazel. Of course, Tania is aware that he is the stud, the babe, the hottie on campus. She knows he knows. She supposes he has known this his whole life. He is accustomed to being beautiful with all the privileges that allows. Being with him is as much about the visceral experience as the visual one. It's as though she can't say no to such beauty. That would be some kind of foolishness. *It's like even when you're not hungry, if a gourmet meal is placed in front of you, do you turn it down?* she thinks.

But then the sex starts and she floats out over the prone bodies or maybe it is more accurate to say she sinks deeper into her own thinking and the act becomes cerebral rather than physical. She does not relax with him and allow the sensations of her body to supplant her thoughts. Thom tosses her around the bed in the ways he likes and she goes along and she thinks she's pretty convincing. He's never asked her, "Did you come?" like some men do. She is not sure if that is because he assumes it's impossible that she didn't or because it's inconsequential to him. She doesn't pretend to know what he's thinking or what his intentions might be.

When he is finished, they lie in the bed for a short time and they talk.

"Did you read that book I lent you?"

"Yes." And they talk about the book and she tries to sound like she thinks he wants her to sound.

He gets up and she watches his body as he moves through the room. "Why aren't you taking classes this summer?"

She shrugs. "Because not doing so provides me an opportunity to work full time at the grocery store, and as such I can experience maximum pain and boredom." But really she needs the money.

He begins to pull on his clothes. He gets antsy after they have sex. Their interchanges are prior to his orgasms. After is for leaving quickly. "You better get dressed. I have a class in thirty minutes."

She does, watching him as she goes. Not allowing him to see her doing it.

"I don't know when I'll be able to call you again. Summer gets really busy for me and my wife. Don't expect a call any time soon."

"Fine," she says. "I'm busy, too." It stings a little and she is not precisely sure why. She feels a suffocating feeling, a sinking in her belly, as if she is going to lose him. He is not hers to lose and she knows this and she doesn't even really want him. Maybe she just wants him to want her. This beautiful form, this coveted man who chose her.

Obviously he does not kiss her goodbye on the street. They part as though they are merely acquaintances, which is somewhat accurate. She is not sure what she is gaining from this or what she wants from him. She only knows that when he calls, she will agree to whatever he says.

So why is she fucking this pretentious, philandering, dishonest man?

The answer is simple: she does not know why. She doesn't know at all.

Tania is terrified that Shea will find out about Thom. Of course, Thom has more to lose than she does, so Tania feels fairly safe. But why doesn't she just stop it with Thom? Something about the terror spurs her on. Some unnamable thing that has always driven her drives her now.

While she is on the road home, her cell phone rings and it is Shea.

"Hi, Shea."

His voice sounds like home. Feels like home. "Where've you been?" he says. "I called a few times." He is neither angry nor paranoid, merely curious and sweet as always.

"You did?" She had heard the quiet beep of her phone indicating a missed call several times while she was in bed with Thom. "I didn't even notice the missed calls."

"Want to meet later?"

"Sure, I have to work until ten, though."

His voice is soft and smooth like warm liquid going down the throat, just a teeny ragged on the edge from the cigarettes she will taste later. She knows he will bring a bottle of sweet wine (she is no connoisseur; try as she might. *Someday* he says, *you will drink quality wine and I will be here to witness it*). And they will sit on a blanket on the beach under the stars and do nothing but see it all and feel it together and make love under it and merge with it.

"I can't wait," she says before they hang up. He is the refuge from the self-inflicted grievance.

December 2, 1987

Dearest sweetest most beautiful Vivvy,

It's hard to believe that it took us sixteen entire years to meet, but the Fates have joined us at long last via their yellow chariot of destiny.

I am in French class. Je suis en fer! (I am in hell.) The bell has just rung not even thirty seconds ago and already I am incredibly and immensely bored bored BORED beyond knowable belief! I just can't begin to deal with my French homework from the last two weeks. Or my term paper (our special friend) due six days from now. No one good is in class today and pretty soon I'll have to start thinking about deviance or something. I might cry. I can expect some kind of lecture any time now from Mrs. G. But I can't even find the French assignments and no one remembers them because they turned them in a long time ago and it's unlikely Mrs. G will allow me to get them from her. That was quite a run-on sentence. I wish I was in the caf eating lunch with you. Alas I am on a different lunch shift, woe is me! I'm starving to death...shriveling into nothing as I dream of potatoes with gravy! And I only have .50¢! Imagine being in jail and counting down the minutes, months, years, decades? I'd go totally nuts, I can't even live through a 25 minute study.

When Dave smooched me this morning, it was like making out with a popsicle. He missed the bus and had walked to school and his face was all cold and his lips frozen. I would BAWL if he broke up with me and be voluntarily mauled. I love love LOVE him soooo much, incredibly unendingly much. Not to get <u>*too*</u> *emotional and dramatic. Oh, no—Mrs. G used the "C" word. You know the one...and I'm going to say it on paper but don't tell anyone. "Cavalier." Whew, I said it. How terribly insulting and gruesome. BLASÉ, PASSÉ, CAVALIER, MEDIOCRE, TAPIOCA, NOT PAYING FULL ATTENTION IN CLASS!*

I have tapes but not a Walkman—"The Big Test and How to Take It." Give me a fucking break. Let's tell them where to take it. And how. I wish Timothy W. Miller III or whatever his title is would shut his loud proper accent mouth. He's bragging about the million and one scholarships he got and saying blatantly, "Are <u>*you*</u> *happy? Don't worry, be happy."*

Soon we must skip school and eat breakfast, lunch and snack at the Green Diner. I will spike your coffee with a love potion. Then I will have you under my spell and entwine you in my trap, my pretty. It'll be so awesome to get stoned and watch "Pee-wee" and "The Wizard of Oz." Soon, ok? Bell beckons. (Oh how pleased would old mean English teacher be of my use of alliteration? I must try onomatopoeia next! OINK!)

I'm starting to feel hungry and it is only 11:30. I have another hour before I can eat. I'm hungry! Hungry! HUNGRY! I need food. I hate French! I hate feeling stupid. I hate being awake all day and now I'm falling asleep. I keep jumping. How totally embarrassing. I have a horrible itch on my leg but I cannot find it. I am getting desperate. It is probably on my head or something.

Love, Raine

P.S. It is barely the Christmas season and I am already interminably nauseated by the Christmas music they pipe into the restaurant day and night. Ugh to retail at Christmas. FaLaLaLaLaLaLafuckingLa.

P.P.S. I am so hungry and the noise from my tortured midsection is like a couple of felines in a ferocious and depraved cat-fight.

Tania turns the notebook over on her lap. Tania never had a friend like this. Tania limited her socializing to study groups and academic clubs. She thought teenage girls were vacuous even when she *was* one. And of course she had Guin.

There is a knock at her bedroom door and Tania jumps. She shoves the notebook under her pillow.

"Who is it?" she calls out.

"Me."

Guin comes in and flops onto the bed. She wears her uniform, splotched here and there with ketchup and chocolate sauce, strawberry ice cream. She smells warm and sweet and salty all at once. She kicks her clunky shoes to the floor.

"Thanks for keeping your dirty geriatric shoes off my pretty bedspread, dearie," Tania says.

"They're comfortable. If you were on your feet all day, you'd go with comfort, too."

"Um, I am on my feet at work. But I wear fashionable shoes meant for a person less than eighty-years old. I believe we young-uns refer to them as sneakers."

"We're not allowed. It's got to be these." Her eyes are closed, her voice drones.

"I know, Guinevere. I'm just giving you shit. What's going on? Where are the kids?"

"Outside with Mom." Her hands are threaded together and rest on her flat belly. She is such a tiny thing, Tania can't help but always notice. "Nothing is going on. Nothing."

"What's wrong?"

"Darlene is thinking of leaving her husband."

"Darlene the Kmart woman? So?"

"Yeah. I don't know."

"Why do you care?" Tania asks.

"I don't, I guess. I don't even know him. I barely know her. I don't know. It's just things breaking apart, you know?"

Tania thinks of Shea. Then tries to hold the image of him together. A cold fear springs up into her throat again. She says nothing about it. She wants to tell Guin about the diaries, but doesn't. Something holds the words back.

"What are you going to do about Shea, Tania?" There is an edge to Guin's voice that Tania is not used to hearing. This is not a tone Guin uses with her.

"You are not being rational about this, Guin," she says.

She sits up, her eyes wide open. "You have to fix it." Guin is close to tears, which Tania can't stand.

When she and Guin were kids, Tania was always the protector. Guin is the eldest by four minutes, but Tania was the guardian. It was less about size, although she always towered over Guin, and more about attitude and a reckless neglect of caring what others thought. She was the mouthpiece. She said whatever she wanted, and when Guin had no voice, she was Guin's voice and she never minded. She rather liked being tough. She wasn't mean about it—she simply would not take anyone's shit. Not that which was aimed at her and not that which was aimed at her sister.

When they were in fifth grade, their school was a half-mile walk from the salon where their mother worked. They used to leave school at the end of the day and walk to the salon where they would stay, working on their homework, until Vivian's last client was finished. One afternoon, they left school as usual, but a couple of older girls from the junior high were right on their tails.

Guin was scared. The girls taunted them, made fun of their clothes, their backpacks, their knee socks. The girls had bottles of water and they spit mouthfuls at Guin and Tania through straws. The backs of their clothes were getting soaked. Guin kept turning around and speaking to them.

"You'd better leave us alone. Our mom works at The Hair Shop, and we're going to tell her."

Tania kept pulling at Guin gently. "Just ignore them, Guin. Just ignore them." But Guin was so scared she couldn't stop. Tania was scared, but she would never let those girls see it. She was angry, too. Guin was only terrified.

"We're almost to our mom's salon. You'd better leave us alone!"

"Just ignore them."

When they turned into the parking lot of The Hair Shop, the girls said, "Hey, we were just fooling around with you guys. It's cool." And they ran off fast.

Guin went inside and collapsed tearfully in her mother's arms. Cried out the whole sordid story.

"Tania, are you okay?" their mom asked her.

"Yeah, I'm fine. They were just jerks," she said.

Later that night when she went to bed and her mother came to tuck her in, she whispered to her, "I know I said I wasn't scared today, but I was." Her mother held her for a while and rubbed her back.

"You were brave, Tania," she said, and kissed her goodnight.

That's the way it is. Tania is the brave one.

"Tania," Guin says again. "You have to fix it."

But she doesn't know exactly how to do it. And she doesn't feel brave anymore. Not at all.

May 5, 1988

I'm writing to tell you how utterly miserable I am. No, not AGAIN! Well, this time it has nothing to do with my one true love. For one thing, my hair looks like barf. I guess I have a different size curling iron than the hairdresser and I couldn't get it to curl right this morning. So I was already frustrated to pieces! Aaaarrrrrgh! <u>And</u> my skirt is too short, very uncomfy. If you (by some rare chance) are not in today, I will be so lonely without you, I will slink to a corner and shrivel up and die! Die, die! Maul! Perish! Right now I am in A-period study and the French homework that I couldn't figure out last night when we were at the library is still not making sense. So I am writing you a note instead. I'm not even in class yet and I am already bored to tears. And (what else?) starving. The cat is acting up.

I got a "Messy" on one of my math homework assignments because I did the corrections on it so I would understand better. Are you kidding me? Does he have nothing better to think about? Wish I had some food.

My chem teacher is giving us a test on Monday! Thanks a lot, man! I really wanted to spend my weekend memorizing the periodic table and then trying to figure out what it all does. Who wouldn't? Thank you! Oh no—the study teacher took out that thick yellow chalk he loves. He gets it in his hair, on his face, on his clothes and the one that cracks me up is that he puts his hands in his pockets and they become yellow! Everyone laughs at him and he is bit of a sad-sack. Maybe I should be more sensitive, but he is sickening.

We're doing our CPR unit and soon we'll have to practice on that dummy. She doesn't even look real and the thought of how many mouths have been on hers totally freaks me out. I am so tired. I can't keep my eyes open. See that scribble in the middle of the last sentence? That happened when I dozed off. The girl who sits next to me said, "Raine, wake up!" She scared the crap out of me and I started giggling. Yeah—that's a normal response...

Okay—have to go. So far, nothing good has happened today! Sorry I ran off on you when you were in mid-sentence before. But I had good reasons. Several, actually:

My teacher shuts the door once the bell rings, I have static cling and I am worried about chem. There are my excuses, take them or leave them. Sorry!

Oh! I thought of something good—I got my info packet from Island camp. So many cool classes like herbology, nature poem writing, tie-dying, wicca...SO wish you could come with me...

Well, I must groove on down that long corridor, babe. Hugs, kisses and scads of love!

Raine

P.S. Dave is getting his NEW CAR this Saturday! Well, new to him. His beloved and long-coveted 1977 Mustang convertible that he has been saving for since he was a mere boy practically. Can't you already feel the wind tossing your gorgeous curls as we hurtle down Route 88? Summer is going to be AWESOME!

Tania's car is an old beater Subaru Brat. It is a dull gold color. Maybe it used to be bright, maybe sort of orange. It's difficult to say now. She bought it in this condition the summer after high school. She saved all her money for an entire year, sacrificing almost everything normal kids like to spend their money on: movies, CDs, pizza with friends. She was practically an ascetic.

Subaru stopped making the Brat a few years after Tania was born. Now they make the Baja, but it's just not the Brat. Hers is a five-speed. Her mother turned her on to manual transmissions and she can't stand the simplicity of automatics. They're too base, too easy. There is no nuance. Not enough interplay between car and driver. When their mother taught them to drive, Guin agonized in their mom's old Sally. Tania recalls her being stuck on an incline forever, in tears, "I can't *do* it!" before Mom gently told her, rubbing her back between her shoulder blades, to pull the e-brake and let Tania give it a try. "You can try again another time, honey," Mom said.

Tania slid right in, popped the brake and with only the slightest roll backwards, engaged the clutch and gas and smoothly moved to the top of the hill, over it and on down to Route 88 and to her grandmother's house over the bridge. Her face held one of those smiles that won't quit.

Frank taught Guin how to drive in his automatic. Tania went on to buy her five-speed Brat.

Shea tipped his head back and laughed outright the first time he saw her car.

"What?" she said.

"You drive a Brat? You never see these around anymore."

"It's a great car! It's a car, it's a mini pick-up. It serves many purposes and solves many problems." She unlocked the passenger door and he folded his long frame inside.

"Manual transmission?"

"Yup," she said. "Only thing I drive."

He put his hand on her knee and a wave of heat ran through her. He looked right at her and said, "There is something incredibly sexy about a woman who can drive a five-speed."

"*Boys* who can drive a five-speed are sexy. Actually," she said, "this car is sexy."

He laughed. "I think the driver makes it sexy. Not just anyone can look cool in a Brat."

She is very attached to her Brat. She believes that a person cannot be deeply connected to a possession and it not become some part of her. Something integral. Although she knows it's only a car, she can't help but love it. It feels like a safe haven inside the Brat. Something essential of herself stays in that car once she leaves it. It stays there waiting for her. It is a great comfort to return to it knowing it will be there.

The Brat brings her back to her core. She needs it. She is disoriented, and it renders her breathless. She finds herself breathing slowly and exhaling largely when she returns to the Brat. She is lost. Something essential to her self has gone missing. Up and left in the night. She awoke, her hands empty in her lap, a shocked expression on her face.

Bereft and lost.

June 15, 1988
   I can't stop thinking about SB. I don't want to—I shouldn't be. But I think there's a vibe there. I swear. I like the idea that it could be there and that I could do something about it. But I know I can't. It is not even a remote possibility. I will just have to pine away from afar. But I wish he would stop looking at me the way he does.

The people on the pages of her mother's diaries begin to come alive. Especially Raine, Dave, Frank. And SB, someone on whom her mother had a major crush. *Who is SB?* Tania wonders.

She glances at the clock. Enough of this. She needs to go to work. She closes her eyes a moment. The store will be a zoo. July third is one of the worst days of the year—in the hegemony of retail it falls right below the co-worst, which is a position shared by Christmas Eve and the day before Thanksgiving. Who waits until the day before a major holiday to do their shopping? Anyone who does not work or has never worked in retail is pretty much the answer.

She survives the throng of customers but the store closes up a bit late because of the rush. Even though the café is cleaned, Tania stays to help the others who get behind in their closing duties due to the crowds. She and a few of her fellow employees buy a twelve-pack of beer and drink it out back near the dumpster and cardboard compacter. They sit on plastic milk crates. They feel like people who have just survived a train wreck together. They are exhausted and most of them did not take more than a ten or fifteen-minute break in the last eight or ten hours. The beer tastes delicious and cold, the sky is pitch and the stars are like pin prick holes in some black expanse of cloth, as if there is some greater eternal light being covered by it. The air is slightly cool and comfortable on their skin. Everything—the beer, the light of the stars, the sounds of a summer night—is better because they have made it to this side of a hellish retail shift. Tania has discovered one of the sweeter things in life: once something arduous is behind her, she can bask in the relief of the difficulty being over. The breadth of the sweetness almost makes the trouble worth the pain.

"All hail retail," says Sue, raising her beer high.

"All hail us cogs in the capitalist machine!" says Tania.

"All hail," the others say.

"I am beat," says Tania. "Beat, tired and pooped."

"You are the youngest one back here!"

But they all nod slowly in agreement.

"The customers who make me most nuts are the ones who come in with the idea that they are the only people who are going to be out shopping. I mean, come on, honey. Don't be pissed at me about a situation you should have been able to figure out. And yet they act like *we're* the stupid ones."

"Summer people suck," says one of the guys. Hail to that.

"The worst thing about summer people is they have all the money so we have no choice but to be nice to them."

"They sure don't make it easy sometimes," says Sue. She is looking up at the stars.

Whenever the conversation turns this way, Tania grows uncomfortable. She cares about the people with whom she works and she shares their same pain and struggle, but she is distinctly separate—she won't be on this side of retail forever, as they seem to have settled into being. Do they know this about her and pretend not to? Maybe they recognize that she thinks it will be different for her, but harbor their doubts that it will be. Maybe once they might have believed the same about themselves.

And she wonders how much is planned after all. How many intentions fall through. All at once, she can see how easy it would be for a life to be drawn by a series of haphazard turns and twists. A yes over a no. A right over a left. Shaped by circumstances, many of which are beyond choosing. She is baffled as to how she could have thought she was above this.

Yet she doesn't want her life to be a string of unconsidered turns.

It dawns in her mind that the idea of control is only that—a groundless concept. She fears this is the real truth and the thought draws panic into her throat. Because what will happen if she does not have the command to determine her own life?

She tips her beer back and it empties in a cool whooshing stream down her throat. She feels a little tipsy but the cool night air and profusion of stars steady her.

"I'm heading home. Happy Fourth, everyone!" she says.

"Be careful, honey," says Sue.

Tania smiles, "I will. You guys, too. Enjoy your day off. Don't even think about this place until July fifth."

"You don't have to say that twice."

She opens the Brat's windows wide and as she drives, the ocean-scented, cooled air floods in and the stars pour down their light. She turns the radio up really loud and in those moments of getting from one place to another, feels truly free.

When she gets home, the house is mostly dark except for a dim light out on the porch and a bright portable light Pickle has set up on the front lawn near his RV. It is just after eleven-thirty.

"Hi, Pickle," she says. "What are you up to?" She sits in the grass.

"Hey," he has a can of beer in one hand and a paint brush in the other. She sees now that part of the RV has been covered in gray primer paint. "Putting on the base coat. I have only about six weeks to preseason. Can you believe that?"

She nods. "How's the new job?"

He is nodding and smiling. "Going good, going good."

"Learning a lot?" she says. He looks a little frightened—she has a way of scaring him. Sometimes she doesn't even mean to.

"Oh, yeah. It's a lot to learn. A lot of things to remember."

"And that's coming together for you?"

"Oh, yeah. Oh, sure. Want a beer? I got a cooler here."

"Sure," she says. "Love one."

Then there is Shea.

"Shea's here," says Pickle.

Tania stares at Pickle. "Clearly," she says. "Hi," she says to Shea.

"Where you been?" he asks, and the tone of his voice sets a distance between them. His eyes are shrouded.

"*Long* shift at work, then a bunch of us drank some beers out back for an hour or so. It was a long night, babe," she says and leans into him. His stiffness softens. He puts his arms around her. "Are you helping Pickle?" she asks.

"Well, I came here looking for you and sort of fell into helping him. He has a real vision for this thing."

Tania nods slowly. "Have you figured out where you're going to tailgate yet?"

"Nope. I figure I'll get her all done up and then cross that bridge when I come to it."

"Good plan, Pickle." She rolls her eyes at Shea.

"Want to take a walk?" Shea asks her.

They walk over the causeway to the island. He takes her hand. It feels so good and right it makes her wants to cry. What is she doing to this man? What damage has she inflicted already? She feels cold with fear.

"I feel like something's wrong," he says.

"No, no there isn't. I've just been busy." These are watery words—she is less busy than usual with no school load to manage.

She has been ignoring Thom's texts and messages, which he sends in spite of his declaration that he would be too occupied this summer to contact her. Ignoring him, she knows, is not necessarily a means of taking control of things but it is at least not making things more complicated by adding further action to the convoluted haze.

With a violent shift, the mere thought of Thom now repels Tania. Maybe it was Guin finding out—his surfacing to the light. Tania wants, without hesitation, to end this terrible thing. But she can't stand the thought of being near enough to him again to tell him.

What was she ever thinking? What was she ever *thinking*? It makes her want to tear at her hair, rend her clothing—purge. She wants it all to disappear—Thom, what she's done with him, the possibility that Shea might discover it. Her insides cringe, her organs contract, she must squeeze her eyes shut against it.

They say cheating is a symptom of unrest in a relationship, but that is not the case with her and Shea. This is problem of unrest in Tania. As though she started an affair to intentionally complicate her life—keep herself very busy with anything but simplicity. Simplicity allows for too much thought. All this seems so clear now, but at the time when this started with Thom, she needed to put some space between herself and Shea because when she was with him she was caught between the love she held for him and her secrets—secrets she still hasn't told him. Not only the relationship with Thom. But that which hastened the affair with Thom. The lie that hastened all the lies. And lies and lies.

Shea says nothing. She can bet what he is thinking and she can't say she blames him one bit. She wants to say the things that will make him feel more secure. That which will make him feel better. But she can't because she doesn't know what those things are.

"If we get some blankets, I think we could just sleep out here tonight," she says.

He smiles. "Yeah? Okay."

They get the blankets, spread them over the sand and snuggle under. The water breaks gently, swooshes up over the rocks and back out. They don't have sex and they don't even talk much but they don't need to—a closeness she can feel and is sure he can, too, settles upon them. He falls asleep first and she watches his face and she knows she loves him. She cries silently, careful not to wake him.

Something must change. She wishes she knew what it should be.

They wake on the beach to the first rays of dawn and then they make love. It is deeper than ever before. He seems desperate to tell her something and she feels desperate to know. They look into each other's eyes as if this is the most important moment they have shared.

Her mind goes clean and blank. She wishes this could last forever because for the first time in a long while she feels free of herself.

Maybe that is all she needs. Maybe that is the answer.

Tania slips into the old stone house before anyone awakens. Shea has left for the morning shift at the radio station and Tania watches the sun rise through her bedroom window. She dozes off in the window seat and sleeps blackly. She awakens cold and confused, her neck crooked and sore. The images of a distant dream fade immediately, but not the feeling of it.

She goes downstairs, gets a cup of coffee and walks out onto the back porch. The day blooms out—sunny, hot but not humid, cool breeze, not too cool, not too weak. She leans far over the edge, craning her neck to get a look down the shoreline to the beach.

"Packed," she says.

"Oh, yes," says Aunt Anne. "They come from *all* over on a Fourth of July like this."

"This is the kind they call 'perfect,'" Tania's grandmother says.

"Making memories," says Aunt Anne. "What are you going to do today, Tania?"

"I don't know," she flops into one of the chairs, her legs hang off the side. "After work yesterday, I don't want to be with any crowd, that's for sure. Ugh," she says, and drops her head against the back of the chair. "Why do they all wait to get their barbecue supplies until the day before? You cannot imagine how many people were in-and-out and more in-and-out and more, and more. We had to stay open an extra forty-five minutes before we could get rid of all of them. It was nonstop."

"Oh, honey." Grammy laughs. "I'd love to be able to run around nonstop for an hour!"

Aunt Anne says, "Any more than that would be a bonus!" she hoots and Grammy snorts.

Tania smiles. "I'm hungry," she says. She thinks about cold cereal, a packet of oatmeal or toast, none of which compel her to move out of the chair in spite of her hunger.

"What do you want?" says Aunt Anne.

She shrugs and gets up. "Guess I'll boil some water for a packet of instant oatmeal."

"Instant what? Oh, no." Aunt Anne lays down her puzzle pieces and stands up. "Come on. We only eat the real thing in this house."

"What?" says Tania.

"Real oatmeal. I'm going to show you."

Tania follows her to the kitchen and watches as Aunt Anne takes the big saucepan from the cabinet.

"That's a big one," says Tania.

"Oh, you wait. Once they smell this cooking, they will all come out of the cracks of this old house." She opens the cupboard and takes an old tin down, clanks it on the counter. "Steel-cut oats. Irish oats. Once you eat these," she shakes the can and the oats rattle around against the sides of the tin, "you will realize there is no other kind of oatmeal you should be eating. Especially that crap in the little packet."

"I like that crap in the little packet."

"Well, you won't after you eat *my* oatmeal." Of this Tania has no doubt.

Steel-cut oats, equal parts milk and water. "Pinch of salt. This is important, Tania. Pinch of salt. You would not *believe* what a pinch of salt can do. It's like a mosquito in your bedroom at night when you're trying to sleep. You never think something so small could make such trouble. A pinch of salt is like that. Only in a good way."

She pours the milk and water in the big pan, sets it to boil. When it rumbles and rattles the cover, she adds the oats. Big stir with one of the old stained wooden spoons. Reduce to a simmer and let it go nice and slow. "Anything worth eating is worth waiting for," says Aunt Anne. "While that cooks, we need to make something sweet to go on top. Otherwise, it's just plain old oatmeal. You need something a little sweet."

She peels and slices up a couple of apples. A glob of butter—"You need at least one generous glob"—melts in the cast iron skillet, a few spoonfuls of brown sugar melting down to amber caramel. The apple slices sink in, bubble and jump in the buttery sugar, turn soft and brown.

"Sprinkle of cinnamon," Aunt Anne whispers. "Secret ingredient." She leans in close to Tania. "Every recipe," she says in a normal level of voice, "should have one and you don't tell it. I'm sharing my secrets with you so you can learn all this and take it with you. There." Now fill up a nice bowl. Dollop of butter, trickle of cream, dribble of real maple syrup. Top with some of the apples.

"*That* is breakfast!" says Aunt Anne. Tania must agree. The scent alone is almost enough. They go and sit out on the back porch. Tania brings a full bowl for her grandmother.

Then Tania takes a bite. "It's so *good*, Aunt Anne. Oh, my God!"

"It makes me think of Mama," says Grammy, eyes closed.

"Oh, now she made a good bowl of oatmeal," Aunt Anne agrees. "Good food can do that, though, can't it?"

"It's akin to a scent you never forget. You catch a note of it and it just sends you right back," says Grammy.

Tania thinks about their accumulated experience and of course it can be tasted in this food. No question. She eats every bite and practically licks the bowl. She gathers all the empty bowls—"Thank you, dear"—and washes them and the pan. Her phone rings and it is Shea.

"What are you doing?" he asks.

"Washing dishes. I just made some amazing oatmeal."

"You cooked? That's a good little woman."

"Oh, very funny. Aunt Anne knows how to cook. I mean, when I say cook, I mean, really cook. And it's not even that hard. I need to start writing it down, though. She does it all from her head."

"Is there any left?"

"Not a spoonful. Sorry."

"Feed me lunch then. I'll be out of here by one. Want to go to the beach?"

"It's absolutely packed," she says. "Let's go to the secret beach." She whispers *secret beach*. "After the assault of humans yesterday at George's, I don't want to be near anything resembling a crowd."

She packs a lunch for them, a few beers in the cooler. And when he arrives they carry their beach stuff over the causeway through the tickling cord grass. It is empty as always. Just a small stretch of pebbly sand and the open ocean in front of them. She spreads a towel flat on the sand and stretches her body prone upon it. She closes her eyes and empties her mind of everything but the sensation of the sun warming her skin. Her muscles melt away from the tautness of her bones, her eyes are heavy in their sockets and she feels as though she is being slowly drained into the earth beneath her. Then Shea's weight is upon her, his face in her neck. He rubs the tops of his feet against the tops of hers.

"Let's go for a swim," he says.

"Let's skinny dip," she says.

They look around furtively, drop their suits in the sand and run, squealing, into the water. They collapse in, come up laughing. He grabs her leg and pulls her to him. He kisses her and tastes of salt and cigarettes. She wraps her legs around his waist. He makes her breathless. The edge of the world begins to fade and all that is left is Shea. She runs her hands down his smooth chest and then between his legs.

"Auntie Tania! AUNTIE TANIA!" She looks to the shore and there is Ethan in his bathing suit and blue sunhat hollering to her. Guin and Pickle are setting up their beach stuff near hers and the twins are creeping around in the sand.

"Shit!" Tania whispers. "Hi, honey! I'll be right out!" she calls to Ethan. "Crap," she says to Shea.

She looks back at Guin who is dangling Tania's bathing suit from her fingers. "What's this?" she calls.

"Toss it to me!"

"Oh, you need this? This here?" She picks up Shea's trunks. "This, too?"

"Toss them!"

"Why don't you have your bathing suit on, Auntie Tania?" Ethan asks.

"Yeah, why *don't* you?" says Guin.

"Come on, Guin!" Tania is whining now. "Like invading our privacy was not enough," she mutters.

She swims in toward the shore, staying low, the water covering her naked body. "Give it," she barks at Guin, as it smacks her in the head.

"Oops," Guin says.

Tania hands Shea his trunks then she wrestles her bathing suit on under the water. She hauls herself out of the water and trudges up to the towels. As she dries herself off, she says, "This is a private beach, Guinevere."

"Ha! We tried to go over to the state beach, but the parking lots are full."

"Glad to see you guys," says Shea. Water drips from his black hair. Water drips from the long black lashes that frame his melting brown eyes. He is so beautiful, Tania wants to tackle him. Or absorb him. Or beg him to love her as much as she does him. Or beg him not to leave in spite of what she's done. Shea leans down and grabs one of the twins. He tosses her in the air and she squeals. The other twin watches, then comes over to demand a turn.

Pickle comes over and hands Tania an icy cold beer. "Happy Fourth of July," he says.

"Happy Fourth of July," she says and smiles.

Her mother is in love.

By January of her junior year of high school, Tania's mother was infatuated with a skinny, pale, mohawked boy she referred to as "SB" Tania would love to see a photo of him. Then she thinks of her mother's yearbook. She vaguely remembers it—its burgundy faux leather cover. But where would that be right now? She goes to the garage and looks for the stack of boxes labeled *Vivian's books*. She's pretty sure the yearbook was shelved in with the rest of her mother's books.

"What are you looking for, sweetie?"

Her mother's voice makes her jump. "Nothing."

Her mother smiles and gives her an odd look. She is standing in the garage in shorts and a tee shirt with a mug of tea.

"Well, not nothing. *Women Who Run with the Wolves*. I need something to read."

"Oh, that's a good one." She puts her mug down. "Let me try to remember where that is. I should probably get these books onto a shelf in my room. The damp out here is so bad for them. Although I'm not sure how much less damp it is in there."

Tania looks in the boxes along with her mother. She spots the yearbook.

"Here it is!" Her mother hands Tania the book for which she believes she is looking.

"Thanks, Mom. Is this your old yearbook?" she says.

Mom groans. "Yes," she says.

"Can I look at it?"

"Sure. Why?"

"Sometimes I just like to flash back to the '80s."

"In which you existed for less than a year," says her mother. "You just want to make fun of my hair."

"It's more fun to make fun of Frank..." says Tania and flips to his large grinning picture. "And not in the least difficult."

"I know. As skinny as he is now, he was skinnier then. And those glasses!" Her mother gazes down at Frank.

"HUGE. A lot of plastic gave its life for those...Look at your hair." She laughs.

"Fluff was in style. Volume was the fashion of the day. Mine wasn't even that big. There were girls who were partly responsible for the hole in the ozone layer with all the aerosol hairspray they used. They would crowd around the mirror in the girls' room and just waft that stuff over their heads. If you'd walked in and lit a match, the whole school would have gone up in flames. I only used mousse."

"Mousse!" Tania laughs.

"Someday someone is going to be laughing at *your* high school photos, you know."

"Never. I have always been and always will be cool, Mommy."

"We'll see."

They hear a car beeping from outside the garage. Her mother looks out the door. "Oh, it's Frank. He wants to go to the beach today. Do you want to come with us?"

Tania shrugs, "Work."

Vivian makes a face. "See you after?"

Tania smiles and nods and Vivian leaves. Tania runs upstairs with the copy of *Women Who Run with the Wolves* in her hand and the yearbook tucked under her arm.

Up in the window seat she has about twenty minutes to flip through this thing before she needs to leave for work. She finds Raine's picture. Jaw-length blond hair, spiked up at the crown, some falling over her forehead on one side. Open eyes, a smile that seems a bit subdued, as if she's not giving it all away. She finds Raine's boyfriend, Dave. But there is no boy with the initials SB.

She stretches and puts the yearbook in the secret place in the window seat. She leaves for work. This stuff of the past is so much more interesting than her own life right now, which she would gladly escape if only she could figure out how. And not merely the mess she's made with these two men and the big lies—but the thing that has been tugging at her, pulling at her, pushing her around. The thing she cannot name.

Suddenly she remembers something...SB...She flips back through months of diary entries, scans the writing. When her mother first wrote about him, she called him *Skater Boy*, Tania suddenly remembers.

So, SB are not initials—they are an acronym.

This doesn't tell Tania much in the way of his identity.

Could SB be her father?

Tania opens up her laptop and does a search on Raine's name. How many Raine Hollands might there be? Would she have a Facebook page? Lots of older people do. Her mother does. I mean, Raine's not even forty—she must have one. But nothing comes up. She searches directly in Facebook, but no. She searches archives of the local newspapers. Nothing. If Raine married and took her husband's name, it could be anything now.

She stares out the window at the everlasting ocean. There is a blackness in the corner of the sky, moving closer.

Her mother has never been quite forthcoming about her own past, part of which is also Tania's. Mom won't refuse to answer questions, but neither is she loose-lipped about any of it. Doesn't revisit her past; doesn't linger in nostalgia. Her stories are cut to the bone and unadorned.

Once, she asked Frank, "Did you know my father?"

He looked up abruptly, surprise and mild alarm awash on his face. Then he shielded it. "No. That whole thing, you know, well, it happened sort of behind my back."

"Behind your back?"

"Without my knowledge. She only told me after. When you and Guin were on the way."

This—the past she is revisiting through the words of her mother at seventeen—is a maze she never intended to enter. Avenues that lead to pathways she can't anticipate, all toward an end that is undefined. As vague as the motives that drive her.

The room darkens and cold rain comes in sideways through the screen. She rushes to close the windows as thunder crashes. It is so loud, it seems to be directly overhead. She runs through the house and she and Guin slam windows down to their sills. The children cry loudly, call for their mama.

"Go to them, Guin. I'll finish these," says Tania. She is inclined to agree with the children—the thunder sounds terrifying, even though she understands it is only clamoring noise. She closes all the windows and she and Aunt Anne grab old beach towels and wipe wet sills and floors.

"That came out of nowhere!" says Grammy. "What is the meaning of all these storms?"

"God is trying to tell us something," Aunt Anne and Tania say together. Grammy purses her lips and shakes her head.

The sun emerges from the clouds—the raindrops glisten in its light. They reopen the windows and all return to what they were doing before the storm came through.

Tania flops down on her bed. She closes her laptop.

Sometimes you search and hope the answers will come later.

Sometimes the only thing to do is keep moving.

The leaves hung in their last moments. Most of the trees were already bare. The sun was wide and low in the sky, and the winds were descending into their long-winter's breath. That constant wind off the churning Atlantic.

That stolen and shrinking day.

The day she thought wouldn't matter. That she thought would be an easy thing to bear. Just another day.

Laid on the table in the hospital gown. The doctor was kind and touched her inner thigh gently and spoke softly of everything that he was doing just before he did it. The nurse asked where she went to school. Tania answered. *And what's your major?* the nurse asked. *Literature and Women's Studies*. And then there was a deep and searing contraction of her insides and she sucked in air sharply and the nurse took her hand and told her to breathe slowly. Deeply. *What do you like to read?* she asked Tania. The machine was loud and she felt very alone.

It was over in a few minutes. Very few.

Really? thought Tania.

But she was relieved as she reclined upright in the bed and ate saltine crackers slowly and sipped ginger ale through a straw from a tiny can in tiny sips. Relieved that it was over—the procedure, all of it. She listened to recorded instructions through a headset they gave her detailing what she should do to take care of herself over the next few days. She looked at her feet, lumps under the white cotton blanket. She sat very still, slightly afraid to move. Then when they said it was time, she moved her legs over the side of the bed, carefully, and walked over to where her clothes were neatly folded and she found that she was all right.

She drove herself home, having lied to them about having a ride.

The house was cold and empty when she got there and she made a cup of tea and curled up on the couch and watched show after show on the Food Network, even though she never cooked. When her mother got home from work, then Guin and the kids, she said she was having a bad period. *That's all.*

She told no one anything.

Not a soul.

Her ambivalence shocked her. Angered and confused her.

The unexpected bruising was tender to the touch.

One evening when twilight is firmly in place, only Tania and Aunt Anne sit in the screen house.

"What's it like to be old?" Tania asks.

Aunt Anne opens her mouth and laughs largely. "Am I old?"

Tania giggles a little. "You know what I mean. I didn't mean it in a bad way."

Aunt Anne pats her hand. "I know, I know. Well, it feels like I'm not old. I feel the same inside as I always have. The body doesn't work as smoothly as it once did. But inside I'm sixteen, thirty-four, twelve, sixty-eight. All of it. All the years."

"Like they overlap?" Tania asks.

"Like they're layers and at the same time all one thing."

"Oh."

The ocean is quiet this night and the air so still. Maybe they can hear the buzzing of the mosquitoes, but it is difficult to say for sure.

It is quiet enough to hear their own breath and the small but steady sound of the flickering wicks of the tea tree oil candles.

7

Vivian—Contain It All

"There's talk, Vivian," says Frank.

Vivian is working on a bride's up-do. It is intricate work. Curlicues and tendrils and pearlescent-tipped bobby pins. The bride watches seriously in the mirror. Never takes her eyes away. Brides hardly blink, Vivian has noticed over the years. Perfectly normal women otherwise. Vivian remembers a time when brides made her nervous— when they were the least favorite part of her job as a stylist. Now her hands work adeptly, move easily around this bride's head, almost on their own.

"What kind of talk?"

"It's common knowledge now. Gary's abdication." He leans against the counter in front of her mirror. The bride shifts over slightly to continue watching the construction of her wedding hairdo.

He exhales through pursed lips. "So far no one has come forward with an interest in the throne, but I think it's only a matter of time..."

"Does everyone know of your interest?"

He nods up and down slowly. "I've let it leak out. And there have been rumblings."

"Good or bad?" She drives in the final bobby pin and takes a bottle of hairspray from the counter. Shielding the bride's eyes with her hand, she depresses the nozzle and waves the bottle over the bride's head. The sweet-smelling mist falls gently on the intricate mass of swirls and curls and twists and tendrils precisely-placed but meant to look accidentally escaped.

"Ehhhhnnn," he makes a sideways gesture with his head, his teeth bared. "Good, I think. So far, there has been no outright opposition to the idea of my potential sovereignty. And, of course, yours, it goes without saying. It's almost too easy, which is what's got me worried. There must be some opposing contingent out there, biding their time."

She primps here and there at the bride's hair. Moves around her to get a look from every angle. "There's no reason to think that, Frank. You're a founding member of the Society, your interest in ruling is openly known. Maybe it just is what it is."

He shakes his head. "Vivian, you are so naive about these kinds of highly political situations. No," he shakes his head again. "It can't be this easy."

"What are you going to do?"

"I've got people on the inside infiltrating all factions. If there's something going on, I'll find out about it. You look beautiful, by the way," he says to the bride. "You're going to knock him out."

The bride smiles. "Thanks!"

"You're all set, Julie. I know you'll have a wonderful day!" says Vivian.

"Thanks, Vivian. It's amazing." She turns her head each way in the mirror. She smiles, cheeks pink.

Julie leaves with her maid of honor, whose hair Vivian also styled.

Vivian falls into her styling chair. "Are you worried?"
Frank sighs. "Not yet."

She narrows her eyes at him. "Are you growing a
beard, Frank?"

He rubs his cheeks with the pads of his thumb and
fingers. "Yeah. I'm going for the King Arthur look. You
know, feel the part, look the part," he grins, then grows
serious again. "I'm going to ingratiate myself to all groups.
I know it's risky to befriend warring factions, but I must
unite them in their support of me in order to gain their
fealty."

She rubs his burgeoning beard. "If anyone can do it,
it's you," she says.

Vivian comes into the house at dusk. She swats away
the mosquitoes.

"Damn mosquitoes," she says.

"And good evening to you, Vivian," says Aunt Anne.

"Hi, Aunt Anne. Don't take it personally—I have a
long-standing feud with these pests."

The table is set. Aunt Anne and Tania are cooking
supper.

Vivian has been watching Tania's interest in cooking
with surprise and amusement. Tania has always been
somewhat disdainful of domesticity and its patriarchal
implications. She does her part—her familial
responsibility, she calls it—but she makes it clear that
when she performs these tasks, they are free of any
institutionalized misogyny. Which, Vivian has always
thought, is implicit in the fact that Tania has only ever
lived with other females—besides Ethan, who is too little
to count. But Tania will maintain her standards, solid and
unwavering.

"Cooking is about sustenance, Mom. There is something unquestionably essential about it."

"Yeah, to keep on living," pipes up Aunt Anne. Vivian's mother snorts loud, titters.

"I'm just saying there is something primordial about it. It's not like being shackled to a vacuum cleaner. It's not like being expected to scrub the family's clothes on a washboard."

"I get it, honey," says Mom.

So, Tania is learning to cook.

Vivian's reasons for shunning cooking are less political. Aunt Anne, in her eternal efforts at peacemaking will always say Vivian's interests simply lay elsewhere. But that was never the real reason.

Cooking makes her miss her father.

Vivian recalls her father's food often. It was simple fare, but nuanced and layered. Chicken, falling apart and tender in a rich gravy with carrots and peas over homemade butter-dropped biscuits. Thick broth beef stew, heavy cream-laden fish chowder. He baked his own bread. It was home—it tasted purely of home. From the time she was little, she sat on the counter and watched. When she was old enough, she helped him with the simple steps. She stood on a chair to reach the counter until she was tall enough to stand on the floor.

Once Aunt Anne took over the cooking, she endeavored to continue teaching Vivian. But Vivian didn't simply shy away from the idea of it, she recoiled. Aunt Anne did not push.

Cooking brought Vivian too painfully close to her father and left her mournfully alone and empty. Unlike gardening, which made her feel as though she were communing with him; perhaps touching the very same soil in which his hands had been immersed. She could feel his presence in the garden; in the kitchen she felt only his absence.

Any cooking she had learned from her father, she seems to have unlearned. There is nothing she remembers even though part of her might like to call it back. None of it was written down—it all came from muscle memory, his hands and his heart. But Vivian never regained interest because the sharp pain of the connection never subsided.

Some things are never learned because of a lack of interest, and some things are never learned because it simply hurts too much to try.

Ever since Tania asked her for her yearbook, Vivian has been thinking about Raine. Between cracking open that old book and her journey to high priesthood, the past insists on creeping in. Lately, she has been thinking of the past so often she wonders if she willed Tania's interest in those old images—a spell she unwittingly cast on her daughter.

Life flows and it's easy to forget origins, but Vivian became a witch because Raine took a Wicca class at summer camp.

"Wicca?" said Vivian, thinking Raine was talking about wicker, but dropping the *r*, as most New Englanders do at the end of one word or another. In some cases all. What Vivian imagined was Raine weaving baskets and chairs at camp over the summer.

"Yeah, you know, witchcraft and spells. You never heard of Wicca?"

"No, I guess not." Although Raine never set out to make Vivian feel foolish, Vivian often felt uninformed and unaware.

"I'll teach you all about it when I get back."

They were in Raine's room. Vivian sprawled on the bed while Raine packed a suitcase. Vivian groaned, "I can't believe you're going to be gone so long! What am I going to do without you?"

Raine laughed. "Three weeks." She flopped down on her belly near Vivian. "I wish you could come. You should have at least asked your mother."

Vivian made an incredulous face at Raine. "Do you think she would have said yes?"

"Not a chance."

"Exactly."

Later that day, with Raine on the bus to Maine, Vivian and Frank sat on a pier in the harbor. Legs dangled. The sun sat on the horizon, red and orange.

"You can just hang out with me," said Frank.

"I already do hang out with you."

"I mean extra." He meant without Raine getting in the way.

While Raine was gone, she sent letters to Vivian. She wrote her a story.

One day, when she was having particularly bad menstrual cramps, Eve decided to get even with God. She lifted her head from her hands, got up from her kitchen table, strewn with the plates, coffee rings and mugs, egg and toast droppings of a breakfast table abandoned, and, stroking her throbbing uterus, walked out the door. Walked straight into the living room, past Adam and the kids watching a hockey game on TV, and not interested enough in her to look her way, down through the breezeway, and, not stopping for her coat, right out the door.

She got up to heaven and tried to walk through the gates and St. Peter said, "Do you have an appointment?"

"No, I do not. Just tell Him it's Eve. I think He will see me."

St. Peter smiled and said, "You'll need to call first and make an appointment with the registration desk."

"Can't you just ask Him if He will see me? If He won't, then I'll leave and call. It can't hurt to try," Eve added.

"What in the world makes you think that? No, you'll need to go home and call first." But he smiled beatifically at her. Innocently, even. He peered around her to see who was next in line.

"Can't I just make an appointment with you?" Eve asked.

He laughed lightly as at an unknowing child or a simpleton. *"I don't make the appointments. Who's next now?"*

So Eve went home, rubbing her throbbing uterus the entire time, and she walked in the door, walked straight into the living room, past Adam and the kids, watching a hockey game on TV and not interested enough in her to look her way, strode past her kitchen table, strewn with the plates, coffee rings and mugs, egg and toast droppings of a breakfast table abandoned, and, still stroking her throbbing uterus, walked right up to the avocado-green rotary dial phone hanging on the wall.

She dialed up to the front office of Heaven.

"Good afternoon, Heaven," sang the receptionist.

"Hello, I would like to make an appointment with God," Eve demanded.

"What is the nature of your business?"

"Well, it's my husband and sons. And this business of my period every month being so painful and messy. And also why does labor have to hurt so much? And vaginal tearing during birth? And nipple pain with breastfeeding? God did all this on purpose! He could have done it any way He wanted and yet He gave us this shit. And I do all the work and my sons and husband are ungrateful assholes."

"But what is the nature of your business?"

"I want—nay!—I DEMAND an answer."

"To what question?"

"WHY!!?!!"

"Why?"

"Yes. Why, God?"

"That is your question?"

"Yes, that is my question."

"You don't need to see God for that. I can answer it for you."

"I think I'd rather hear it from Him."

"He won't see you for this. It is too elementary."

Eve sighed. "What then?"

"It's because of the apple. It's all your fault."

"What is?"

"Everything. Every single thing that has gone wrong, is going wrong, will go wrong. All of it."

Eve gaped at the phone. "Are you serious?"

"Stew in it." And then all she heard was a dial tone.

At the bottom of the story, Raine wrote, "Is that the God you want?" The story was written on notebook paper, the little frillies still attached as always. And Vivian thought, *There can be another?*

That single thought changed everything.

She and Frank filled the three weeks Raine was away with outings to the beach and their part-time jobs and working on their costumes for the Renaissance Faire coming in the fall. Vivian was sewing an ornate faux velvet gown and Frank was working on an elaborate and historically authentic suit of armor. Lots of research. It was the first time they were attempting chain mail. They spent a lot of time in the air-conditioned cubbies of the university library poring over books with illustrations and photographs of the outfits they were fashioning.

"I knew you would love the Faire as much as I do if you gave it a chance."

She didn't look up from the book through which she was leafing. "Yeah, well, we don't have to let that get out."

"Why not. Who cares?"

"I care. You have to admit it's leaning toward the dorky side."

He crossed his arms and looked up at her. "It is not. And even if it were, who cares what anyone thinks? You care too much about that crap, Vivian."

"I do not!"

He was back to looking at his armor photos. He tossed his head a little and said, "Well *that's* a convincing argument."

"Shut up, Frank. God." Maybe this was too much time with Frank. Just a few more days and Raine would return.

Vivian arranged with Raine's mother to go pick up Raine for her. "I don't mind at all."

Raine's mother touched Vivian's cheek. "You are such a nice girl, Vivvy." Vivian smiled. She was nice, she supposed, but mostly going crazy without Raine.

Raine bounced off the bus and ran screaming, "Viiiiiiiiiiii-veeeeeeeeeeeeeeeee!" They embraced and jumped up and down. "We're like idiot cheerleaders right now and I don't care—I'm just so happy to see you!"

"I would do a herkie right now if I actually knew what that was. God, I missed you! I didn't think this place could get worse and Frank is about to make me go nuts." They hugged again.

"Oh, Viv! It was so much fun! Even better than last summer. And I cannot wait to see Dave. I am about to explode if I can't get my hands on him soon."

"What did you do?"

"Hiking, canoeing, crafts."

"And the Wicca?"

"Yeah, that was my main workshop every morning. Goddess and Earth magic. I feel so attuned right now."

Vivian had tried to look up some books, but found nothing. She wanted to ask the reference librarian but since she wasn't entirely sure about what she was asking, she decided to wait. She could just ask Raine. She could ask Raine anything.

Raine handed her a book. "Here. You can check it out." Then she wanted to go find Dave, so Vivian took her home. They would go to the beach tomorrow, they promised, hugged and squealed some more. Those three weeks may as well have been years. Vivian remembers that this is how time works for the young. It moves so slowly, it is painful at times.

When Vivian got home, the house was blessedly empty. She closed the door to her room. She opened the book and read:

Thousands of years ago, before the emergence of the patriarchy, humans worshipped wise Mother Goddesses: She who gave life, She who took life, She who cycled, She who was fertile, She who grew old. All women are the natural manifestation of Her. She is mother, virgin, lover, warrior, creator, destroyer, artist, sorceress and healer. She is wisdom, creativity and evolution. She is within every woman.

The time has come to honor the Goddess once more.

Vivian was a goner from the first word.

The stories we live and that which comprises them— the circumstantial, the intentional—unfold, moment by moment. Vivian has learned that she can look back at the folds, the wrinkles, the tears and repairs and recognize some semblance of a coherent story. She can allow it to define her, she can succumb, she can wallow.

Or she can rewrite.

She can begin again. She can take up the pen, and write a new story.

Given the option between one choice and another, there is a third: neither, then start over.

Another black sky bears down, barreling in off the water. The rain hits the car, sounds like stones hitting metal full-force. Vivian turns her windshield wipers to the highest setting and it is not sufficient. She pulls over to the side of the road to wait it out. Old Sally tilts and rocks with the gusts of wind.

When it passes, the sun shimmers up from the wet roads and the sky is blue, blue and calm. As though nothing happened.

Vivian arrives at the salon and the little bell chimes when she opens the door. "Hello?" she calls out.

"Hi! Vivian?" calls a voice from the back. Audrey, one of the older stylists comes out from the kitchenette. "Just making a pot of coffee," she says. "I beat you here today!"

"I got stuck in the storm. Had to pull over and wait it out."

"What storm?" asks Audrey as she starts organizing her tools.

"The one that just blew through!"

Audrey shrugs. "No storm here."

Vivian looks outside at the pavement, leaves in the trees, cars in the parking lot—all dry. "These storms that have been coming through this summer have been so strange."

Audrey agrees. Vivian can't help but wonder what they might mean. Fierce but brief, what is it they are precipitating? They feel ominous to her and she wonders if she is simply being suggestible. But it feels as though something is unsettled.

Alison comes in and Vivian starts working on her haircut.

"How are the kids?" Vivian says.

The bell jingles and Frank strides in.

"Good morning, Alison." Vivian doesn't know why Frank insists on such a formal tone when he speaks to Alison—he sees her at least once a week when they do the kid exchange, and usually more often because of the kids' different activities.

Alison adopts his tone, "Why, hello, Francis."

Frank turns his attention to Vivian. "It's done, Vivian. Gary has given his endorsement!"

Vivian is genuinely shocked. "How did you make that happen?" Frank and Gary have a rather turbulent and adversarial history.

"*Iron Man* number fifty-five."

Vivian gasps. Frank must want this more than Vivian ever imagined to give away that comic book—it was his prized possession. *The centerpiece of my collection.* A phrase she had heard ad nauseam since she was fourteen.

"All's fair game in politics of this delicate nature," he says, his hands up, palms out.

"You gave away *Iron Man* number fifty-five? In which we witness the first appearance of Thanos?" Alison is as shocked as Vivian. She had to co-habitate with that comic book collection for a good number of years. An arduous endurance and one about which Vivian heard no end. Until the divorce, of course. Frank was frantic she would try to claim a portion of the collection in the divorce settlement. She threatened it, but Vivian never believed Alison would go through with pursuing it. She did it to stir him up. And to make it a lot easier to sweep everything else out from underneath him when she acquiesced her claim on his beloved comics. In light of almost losing his comic book collection, losing everything else seemed much more tolerable to Frank. Vivian was angry about it, but couldn't help but think it clever, if not a little evil.

"Never thought I'd see this day, Frank," says Alison. "What did you get in return?" She leans forward in Vivian's chair.

"The crown," he says grandly.

"Oh," she says flatly, falling back into the chair. "The Society."

"Yup," he smiles broadly. "I finally achieved it."

"Through bribery," says Alison.

"How do you think they did it hundreds of years ago?"

"Oh, you mean when serfs were chin-deep in the clutches of the bubonic plague, leeches were a primary medical solution and they thought the world was flat? Who cares!"

He disregards her finer points and says, "Bribery! Coups! Regicide!" he points at her with the last pronouncement. "Whatever it took!"

"In this case, *Iron Man* number fifty-five."

"Whatever it takes," he repeats and turns to Vivian. "We'll need to start working on our coronation garb."

"Vivian is going to be queen?" asks Alison.

"Oh, yes!" says Frank.

"Well, he did always want you to be his queen," says Alison.

"You always thought the Society was stupid," Frank says.

"Okay, you two..." says Vivian, all the while continuing work on Alison's hair.

"The Society *is* stupid!" says Alison.

"Frank, don't you need to get back to the store?" Vivian says.

"No. Joey's working. You, Alison, were never generous enough in spirit to try to take my interests seriously!"

"That's because your interests are most often shared by twelve-year olds!"

"Not true!" shouts Frank.

Vivian turns the blow dryer on high. She grabs a round brush and begins to dry Alison's hair. She can see Frank gesturing to her, but she ignores him. He grabs the blow dryer out of Vivian's hand, turns it off and says, "I am leaving, Alison. Good day."

"All hail the king!" she calls.

Vivian turns to Alison in the mirror. "This is a big deal to him, Alison," she says.

Alison sighs and shakes her head a little. Her glossy hair catches the light, flashes blue. "How do things just go so far off the rails, Vivian?" Alison asks Vivian's reflection.

Vivian can look back along the road of memory and she can see exactly where things went off track. But in the moments themselves, it is never that clear. Even though she is prone to wonder, *How did I not see it then?* she knows that in the moment, the most you can do is give it your best guess and commence to hoping.

"I am the last person to answer that," she says, turns the dryer back on, finishes her work.

Carol is fading.

Vivian sees it more and more clearly. They meet and Carol has difficulty staying awake. She is thin and weak. She is in visible pain.

This morning she tells Carol that it will be their last meeting. She is ready and Carol should be free. Carol can let go of the coven because Vivian is ready. At their last Sabbat, Carol told the women this would be her last ritual as their High Priestess.

"The Goddess has chosen Vivian to guide and support this group as your next High Priestess." The women wept with Carol and embraced Vivian joyfully. Vivian wept for Carol and for the love she felt from the women with whom she has shared her spirituality for so many years. Why had she been so worried? She must decipher the lesson in this, internalize it and recall it in her very bones.

(I am good, I am *good*.)

Vivian and Carol plan her crowning ceremony. Then Carol says, "I will not be at the ceremony."

"You won't?"

Carol shakes her head and smiles. "I do not bestow the power, Vivian. The Goddess does. You go to Her. This is Hers to give you, not mine."

It is night and Vivian lies in bed and cannot sleep.

She hugged Carol close and delicately for a long time, tried to make her touch as gentle as air, shrouded Carol's aura with her own. Mellifluous and honeyed, like breath. Then Vivian went to work and cut and styled hair all day, her mind and spirit nowhere near the salon; her hands running over curls and smooth tresses, over foil, over curlers; her fingers in scissors and on blow dryer and straight irons. She is grateful to those hands for their skills that require little of her conscious attention anymore. They simply execute the work. She can be far away in her thoughts. Today, her heart ached and her spirit sank low for Carol.

Now tonight she lies in bed and cannot sleep.

The air from her window flows over her, cool and slightly salty. Sweet and blowing the thin curtains lightly. Cool air on her body, covered lightly only with a worn bed sheet, is one of the beautiful indulgences of summer. Here, so close to the shore there are few leafy trees, but her old house was surrounded by tall willowy oaks and she loved the sound the wind made through the leaves in the quiet of night. Complete in its composition and tune.

It is very late and the house is nearly soundless, everyone but Vivian asleep, and she listens to the ocean rolling. The sound of the waves breaking is restrained, so the ocean must be rising and falling peacefully tonight. Spilling gently. She rises from her bed knowing with an urgent sureness that she must commune. She must dissolve something of herself in all that water. That mothery liquid.

She slips quietly out the back of the house and walks on bare feet over the cool sand. It sings beneath her feet. The moon is high and bright white, its light bobbles and nods on the water. Winks and invites. She slips the clothes from her body and walks into the water, not slowly but not hurriedly, and when she reaches the point where the water meets her waist, she glides under. A peace only the ocean provides envelops her. It never fails to overcome her with its enchantment. It is a filled-up, almost too-much love kind of way. And she is so grateful. So she floats on her back sustained and buoyed by the Mother, shone down upon with clear white light by the Mother. The moon, the water—two expressions of the Mother's multitude of forms.

She stays out there for a long time. She senses the moon has shifted in the sky. She feels the tide has pulled out. She has no urge to leave.

So she stays.

Mother.

Vivian and her mother were two separate planets orbiting around each other in that big stone house by the ocean. It was as though she were living with someone else's grandmother. A woman who had nothing and yet everything to do with her. She loved her mother, but she felt unfastened; out there on her own. Attached to that woman and that house but floating out of earshot somewhere out in the blue. It was a matter of being misunderstood, not unloved.

She began of necessity to mother herself.

Once she realized that part of the nurturing she craved needed to come from her own self, she could begin to forgive her mother for not being perfect. For not fulfilling an image. She could also begin to forgive herself. It was not an absolute necessity to have someone out there holding her up. When she let go of that idea, she realized she was not alone. She had never been alone.

But she learned to be fierce about her own joy.

This night, as she is supported by that mother water, she exhales slowly and centers her concentration on the white orb in the sky to which she has turned so many times for solace.

And She is there. As She is always.

Vivian exhales slowly but surely as she treads water.

The women gather on the beach at next full moon.

Vivian goes to the Goddess and She comes to Vivian. The women cover Vivian in flowers. The moon is immense and fulgent.

And Vivian is filled, filled, filled but finds she can contain it all.

When the air is as active as it is this night, they don't have to go to the screen house. The mosquitoes are simply blown away.

This night the moon is full and seems to be resting right upon the rippling water. A silvery wash. A ribbon, wide to narrow, floats on the surface of the water.

Vivian is very quiet, but there is a fullness that her daughters sense. They know this was the night of her ceremony, but they don't ask. There is something sacrosanct in their mother's demeanor and they instinctively know that tonight is not the time to ask. They bask instead.

Anne and Millie drowse in their comfortable chairs on the back porch that faces the moon ribbon water.

Everyone is quiet and still, except the wind.

And what is the wind?

The screen house sits empty this night.

There are times when they don't need it.

8

Guin—Enough

The circle of Guin's life is tightening. The perimeter—the places where she can easily breathe—is closing in. It is more and more difficult to escape the smothering. She tells herself this is merely a body sensation—not unlike a headache or indigestion—a thing that is harmless and will pass, but believing such logic in the worst moments is nearly impossible. The center of safety is home and the safety circles out and out in a spiral which is a beautiful image, except the farther out the spiral spins, the less she is able to breathe. In those far-away spaces, she feels an urgent need to get back to the safe sphere. It is a landscape of widespread fear.

It is a dark shroud.

Guin sits in Dunkin Donuts with Darlene.

"Do you know what they're finding in the drinking water now?" she says to Darlene. "Birth control hormones, rocket fuel, heroin." She takes a sip of her piping hot tea and sighs. "Do you know what I found out my sister is doing? I probably shouldn't even talk about it."

"I don't know her and I won't tell anyone. You can tell me if you want to."

"No. I trust you. It's just...let's just say it's...she's doing a thing that is so far from who she is and I don't know why and neither does she."

Darlene is quiet.

"Is anything what we think it is?" Guin asks.

"I don't know, Guin. What does anyone know?" Darlene says this slowly and sadly and Guin can only nod *yes*. Oh, yes.

Guin could not answer if she tried. A sort of hysterical sensation bursts through her. She is not sure what causes it or what it means. She only wants to feel safe again. She wonders why she simply and firmly accepts this anxiety and the circumstances that deepen it. The very circumstances of the way she lives. The panic simply descends upon her and she stands, silent and still, a passive presence in her own life.

Then Darlene tells Guin she is going to leave her husband. She has decided.

Guin is shaken by this and for a moment, she slips into a small panic until she recovers herself. Another instance of that little shudder and spin and sliding of solid ground. This news and learning of Tania's infidelity—things are cracking apart around her. She feels left out in some odd way yet she knows that none of this is anything she wants to know firsthand. The idea of things coming apart and changing jars her. These things that people do—what pushes them to their limit? And for the first time she wonders, *Can I be pushed?* She wonders where the line might be—what the final straw would look like. Would it be heavy or light? Something entirely different or just more of the same. *Can I be pushed?*

Guin says, "What will you do?"

In the few short weeks since they began, these cups of tea with Darlene have swiftly become a sort of preservation. Some sanity and relief for Guin.

"It's not like I'll be any worse off," Darlene says. "He doesn't hold down a job now, he barely gives me any help with the kids or the house. I do everything myself and he's a grouch most of the time. He says I'm always all over his ass and he's sick and tired of it." She shrugs. "Maybe I am, but you know what I think is the root of all this? I think he got stuck with us and that's why he's unhappy."

Guin could never speak those words without a searing pain accompanying them, but Darlene doesn't seem hurt by them, more like worn down. It would tear Guin apart to admit a thing like that about Pickle.

"But don't you love him?" Guin asks her. Except for the grouch part, Darlene's husband sounds too much like Pickle for comfort.

Darlene sighs and looks out the window, then back at Guin. "Yeah. But sometimes I wonder why. I'm making him sound terrible!" She laughs a little. She stops and is quiet, looks out the big window of the coffee shop. "He has his good points and I know he loves me in his way. I guess that should be enough." Guin waits but Darlene has nothing more to offer on that thought. Guin can't help but add to Darlene's sentiment, *But it's not*.

What is enough?

Guin shies away from gathering expectations of Pickle, piling them up to an insurmountable elevation. But the needs and desires she suppresses are rising and noisily refuse to be ignored.

She notes that it is strange how when an idea floats around in the mind, things crop up out of nowhere to highlight it, as if the world and people are inexplicably aware of the train of thought and want to add to it. At times she finds this converging gleefully surprising and other times somewhat unsettling. Just the other day Mrs. Fournier talked to her about Pickle.

"Honey, how's Pickle's new job? He won't tell me anything. Even when I bug him." She leaned on her counter with her ever-present mug of coffee. Guin always wonders how the woman sleeps with all that caffeine coursing through her. She smokes cigarettes, too, but never around the children. She no longer smokes in the house at all since she learned about secondhand smoke. For years now she has smoked out on the upstairs porch of the triple-decker house she and Pickle's father own. Some of Pickle's siblings live on the other floors. In winter, Mrs. Fournier puts on her calf-length puffy coat to smoke in the cold. Her smoke mingles with the warm air from her lungs creating an ever-disintegrating halo around her head.

"I think it's going good. He doesn't talk about it much with me, either. He never talks about his jobs much at all..."

She snorted, "When he *has* a job. Listen, honey, I know Pickle's kind of a screwball. And I feel responsible. He was the sweetest little boy and I spoiled him all his life. Now he's your problem and I feel sorry about that."

"I don't think of him as a problem."

"Oh, honey, I know you don't. It's just, well, it's almost like another baby for you." She laughed. "I guess that's the last thing you need!"

Guin just smiled. What else could she do?

"Don't be too hard on him. It always comes down to the women in the end, doesn't it?" Pickle's mother said.

Guin is never hard on Pickle.

"It's the same with Pickle. I love him," she tells Darlene. "I never give him a hard time about anything. Sometimes I try to tell him he really needs to hold on to a job and help me out, but then he gets upset and says I make him feel like a loser and then I end up saying sorry. But it's hard doing everything and it's almost impossible to make ends meet with the money from the restaurant. No, not almost—it is impossible." She takes a sip of her tea and weighs her words. She says things to Darlene that she is often afraid to inspect even in the privacy of her own mind. But here they flow and it is a great release of pressure she wasn't aware had built up inside her. "Sometimes I am so sick of babying him. Do you ever wonder who's going to take care of *me* for a change?"

Darlene nods. "You hit it on the head. Sometimes I am so tired I feel like there's no way I can make it through all the stuff that has to get done before I can just *be* done."

There is no done, thinks Guin. "Yeah, and it's not even like it's just in my body," Guin says and it's difficult to articulate exactly what she means, but it seems Darlene understands without explanation. Guin feels thin. She could blow away. She might fall over at any moment. She cannot keep it all going. She might break. She is often amazed when she gets to the end of the day and she realizes what she has accomplished—just how many things she has done. Yet instead of being satisfied or proud, she tends to reflect on where she thinks she has fallen short. And always present is the looming fear. And she never knows what it is. And she knows all of it will have to happen again tomorrow, which is especially exhausting.

"It's all so exhausting," is all she can say.

All Darlene can say is, "I know."

Later, after supper and baths, Guin rocks each baby to sleep after nursing. She knows they say you shouldn't, but it's too sweet and she simply can't resist. Megan, already asleep, breathes evenly from her crib. Laura rests in Guin's arms, eyes just now fluttered shut, her small body warm and weighty with sleep. From one corner of her slightly parted lips, a trickle of milk flows down to her round chin. Guin gently wipes it away with her thumb. She puts her face close to her baby's neck and inhales her scent. Honey.

The sun is setting over the water and a cool breeze blows across their bodies. Guin lays Laura in her crib and pulls a light blanket over her. Each baby wears only a onesie and Guin loves her babies in only a onesie—their plush limbs, narrow shoulders and skinny necks, big round bellies on full display. Guin runs her hand lightly over each baby's back. Between their tiny shoulder blades. She leaves reluctantly, as she does each night, as if she is going to miss something that must be witnessed. She always must remind herself that there will be tomorrow with them.

And for this her gratitude is almost too much to bear.

The car makes that sound again. Metal clashing against metal. She makes a face and turns the radio up louder. Steve Perry croons about only the young.

"Guin, what is that?" asks Pickle.

"What?" she asks.

"That grinding sound? You don't hear that?"

Guin hears it. Has been hearing it. She turns the volume a bit higher.

"Oh, that. Yeah, maybe it's the ABS? That light has been on lately." She has no idea what "ABS" means.

"Oh," he says.

"So, what does that mean?" she asks him.

"Um, I don't know."

"You're learning how to fix cars, right?" she asks.

"Well, I don't know everything yet!"

She shakes her head back and forth. "I don't think it's anything. Maybe the brakes just need a tune-up, or whatever. Maybe you can look at it."

"Sure," he says and looks out the window.

Free to fly…

Guin's first memories of Pickle are from the halls of high school. They were fifteen. He was the most beautiful boy she'd ever seen. She almost couldn't tolerate how he made her feel—hot and flushed. The mere thought that he might like someone else could take her down at the knees. A breath-stealing punch to the stomach. It would have meant the end of the world. When she saw him in the halls she was afraid to make eye contact so she watched him peripherally and then asked her girlfriends, *Did he look at me?* They responded, *He definitely looked at you!*

Guin went out of her way to put herself in his path. She had memorized his schedule with the assistance of a girlfriend who helped out in the office and copied it from his file. She craned her neck looking for his dirty-blond hair; she made sure he'd pass by her several times a day. She never knew where to look when she saw him; she was hyper-conscious of her body when he was near. Pickle was so soft and pretty. She longed to feel the softness of his hair on her fingers, touch his cheek.

Guin will never forget the day Pickle first spoke to her. It was between third and fourth periods. Guin was strategically positioned to his view in the corridor leading to D-block where the gyms were located. He had gym third period and she had it fourth. This was one of the easiest encounters she'd arranged.

She watched him approach through lowered lids. The pink rose in Guin's cheeks. Pickle's face angled slightly to his right, toward a friend. He turned his head just as she was within a few feet. A piece of his longish, dirty-blond hair fell across his forehead as he turned toward her. He reached his right hand up and brushed it away. His eyes— the color of the sky on a fall day—slowly turned to Guin's. He blinked slowly as one side of his flawless lips turned up in a smile.

"Hi, Guin."

She almost died.

He'd spoken to her.

She forgot to breathe. Warmth spread through her.

Later, Guin was putting some books in her locker, rifling around for a notebook, hurrying in the five minutes before the next class.

"Hi, Guin."

She froze for a second that felt like hours. Days. *Oh, God, what do I do?* She turned around slowly, hoping the look on her face did not reveal the terror that pulsed through her.

"Hi, Pickle," she said softly, smiling up at him.

"What's up?" He leaned in close to her, grinned a half smile. He smelled so good. Like very clean air. Like babies, like cookies. It was intoxicating. His body slim and his hands lovely. His eyelashes so long. She had an unbearable impulse to reach up and gently brush the backs of her fingers across them. She had never seen anyone so beautiful this close.

"Nothing," she said.

"What're you doing Friday night?"

"Nothing," she said.

"A bunch of us are going to the game and then to the beach," he said.

Oh. My. God.

"Oh yeah?" she said.

"Yeah. Thought you might like to go."

"Oh, yeah, sure. That'd be cool."

"Cool. I'll pick you up at seven?" he said.

She nodded.

"Cool. See you tomorrow."

She nodded some more.

The bell rang. She ran grinning all the way to math.

That night, she lay in bed and thought of him as she looked up at the ceiling where someone who'd lived there before had stuck glow-in-the-dark stars. They glowed a pale green. They looked nothing like real stars. And the room was a little dumpy, like the rest of the place. But that didn't matter at all tonight. Nothing did. She lay there thinking only of Pickle. He was extraordinary. She got up, turned on the light and looked in the mirror. She could hardly see herself. She stared at her face until she got that feeling like when she repeated a word over and over so that it becomes a random sound, losing its intended meaning. Oval face, strawberry-blond curls, fair skin, high pink color in her cheeks. Hazel eyes.

She was not extraordinary. But he saw something there. Something unusual, which was almost as good as extraordinary.

She has been with Pickle ever since.

When she gets home from work, Pickle is in the driveway working on the RV. He has outlined the Patriots logo and started painting in the blue. It looks very authentic and Guin is surprised by how good it is turning out.

She brings the kids into the house and goes back outside where Tania sits watching the painting. She is drinking a bottle of beer and Guin takes it out of her hand and takes a long sip.

"It looks really good," she says.

"It does," says Tania. "You sound surprised."

"Oh, like you're not?"

"Well, you wouldn't expect me to be anything but."

"True." She nods again. "It really looks good. It's not that I don't have faith in Pickle, but…" says Guin.

"You don't have to tell me."

I surely can't tell him, she thinks.

She looks closely. He has gotten a lot done suddenly. She tips her head toward one shoulder, wrinkles her forehead. "Did he just start working on this when he got home from work today? I don't remember it being so far along."

"I had the day off but I was out all day at the beach. I can tell you he was here when I left and when I got back."

"What about work?"

Tania shrugs her shoulders and gets up. "Ask him. I'm going to get another beer. You want one?"

"Yes, I think I do."

Guin walks briskly over to Pickle. "Looks good, hon," she says.

He smiles and jumps off the ladder. He pulls her into a hug and kisses her. He is sweaty and smells of beer. "When did you get all this done?" she asks him.

"Today." This is all he says.

Today happens to be an ordinary Thursday. She holds on to a thin thread of patience.

"What about work." Her voice does not lilt as with a question.

"Oh, well, Guin, I'm not sure that's going to work out."

She takes a breath and exhales slowly. "Why not?"

"Don't yell at me, Guin!"

"I didn't yell." She is still not yelling. She is not sure how long she will be able to say that, though.

He says nothing, keeps drinking his beer. On his face is a look of fear, the look an animal gets when it thinks it needs to fight or flee. She has seen this expression on his face too many times before and it raises a disgust in her. She is disappointed in his behavior but also repelled by the way he cowers to her.

"Pickle!"

"What?"

"The job. What's wrong with the job?"

He sort of kicks the ground around, the broken seashells and the mixed-in sand. "It's just a lot to learn,

234

and I don't think I'm very good at it. The guy is always yelling at me. I don't have to take that shit!"

"Pickle! It's been a month. A month! And I think what you call *yelling* is just a boss telling you what to do which he has every right to do since he is the *boss*!" She stops talking and walks in a little circle. She is trying to collect herself. She stops right in front of him. "Did you quit?" she asks quietly now. She sort of holds her breath without meaning to. Her whole being is holding itself somehow, waiting to hear what he will say.

He exhales and just stands there looking at her.

"Did you?" she asks again, steadily.

He opens his arms out to his sides, his palms are facing up. "Guin." He says her name quietly and it is laden and husky with things she knows he does not want to say.

"You did. You fucking did. Oh, Pickle!" She sits down on the little step of the RV. She rubs her eyes. It is a hot evening, the end of a late July summer day. Her skin feels scorched and raw. She hates this kind of heat. And the mosquitoes are starting to act up. Right now the sun is beginning its inevitable descent—the sky streaked a little pink, and soon the sun will drip orange and purple over the water. She can hear her kids playing out on the porch, their voices light, brimming and spilling over with laughter. She needs to think about their supper right now, not this again with Pickle. This has happened too many times. Too many times.

And she says so. "Pickle, this has happened too many times." Her voice is no longer loud.

"Guin, you can't just expect me to be miserable at work with some job I don't know how to do and some guy yelling at me all day."

"Yes, Pickle, I can, because those kids need food and shoes and diapers. Do you think I've loved being a waitress at The Grille and Creamery since I was sixteen years old? Is that my dream job? Is this my dream life? Is it, Pickle?"

"No, but at least you're good at it and your boss likes you."

"Really? I'm good at being a waitress? Well, thanks, hon." As if that's the biggest accolade in the world. As if this is what she wants for her life. Not that she knows explicitly what she wants for her life but she's finally realized it is not this.

She hears the bang of the screen door and then Ethan tugs at her. "I want my lunch, Mommy."

"Supper, honey," she says automatically.

"I want my supper!"

The twins follow close behind him, "Mama," they say as they touch her body, as high as they can reach. She bends down and deftly picks up each of them, brings one to each hip. Laura touches Guin's cheek and Megan's hand weaves through her hair. Sometimes, especially at a time like this, she just wants to go. Go and recall what freedom feels like. That state of being she took for granted while she had it. Knowing she will never have it again makes her ache a little. But then she looks at these babies and she is grounded once more. She turns to Pickle.

"You have to go," she says abruptly. "Now—just go. Go away. Go."

Pickle puts out his hands. "Go where, Guin? Where am I going to go?"

"I don't give a flying..." she pulls herself up short, "crap. Go to your mother's, sleep in this smelly piece of junk. You don't even live here!" She stops. "You know what? Enough! I am not doing this for you, too. I worry about everything for our kids, I ask my mother for a place to live, I hold down a job, get the kids to the doctor, to your mother's, everywhere, everything. You think I want to do everything? You think I don't want my own place to live? You think I don't want someone to take care of *me* every once and a while?"

"I do anything you ask me to do, Guin!"

"Not really, Pickle. Figure something out for yourself for a change. I am tired of thinking all the time!"

"But where am I going to go?"

"I am kicking you out of my grandmother's yard and I am not doing this for you. Figure it out on your own!" she screams. The babies get silent, stare at her. Ethan cowers at her feet.

Tania slips in and gently takes the babies from Guin's arms. She ushers Ethan inside.

"You're dumping me, Guin?" He is not yelling anymore. He is crying now. His voice has softened, thickened with tears and a sadness that Guin feels in the very center of her body. "Guin, are you dumping me?"

And she must say the most difficult word: "Yes."

"But, Guin!" He wipes his nose with his sleeve.

She turns and walks inside.

"Guin!" he calls.

"I have to go in now, Pickle. I need to take care of the kids."

He calls to her softly.

"I have to take care of them, Pickle." She keeps walking, steps inside and closes the door, leans back into it and listens. She listens and there is only silence punctuated by the calls of gulls, the persistent movement of the water. Then she hears the RV sputtering and the crunch of tires on the crushed-shell driveway as he drives away. She breathes slowly.

She walks out back and everyone is quiet. They all look up. She begins to sob. They leap to her.

Everyone sits quietly on the back porch. They share space and breath and spare but gentle speech.

The phone jingles. An old table phone—used to be shiny, now a dull black. Aunt Anne answers, "Hello?" Guin lifts her head from her sister's lap and steels herself. She doesn't want to talk to Pickle, but it's not him. "Prayer Line, Millie."

Guin watches her grandmother take her small steps over to the phone. She reaches into her pocket and removes the little pad and a stubby pencil. "Hello?" she says. She nods slightly, sighs. "Oh, my. Yes. Thanks, Arthur." She pushes down the disconnect buttons.

"What is it, Millie?" Aunt Anne asks.

"Terrible accident up on 88." She dials the number of the next person on the chain. "Hello, Jackie? Hi, sweetheart. How are you? Got a call about an accident up on 88. Yup, when the storm came through about an hour ago. Young man and young woman, both airlifted to Boston. Pretty serious it seems. Okay, thanks. God bless you, too, Jackie. Bye-bye."

Everyone is quiet. There is a heaviness on the old stone porch and they are stuck in deep. Even the children play more sedately than usual. Everyone moves to the table and eats without much talk.

"I sent Pickle away," Guin says out loud. As if they didn't already know.

"Hooray! When's the party?" says Tania.

"Hilarious," says Guin.

Then her mother comes in, tired, and sits heavily and begins to eat. As Guin turns her back to the table to clean up the kids, she hears her mother whisper, "Where's Pickle?" and someone whispers back, "He's gone," and her mom says, "Where?" and someone says, "Guin told him to leave," and her mom says, "Did he lose another job?" and Guin says out loud, "Yes, he did, Mom, and I am not as upset as you all think. I know you are all waiting for me to break down since that's what I usually do but this time I will not."

Vivian spreads butter over her ear of corn. "You've never kicked him out before."

Guin turns with the wet cloth in her hand. "He's never quit the seventh job in three years for no good reason before. Well, the *no good reason* part we've all become accustomed to, but not the seventh job in three years part. Something snapped." Then she begins to cry again in earnest. She growls, "He doesn't even really live here!"

"Tania, why don't you put the kids to bed," says Grammy.

Tania does just that and Vivian puts her arms around Guin, and they sit down on the old wicker couch near the window.

"I am not upset! Why am I crying?" says Guin.

"Anne, let's clear the table," says Grammy.

Guin says nothing more and neither does Vivian. Guin simply rests on her mother and cries. She lies with her head on her mother's lap, which no matter how old she gets always feels right. Vivian strokes her head and Guin remembers that there is comfort for her, she is not alone; she is not carrying the heaviest burdens without being shored up. How could she have forgotten? Life has a way of doing that. But she won't drown in the difficulties as long as there is a lap upon which to lay her head.

The children asleep, the table cleared, the women gather in the screen house. Aunt Anne lights the small silver buckets of tea tree oil-infused wax candles that she makes every spring.

"Those smell a lot better than the ones you get at the store," Grammy says.

"They work better, too," says Aunt Anne. Aunt Anne has many homemade remedies to ward off mosquitoes. Guin would not be surprised if she has rituals that she performs in the dark of night or the first rays of dawn. "The best thing I have found is to combine flat beer, antiseptic mouthwash and Epsom salt. Pour the solution in a spray bottle, and squirt it anywhere you want to keep the mosquitoes at bay. Works like a charm."

"Now if you only had remedies for men," says Tania.

She laughs. "I've never been any good with men, girls. You can't ask me about men. I have my insights, but no perfect answers. And I only have the insights now that I am too old to put them to use."

Grammy says, "Don't shortchange yourself, Anne. You know lots about men. Or a little about lots of men." She titters.

Aunt Anne laughs aloud. "There was a time when all she did was lecture me about my male friends. Now she laughs."

"Lots of men?" says Tania.

Aunt Anne just nods a little. "A few."

Grammy snorts and leaves it at that.

Grammy settles herself more deeply in her wicker chair. It is a rocker and Guin can hear the old cushions shifting around. "If only my husband had lived longer. He was a good man. Or what we thought of in those days as a good man. I think our standards cannot be measured against yours nowadays. They wouldn't match up at all."

"What was a good man?" asks Tania.

"A good man was one who provided for his family, was kind to his children, respectful to his wife, didn't drink too much. I don't think we expected what you girls have come to expect from your men."

Guin says, "Pickle can't keep a job—he doesn't provide for us. He's all those other things, though." She sighs. She is ashamed to admit even to herself that she misses him already. She will not admit it out loud. They can probably read her mind anyway. A little stream of quiet tears trickles from her eyes.

"It does seem our Pickle can't keep a job," sighs Grammy.

"He's such a love, though," says Aunt Anne.

Guin feels a sob rise, but swallows it down. "He's wonderful," she chokes out. Then she growls, "Ugh!" More tears fall on her mother's lap.

"I feel sorry for you girls now. It's so much harder in some ways than when we were girls," says Grammy.

"I think you're right. Although we can't surrender the strides we've made as women," says Aunt Anne.

"I suppose not," says Grammy.

"What do you mean, 'you suppose not'?" says Tania. "We can't surrender anything!"

Aunt Anne says, "I know exactly what you're thinking, Millie. It's that men and women are all mixed up right now."

"It's true," says Grammy. "It used to be that what women did, women did and what men did, men did. Now, thanks to women's liberation..."

"Feminism," Aunt Anne corrects her. "Which, by the way, I have always supported and continue to support."

"Yes, Anne, we know."

"Well, I know what you are about to say, and although there may be some truth in it as pertains to the root of the problem, I still think that women had no choice but to rise up," says Aunt Anne.

Grammy nods and says, "It's all a big mess, now, though. No one knows what they are supposed to be doing. Who is working, who is taking care of the kids, who is supposed to be the breadwinner. Worse than all that, which is, after all the practical business of everyday life, worse than all that is that women expect men to be their friends. I think that is the root of the problem."

"Men and women shouldn't be friends, Grammy?" Tania says, indignantly. Guin can tell she has her back up already. Tania attends classes on this stuff and reads books and takes it very seriously. Guin would like to learn more herself but she is too busy and, although she had thought of going to college once, that seems like a long time ago.

"Yes, spouses should be friends. Take care of each other and put each other first. But you can't expect a man to include you in his boys' club activities and you shouldn't expect him to care too much about your women's interests. That is what sisters and girlfriends are for. Women simply expect too much from men nowadays. I don't mean money, or possessions, or help with the kids. For all that I think a balance could be struck. Women want to be buddies, and that's the problem. Why can't some women be happy with other women as their friends? What is this need to be 'one of the boys'? What do these women think they are missing? As far as I have seen, not a whole lot."

"Women want equality, Grammy. Not exclusion." Tania sits straight up in her chair. She is stiff and rigid with offense.

Aunt Anne says, "Equal is good."

"Exactly," says Tania. "How can we go forward in the shadow of the patriarchy as we have for hundreds, no thousands, of years? You know what Simone de Beauvoir said? She said that when a person is made to be in a state of inferiority, she becomes inferior. We have to *be* equal."

"Honey, what does that even mean? All I'm suggesting is that we accept that we are different, and different is fine. We can't become one big homogenized group. Men and women are different. When we accept that, then we can start thinking about equality."

"Mom taught us about Goddess," Guin says, her head still in her mother's lap. She feels surrounded and enveloped and it is such a welcome and needed feeling.

"It has been postulated that the Goddess is merely a reaction to the patriarchy," says Tania.

"No, She is not," says her mother. "She has been around for a lot longer than the gods who currently hold all the attention."

"Not this Goddess talk again," says Grammy. Her voice is tinged with impatience.

"No, Mom, not this 'Goddess talk' again." Mom is more impatient.

Aunt Anne pipes up and changes the direction of things. "I saw a bumper sticker once that said, 'Women who seek to be equal to men lack ambition.' If that doesn't say it all, I don't know what does."

Grammy snorts, "Oh, Anne, you're terrible!"

Even Tania laughs.

Mom says, "The years have taught me that the work of life—I mean taking care of family—is impossible to do on your own." She sighs. "Maybe it *was* easier when we knew who was supposed to do what."

"Or when you each have each other," Guin says.

"Yes, that too," Mom says and rubs Guin's shoulder. "Somehow we do always find a way."

It's five in the morning and Guin hasn't slept at all, and she has given up trying. She checks on the babies and they are sound asleep. Ethan, too, is sprawled out on his small bed, arms and legs flung out with the kind of abandon only small children surrender to sleep. She touches the impossibly smooth skin of his forehead, his arm. His breath catches slightly then falls back into a deep and regular pattern.

She creeps quietly outside and carefully walks over the stones that line the stretch of beach out behind the house. She sits down in the cool sand, gathers piles of it in her hands and lets the tiny grains slip through her fingers. Over and over. It is a soothing sensation.

She is in awe of what she did yesterday. What is life without Pickle? She hardly remembers—it was so long ago that she lived her life without him. She doesn't want to be without Pickle, she just doesn't want to be with him like this anymore. Even though what she did feels like a great surprise, she knows everything has been culminating to this very moment. Now, right now. And she knows it could only have ended here on this beach with these grains of sand falling through her fingers while the children sleep.

She sits close to the shore and her mind feels emptied out. She watches as the sun slowly breaks wide over the horizon. First one ray, then another few, then a bursting and it is day. The sky is blue-black up high above the earth and white along the horizon where the sun breaks it wide open. The gulls begin to call and the sandpipers are suddenly upon the shore, chasing the tide in and out, pecking at the wet sand. The cord grasses sway. The sun dots the rippling water with light.

She has no plan. She has never had a plan. She was in high school, worked at The Grille and Creamery, loved Pickle, got pregnant, then pregnant again, still works at The Grille and Creamery. That is it. That is where it starts and ends.

But where will it go?

Tania creeps quietly outside and finds Guin in the screen house. She opens the door with a loud creak.

"I tried to sit on the porch, but got bit too many times," Guin said. "They're just as bad in early morning as they are at twilight," she says.

"That's what Mom always says," says Tania. "I woke up and felt compelled to come outside, even at this ungodly hour."

"Twin perception," says Guin, an idea at which Tania scoffs, but which Guin believes wholeheartedly. "You knew I was down here. Lonely and lost."

"Right, right, right," she says. "Are you lonely and lost?"

"Kind of," Guin says. Tania sits down next to Guin and takes her hand. "What now?"

Tania shakes her head slowly. "Fuck if I know."

They sit quietly and watch as a new day begins. They both think—although neither one knows the other does— maybe it's okay, on this day, not to know. Maybe it's okay.

Maybe I'm okay.

9

Tania—Unravel

June 30, 1988
Helloooo my dearest Vivian!
I'm writing in black today as a sign of mourning, not to be melodramatic or anything. I just know there is something wrong with Dave and I can't tell what. It's a vibrational thing. I can sense it. So I am being clingy and he is being aloof. Aaahhh-looooof! God bless me. (See? I am not completely incapable of humor.) Dave better not try to break up with me tonight. I'll HAVE to talk him out of it somehow. Seriously, breaking up is the LAST thing I want to do right now, even though he has been annoying and hurtful just lately. I've invested too much in this relationship just to trash it like he wants to. Maybe my whole idea is wrong and he just wants to talk about it or something. Oh well, at least he is still driving me to school. He was quiet this morning, wearing his cold mask of indifference. I still love him, though. No one loves him more than I do! I might tell him that one of these days.
Sorry my notes aren't funny and entertaining like yours but my creative thought processes are running out

with still eighteen minutes to go in my lunch break. At least I am eating right now...

Tonight I'll just tell him how I feel and ask him what he plans to do. What more can I do about it? I hope you're right and it'll all turn out for the best.

Well, I gotta go—the bell beckons.

Love you, love you, more than even you love me or life,

Raine

P.S. Summer has just begun and it sucks and it had better improve. It's supposed to be AWESOME. Hope my prediction comes true...

Tania matches up the dates of notes and letters from Raine with entries in her Mom's diary and a clear picture begins to form. A story. Her mother's history.

July 3, 1988

I am on break at this zoo they call the supermarket. The day before a holiday SUCKS. I fear this shift will never end. If I look at another package of hot dogs, I might puke. What the hell do hot dogs have to do with independence? Is this what Americans have evolved into? Hot dogs, charcoal briquettes and fireworks. Yay, freedom!

There is no one to tell about SB except this diary and I hope no one sees it because it would be a major disaster. Beyond major. Is there a word bigger than major? Total is bigger. It would be a total disaster. Nuclear is even bigger than total.

A couple weeks ago, a bunch of us went out. Frank was busy, so at the end of the night it was just a few of us. I dropped everyone off and then was going to take SB home and he starts flirting with me—more than usual. We got to his house and he says, like always, "Where's my hug?" So I leaned over and hugged him but he kissed me goodbye. I mean he KISSED ME GOODBYE. I didn't expect it at all. I mean, I have been in love with him for so long, but I never said so.

But then we went out alone last Friday night when neither of us happened to be working. We were just going to hang out until everyone else got out of work. But we went out to the dark side of the island and we did it for like two hours straight. SB had rug burns on his knees and my thighs still hurt! Then we drove around and picked up everyone and went to a bonfire party on the beach. I had to pretend for the rest of the night that "it" hadn't just happened with him. I haven't really talked to him since. Better keep it that way. Raine is on the verge of a break-up—I can't just throw this in her face. OH MY GOD, it's so messed up.

(But I am totally crazy about him.)

Of course Tania can't ask her mother any questions about what she is reading. She considers finding roundabout ways of asking Frank, but he would be suspicious and he'd never betray her mother. If there is a secret he harbors, he will keep it.

What does SB have to do with Raine? The boy Raine was crazy for was Dave.

This mystery is quite a lovely distraction and has allowed Tania to dodge real life. She is also dodging phone calls from both Thom and Shea.

In the moments when she is not immersed in the diaries trying to unravel her mother's mystery, she can't stop thinking about what she has done.

Because she is not returning their calls, she suspects Thom's annoyance will be growing, but she knows Shea will be confused and hurt if she keeps this up too long. She is certain she is losing the ability to behave normally around him. She fears she will slip and her lies will spill.

The sky outside is that perfect blue of summer skies with only a few fluffy clouds puffing around. She moves to the window seat and looks down the shoreline. It's only nine-thirty and the beach is already filling up. She wishes she could go, too. Sit in the sun, take a swim, a long walk. The ocean soothes her in a way that, at worst, allows her to forget her troubles for a little while, or, at best, smoothes things out into a new perspective.

She picks up the letters and diary again. Some of the information is not meeting up, and some of it seems cryptic because it is only one side of the conversation. Maybe as she keeps reading, it will become clearer. She is getting close in the timeline to the point when she and Guin were conceived. She still doesn't know who SB is. She's gone through her mother's entire yearbook and plenty of boys look like the skater type.

There is a rap on her door and she jumps, jams the notes, open diary and yearbook under her pillow. "Who is it?"

"It's Aunt Anne. Can I come in?" Aunt Anne sings.

"Yes," Tania mimics her tone.

"I need to bake a cake," she says.

"Why?"

"Well, what will we eat for dessert if I don't?" asks Aunt Anne.

"Bag of Oreos?" Tania suggests.

"Uck," Aunt Anne makes a face of disgust. "No. Come on. You've never made dessert."

"What kind of cake?"

"What kind do you like?" asks Aunt Anne.

"I like carrot cake."

"Oh, me, too. With cream cheese frosting." They reach the kitchen and Aunt Anne starts clattering around. "First we've got to make sure we have everything we need." She doesn't consult a cookbook, just opens cabinets and closes them, pokes her head in the fridge. "I think we do," she says conclusively. "Okay, so grease the pans, honey."

"What the what?" says Tania. "You should know I've never baked a cake. I've never even witnessed a cake being baked."

"What about your birthday?"

"You always bake our cakes," says Tania.

"Oh, yes. Yes, that's right. Okay then. Run a lump of softened butter around the pan. Don't be chintzy about it. If you don't do this, your cake will never come out."

Tania shrugs, "We could just eat it out of the pan."

Aunt Anne looks at her. "No," she says.

Tania does what she's told, then dusts the inside with flour and taps it out after Aunt Anne tells her to do that, too.

"Now *here* I am going to teach you a really good trick. Take your pan and place it over a piece of waxed paper. Trace the pan and cut out the circle. Smooth that circle of waxed paper into the bottom of the buttered pan. See! You do that and your cake is certain not to stick. It may seem like a fussy step, but I guarantee it is worth it. You have one cake that refuses to disengage itself from a pan and you'll never skip this waxed paper trick ever again. Mark my words."

They grate some carrots very finely. They clabber milk, add vanilla, eggs, raisins soaked in a little bit of warmed apple juice. Walnuts ground up small. Cinnamon, clove, ginger. Sift the flour and leavening. Cream the butter and sugar. Smooth batter into the prepared pans. Bake until the kitchen smells almost unbearably good. And while the cakes cool on the wire racks—"See how easily they come out of the pans? Waxed paper circles!"—whip up the cream cheese, butter, powdered sugar and vanilla.

"That's a cake," declares Aunt Anne after she teaches Tania how to frost it. "Bag of Oreos," she mutters. "You kids."

"Hey, Oreos are good!"

"Well, then you can have some while I eat this cake," says Aunt Anne.

"Nah, I'll eat this lousy cake," says Tania. Aunt Anne throws an arm around her, squeezes.

"Wise choice," she says.

After they bake the cake, Tania heads off to the university library. She visits the microfiche room and spends the entire afternoon—a coveted day off from George's—combing through old newspaper archives for anything about Raine Holland. She moves backwards from 2000, a randomly chosen date, to 1990, right around the time she and Guin were born. She searches for four hours and finds nothing and begins to think this endeavor is pointless. She leans back and stretches.

"I give up," she says aloud. Someone says, "Ssssshhhhhh!"

She goes home and takes up one of the diaries and reads for a while. She rolls over onto her side, slides the diary under her pillow.

She thinks about Raine and her mother, their closeness, and wonders about her mother's reticence. Tania has shared none of this with Guin, neither the diaries nor her own secrets. It is all too furtive—uncomfortable and itchy. They have spent their lives sharing everything. She feels as though she is splitting apart and if she speaks of it, then the last shred of whatever is holding her together will come undone. Keeping quiet is the glue.

She is meeting Thom today at the apartment. She is going to break it off. She assumes he won't care. If he wants to, he will find another. She is sure of that as much as she has grown sure she is not the first woman.

She drives down to the city and meets him in front of the apartment.

"Hello," he drawls, pulls her to him as soon as they are alone.

She pulls away. His touch makes her queasy. "Thom, I think it's time to put an end to this."

His brow furrows. "End it? Are you breaking up with me?"

"Yes." She feels only coldness for this man now. She can't imagine what she was thinking before. It has less to do with him than a newfound awareness in herself.

"Why?" He is cold now, too. She can feel him detaching.

"You're married. What is the point of this?"

"Why does there need to be a point? Can't it exist for the sake of itself?"

"I just don't want to be your fuck-buddy anymore, Thom, that's all."

"I'm sorry I couldn't offer you more." He says it in a way that is clear to Tania that he is not at all sorry. He offers exactly what he wants to offer.

"I don't want more from you. I never did. Don't flatter yourself." She is sorry she added that since it makes it sound like she cares more than she does. "I'm not angry. I just need to simplify my life."

"Fine. Simple it is. Now go."

He is more angry than she imagined. She did not expect him to be angry at all.

"It's not just that—there's Shea." She says nothing more.

He laughs, but it is bitter. "Oh, right. Your boyfriend."

She says nothing, just looks straight at him.

He is quiet, his eyes bore into hers and it is difficult to hold them. She feels young. "Let's have a drink," he says.

"I don't really have time," she says.

He gives her a look and she shrugs. He gets her a beer and he pours himself some scotch.

She has nothing to say so she drinks her beer and watches him. "You're going to stay with him, aren't you?" he says.

She is struck once again by just how beautiful this man is, yet realizes she is repelled.

"I love him," she says simply.

"What if I said I'm in love with you?"

She nearly chokes. "What did you say?"

He leers and says, "You heard me."

She gapes at him. She can't make him out. She realizes she has no access to his truth. But she calls him on it, on mere instinct. "No, you're not, Thom."

She doesn't want to know him. She is gripped by a sudden and suffocating fear which is followed by a crushing need to touch Shea, to be sure of him. She wants to erase everything with Thom. She needs to run.

She puts her beer down, even though it is half full. The condensation forms a little pool on the table. She smirks a little. "You just want me because you can't have me."

"That's a reductive answer, Tania."

"Thom, go home to your wife."

He looks at his bourbon, then back up at her. "Well, that will be impossible because she's gone."

"Gone?"

"She left."

"Because of me?"

Now he laughs and it is much more genuine than hers. And he is mocking her. "No, dear. She didn't know about you. It was a heap of stuff on a long and twisted road. I don't know. Maybe she did know about you. I'm not really certain. But I doubt it. There's always the history."

"I wasn't the first."

He tips his head to one side. "What do you think, Tania?"

"Why did you tell me I was?"

"Why do you think?"

She stands, gathers her things. "I have to go." And she leaves and does not look back at him.

She pulls her car from the curb, barely glancing back for traffic and rushes home as quickly as she can. She needs to put distance between them. She is desperate for it even though she realizes distance won't change anything. But she must go. She drives over the causeway near her grandmother's house. She does not bother to stop and park her car in the driveway and walk over. Instead she parks in the small sandy lot near the pick-up trucks and vans of the guys who fish off the rocks of the causeway. She runs down the path, her heels digging and twisting in the soft sand. The path is lined with beach roses. They smell sharp and they make the air feel close and warm, too hot. She runs faster toward the openness of the expanse of beach, the span of shoreline, and as she breaks off the path into all that openness she feels her lungs expand again. There is no one here. It is rocky and unguarded. She removes her clothes down to her panties and bra and blazes into the water. Her feet scrape over rocks—they dig into the soft middle part, they jab and burrow into her heels, tear her toes and she doesn't care because it is almost as though she is not feeling any of it except the water as it gushes over her skin and then, when it becomes too deep and she can no longer move her legs forward, it cradles her as she falls forward, submerged in all that salt and liquid.

Salt is the cure.

She hopes it will cure her. She weeps as she floats on her back, looks up at the sky, endlessly broad, unreservedly blue, and she is made small.

How can she be cured when she doesn't know exactly what needs healing? And yet, doesn't she? It is not Thom. It is not even Shea. It is herself. She thought she was square with it. She was wrong.

What will she do next when she has taken a grain of sand, gritty and irritating, and worked it and worked it? The oyster makes a pearl. Tania has rendered hers into something large, rough and uneven. Coarse and unwieldy. The path to this place has been nearly obliterated—smudged, smoothed, raked until it is unrecognizable—how will she backtrack? All the crumbs have been eaten and Tania is stranded. She worries that the damage is too great for repair.

Can she go back?

Oh, she wants to go back. This is why she cries. She does not know how to get there. She has made such a terrible mess and she wants to fix it before anyone can see just how bad it is. Wipe the tears, drop them in the ocean, and go home, she tells herself firmly. She does. She climbs into the Brat all wet and doesn't care. It doesn't matter. Move forward. Begin to mend.

Then on the ride home, some things start pulling themselves together in her mind. Thoughts start flowing, clicking, as if this purging of Thom, of the mistakes, has cleared something.

When she gets home, she runs upstairs—does not even say hello to anyone—goes to her room and closes the door. Clicks the little lock on the doorknob. She flips back through her mother's diaries, reading fast and she finds it—not long after her mom met Raine, they were already the closest of friends. There it is—the first mention of Skater Boy. The boy her mother loved.

I'll call him "Skater Boy." I can't like him—but I do. I love him. She would hate me for it. I love her too much. She cannot hate me.

She turns pages frantically, skips ahead to December 1988—eight months before she was born.

December 2, 1988
I am in my most boring class which is economics. Why do I need to know this stuff? I am so depressed. Raine

keeps asking me why and I can't tell her. Obviously. I'm surprised she even notices me or my mood at all since she is so ecstatic that her relationship is back on track. SB has paid me no—zero, that is—attention since I broke it off with him. I guess him staying away from me is what I wanted. Well, what had to happen. But I'm so sad. I guess a part of me didn't believe it would truly be over, even though I knew it had to be. I don't even know if he had real feelings for me or if it was only about sex. And I really love him. No one will ever know how I feel and thank Goddess.

Here's the kicker—I haven't had my period in two months. I should be freaking out, but I feel frozen. I know I have to get a test, but I don't want to do this alone. I need Raine. I have no one but her. Like I could ever tell my mother...Raine is so lucky and sometimes she doesn't even know it. Her mother is so cool, she can talk to her about anything. She BROUGHT Raine to the women's clinic to get the pill. My mother, on the other hand, would give birth to a litter of kittens right there on the kitchen floor if I went to her with this. I've thought about this a lot and I can tell Raine without saying anything specific about the boy. I can say it was the friend of a friend from work who lives far away, and I don't even remember where, but he was visiting. Raine doesn't have to know. SB can <u>never</u> know.

Her mother loved her father. How did Tania miss it?

It's Dave—Raine's boyfriend. Dave Rodgers. Dave Rodgers is SB, Skater Boy. She pulls the yearbook from under her bed, flips to his picture. The pages drop open. David Rodgers—her father.

Where is Tania?

"Where is Tania?" asks Vivian.

"Don't know." Guin sighs with her eyes closed and stretches back in her chair. She wears her waitressing uniform and her clunky, comfortable shoes.

"I feel like I haven't seen her in days," says Vivian.

Outside the screen house, the sky is separated into bands of orange, purple, indigo. The stars puncture the deep blue high in the sky.

"She hasn't been around much these last few days, now that you mention it," says Anne. "I wanted to show her how to make drop butter-biscuits tonight."

"Oh, I love those," says Guin, eyes still closed.

"I'll make them tomorrow, honey, whether she's here or not. Just for you."

"Where could she be?" says Vivian. She takes out her cell phone and presses the buttons. "Straight to voicemail."

Guin sits up, eyes wide. "Do you think we need to be concerned?" she asks.

"I don't know. You try to call her in a little while. See if she answers."

"Oh, I'm sure she's fine," says Millie. "She's got something brewing around in her head or heart. I can sense it."

Anne nods. "She's working on figuring out something. I think so, too."

They sit in the screen house and worry—a little or a lot, depending.

It will be contained.

10

Vivian—Myths and Patterns

Tania continues to slip in and out, a wraith. When she finally stays put in the house for a while, her mood is volatile. Like those storms they have experienced all summer. The ones Vivian seems to notice more than anyone else does.

When she is around, Tania is icy cold. Stone. Her eyes have a closed-up, a veiled look about them. She barely speaks. Then Vivian notices that she is the only one being assaulted with silence—to everyone else, Tania's tone is almost normal.

"What is it, Tania?" she asks her daughter.

"What?" she says with utter calm and nonchalance.

"You seem, I don't know...are you angry with me?"

Tania stares at her for a few moments. "Why would I be angry with you?"

"What's going on, Tania?" says Guin. Vivian hears the tension in Guin's voice—Guin doesn't like confrontation, even that which is not her own.

"Nothing. I was looking at your yearbook again, Mom. I was closely reading some of the inscriptions. You had some good friends."

"Sure," Vivian says. Tania's tone alludes to something.

"Oh, what was his name? A boy...maybe a skateboarder?"

Vivian is chilled to the bone. She says nothing. Looks into her daughter's eyes, striving for steadiness. She consciously works at keeping her face still.

"Dave! That's what it was—David Rodgers! You ever hear of him, Guin?"

Guin is packing the diaper bag while attempting to encourage the kids out the door at the same time. "What? No. Who?"

"Dave Rodgers. And you seemed really friendly with that girl, Raine. Whatever happened to her?"

Vivian's mouth is dry. "I'm not sure." Her mind is racing back to that yearbook. What could be in there? She doesn't recall anything particularly telling, particularly revelatory. She is suddenly consumed. "We lost touch. I have to get to work, sweetie."

"Sure, Mom," she says, words clipped, every nuance of sound clear and sharp. "Have a good day."

Vivian gets into Sally and turns the music up loud— an old song by The Cure. She doesn't actually need to be to work for a while and she drives over the causeway and parks the car. She gazes at the ocean and allows its movement to soothe her. She goes back over the conversation with Tania. Goes back in time, deeper and deeper.

David Rodgers.

She conjures Dave's face and inhales sharply at the wave of feeling through her belly and across her chest. The intensity should be surprising, but she is not surprised.

Once Dave kissed her, nothing could be the same. It would have been fine if she hadn't wanted him. Then she would only have had to deal with what to tell Raine about his unfaithfulness. But she did want Dave and that was the difference that complicated everything. She knew it was wrong and in spite of it she was drawn. She was powerless.

Raine was over at Vivian's house. She sat in the window seat on the flowery cushion and looked out to the ocean, rolling and rolling. It was a Friday night, late summer, and they had just come home from a night out with friends. It was after midnight and Vivian's mother was asleep. The girls shared a bottle of sweet wine. They passed it back and forth between them and ate peanut butter spread on round crackers. They played music quietly on the radio.

Raine looked out at the ocean then at Vivian. "Something is wrong with Dave. He's so distant."

Vivian felt her face go hot at the mention of his name. "Yeah, where was he tonight?"

Raine shrugged and her eyes filled with tears. "He never called me even though he said he would so I have no idea." She cried more fully now. "I think he's screwing around with someone else. I swear, Vivian, I will die if he dumps me. I don't even care if he is fucking someone else. I would forgive him if he just came back to me."

Vivian joined Raine on the window seat and put her arms around her. Raine put her face on Vivian's shoulder and Vivian could feel her warm tears seep through her tee shirt. "Raine, he hasn't left. You can't assume the worst when you don't even know what's going on."

"I can just tell," she sobbed. "He's not the same. I have known him forever and he doesn't want me anymore. I guess he stopped loving me." She was so sad that Vivian's heart hurt.

Vivian had been sleeping with Dave for several months and although she kept meaning to stop, knew she ought to, she just couldn't seem to say no. It became a mantra, just this once, just this once, just this once, and it never was just once. The problem was that although Vivian had never admitted it to anyone, least of all Raine, and not even Frank to whom she told almost everything, she had been in love with Dave for a long time. She never once initiated anything and could hardly admit it to herself. But the feelings had been there all along and when he came to her, she should have said no, but she couldn't.

"I just wish I knew what was going on. I wish I knew what he's thinking. The not knowing is driving me crazy!" Raine said.

Vivian knew exactly but to tell was to risk everything. She couldn't believe she was lying to Raine so easily, so smoothly. Not without guilt or remorse, but lying nonetheless. Lying to her mother was one thing, that was easily justified, but to Raine, the person she loved most— how could it be possible? Yet it was.

The next night while Raine was at work, Vivian called Dave and asked him to meet her at the beach.

When he got there, he immediately pulled her to him and kissed her. She melted into him. She felt an eagerness in her body for him that she had never experienced before. It was burning and insistent. He had his hand down inside her panties before she could even say a word.

"No, Dave. Wait! Stop."

"Why?" he said, kissing her, his eyes still closed.

"I didn't call you here for this. We have to stop. That's what I wanted to talk to you about. This has to stop."

His finger was inside her and her body reacted to it. She moved along with the motion of his hand. She wanted him. Oh, how she loved this beautiful boy. She knew she would do anything for him. It was out of her control.

"No," she said. "Raine is so worried. She knows something's up."

"Does she know anything about us? Did you tell her?"

"No! No, of course not. Dave, she can't know. She will hate me."

"She'll hate me, too."

"But she'll forgive you. She won't forgive me. We can't hurt her."

"I know."

"Do you want to be with her?"

He didn't answer but buried his face in her neck. His hands were on her body. It felt like love.

But she was here to end it.

"No more. No more—this ends tonight."

"Okay. You're right. One last time, okay? One last time and I swear we can forget this ever happened between us."

She let herself be carried away. Because she loved him. And it was one last time.

"One last time," she whispered.

What followed would change everything with no way back.

One last time.

Now she closes her eyes. She can recall the intensity of those old feelings. The song plays on the radio—the raging sea that stole the only boy she loved. So far away—he could not see.

She glances out at the water again, relinquishes the memories to that raging water, starts the car and drives to work.

Vivian stands in the center of the women during the first new moon following Carol's death. She inhales deeply and begins to cast the Circle for the first time. It is Carol's transition rite—Carol has moved on to her next incarnation and they gather for her memorial ritual. There are candles set in hurricane lanterns in front of each woman. Vivian walks the Circle and lights the candles one by one.

"This is a ritual of passing for Carol who was born to this earth and has passed on to await her rebirth."

She recites a poem to the Goddess. A prayer. The women each place an item that symbolizes rebirth to them into the ritual cauldron.

"Carol was our sister. She was an incarnation of the Goddess, as are we. She is now one with the Mother, in death as she was in life," says Vivian. "As are we, too, and will join her one day in death."

They share ritual cakes—the first Vivian has baked with her own hands—and Carol's favorite ritual wine. They tell stories of Carol and laugh and cry together.

They hold hands and raise the cone of power.

Vivian closes the Circle and the women embrace and slowly begin to disperse. Vivian then finds herself alone on the beach. She packs the sacred ritual tools into the chest on wheels that Carol bestowed to her. She removes her white robe and sits on the beach in her regular clothes. It is a new moon, for rebirth, and the stars are fully burst open and far flung in the expanse of the deep, deep black of the sky.

The enormity of her new role settles into her bones. It is terrifying and exhilarating all at once. She feels completely raw and open, but it is neither painful nor unwelcome. She feels fully herself and utterly dispersed into the Universe. These are the moments when the idea of oneness is clear to her. She doesn't want to let go if it.

This kind of joy.

And she thinks once again about stories.

The stories we tell each other. The stories we tell ourselves. The ones we believe. The ones we don't but identify with in spite of our dubiousness. The intentionally misleading. The complex mythology of the individual. The stories that comprise a family, a town, a nation, a world. The myths that construct us.

She remembers back to the moment when she truly comprehended the idea of myth. She recalls exactly where she was—taking a walk along the beach in late spring, her bare feet in the ocean for the first time that year. She was immersed in the Wicca book Raine had given her as well as a book on comparative religion she had withdrawn from the university library. Her mind was opening to ideas that were so different from those in which she had been submerged since birth. She had just read some Greek myths and was thinking about them as stories when it suddenly became clear to her: they're all myths. A bolt from the blue of the sky. The myths with which she grew up were no more real than Greek myths or Chinese or Hindu. Myths are just the telling of the same stories in different ways. *It's not real*, she thought. She meant everything she had been taught and the fear and guilt and shame and confusion those lessons held. In which she had been steeped. *They're stories. They're myths. And I don't have to believe.*

She felt free. She had never felt so free. She exhaled a lifelong breath. She smiled.

That was a moment to remember. A moment on which her own story turned. A moment of pure liberation.

She looks up into all those stars this night and feels it to be another pivot in her story. In the myth of Vivian. She wonders where the story will traverse next.

And she is not afraid.

"So, what's your plan?" asks Frank.

They sit outside behind his house. The yard backs right up into the salt marsh. He is cooking chicken on the grill and a big pot of water is coming to a boil for corn on the cob. They sit in his cedar adirondack chairs that overlook the marsh and drink cold beers and shuck corn.

"Is this Silver Queen?" Vivian asks, taking the first ear form the brown paper bag.

"No, too early for that. It's butter and sugar," says Frank.

"I love that name—butter and sugar. It just sounds good." She pulls the husk from the cob and carefully removes the silk. "To answer your question—I'm not sure yet. My credit is shot and it won't recover for quite a few years. I don't know." She tosses a husked ear onto the platter with the others. "The Universe will reveal it. I just have to be patient."

"You and your Universe," he says. He carries the platter over to the big pot, removes the cover and drops each ear in carefully. She sits back and stretches her legs, sips her beer.

"Why not just make a decision and execute it?" asks Frank, sitting down and stretching out himself. "That wouldn't be you, though, would it?"

She smiles. "I believe that it will become clear to me. Just like everything else."

They are quiet for a while. It is good to be quiet with your best friend, drink cold beer and watch the light from the sun setting behind you cast purpled light onto green cord grass.

"My mom and Aunt Anne are old, Frank," she says.

"This is news?"

"Your parents are twenty years younger than my mom and aunt, Frank. Those women are *old*." They are quiet again. Long-legged herons look for their supper at the edge of the marsh. "My mom has congestive heart disease," she says finally.

He takes her hand. "Is she going to be okay?"

She shrugs. "Special diet—beer and brownie suppers need to come to an end, yet something tells me they won't entirely—medication, rest. It won't kill her right away. Someday," she shrugs, "it will. I just don't think Aunt Anne can do it on her own, although she insists she can. But there will be more medical appointments to get to. And that's a big house. It's full right now, but it's big. They can't take care of it and they won't leave it willingly. I don't know, Frank," she takes a sip of beer and watches the herons in the purple light. "I think they need me to stay."

They didn't actually tell Vivian about the heart condition. Vivian took a call from her mother's doctor and the message was cryptic enough to raise her suspicions. She had to wheedle some information out of Aunt Anne and then coerce her mother to admit it.

"Mom! You can't keep this kind of thing from me!" she'd exclaimed, on the verge of anger.

"Oh, it's nothing. I didn't want to worry anyone."

"You're right—a debilitating heart condition is nothing. It's not like you *need* your heart. Oh, wait—yes you do! Mom, this is not a thing to hide."

"Don't treat me like a child, Vivian!" she says. "I am a grown woman."

"You are an *old* woman!"

"Oh, Vivian," said Aunt Anne.

"You are, too," Vivian said to Aunt Anne.

"Maybe we are, but we still have a right to privacy. We still have a right to make our own decisions."

Respect for the crone, Vivian remembered to consider. She took a deep breath. "Yes," she said more gently. "You do. I'm sorry. Mom," she spoke softly, "but please don't shut me out."

Her mother put her hand over Vivian's. "Oh, Vivian." They looked into each other's eyes and for the first time that Vivian could think of, she thought that perhaps she and her mother were seeing one another. It was connection that she could not remember feeling for a long time, if ever.

Now she thinks back on all the years that she and her mother simply missed one another. They saw each other frequently, spent time together, rarely argued since her teenage years and yet seemed only to float around each other. They didn't understand one another, but Vivian always believed that was no reason not to connect. Maybe it was about to happen. Better late than never.

"I think the Universe has spoken," Frank says.

She nods.

"Is that okay? What the Universe seems to be saying?" he asks.

He gets up and lights a fire in the stone pit in front of their chairs. The flame takes quickly on the seasoned wood. It crackles and warms her outstretched feet. The wood smoke shoos the mosquitoes away. She watches the fire twirl and skip and shimmy.

"I'm not sure yet," she says finally. "They haven't asked me to stay. We haven't even talked about it. But it seems like we'll have to sooner rather than later." Vivian won't push them. She will allow it to unfold. This is yet another thing which she has not planned. She is not even forty years old. How is her life meant to unfurl?

"So, I have news," he says. "We're in. It's official."

"We are?" she sits upright.

"We are! Gary leaves for Connecticut in three weeks and our coronation will commence at the following meeting of the Society."

"Frank, that's amazing!" While Vivian has always enjoyed the Society, she knows this means so much to Frank. "Congratulations."

"And the same to you, my queen."

She shakes her head and closes her eyes. "You are such a dork, Frank."

"Oh, you love me," he says.

"I do," she says. "I don't know why." But of course she does and she knows he knows it, too.

It is a good thing to eat a supper of fresh corn on the cob and barbecued chicken with your best friend while the sun sets and a warming fire dances at your feet. It is good, and of this Vivian is sure.

What does Vivian want?

The idea of "plans" ended when she found herself pregnant at seventeen. Since then her life has been more of a reaction to itself than a thing that was being intentionally propelled forward. More of a somersaulting than a brisk and straight walk forward. Now her mother's health. Another thing pushing her into a forward flip, knocking her feet out from beneath her. This has been the pattern for the last twenty-three years.

Perhaps, she is beginning to think, this *is* the pattern of life.

This evening a storm blows in. Not one of the swift and violent storms, but the usual kind—slow-moving, stuck and stubborn. They sit on the back porch and look out at the lightened sky, illuminated by low-lying rain-heavy clouds.

Mosquitoes don't come around in steady rain like this.

The screen house sits empty. The gusts of wind that accompany this little everyday storm are too mild to shift the screen house in its little sand footprint. It stands steady and waiting, as it always does.

They sit quietly on the porch. It seems the sound of the rain has rendered them mute. Maybe there is not a lot to say this night. And maybe there is too much to say.

Sometimes it is good to let the words hold on in the mind. Sometimes silence is best.

11

Guin—Discovery

Guin wakes in the night, the fear a tight ball in her belly. Alone in the bed, she rolls over, curls up and tucks her pillow down close to her abdomen. Maybe it forms a barrier of some kind, she doesn't know, but it calms the thing twisting inside her.

When she was a kid and woke fearful in the night, she tiptoed to Tania's room and gently pulled back the covers and slipped in close next to her sister. Tania scooted over and Guin was never sure if she was asleep or half awake, but she always made room and never complained. Guin was able to sleep in the warmth of Tania's body, up close to Tania's breath setting a rhythmic pattern that put the night and the fear into some manageable shape.

Guin wakes in the middle of the night now and is tempted to go to Tania, but doesn't. Instead she rolls over and looks at the clock. Two-thirty. Always two-thirty. There is nothing good about two-thirty in the morning. Everything is at its worst, at its most frightening. Nothing is manageable; problems are too confusing and mysterious ever to be unraveled.

To occupy her spinning mind and set it to some order, she thinks back to her tea today with Darlene, who enrolled at the community college.

"It's the paralegal program," she said, taking a big sip from her styrofoam cup. "In two years, I'll graduate and I will finally get a professional job and some decent money."

"Wow, Darlene. That's really awesome," Guin told her. "Wow. I just can't imagine having that kind of direction."

"Why not? There must be something you want to be. If I can do this, so can you. They're giving out all kinds of loans right now for education. It's one of the things the president's doing to fix the shitty economy."

"Yeah?" said Guin.

"Yeah. Just go see someone at the financial aid office. They can explain it to you."

"I should." She looked down at her cup, toyed with the tea bag tag that dangled from the side. "But I don't even know what I'd study."

"Didn't you ever want to be something?" Darlene asked.

She sighed. "Well, sure. I used to want to be a preschool teacher."

"You can do that—get a teaching certificate."

"I don't know..."

"Go ask about it—you have nothing to lose, Guin."

Guin said maybe.

Lying in bed at two-thirty, Guin recalls a time when she had it all figured out. When she knew what she wanted to be. When she possessed self-confidence. Where had it gone? She rolls over to her side and presses the little pillow to her belly.

Her mother always says to visualize the thing that you want in order to manifest it. Then she says things about giving it to the Goddess and lighting a candle or burning your worries or something like that, but right now Guin forgets about all that and simply imagines herself in a classroom. Circle time and singing songs and reading stories. Art projects and snack break. She imagines the scent of apple slices and Ritz crackers. She can smell them—she really can.

She falls asleep without trying and when she wakes in the morning, she almost feels like it could be true, that it could be a thing she could achieve.

That day The Grille and Creamery does not feel as bad as usual because it does not feel like a thing she has no choice but to do.

It does not feel like the rest of her life.

When she rounds the corner to her Grandmother's house, she sees Pickle's RV squarely planted in the middle of the crushed-shell driveway. This is not a night he is coming to get the kids, so he must want to talk. She sighs. She must gather strength for this. She has not seen him since the break-up—every time he comes for the kids, she makes Mom or Tania deliver the children while she hides out back.

She shuffles the children inside then walks straight-backed to the driveway where he waits. When she sees him, she melts a little. But she stays firm.

"Hi, Pickle." She stops several feet away from him.

"Hi, Guin." That's all he says. He looks down at his feet and pokes around at the broken shells.

She wants to reach out and touch his face, his silken hair, push away the lock that has fallen over his eye. The lock that always falls over his eye like that. She folds her arms across her chest.

"What do you want, Pickle?" she asks softly, and not unkindly. "Why did you come here?"

He looks up into her eyes. "I don't know, Guin. I just...I miss you. I can't stand it." Tears spill from his eyes unchecked. He wipes them away roughly with the backs of his hands. "I don't want to be broken up."

"What *do* you want?"

"What do you mean? I just said—I want to be together."

"Okay. What do *I* want?" she asks.

"I don't know, Guin. Tell me," he pleads.

"Pickle! I already told you—I cannot do this for you."

"Do what?"

"Figure this out! You have to figure out your life before we can have one together," she says.

"Just tell me what to do, Guin. Please."

He sounds so sad that she almost answers him. She almost tells him everything he needs to know. But she can't.

"I have to go in now, Pickle." She starts to turn away.

"But I love you! Please," he says.

She turns back to him. "I love you, too, but this is not going to work. Not until you get your life together. Not until you look at this...*life* we have together and see it, really see it. I mean, do you think this is what I want anymore, Pickle?"

He says nothing. Just looks at her sadly. "Guin..."

"I have to go in." She walks up the stairs.

"Please, Guin," he says again.

"I have to go." She longs to hold him, be held by him. She longs to tell him exactly what to do to make it right. She keeps moving into the house. She hears him calling to her.

Some things cannot be done for another. Even when you want to.

Some things require their own discovery.

Guin tells Tania she is thinking about going back to school. She is lying around on Tania's bed like she always used to before she had kids. She stretches out on the bed and her arms stretch out under Tania's pillows and her hand bumps into something hard. She rolls over and pulls out a black and white speckled composition notebook.

"What's this?" she asks Tania.

Tania snatches it from her hands. "Nothing. Just a notebook." Guin watches as she tosses it under the bed.

"All your secrets?" she drawls at her sister.

A strange look comes across Tania's face and she looks away from Guin.

"I was kidding, Tania. You all right?"

"Yeah," she almost barks.

"You don't sound all right."

"What did you want to tell me, Guinevere?"

"Fine, Titania—I will let it go." Tania will never be coerced into speaking. Guin is tempted to spill at the slightest provocation, but Tania is a vault. Guin tells her, "I think I want to go to school. To be a teacher. I mean, I can start with a two-year degree and go from there."

The kids are with Pickle. The freedom is liberating and disorienting at the same time. She has forgotten what to do when time opens up. She feels a bit lost and untethered.

"You should, Guin! You always wanted to be a teacher. You always said you would be," Tania says.

"I did, didn't I?" Guin is genuinely surprised.

"Yeah, you did. You don't remember?"

She does now that Tania recalls the memory. How is it possible that she had forgotten? Yet she did.

"I'm not as smart as you," she shakes her head as if to dismiss the entire idea.

"Not too many people are," says Tania and she smirks at Guin. "That shouldn't stop you, though."

"What if I can't do it?"

"What if you can?" says Tania.

She wonders how she strayed so far and in the same moment realizes that it is probably the easiest thing in the world to do.

Isn't this exactly what happened to her mother?

"Something unexpected happens and then you take what is a logical step in that moment and then another and another. You can't always see far ahead," her mother says when Guin talks to her about it. "You make the best decisions you can in the moment and you try to imagine what the future you want looks like. Then you make the big decisions to get there."

"I can't see anything," says Guin.

"Yes, you can," Mom says simply.

Can she?

She walks over the causeway to the beach that they all think of as their "secret beach."

She is twenty-two and she cannot deny that her life is merely happening to her. That is not to say she is entirely unhappy with the way it has begun to unfold. But she is just starting to realize that the unfolding is not predestined. That life is something she builds. Not only with Pickle, their combined life, but her own individual path. The paths that run parallel, with their own trajectories, but concurrent with a fine-tuned harmony.

She thinks about the story she has been telling herself. She has been watching and fearful and getting by the best she can. Is this the best she can? Maybe it is time to begin rewriting the story.

She stands up from the sand and brushes off her bottom. She makes a visor of her hand and looks out over the water. A stormy blackness is billowing and moving forward quickly.

She walks along the shore, her shoes dangling from her hand. The water feels cool over the tops of her feet. When she is present like this, she is able to breathe and see forward with clarity. Can she see far enough ahead to choose? She breathes and if she can remember to continue to breathe, then maybe.

It seems, yes, maybe.

Yes, she thinks she can see.

She gets home as the first fat drops of rain spot her tee shirt—moments before another storm moves directly overhead.

Another slow Tuesday and Guin drives the kids to Pickle's Mom's house.

Ethan asks her to turn up the Journey song and she's grateful because the car is making that grinding sound she does not like. The very idea of another slow Tuesday at The Grille and Creamery both wearies her and raises her anxiety. Her chest constricts thinking of all these boring hours ahead of her. Slow-moving time is unbearable. She tries to take a deep breath. She pushes her shoulders down, which have moved without her willingness up near her ears—inhales, exhales. Her chest loosens slightly. *Don't think about work,* she tells herself. *One moment at a time—one breath at a time*, she tells herself.

She joked with Darlene at Dunkin Donuts the other day that instead of taking things one day at a time with her car, she takes it one trip at a time.

"Someone told me to talk to it, but when I do, it makes that noise anyway. I don't think it cares what I say."

"One trip at a time," Darlene smiled. "I like that. Maybe that's how we should think about everything. Maybe a day is too much all at once."

Guin thinks that Darlene is probably right.

She hopes Pickle is not at home. Guin is still not sure how to be without him and seeing him deepens her sadness and loss. She carries hope around like a little light that she won't allow to go out. She would rather be hopeful than think she and Pickle are doomed. She is certain of two things: that Pickle is not stupid and that he loves her. And the knowledge of these is what keeps the hope lit. *Please, Pickle. Please, please, please, Pickle,* she thinks.

Without him, she has been forced to feel what it means to be on her own—something she hasn't experienced since she was fifteen. And when she was fifteen, she didn't know anything about being on her own in the first place. So, in essence, this is all new to Guin. While she knows she should embrace this opportunity for growth, she feels mostly sad and ungrounded. Tania keeps telling her that women must relinquish the reliance on the patriarchy, be their own persons free of the restrictive male gaze and free of dependence. Her mother says the Universe will provide the answers, and all Guin need do is possess patience and openness.

But Guin just misses Pickle.

She wonders, does it matter why she misses him? Does it matter—is she deficient in some way because she does? Is she not a feminist? Not a willing participant in the workings of the Universe?

When she gets to the Fourniers', Pickle's RV is not parked out front and Guin sighs with relief.

Pickle's mother is smoking up on the balcony. "Hi, honey!" she calls down. Guin watches her stub out her cigarette, spin around quickly to get inside her kitchen. There Guin knows she will wash her hands then run to the bathroom to rinse her mouth with mouthwash. She always smells of very minty cigarettes. Guin appreciates the effort and loves her for it. She climbs the stairs behind the kids, carries the heavy bag of their stuff.

"Hi, sweetie," says Pickle's mom. She gives Guin a hug and kiss on the cheek. She bends down, "Hi, loves! Are we gonna have fun today?"

Guin can't help herself and asks, "Is Pickle here?"

"No, honey. He knew you were coming—I think that's why he cleared out."

"How is he?" These are words she has been waiting to say. Savoring the moment when she could ask them and hear the answer; when she could talk about him. It makes her feel almost close to him—it is as close as she can get right now.

"He's all right, I guess." She pauses and seems to be weighing her words. "He misses you, honey. I'm not saying that to make you feel bad."

"I know," Guin says miserably. "I miss him *so much*." And she embarrasses herself by beginning to cry.

Pickle's mom rushes over and takes Guin in her arms. "Oh, honey," she says. "I know, I know." She pulls away and holds Guin at arms' length. "You know I'm here for you, no matter what happens. I love you, honey, and these babies are my grandchildren and I will always take care of them if you need."

"Thanks...Mrs...Mom," Guin stumbles over the words.

"Mrs. Mom!" she chuffs.

Guin laughs. "Thank you, Mom. I mean it. I don't know what I'd do without you."

She leaves for work and knows exactly how to make this right—all she need do is simply tell him. Lay it all out for him. It is tempting. But she wants him to figure it out and believes it is the only way any real change can happen for them.

At the end of the day, in the car, Ethan says, "Mommy, put on the song about the sky and the wheel." They are on their way home.

"Did you see Daddy today?"

"Yes."

Is it wrong to spy on your whatever-Pickle-is through your three year old?

"Really?" she says this in a sweet and thick tone which she wonders if kids find as annoying as it sounds to her own ears. She waits.

"Yes." He is looking out the window and concentrating (it seems) on the song.

"What did you guys do?"

"Nothing."

"Nothing," she says. Nothing. Well, she supposes, that sounds about usual. "Did you guys play?"

"Yeah."

"What did you play?"

"I don't know."

"Was Daddy coming home from...a job? Or was it morning time?"

"I don't know."

"Did Memère say Daddy has a job?"

"Mommy. I am trying to hear the song!"

"Okay, honey." She wishes the twins could hold a conversation. She turns up the music a little. "Good?" she calls back.

"Yes. Fanks, Mommy."

"You're welcome."

She sighs.

She wonders if she will ever figure out how to *be* without Pickle. She wants to feel free, as Darlene does now that she left her own man. But Guin doesn't feel free. She feels lost at sea—an unfathomable distance between herself and solid ground.

She misses Pickle, simply. She loves him, simply and surely.

The weeks pile one onto another and she leaves work early on yet another quiet Tuesday.

She finds herself driving. She listens to *Don't Stop Believin'* and then rewinds it and plays it again as soon as it ends. This song always makes her feel good. It gives her hope. Makes her feel as though there can always be possibility.

She wonders for what seems like the thousandth Tuesday in a row why they even bother opening on Tuesdays. It's always just a few of the same customers— same old ladies having tea, same old guys having coffee. They are regulars and Guin is happy to see them, but what strikes her on this Tuesday is that this might be her four hundredth Tuesday. She tries to do the math in her head and can't quite come up with the number, but she knows that if not exactly four hundred of her Tuesdays have been spent at The Grille and Creamery, it has been altogether too many. Too many Tuesdays. And she thinks the thought that until now has only been an abstract idea: *Maybe I should quit.*

In between the song she keeps repeating and the idea that has formed concretely in her mind into actual words, she believes truly that it is possible.

She can quit The Grille and Creamery.

She can quit. She can't just *up* and quit but she can work toward quitting, and with these thoughts the entirety of the wide world opens up and she realizes that the possibility was always there; she simply failed to see it. Now that she can see it, it is a thing that can, without a doubt, be.

She feels giddy and breathless.

The sky opens wide as she drives fast down Route 88 toward the beach.

Lately the screen house has been too full.
And too empty.

12

Tania—The Best You Can Do

December 3, 1988

I told Raine I'm pregnant and she was shocked. She actually could not speak for a moment. She said she had no memory of even how to speak for that minute. She was mad at me at first for not telling her. She kept asking me, "Why didn't you tell me?" I told her it was because I felt totally used. I said I was too ashamed to talk about it. She said it was because of being a Catholic. (For once I was happy to be Catholic.) She said we totally needed to work on my inner Goddess, but first things first. Once she was over the shock, she went right into Raine action-mode. She devised the perfect plan to figure this whole thing out. It's Friday and I told my mother I'm sleeping at Raine's tonight. After school we went to CVS and walked right up to the cashier who was this old biddy and paid for the test. All the while, Raine and I looked the old broad right in the eyes. I am sure Raine was just hoping the woman would say something to us so she could go off on her. But all the biddy said was, "Do you want a bag for this?" And we were like, what do you think? But we just said yes please and left it at that. Raine said we need to do it in the morning which is the best time. I'm so scared. I keep saying that and she says not to be because we'll figure it out together. I feel like a terrible person asking her for so much help and support because of what I've done. But for tonight I am not anything but me and for tonight I just want to forget.

Tania knows what came next.

Experience overlaps. It repeats.

Tania believed that her conception was a haphazard, possibly drunken, outrageously foolish teenage escapade. But it was not whatsoever. Of course not, she thinks. Why was she so foolish and immature to think there would not be a story? A real and complicated, full story. She imagined there were no emotions involved, but she knows her mother well enough to have been able to surmise this at the very least, in spite of the story her mother told with spare words. Now that she knows the truth, the notion is simply ridiculous. It is as though she looked back at her mother's life and saw facts only, colorless and streamlined, and could not imagine that her mother possessed thoughts and feelings. It seems so foolish that she ever thought about it that way.

December 29, 1988

How's my beautiful gorgeous breathtakingly lovely Viv?

I have to go to the bathroom. I am sooooo hungry. The cats are acting up. I also need a few weeks of sleep.

Vivvy, I am so dim. Mrs. S gave us a poem to analyze. I'm usually off a bit, but no big deal. Well this time, my best girly friend, I turned "The Love Song of J. Alfred Prufrock" into the biggest sex orgy! Wow—talk about waaaaaay off. It was about sterile society and a man who is afraid of sexuality. I had him with prostitutes and lovers.

*God, Mrs. S. must think I am the biggest perverted idiot.
Oh, well.*

*Want to hear something ridiculous? On Mrs. H's
board there is a poster which says:*

1) Be ready: have notebook, lesson, etc.

2) Have homework ready to be checked

3) There is NO talking

4) Lift your hand for teacher's attention

5) If you talk:

    a) 1ˢᵗ time, eye contact warning

    b) 2ⁿᵈ time, verbal warning

    c) 3ʳᵈ time, detention

*Who the hell reads this besides me? How the hell can
you know if your teacher is giving you eye contact
warning? If my teacher gave me major eye contact, I
would probably smile because I didn't know what else to
do.*

*Vivvers, I know I am just babbling on and on about
nothing while you are going through one of the worst
things of your life, but I want you to know everything is
going to be okay. Please let me tell my mom. I know she
can help us. I know you said <u>no</u> 1,000,000 times but please
just think about it. Please. It's going to be okay. It will be.*

*Love, forever and ever and never forget it and I will
always be there for you—Raine*

*P.S. Off to gym. Whenever I play floor hockey and
miss the ball, I say "Eeesh." Even if I tell myself "Don't
say eesh this time, don't say eesh this time" every time I
still say "eesh." It's mortifying.*

*P.P.S. I just said something in French and it didn't
sound like my voice. It actually sounded French. Mrs. G is
bursting with pride I can just tell. She will try to take
credit for this progress of mine no doubt. Now she just
made me go to the board and conjugate the verb "loger"
which means "to lodge." As in I would like to lodge my
French book in Mrs. G's <u>FILL IN THE BLANK</u>. I am
leaning back in my chair and my sweater is picking at me.*

I am bored. I usually wear a belt with these pants. Now I know why they feel loose. S-T-A-R-V-I-N-G. I think other people can hear the cat. I think it's at least three, actually. People are looking at me funny. Someone is knocking on the door to get into the classroom. The door is cracked open. And who knocks to get into a classroom? I just read this note back to myself and almost died of boredom. I'm going to give it to you anyway.

Tania places her mother's diary down. She knows that sometimes it feels as though there is no one to tell and no one to help and when it comes down to it, we're all alone in the end.

Ever since she found out about Dave, Tania has been filled with anger. She came from love—her mother loved her father. She doesn't understand why her mother allowed her to believe otherwise and she could have known him all this time. Her mother stole that choice from her and Guin. She hasn't known what to do with the anger or with herself. It has been taking over. There has been no one with whom she isn't cross—customers at George's, coworkers, family, Shea. Even the little kids. She wonders if she ought to be locked up in a box until it passes. Shea hasn't called in a couple of days. She would consider calling or texting him but she doesn't trust her mood. Doesn't trust the words that she will conjure.

But reading the entries and notes her mother and Raine wrote in the wake of the positive pregnancy test deflates her anger. She vacillates between abject sadness and a rage that seems to possess no roots.

All she wants is to hole herself up in the far-most corner of the top floor of the university library with a smuggled thermos of coffee and a stack of books to occupy her mind until she is kicked out, the doors locked behind her.

From the window seat she watches a vicious storm out over the water. The sky is charcoal gray, a drenched opaque hue. Rain pelts the closed windows fiercely. The wind threatens, presses up against the glass. This storm is a real menace.

It matches her temperment.

As soon as the storm passes, she decides, she will go to the university. It may help her shake this mood, it may not, but she feels pent-up and needs to move.

She waits until early afternoon when she is fairly certain everyone has left the house and her aunt and grandmother have tottered out to the sun porch to work their puzzle and read their tabloids.

She opens her door a crack and listens to the quiet. She opens it a bit more and listens longer and harder and there is no noise but the sound of the ocean coming through the windows, the cry of gulls, the rustling of paper from the sun porch.

She makes her way on tiptoe, her feet silent on the smooth wood of the stairs that lead down to the first floor. Her sandals dangle from her fingertips, her small bag hangs from her shoulder. She rounds the corner to the kitchen, turns her head to look back to be sure neither Aunt Anne nor Grammy have seen her. As she turns her head forward to make her escape out the kitchen door to her awaiting Brat, she smacks into her mother. She screams. Her mother yelps and drops a glass of iced tea on the floor.

"What in heaven's name!" exclaims Grammy from the sun porch.

"Everything all right?" calls Aunt Anne.

"Fine," call Tania and Mom at the same time.

"What the hell, Mom?" snaps Tania.

"What the hell, yourself. What are you sneaking around for?" But Mom is not angry—she grins at Tania. She picks up the broken glass carefully and mops up the spilled tea with some old rags, then moves to the refrigerator and pours herself a fresh glass.

"Where were you? I didn't hear you." It is accusation, which Tania knows sounds ridiculous since her mother has done nothing wrong in simply being home.

But there is so much wrong.

"I was outside for a walk. I have the day off," says Mom. "Tania, what's wrong. You've been so..." she pauses. "Unhappy."

"Bitchy, you mean?"

"I wasn't going to say that."

"You were just thinking it." Tania is going out of her way to be insulted when she knows she is being babyish. She wants her mother to feel badly. Her mother says nothing, looks at her quietly. Tania knows what her mother is doing—this is one of her parenting techniques. Not that her mother would call it that. It is a thing Tania recognizes as one of the ways her mother has cultivated to pry information from her and Guin. It is a gentle means, that is its intention, and yet it has come to be a huge source of aggravation for Tania over the years. Works like a charm with Guin. But Tania prefers a more direct method.

"I know what you're doing, Mom," she says caustically. Spits the words out. Her mother says nothing. "Don't just look at me like that."

"Tania, what's wrong?" she asks, and reaches out to touch Tania's arm.

She pulls away sharply before her mother's touch reaches her body. She stares at her mother. "What's *wrong*? Want to tell me about your friend, Raine? And how about her boyfriend, Dave?" She glares and watches as her mother's face collapses a little. Tania abandons her sadness, drops any conflicted feelings, any semblance of understanding and compassion. She grabs hold of her anger and allows it to guide the moment.

"We were friends in high school," her mother says and this is all she says.

"Friends, Mom? Hmmm. I question your idea of friendship. I question your very idea of honesty. Mom, did you screw your best friend's boyfriend? You did, didn't you. Wait here." She turns and sprints upstairs. She grabs one of the diaries and her mother's high school yearbook and runs back down to the kitchen. The running, fueled by her anger, makes her breathless. She inhales and exhales fast and hard and struggles to moderate her breathing. When she gets to the kitchen she tosses the diary on the counter. It lands with a thud that seems to echo in the quiet of the house. Tania opens up the yearbook to Dave's picture and slams the book down next to the diary.

"Where did you get these, Tania?" Her mother's face holds a balance of confusion and anger.

"That's beside the point, don't you think, Mom?" She pokes her finger hard at Dave's picture. "He's the one, isn't he?"

"The one what?" She clips off the words, a sharpness in the voice with which Tania is not accustomed.

"My father, Mom. Our father. It's him, isn't it? Your best friend's boyfriend."

"How did you...?" She eyes the black and white composition notebook.

"I read all of your diaries. It took me a while. Dave is Skater Boy—SB—right?"

Her mother picks up the diary and folds it in her arms, close to her chest. "How could you read these without asking me?"

"How could you hide my father's identity from me for twenty-two years?" she screams.

Her mother stares at her, eyes hardened. "How could you read these? You...who prides herself on honesty at any cost."

"Where is he? Where is Raine?" Tania feels insane. It is as though she knows these people and is desperate to see them again. "You said you didn't know my father—that he was a one-night stand. An accident. But this was someone you loved. This is someone we could have known—we could know him now! Did you ever tell him about us? Maybe Raine would have forgiven you. Did she know? Did he know?"

Her mother sighs and closes her eyes. Her anger seems to have seeped away. "They knew," she says quietly.

He didn't want to know her and Guin. That was it. "You had no right to keep them from me, from us. Even to protect us."

"That's not it, Tania."

"What is it then?" she is shouting again.

"They're dead. They died before you were born."

"What?"

"It was a car accident, the summer after high school. You weren't born yet. And we were trying to work it out. Yes, you would have known them. They would have been in our lives. But they're dead."

"Dead?"

And the house is silent once again for this terrible moment.

The phone rings. Neither Tania nor her mother move to answer it.

"Hello?" Tania hears Aunt Anne answer it from the sun porch. Their voices carry to the kitchen. "Prayer Line, Millie," says Aunt Anne.

A pause. Tania continues to stare at her mother.

"Hello, Arthur. Yes, got my paper and pencil. Okay, shoot." A silence and then a gasp. "I need to go, Arthur. I think that's my granddaughter!" The phone clatters on its stand. Vivian is already running out to the sun porch. Tania follows.

"Vivian!" her mother yells.

"What did he say?" asks Vivian.

"A bad accident up on 88. A young woman in a car that sounds like Guin's."

They stand frozen in the sunshine of the sun porch. Her mother's cell phone chirps.

"Hello? Yes, this is she. I'm her mother..." Tania stares at her mother's face, her eyes wide, her mouth and hands trembling. She takes a deep breath and relief floods her expression. She looks up at Tania and mouths, "She's alive!" She snaps the phone shut and it seems she can't move.

Tania pulls her mother's arm and they run to Tania's car. "We'll call as soon as we get to the hospital," she calls over her shoulder to the elderly women.

Guin is unconscious, her head bandaged and her face purpled. There are numerous cuts that have been cleaned up.

"She looks terrible," says Tania. The doctors have assured them that she looks worse off than she might be, and if she wakes soon, she should make a full recovery. But that is as sure as they can be. Maybe and might be are as close as it gets to certainty.

Tania and her mother sit beside the bed. Guin is still sedated from the emergency surgery. Her arm is fractured in several places, and she has sustained a bad concussion, several cracked ribs and a collapsed lung. She looks small and broken.

"She looks terrible. But she's going to be okay. She's going to be okay." Her mother has spoken those words repeatedly in the last two hours. Tania is not sure if they are meant for her benefit or her mother's own.

Pickle paces in front of the windows. He has not been still except for when he held Guin's hand and cried into her neck. He only peeled himself from her because Vivian wanted to sit by her. And now he can't keep still.

"You're going to lose ten pounds before she wakes up, Pickle. Come sit, honey," says Mom with an outstretched arm.

"I can't. I'm too nervous," he says.

"It's so annoying, Pickle," gripes Tania.

"Tania," Mom says low.

"Well?"

"Pickle, honey? Here—take this." Mom fishes ten dollars from her pocketbook. "Can you run down to the Dunkin in the lobby and get us some coffee? You know how we like it. Get yourself one, too. Okay?"

"Better make it decaf," Tania mutters.

Mom lets it go. She rubs Guin's hand softly.

Tania watches her sister's face intently. The idea of losing her is too grim for Tania to dwell upon for too long. Too fearful a space to go. This face she knows so well, better than any other. Guin is like an extension of herself and while she doesn't ever take it for granted, it is too easy to get caught up in the business of living and forget how important this face is to her life, to her very existence. Her eyes blur with tears and she sees Guin's eyelashes flutter. Tania swipes at her own eyes. She wonders if it is a trick of tears and imagination, but Guin is waking.

"Guin," Mom says softly. "Oh, honey. Oh, Guin."

"Guin!" Tania squeals. "Thank God!"

"And Goddess," her mother echoes automatically.

"What happened?" Guin whispers.

"The police said your brakes failed. It was during the storm. They think you hydroplaned and then your brakes wouldn't catch."

"I have been having some trouble with them for a while..." Guin says weakly.

"Why didn't you get them fixed?" Tania says.

"Not now, Tania. Everything's okay."

"How's my car?" Guin asks.

"Well, everything is okay, except the car. The cops said it's most likely totaled."

"Thank God the kids were at Pickle's mom's..." says Guin with an exhale of relief.

"Guin?"

"Pickle," she sighs.

He puts the coffee down hastily and runs to her side.

"Come on, Tania," says Mom.

They go out into the hallway and Tania watches Pickle place his head on Guin's belly. She gently strokes his hair and Tania can tell he is crying.

"I hope they work it out," says Tania. "Did I just say that?"

"I can't quite believe you did," says Mom and laughs a little.

"Truth is, it's not the same without him around. If you tell him I said that, I will deny it," she points at her mother. Mom makes a zipping-up motion across her lips with her thumb and index finger.

After Pickle leaves, Mom says she's going out to get them some supper. Tania and Guin are alone.

"How are you feeling?" Tania asks her sister.

"Good meds," she says.

Tania suddenly, as much to Guin's surprise as her own, begins to cry. Large gulping sobs, wet and uncontrolled.

"What if you had died?" she squeaks.

"I didn't." She takes Tania's hand. "Come up here."

"I don't want to hurt you."

"Yeah, please don't," Guin teases.

Tania curls up close, not quite touching her sister for fear of hurting her. Her head is next to Guin's on the pillow.

"It's such a mess, Guin," Tania says softly.

"What is?"

"Everything."

"I know. Me, too."

The light is on the wane. The very last of this day. Ever. She feels Guin's hand close around hers. Their fingers lace.

Tania closes her eyes and discreetly sniffs Guin. The vary faint aroma of warm ketchup and French fries. She closes her eyes and basks in it.

Guin's accident has loosened something in Tania. She is unraveling—the tight coil is coming undone. All that was carefully and meticulously folded is reeling out. Loosened and blowing about.

She spends every moment of hospital visiting hours with Guin. She calls in sick to work, she gives away shifts. When she does have to work, she stays with Guin for as long as she can and then returns as soon as her shift is over. Mom is there as much as possible, too. But not as obsessively as Tania.

"Tania, I can tell something is wrong," says Guin again.

But Tania says nothing.

One morning she comes in to find Guin crying. Tomorrow Guin goes home. She is healing well. The doctors are happy with her progress.

"What's wrong?" Tania asks.

"I'm going home tomorrow."

"This is a bad thing?" Tania says, sitting down on the edge of the bed and taking Guin's hand in hers.

Guin laughs a little. "No. It's just...that when I go home, the problems all come back."

"Tomorrow makes six days—I thought you were eager to get home," says Tania.

"I am—I miss my kids so much. I even miss The Grille and Creamery."

Tania feels a terrible and sharp tug deep in her belly. "Guin, you didn't do this on purpose, right? The accident?" she asks her sister.

"No! No, it's just...I've felt so lost lately and since I've been here, it's been, like, a little break. From all the stuff I sort of don't know what to do about. Now I have to go home tomorrow and it will all be there...waiting."

Tania sighs. "What is the stuff?" she asks.

Guin takes a deep breath. "I feel scared all the time, Tania. I can't breathe. I hang around in the hospital parking lot because it's one of the only places I can breathe. My stomach is always in a knot. Always jittery. I feel like the tension in my body," her voice breaks, "is what holds me up. I'm just a rag being carried along by the anxiety. The buzzing and humming of it." She sobs. "I'm so tired, Tania. I have so much to figure out and too much to do and never, ever enough time."

Tania says, "I know. I have stuff, too."

"Tania, what is it? Please tell me."

The warm tone of Guin's voice breaks Tania.

It is Shea and her vast love for him and her fear of losing him so she pushes him away which is counterintuitive, but there it is. And this terrible thing she has done with Thom. All the things she thought she could control but now knows she can't. She read Mom's diaries without asking and blamed Mom for everything. She found out who their father is and he's dead. She tells Guin everything she learned from their mother's diaries. And she got pregnant herself, didn't tell Shea, went to the clinic and had an abortion and drove herself home. And she thought she was okay, she thought she had it all figured out—turns out none of that is true. None of that is true. And she is lost, lost, too. And she is falling to pieces.

"Oh, Tania. Why didn't you tell me?" Guin strokes Tania's back.

"I don't know," she cries in her sister's lap. "It's like the words weren't there. Everything I've done in these last months—all these crazy things—I'm not even sure why."

The room fills with their tears, their sadness.

Mom comes in and stops abruptly when she witnesses both her daughters sobbing together.

"What is it?" she asks.

Tania and Guin laugh a little and Tania sits up.

In this safe circle with slow deliberation, both Tania and Guin find the words that have been eluding them.

"Did you want the baby?" Guin asks.

Tania shakes her head, "No. Not yet, but I thought it would be easy. Some great 'feminist expression' as if I weren't a person but a political argument to be won. I don't want a baby right now, but I didn't want to go through it alone." She couldn't say she felt a fool for allowing it to happen because to do so would be to pass judgment on her sister, her mother. She could not hurt them like that, and she was ashamed now to even have conceived such thoughts at all. To have imagined herself as better.

"You wouldn't have been alone," Guin says.

"We never talked about everything. You know, the diaries and Raine and Dave," Tania says to her mother.

Their mother takes a deep breath. "I always meant to tell you. I kept thinking the right time would come but it never did. I never set out to hide it—even though it appears that way."

"Mom, I'm sorry—for reading your diaries without asking. And for the way I treated you."

"I wanted you to think you came from something better than the betrayal of a best friend. I was ashamed.

Never of you," she touches Tania's hand and Guin's hair. "Only of myself. I thought if I kept the story simple and didn't talk too much..." she trails off. "Then time kept passing and I worried you would be angry that I had kept my story, your story, from you." She tells them that all the years piled up over the lie and she didn't know how to unearth it. "And then I was scared you would be angry that I had misled you for so long. All I could imagine was losing you girls to my dishonesty."

Mom explains that in the end she told Raine that Dave was the father; that she loved him. At first she thought it best to keep it a secret from Raine and Dave. But then she wondered if in telling the truth to Raine, the virtue of being honest would somehow exonerate her own actions. If not exonerate her, somehow render the whole mess less terrible, make the terrible thing less a betrayal. But Raine was destroyed and furious. It didn't turn out anything like Vivian thought it would. Or maybe exactly as she feared it would.

"But then some time passed, and Raine began to forgive me. Little by little. And she and Dave and I were trying to figure it all out. We were trying to form some kind of new family. We were starting to believe it was possible. That was the way Raine and I were—we believed anything was possible when we were together."

"What happened?" Guin asks.

She takes another deep breath. "They were driving too fast on 88 in Dave's Mustang and someone else was driving too fast in the other direction. Seat belts—we didn't really think about them in those days." She shrugs.

"I wanted to find her for you, Mom," says Tania. "You had this almost magical relationship with her. When I figured out about Dave, I felt betrayed for her. For me."

"I'm not proud of it, Tania. It was a huge mistake. But then I got you two, so how can I look back and be entirely sorry?"

"Oh, yeah, because having us made life so easy for you," Tania scoffs.

"I wouldn't change a thing," says Mom.

Tania reaches for her mother's hand. "I'm sorry. I'm just so sorry." Her mother holds her and Tania lets go of everything, abandons all of it, and cries into her mother's warm neck, the soft curls that have always been there.

Tania knows she has so much to fix, so much to confess and make right. She is scared. She must start with Shea. As she thinks about him, her phone signals a new text message.

She reads it and grabs her bag. "I have to go meet Shea," she says. She says goodbye and runs out of the hospital and to her car. Forces are converging and there is nothing she can do to stop or control any of it.

She has a feeling—she knows he knows. And she doesn't know what she will say. She has no idea how to undo the damage.

There is too much to say. She fears there are no words for it.

The message says: *Meet me at the beach. 20 minutes. Please be there.*

She is cold at once. This is not a good message. This is not how Shea expresses himself to her.

She speeds to the spot on the beach where she knows Shea waits for her. Her hands are freezing on the steering wheel even though it is August. She rubs them together. Her mind is rushing from thought to thought. What will he say? What does he know? She tries to calm herself. She tries to tell herself that this is not necessarily bad. But as soon as the thought forms, it is immediately countered, and she knows the second sentiment to be true. In her bones.

She bumps over the causeway. She parks and runs through the cord grass that lines the sandy path to their beach. She is out of breath by the time her pace slows at the end of the path that opens out to the wide sand and the endless ocean.

He sits in the sand, his long legs outstretched in front of him. He leans back on his elbows. He gazes out at the ocean, his face, from where she is standing, in profile. He is utterly serious.

"Hi," she says.

He turns his head slowly. And she sees that he is not so much serious as broken. And in that moment she is certain he knows.

"Hi," he says and stands. He stops a few feet away from her. "How's Guin?" he asks.

"Much better. She comes home tomorrow." She fights the urge to chatter, and waits for him to talk. Waits for the inevitable. Waits for the hammer to drop—hard and quick and finally upon her.

"Juliet told me. About Professor Clarkson," Shea says.

Juliet is Thom's wife.

"They're splitting up," he says.

Tania nods.

"You knew? Hmm," he snaps his head over and back sharply. "I guess that's no surprise."

Tears run down her face. "Shea, I'm sorry."

"That's it?" he says.

"I messed up. I'm sorry!"

"I love you!" he shouts. "You *messed up*?"

"There's so much, Shea. I love you. I love you. Please." She is sobbing.

"What are you talking about? You slept with someone else. What else is there?" he cries too.

"It's not that simple. Please, Shea!"

He shakes his head. "There is nothing more simple, Tania." The way he says her name is nothing like the way he usually says her name. The way he says it now sounds terrible. And she is scared. Struck numb yet tingling with fear. She has not been able to figure this out and doesn't know what to say to him. She considers frantically, and thinks there must be some perfect balance of revealing and concealing that will repair everything.

"Shea, I..." But she has no idea what it is.

She looks at him. He is torn up and raw—his eyes deep in his face, dark and sorrowful, red-rimmed. Suddenly she knows the only way to salvage this—if that is indeed possible—is to tell everything. To purge. Let it flow from her and see where everything lands.

She takes a deep breath. "In November, I discovered I was pregnant. This was long before...Thom. The thing with Professor Clarkson. I didn't tell you. I didn't tell anyone. I went to the clinic and I...had an abortion."

She watches as his face cracks a little. "Mine?"

She nods her head up and down slowly. "Yours," she whispers. "I thought it was the best thing to do. I thought it was what we would decide together anyway. It wasn't the right time for a baby, and so I just did it."

"Making that kind of decision without me is really fucked up."

She moves toward him, but he backs away. She drops her hand to her side.

"I made this choice, and I thought it was best for our future. But I felt so alone. And then I was so scared of what you would do if you found out. And I just started...I went kind of crazy. None of this is meant as an excuse, Shea. I'm so confused right now. But I know I love you. And I am *so* sorry."

He continues to stare at her. She can hear their breathing. The ocean crashes in between their breaths.

"Were you ever going to tell me any of this? If you hadn't been caught?" he asks quietly. He looks right into her eyes. She opens her mouth, but no words form. Her mind is stripped. Time ceases to matter. It ceases to move forward—time means nothing.

After a while he speaks. "I have to go," he says quietly. And he begins to walk away from her.

"Shea!" she calls after him. "Shea, please!" she cries. He does not turn. "I don't want to be without you!"

"You should have thought about that a long time ago," he calls back. He does not turn.

"Please, Shea!"

But he keeps walking.

She stands there for a long time. Then she slumps down into the sand and there she sits until the light begins to slant and an early evening chill across her skin jars her. She takes a deep breath, walks to her car and goes home. She doesn't know what else to do.

Tania is heartbroken.

She sits on the sun porch and sobs. Mom is still at the hospital with Guin. All Tania tells Aunt Anne and Grammy is that she and Shea broke up and they don't ask why, for which she is grateful. There is no way she could explain the murky details to these two elderly women.

Tania cannot stop crying. She checks her phone every few minutes to see if he has sent her a message. But she knows he won't. Yet, she can't stop herself from checking. Hoping. Finally her sobs subside and she feels scraped out. And exhausted.

"Come on, Tania. The best thing for a broken heart is busy hands," says Aunt Anne.

"I don't want to," she says miserably.

"Trust me. Come to the kitchen. I have a recipe for a broken heart."

Tania follows because she has no idea what else to do and she's too weary to protest.

"You need something warming and rich. Grab the canister of rice. That starchy Italian kind."

Tania goes to the shelf where they keep the big canning jars filled with beans and grains, all lined up. She finds a jar of pearly white, short-grained rice.

"This one?" she asks.

Aunt Anne peers at it over her glasses. "Yes, that's the one. Now measure me out one and a half cups."

Aunt Anne pulls out one of the bigger sauce pans. She measures in some water, pours in the rice, a stick of cinnamon that she pulls from a clear jar, a pinch of salt and puts it to the boil. Once it boils, she brings it down to a simmer. Tania watches as the water is absorbed by the rice.

"Now, milk. Can you get it from the fridge, honey?" Aunt Anne says. "One cup at a time now. Once one cup is absorbed, you add another. And some sugar—not too much. You want it lightly sweet, but not cloying. Now we wait and watch. Isn't it nice and warm here by the stove? The nights are starting to get just a little chilly, have you noticed?"

It is nice and warm, and Tania gives the rice a stir now and then, and adds the milk when it is the right time.

"Oh! Vanilla—I almost forgot. A splash of vanilla. Take a little sniff while the bottle is open." Tania does. "It's a thing you should always remember to do with vanilla."

When the pudding is done, Aunt Anne tells her, "Finish it off with a generous splash of heavy cream and a big pat of sweet butter."

Tania pours a stream of cream in a circle over the pan. She watches the fat square of butter melt in. And she stirs it all gently.

"Let it sit for a few minutes off the heat and set a bit," says Aunt Anne. They are quiet. The kitchen is lit dimly by the light above the stove, scented by sugared milk, warmed cinnamon.

"You know, you get to the end of the day and the best thing to do is sit in that hour of amber light, just as the sun sets. You know, when the sky is all those hues of orange and pink—the warm colors—and just recall the good you did this day. It's the best thing you can do," Aunt Anne says. "I think the rice pudding is ready now."

They carry bowls of the steaming rice pudding out to the sun porch. Aunt Anne hands one to Grammy, who says, "Oh, lovely, Anne."

"Tania made it," says Aunt Anne.

"Delightful, Tania," Grammy says, after taking a bite.

Tania sits in the golden light and holds the bowl with cupped palms, enjoying the smoothness of the ceramic in her hands, the warmth it emanates. She takes a taste, and it is so good and warms her belly in a way that is greater than merely good food in a belly.

"Thanks, Aunt Anne," she says.

Aunt Anne only smiles.

Tania tries to think on the good of this day. Truth is good. She remembers for the first time in a while that truth is good. And she hopes it proves its goodness. There is nothing to do now but wait and see.

Tania cannot sleep.

She hears her mother come in from the hospital, get ready for bed. Then her door closes quietly. Tania is fine being alone tonight. Somehow that feels right.

She creeps out to the screen house. The mosquitoes have long since quit for today, but the world outside feels too big and wide and open this night. She prefers the containment the screen house provides. She can still see the ocean through the small mesh of the screens. She can still hear and smell the moving salted water.

The screen house is a great, lovely filter.

She pulls her legs up to her chest, perches forward on the edge of the chair. There is no relaxing for her this night. No rest. Nor peace. She closes her eyes and conjures Shea's face. The curves and contours. The textures. Every detail is there behind her eyes.

Is this all that is left? Is this—this image, as beautiful and cherished as it is—all that is left?

How could she have been so careless with his heart? So light-handed with his happiness. She should have treated him like glass.

It becomes too difficult to look upon the image of his face so she opens her eyes and peers out through the little mesh squares into the darkness. She can just make out the white of the breakers—their steady rows. Predictable and reliable.

She walks out of the screen house and the stars spread out farther than seems possible. She wanted to feel contained but now all she wants is to feel small. The night sky will provide. It will reduce, but expand her into the vastness of everything. Problems slightly absorbed, a little dissolved.

She closes her eyes again and turns slowly under those stars, arms stretched out away from her body.

She stops, opens her eyes and realizes that as sad as she is, as heartbroken, it is Shea's heart about which she worries. That is where her concerns lie. And it occurs to her that this is the most honest and authentic she has felt in a long time.

That stops her up short.

This is where we begin to find ourselves, she thinks, maybe. Maybe.

13

Vivian—Love and the Spirit

Vivian brings Guin home.

Guin's children bounce around her, jumping over and over, joy spilling, "Mommy! Mommy! Mommy!" They are little leaping bugs.

"Careful, guys," Vivian says. "Mommy still has a few boo-boos."

"Show me the boo-boos," says Ethan. Guin shows him the bandages on her arm.

"Gross!" he says gleefully and hugs her. With help, Guin carefully gathers the twins near her on the couch and they bury their faces in her hair, her neck. Guin closes her eyes and Vivian watches her breathe them in.

Tania comes out of the kitchen and tells them to come to the table for supper.

"I cooked!" she says.

"She found a recipe and made it herself," says Aunt Anne. "She wouldn't allow me to help."

"I'm getting good at this," says Tania.

After supper, Vivian helps get the little ones bathed and settled in bed. Then the women convene in the screen house.

Vivian never meant to have children when she did—this is no secret. She thinks that she would have eventually, had her life gone the way she planned: go to college, find the man she was meant to marry, teach. Have children. Be a teacher and a mom. But the idea of planning is only that: an idea. Sometimes life goes the way you imagined and sometimes it does not, and Vivian wonders how much choice we really do have.

Looking around the screen house this night, she witnesses the life she's built. This is the life she has created. And there is no doubt that it is good.

Guin and Tania giggle together about something. It makes Vivian think back to when they were little girls. Always with their heads together—strawberry blond curls and sleek deep-brown tresses. Entwined.

"Daughters are a blessing," says her mother, out of nowhere. She leans in close to Vivian and whispers the words. Vivian feels as though her mother has read her mind.

"What did you say?" she asks her mother.

"I see the way you're looking at them—your girls," she says. Her mother places her hand on Vivian's. "Daughters are a blessing," she says again.

Vivian smiles and places her other hand over her mother's.

They stay out in the screen house long past the time when the mosquitoes fly. The elders head off to bed and Vivian and her daughters are left alone together.

"It's so good to have you home safe," Vivian says to Guin. But she is really speaking to both of her girls. Here, safe in this screen house—everyone together. *Everyone* as they know it: Vivian, Guin and Tania. It was so much easier in some ways when they were small and she always knew where they were—when they were always near her. The thing they don't tell you is that the letting go is terrible. It is just about the worst thing a mother has to do. All those years when they were small and needed her so much, the weight of it simply wore her so thin she thought she might not survive it. And now, the need lifted gradually over the years, it is easy at times for Vivian to feel like too much of a husk.

"Listen," she says to her girls. "I think it's time to tell you everything about your," she pauses because the word feels so strange in her mouth, "father. And my friend, Raine."

Guin and Tania turn to her.

"I loved both of them. I think we were on the verge of creating a new kind of family for all of us." She shakes her head a little and is surprised by her tears. A small sob escapes. The feelings are more raw than she might have imagined. Even after all this time has passed. There are things that are difficult to say. She has held much of this close to her for so long. She thought she could ignore the past—wipe it away and start with the birth of her girls. But the stories go back. And it is their story, too. She takes a deep breath and in the screen house this night, she tells them everything.

Coronation day nears.

This summer she has become a high priestess and a queen.

She stands in front of the mirror and turns around in her gown. She can't help but smile. She pulls another bobby pin from the box in front of the mirror and pins up another curl. She is testing out her outfit, how she will wear her hair when they are crowned. And she must admit, she is excited.

She told Frank that she confessed everything to the girls—Dave, Raine, all of it. They sat in his yard, enjoyed a fire and the stars. Good, cold beers.

"How did they take it?" Frank asked.

She tells him about Tania and the diaries. "She figured it all out. I was scared, Frank." She began to cry. "What if they had been so angry that they never wanted to speak to me again?"

He took her hand. "That didn't happen. Can you really imagine such a thing?"

Vivian didn't want to try. "I'm glad the truth has been told." She took a sip. "I kept this secret for too long. I didn't even know how much it was weighing me down. Or maybe I got used to its heaviness." When she shed that secret, some shame and unworthiness slipped off her, too.

"Frank?"

"Yeah?"

"I want to thank you for being there for them all these years. And for me. I don't think I've ever said that, but I have thought it many, many times."

He only squeezed her hand. What else needs to be said after fifteen years, twenty, going on twenty-five?

Just carry on.

"Are we really almost forty?" she said, her head resting on the back of the chair, her eyes resting on the Milky Way.

"Who cares," said Frank.

"Not me!" said Vivian. There is so much more life. There are so many more stories.

She hears a knock and goes to the kitchen, enjoying the velvet of her dress heavy and luscious around her legs. She opens the door and Frank comes in. He stops short and grabs at his heart.

"My queen!"

She rolls her eyes, but laughs. "Will you ever, ever stop being a dork?"

"No, m'lady. 'Twould be too much of a departure from the norm. Much too shocking for the masses. For my subjects." He bows deeply, then stands and holds out his hand to her, which she takes. "You do truly look lovely, Vivian," he says.

She looks again at her reflection in the mirror.

It is late summer and the Society will be reconvening in a few weeks. Frank is here for a fitting on his new costume. Over the years, Vivian has grown to be quite a good seamstress out of necessity by this hobby of theirs.

"Stand on the step stool, please," she tells him. She adjusts his outfit in a few places, sets pins where she needs to make slight adjustments. "Stop the fidgeting, Frank. Do you know," she pauses and looks up at him, "that I have to tell you that every time?"

"Many apologies," and he bows.

"Does the bowing help, do you suppose?"

"It doesn't hurt."

This summer passed quickly. She cannot recall another summer quite like this one—so many changes. Similar to the first summer she shared with Raine. Big highs and deep lows and all of it somehow set above normality. Heightened, brighter. Too much and just enough.

It occurs to her that there hasn't been a storm since the afternoon of Guin's accident. She turns and looks out the window. Bright blue sky. Clear August blue. Almost September.

"All set," she tells Frank.

He faces the mirror and pulls her to his side. He shakes his head a little. "Can you believe it?" he says.

She smiles at him. It is a beautiful thing when someone you love realizes a dream.

Queen. High Priestess. Mother. Goddess.

"I'm going to stay here, Frank, and look after Mom and Aunt Anne," she tells him.

"The Universe has spoken?" he says.

"It seems the Universe has spoken."

"But what about *you*?" he asks.

She sighs, but not with sadness. "Some parts of life choose you. Then you choose from there. It's good."

Caretaker of Crones.

Her idea of *Mother* is expanding.

"You always find a way, Vivian," says Frank. "It's one of the things I love about you."

Vivian hopes so. Sometimes she thinks Frank has bigger ideas about her than actually exist. Or maybe he sees things in her that she doesn't recognize herself.

Maybe it's time for her to look harder.

"Thanks, Frank. I try."

And she does. One foot in front of the other. One moment at a time. This is how she contrives her life. This is how she writes her story. All the roles she plays. All the care she gives out. Heart and soul, love and spirit.

Love and the spirit.

This night a soft rain falls. It has been damp and cloudy all day.

The kind of weather mosquitoes adore. This night they swarm.

The elder women have gone off to the warmth and dryness of the living room with cups of lemony tea. Vivian, Guin and Tania sit inside the screen house.

"So, as it turns out, I'm going to stay on here and help take care of Grammy and Aunt Anne," Vivian tells her daughters.

They are quiet.

Guin speaks. "I'm thinking of getting a place. Maybe with Darlene, or on my own if I can swing it."

"That's great, Guin," says Tania. "I think it's time for me to figure out something, too. I've been looking in the classifieds for an off-campus apartment. Everything feels so out of whack right now." She shrugs. "Maybe a big change will be good."

"Yeah," agrees Guin.

It seems they have all been giving thought to the same thing in the confines of their own minds and hearts.

"It will be strange to be in different places," says Vivian.

The young women agree. In their hearts they feel it more than any are able say.

They are quiet for a while, each thinking her own thoughts. The ocean rushes in and flows out. The sound of water over the rocks is like music. A sound they know so well.

"It will be weird," says Tania finally.

"Kind of scary," says Guin. She sighs. "It all feels very big right now."

Neither Vivian nor Tania ask her what she is talking about. They understand. They know what she means is life—the balance of it. The choices.

The stories they all write.

No matter what happens, keep writing.

14

Guin—Something Like Hope

Guin and Darlene sit across from each other at Dunkin Donuts.

"I got a roommate," Darlene says today. "My cousin and her two kids. She just left her husband." Darlene shrugs. "A lot of that going around."

Guin recently told Darlene that she intends to get her own place. "Not that I think it wouldn't be great to live with you," she said last week at their table at Dunkin Donuts. "I just think it's time to be on my own."

Darlene put her hand over Guin's and smiled. "I understand. Really, I do."

"It's sort of a joke since I have no idea how to pay for all of it myself," Guin said.

"You'll figure it out—don't worry," said Darlene.

Today Darlene dangles a set of keys in front of her face. "My apartment!" she sings.

"Oh, Darlene! Congratulations." Darlene has been living with her mother since she left her husband. But it's not like Guin living with her mother.

"We are like oil and water if oil and water are a spark and leaking gas container," Darlene has said. "You're lucky to have a mother like yours."

"Yeah, I am lucky," Guin said and smiled.

"Are you going shopping soon?" Guin asks.

Guin and Darlene have joked about shopping the Martha stuff at Kmart.

"I'll wait until you find a place," Darlene says.

They open the morning newspaper and Guin and her friend look through the apartment listings. She looks for places in the city because the apartments are a lot cheaper than the places out near Grammy's. Guin has a red marker and circles the ones they think might be good. Darlene tells her which neighborhoods are good and which do not get a red circle. Darlene grew up here.

"Oh, no. Not that block. Actually—stay away from that whole street," Darlene says. "You want anywhere in the North End pretty much or the South End down near the beaches. But you've got to be a little picky down there."

Fear. Guin works not to allow it to crawl through her. She has not told anyone, but the day of the accident, when the storm consumed her, she was in the middle of a moment of collision between panic and elation. It all came together—the black clouds and driving rain and absorption in her newfound freedom and a consuming panic. A culmination of euphoria and desperation. All in a single moment when the storm crashed down on her old Subaru.

Fear is not what she wants as the basis of her story.

The way she has thought about her story until now has been a sort of waiting. Waiting for the life she wanted as if it would simply materialize with no effort on her part. As though that life were out there waiting for her to meet up with it. As if she could walk up a road as this Guin and meet up with another incarnation of herself, shake hands and walk right into that other Guin's life—that *out-there* life she imagines about now.

But the fear is what she must conquer over all else.

She has spent too much time butting up against it. The fear has become an embodied creature. Some *other*. It is with her always in some shape. At times it leaves her mostly alone, its back to her, turning its gaze upon her briefly here and there with a turn of its head and then a retreat. Other times, it lends her its full brute force. Affronts her body and mind, her very soul, with its wrathful attention. Its mean purpose.

She tries to outrun it.

But it is faster than she and possesses a greater stamina. So she must wearily succumb and be consumed until it decides to settle down to a simmer once again. Guin waits for its return, wary and tired.

Maybe this has been her error. The running and the acquiescence—the acceptance of the violence. Perhaps it is a power struggle which she has no way of winning. Maybe it's a matter of eliminating the struggle. Giving up her power, that is, which sounds counterintuitive. But fighting is not working.

It's like when she and Ethan are engaged—locked— in a battle. He is crying at bedtime and wants her to put the blankets on his legs, so she does and he kicks them off and then insists she put them back on. Then he kicks them off. They do this a dozen times. All the while, he cries. Finally he leaves the blankets alone. But he's not done. And he's still crying. Now he wants her to sing songs but every song she starts he says, "No, not that one," until she is out of songs in her repertoire. All the while, he cries. They do this a dozen times. Finally he settles on a song, so she begins to sing. After the first line, he says, "Start over." They do this a dozen times. All the while, he cries. Finally, he allows her to continue the song. Eventually he hushes as he clasps her hand. She watches his face soften, his eyes drift closed, and flutter open and drift closed. All the while she sings and strokes his hand. Finally his eyelids close and his breath slows, becomes even, smoothed-out. She slides her hand gently from his. She touches his hair, brushes her hand gently across his soft cheek.

She gives up all her power and lets him rant until he wears himself out. Until it's all spent. And it takes a little while and she must grit her teeth sometimes and she must draw upon every bit of patience she possesses, but it works if she does not insert her desire for power into the struggle. Before she figured this out, she would, in the best moments, attempt to reason with him and, in her worst moments yell, curse under her breath. She had to dig deep to the very bottom of her limited well of restraint not to squeeze or claw him. These are terrible and terrifying feelings to which to admit. They make her feel breathless with their depth of evil—that she could be possible of such treachery, such black vitriol.

Then she learned to soften.

Maybe this is what she must do with the fear. Not tense up against it. Take away its power by refusing to participate. Be steady, be still, stand fast and move through it slowly and little by little. Maybe it will go away; maybe it will dissipate slowly. Maybe she will make space for it in her body. Just like anything else, this is a place to start.

This is the starting point of a story written with deliberation. These are the *first* words, the beginning. Because the beginning can start anywhere along the line, and there can be more than one, too.

When she was in the hospital, she and Pickle spent one entire afternoon together. Vivian was at work and she finally told Tania to please get on with her life—"I'm better, really! Go to work," she assured her. And she and Pickle were alone for a long while for the first time since the break-up.

"I think I've figured it out," she told him. "Well, not figured it out, but figured out a starting point where we can start figuring it out." Her stubborn resolve to withhold answers from him shattered in the car wreck—she can see that there is too much to lose and it can happen too fast to cling to obstinacy.

He looked at her with confusion.

"I want a real life," she told him.

"What do you mean?" he asked.

"I mean my own little family together night and day. My own home—not a house, just an apartment is fine. My own pots and dishes, my own bathroom to clean. My own quiet when the day is done. You and me," she laced her fingers through his.

"I thought you didn't want me," he said.

"I never said that."

He stood and turned from her, paced around the room. "I don't know what you want, Guin. I want to do it, but I don't know what it is."

"I just told you."

"But how, Guin? How? Tell me how I'm supposed to do all that," he said.

"I can't do all that. I can't tell you and I can't figure it out for you, Pickle." This he must do himself if they were to grow, paced together.

"Why not? If you know then just tell me," he pleaded. "Please, Guin."

She shook her head. "I can't. I just can't." *This isn't mine*, she thought. *This is not mine to do—I am already doing my own work.*

"Please," he said again.

"You'll figure it out," she said.

He looked pained and afraid. "What if I don't?"

She could not say anything to that. It was too terrible to fathom. She shrugged. "I don't know," was all she said.

They sat in silence until the light in the room changed. A nurse came in to bring her supper and the mood was lightened. Pickle left then and she has not talked to him since. She is not sure how to feel about his absence.

317

She is equally used to it and hateful of it. She is waiting and yet moving forward slowly, tentatively. A part of her is standing still and another part taking small steps.

That is the key, she thinks. Small steps.

Today, Tania drives her to The Grille and Creamery. Guin is still not cleared to work or drive. But she does not go there to work. She goes there to tell Mr. Whiting that she will not be returning.

She walks in and everyone says hello—the waitresses and the regular customers who know her by name. She stops at the tables and tells her car wreck story as many times as she is asked. They tell her about the latest in their lives. They tell her they miss her. The other servers tell her it's not the same without her around. They ask her when she'll return and she doesn't know what to say, so she says she is not sure yet, and swallows hard at what she will be leaving behind. Leaving behind that which she never would have thought she would miss. But of course she will. Of course.

Mr. Whiting is in the tiny back office. It is not much more than a closet off the kitchen. It smells of food—whatever is being cooked. Breakfast, lunch or supper. She stands back a little and watches him. His back is to her and he looks at the computer screen, a spreadsheet of numbers. His pants are always a little too short and they hike up to the middle of his shins when he sits. His shirt stretches across the small of his back. His foot bounces a little on the floor. He removes his glasses and rubs his hand across his eyes.

"Mr. Whiting?" she says quietly.

He turns, "Guin! How are you?" He stands and puts his arm around her awkwardly. She flinches slightly—he's never touched her before. He's not that kind of man.

"Oops—did I hurt you?" he says.

"Oh, no. The arm is still sensitive, but it's better. Much better," she says.

"Good, good! We were all shocked to hear about your accident. Everyone was worried sick. All the regulars ask after you all the time."

She smiles and there is an awkward silence.

"So," he says. "Coming in to tell me when we'll have you back around here?"

"Well, no actually."

"Few more weeks?" he says.

"Mr. Whiting, I wanted to tell you that I won't be back."

He stares at her. "Not a permanent condition, Guin? I thought they were going to get you all fixed up."

"No, nothing like that. I've just had a lot of time to...think, and...it's just time for me to move on."

He smiles a little sadly. "We hate to lose you, Guin."

She realizes that in some ways she hates to go. Not just because she is a little scared to leave behind this place she knows so well, but because there is a lot more worth having here than she recognized. She thinks that maybe she knew it once, a long time ago, but she has clearly forgotten.

"I will miss it," she says. "But I'm thinking of going back to school. For teaching. I've always thought I would like that a lot."

"Well, good for you, Guin. You'll be hard to replace." He hugs lightly, for real this time.

They leave the office and walk into the restaurant. Mr. Whiting tells everyone that Guin is moving on to new things. He says—*new horizons!*—and everyone says *what?* at first then *good luck* and *we'll miss you.* And *you'd better visit.*

"I will. I promise," Guin says.

On the drive home, she is quiet.

"You okay?" Tania asks.

"Yeah. I am," says Guin. She really is. There is a bubbling in her belly and it's not fear or anxiety. It feels something like hope.

Guin and Darlene sit on the back porch at Grammy's.

"Wow—look at this view," says Darlene.

Darlene starts school in a couple of weeks.

"It's not too late to register, you know," she tells Guin.

"It's not? I haven't even applied or anything."

"Guin—it's community college. Anyone can go."

"Oh," says Guin.

Darlene pulls the course book from her bag and opens it to the young education program. "Here are some of the classes you have to take. This list," she points. "Go down there, Guin. What do you have to lose? I am going to drive you. Right now. Let's go—we're going."

She smiles. "Okay—let me see if Tania will watch the kids."

She goes up to Tania's room where she finds her sister cross-legged in the window seat, reading. How many times has she come upon Tania this way?

"Where are you going?" Tania asks her.

"Darlene is going to drive me over to the college so I can..." she pauses and wrinkles her face a little. *Am I going to do this?*

"Register?!" Tania yells and jumps off the seat.

"Um, yeah," says Guin.

"Yes! Yes! Go!" She follows Guin downstairs.

Darlene brings Guin to the financial aid office and the registrar and—suddenly—she is a student.

She marvels at the simplicity of it. One small step then another.

And then as she and Darlene walk back out to the car, they pass an office. "Career Center," the sign reads.

"Wait. What's this?" she asks Darlene.

"They help students find jobs," says Darlene.

Guin walks to a bulletin board where flyers with job openings are posted. There is one, printed on pastel paper, the letters typed out in bright primary colors. It is a preschool she saw down near the beach in the South End when she and Darlene were riding through the city looking at the different neighborhoods. It's called Spruce Street Nursery School. They are looking for a teacher's aide.

"I don't think that's a professional position, though," says Darlene.

"I know, but I'm not a professional person," says Guin.

"Yet," says Darlene.

"Right—yet," Guin smiles. "But that's why it's perfect for me." She touches the flyer. "Think I can take this?"

"I won't tell."

Guin removes the pins, folds up the paper and puts it in her bag.

When she gets home, there is a strange car in the driveway. It is an older model Volvo station wagon. Not ancient, she thinks, but not new, either.

Darlene drops her off and Guin goes inside. Ethan comes running to her. "Daddy's here! He brought us a new car!"

"What?" says Guin. Pickle walks into the kitchen. "What's going on?" she says.

"Can we go outside?" he says.

"Sure. Mom!" Guin calls out.

"Yeah?"

"Can you take the kids out back? I need to talk to Pickle," she says.

"I'm right here," says her mother. She smiles. "Go talk to Pickle. I'll watch the kids. Come on!" she calls to Ethan, reaches out and takes his hand. The twins toddle along with her.

Guin and Pickle go outside. He sits on the stone fence that borders the front yard. She sits down next to him.

"I thought a lot and I think I know what you were talking about." He pauses. "I sold the RV. I bought you that Volvo. I checked around and they say they're really super safe. For you and the kids. I got myself a little car, too. An old Toyota."

She is quiet and watches his face. She watches his hands. They are still and loose in his lap. His face is calm. A little flame lights in her belly. Her breath is catching slightly. But she is okay.

"You got two cars?" she says.

He nods his head. "Yeah. I got a job, too. Out at Stinson's Dairy. I deliver the milk."

"You deliver the milk?"

"Yeah," he smiles. "I'm really good at it, Guin," he says softly.

"I'll bet you are," she says.

"And I really like it, too."

She takes his hand. "I'm so glad. I'm so happy for you."

"I have money left over, too," he says.

She waits.

"We can go look for an apartment," he says. "I have enough for first and last rent."

She says nothing, just looks at him. She reaches out and pulls him to her. She hugs him fiercely. Holds on tight. Cries onto his shoulder.

"I figured it out, right?" he says.

She laughs and pulls back to look at him. "You did."

They kiss and he touches her hands, her face, her hair, as if he were dying of thirst and she is water. She understands as she touches his hair, his soft face, his lovely hands. She feels the same.

"I wasn't trying to manipulate you, you know. I just..." she stops because she can't quite find the words to embody the feelings.

"I know. Once I thought about it, I started to imagine what it would be like and then all the answers started to come—boom boom BOOM. It was so simple."

She is nodding her head up and down. She feels as though her smile might burst her cheeks.

"So simple," she says. "That's exactly right."

He pulls a key ring from his pocket. "Try it out?"

"Yes!" she says. She skips over to the Volvo. "I can't drive yet, though. Not for two more weeks."

"That's okay. Check it out and I'll take you for a spin. It rides real nice," he says. "For an older car, you know."

"It's just great, Pickle." And it is. The paint might be a little dulled, but the color is a lovely pearled oyster white. She can see through the window that the interior is fawn colored. It is a boxy station wagon—a car a mom drives. And she loves it. She opens the driver's side door and starts to bend over to sit down behind the wheel but then stops. There on the seat is a small box. Pickle comes up behind her and takes it off the seat. She turns to him.

"Pickle?" she says.

He opens the box and in the black velvet sits a ring. A perfect, round pearl in a gleaming gold setting.

She can say nothing.

"Guin, I want to know if you'll marry me," he says. "There has never been anyone but you for me."

All she can do is nod but she knows he understands.

"Yes?" he says.

"Yes! Yes yes *yes*!"

He puts the ring on her finger and they hold each other for a long time. She might never move again and that would be okay.

"So you want to go for a ride?" he says finally.

"Yes!" she says. So much *yes* today.

She trots over to the passenger side and sits down. She wiggles around and settles in. The car smells good— almost like a new car. She runs her hands along the cushions. She fiddles with the radio and CD player.

"No more tape deck," Pickle says. "Hey, I almost forgot—open the glove compartment."

She does and there is a CD with a bow taped on. She laughs. "*Journey's Greatest Hits*," she says. "What would I do without this?"

She opens it up and pops it into the player as Pickle backs the car off the crushed-shell driveway. She forwards it to track two.

"I love this song," Pickle says as the song begins.

"Me, too," she says and threads her fingers through his, aware of the ring on her finger.

Don't stop believing.

Guin meets Darlene at Kmart. She spots Darlene's car and parks right next to her. "Am I close enough?" she asks Darlene.

"Right up my ass," says Darlene. She gets out of her car and comes over to Guin's. Guin steps out and stands next to Darlene. "Fancy ride, sistah." She picks up Guin's left hand. "Fancy finger, too." She smiles.

"Ready to shop?" Guin asks.

"'Til I drop," says Darlene.

As they walk through the doors, Guin puts her hand inside her pocketbook and touches her wallet briefly. There is money in it. Actual cash that Pickle gave her and some from her final paycheck from The Grille and Creamery. She is not playing house today. She is not pretending which curtains she will buy, which color towels. She is buying these things—she is choosing.

It occurs to her that she hasn't thought about the hospital parking lot in a while. And even now that she can drive again, she doesn't think she will need to go there anymore. It's good to know it's there—but it's also good to say she used to sit in the hospital parking lot to breathe, but doesn't anymore. She wonders about those birds. Maybe they found a new place, too.

"My mom gave me her old pans and dishes and kitchen things. She doesn't need them now that she's moving in with my grandmother and aunt permanently," she tells Darlene. "Oh, look at this," she says, touching a set of place mats. They are hues of turquoise and celery green, the edges touched off by delicate bead work.

Darlene leans over and looks. "Get them," she says.

"I will," and Guin puts them in the cart. "I got that job. At the nursery school," she says as they walk up another aisle.

"No way!" Darlene stops. "It's all kind of, you know, coming together for you, Guin." She sighs and smiles. "Guin, listen—I'm really glad you stopped me that day at the beginning of summer." Guin senses she wants to say more, but sometimes it's hard.

"Me, too," she says. There is more she would like to say but the simple words will have to suffice for now. She believes she and Darlene will be friends for a long time and more words will flow when the right time arrives. She feels lucky and she knows it was not luck exactly, just a moment when she listened to that small voice inside her. Her instincts, she supposes. Intuition. Her mom would say it was the universe speaking to her.

No matter. It can be called by any number of names. She is simply glad she heard it—and that she listened.

She and Tania have been talking a lot about learning how to remember and let go, determining how to decipher. Tania calls it *filtering*.

"We have to figure out how to not let it all in—keep some of it out. Or at least let it flow by. You know, filter it," said Tania.

They walked along the beach together. The water flowed over the tops of their feet. When Guin is walking at the shore, she can never decide whether to watch the water flow over her feet, gaze at the horizon or at the expanse of the ocean itself.

"I never know where to look," Guin said simply to Tania. Tania looked over at her and nodded.

"I know," she said. "Me neither."

Guin was not sure upon what they had just agreed and she knew unflinchingly that it didn't matter. It could mean one agreed-upon thing or many things. The meaning can overlap.

"How do we filter?" Guin asked.

Tania shrugged. "I'm not sure," she said, and they walked along quietly for a while. "Maybe we just have to be a little more selective."

"Maybe we just have to be better about letting go," said Guin.

The light began its slant—that moment of the day when there is a subtle shift. One of those liminal moments like when the seasons change. Easy to miss but when you catch it, you can sense and see, hear and almost touch the movement between the moments.

"Filtering," said Guin. "I like that."

"Letting go sounds good, too," said Tania.

And they walked further into that slanted light, that liminal moment. That moment in between.

Now as Guin chooses the things to create her home— her own home—she prepares to take this big step. This big step that is scary and exhilarating in equal parts. She is breathless and filled up.

Guin takes a deep breath and she leaps.

"These are delicious, dear," Anne says to Tania.

"Delightful, honey," says Millie.

Tania has been watching the Food Network.

"It was one of those things from that Southern woman," says Tania with a half-full mouth.

"Oh, I've watched her—she makes good things," says Millie. She moves around the screen house pouring tea from her favorite china teapot. "Jasmine oolong," she says as she pours the amber liquid. It smells more like perfume than food, and the flavor is sublime, better than can be imagined even from the scent of it.

Tania likes to cook. Who knew? She often wonders.

Macadamia nuts, cherries, white chocolate in a soft and chewy buttery crust.

"And they're still warm," says Guin, swooning.

"That's the only way to eat them," says Anne.

"You did these all on your own?" says Vivian. Tania nods affirmatively.

The mosquitoes move thickly through the twilight. The women can hear them. Or maybe they imagine so.

Light the tea tree oil candle. Sit safe inside.

15

Tania—Build the Woman

Tania has given up reading the diaries. It has come to feel like too much of an intrusion. It always was; she simply refused to acknowledge it. But now she does.

She packs up her room. She is moving next week and must put all her things back in boxes again. She found a group of girls who need one more roommate in a big, old house they rent down by the harbor in the city.

"It has a widow's walk," Tania tells everyone. "There's a view of the harbor from every window up in there." It's amazing. Not that she doesn't have a lovely ocean vista here, but she imagines sitting up there in that widow's walk with a hot cup of coffee and a book, all that glass suspending her above everything.

It's going to be beautiful when it snows, she thinks.

She brings a box up from the garage and starts to pack her mother's diaries and notes. She does not regret that she read them, but she is saddened by her dishonesty.

Tania dreams of Shea. Often.

One morning, she wakes from an especially vivid dream of him. So visceral that when she wakes, she feels almost sick from the want of him.

In the dream, they are in a strange house in which they seem to be staying for a period of time, although she is not sure why. She follows him around the house making small talk and he's not ignoring her, but he seems very busy. He is moving bags around. She doesn't know why or what they might contain. She throbs with the need to touch him. She wants to feel his body near hers—it is an absolute ache. Then he takes her by the hand and tells her he still loves her. And in between each of the words, he kisses her lightly. Her dream body responds to it as though it were real.

I...

still...

love...

you...

Accompanying each kiss is a hot flicker deep in her belly.

The dream, the feelings it evokes, stays with her all day, like a specter following her. A dream hangover is what Guin calls it.

"Oh, you're having a dream hangover."

"It was so *real*. I could feel it. All of it. I was so happy for a minute until I realized that it was only a dream."

"Oh, I hate that," says Guin.

Every morning, Tania wakes up and for a moment everything feels normal until the remembrance of her distance from Shea hits her hard in the stomach. And she must lie back on the pillow and breathe slowly until the throbbing ache subsides.

In returning to honesty, she has discovered a new facet: that honesty is reality as it is, not as she wants it to be. Not some ideal. This is where she must begin. The first page, the opening words of her story. And she must ponder the new and hard-learned knowledge that she will never possess all the answers. She can only hope to find her own. That might be the most honest she has ever been.

Tania needs to begin exactly where she is.

She carefully places the diaries and the notes in the box.

She finds a lavender colored envelope on the floor. She opens it. It crackles.

March 12, 1989
    Dear Vivian,
    I'm sorry I haven't called you back. I know you've called a hundred times. I'm trying really hard to deal with this. Dave and I have been talking a little. I know it makes no sense that I would talk to him and not you. And I know it's not fair. Which is why I'm thinking about this. I don't ever want to be like everyone else, I guess.
    Dave says that even though this is really messed up and what you guys did was wrong, this is more than just the three of us. He says maybe we can try to be a family. Like me and you and Dave and the baby. I mean, not like <u>*you and Dave*</u> *exactly—I can't really do that, Viv, I'm sorry. I mean, maybe we can make it work. I think, you know, just* <u>*love*</u>*.*
    I'm trying.
    And I love you no matter what has happened. Even if I'm mad and, I don't know—I think we should try.
    We're going to Providence today to hit the good record shops. Maybe I'll find some rare forty-five for you, Gypsy!
        Love your friend,
        Raine

Tears fall from Tania's eyes. There is a deep sense of loss in her heart. She realizes it would have been a different story. Although she doesn't want a different story than the one she has, it's nice to know there was more, even if she never knew it. Its cosmic presence, its spiritual existence is something real.

That is an idea she knows her mother would love.

Tania goes to school to register for fall classes. She is both nervous and hopeful at the prospect of bumping into Shea. But she doesn't and then feels only disappointment. She thinks about the stories that emerge as she moves around the green campus. Who she thinks she is is only a story—a story that has been running her life.

There can be another story.

She decides on a slow cup of coffee. She sits in the coffee shop near campus, indulging in her wicked—but hopefully not conspicuous—habit of eavesdropping. A middle-aged couple sits at a table next to hers, their conversation intense and serious. Snippets glean trouble with a friend or maybe an adult child; she's not quite sure. Two women sit across from each other, a cribbage board between them, cards in hand. A man and woman come in together, get coffee. They go outside to smoke, return, sit down without removing their coats. The woman makes a quiet yet terse phone call on her cell, then snaps at the man to follow her out. Two women sit across from one another, open laptops in front of each, over which they speak lightly and laugh easily. All those words that seep, slip and drop, plummet and topple from their mouths, dissipate into the air, rendered into the sunbeams teeming with dust motes. Dissolved.

The sounds of words, round and heavy, fade, but their meanings remain to form relationships. One by one, layered bricks. Words, too, build individuals. Every thought, every interaction—building. They create irrevocable change, for good or bad. Their sounds disappear, but their essence endures, informs, creates, destroys. Consciously, subtly, unconsciously, indelicately. Words are not vapor.

Words forge meaning, articulate context, content, nuance, symbol. These words built her, continue to assemble and shape. She cannot compartmentalize the elements that comprise her. She defies categorization. Daughter, sister, granddaughter, niece, twenty-two years old, student, supermarket cashier, friend, girlfriend, cheat, woman trying hard to change. Woman full of hope. She is not one of these—she is all of these. A singular, irreproducible coalescence. Built from words and stories: words she's shared, stories she has been told, stories she tells herself.

Tania's work is to create context, to assemble order. To proscribe disappearance. Take the words, arrange them, ground the individual, forbid the words to dissipate into the sun beams. Build the woman.

Tell her story.

Tania helps Guin with her packing.

"God, you have, like, a ton more than I do. Obviously," says Tania to her sister.

"Ugh...it's miserable, isn't it?" She folds yet another teeny item of clothing into a box.

"So," says Tania, hedging. "I tried to call Shea today."

"You did?" says Guin. It is no secret that Guin wants Tania to fight for Shea. Tania intends to, in spite of the deflated feeling that hers is a lost cause.

"Yeah. He hasn't called back, though."

"Well, he might be busy and it hasn't been that long," says Guin.

"You don't need to try and make me feel better, Guin. I know I don't deserve anything from him."

She wrote him several letters, too. She didn't try to explain or make excuses. She simply talked about how much she loved him, her sorrow at her actions, her knowledge that he deserved better. She followed it up with her thoughts and promises on the future, should he give her a chance to have one with him.

Oh, she hopes he will give her that chance. She wants it more than anything.

She has to work not to dwell on the aching remorse, the lamentation that leaves her breathless.

Guin pulls Tania to her in a hug. "I hope so much that it works out, Tania." She pulls away. "Don't be mad at me..." she says shyly. "But I sent him a letter, too. Just a simple card. I told him how much we all love and miss him and that I hope you guys find a way to work it out. I told him how much you love him. That's all. Don't be mad."

"I'm not mad. Thank you. That was sweet."

Tania goes down to the kitchen when Aunt Anne calls to her.

"We need to make a few more suppers together before you move away to your new home."

"What will we make tonight?"

"Corn chowder. I picked up some Silver Queen."

It is late August and the Silver Queen corn is finally ripe. First fry up a few slices of bacon in some olive oil. Once it crisps, remove it to drain on some paper towels. Diced sweet onion, very small diced red, yellow and orange peppers. Strip the corn from the cob and add it to the pot.

"Really scrape it down—get all that milky juice. That sweet starch," says Aunt Anne.

Sprinkle over some flour, pour in some chicken broth. Cover the pot and let it bubble and thicken. Slow drizzle in a good cup of fresh heavy cream, drop down the flame and let it simmer. After a little while, add in some freshly shredded mild and creamy cheese. Stir it in and watch it melt. Salt and pepper it.

Just as the kitchen is smelling too good to be true, Tania hears her phone buzz a text message.

Would you meet me at the beach later? I think it's time to talk. 8:00.

She can't move or breathe.

"What is it, honey?" says Aunt Anne.

"Shea wants to talk," she says.

Aunt Anne smiles.

"Guin!" she yells, pounding up the stairs. "Look!" She shows her sister the text message. Guin grabs her and they squeal and jump.

"What are we—cheerleaders?" Guin laughs.

"Oh, gross. Cease immediately." She falls back on the bed. She is too afraid to hope and she can't help but be filled by it. She is bursting with hope.

"I hope I can say the right thing," she says to Guin.

"There's no right thing, just speak from your heart."

Tania nods.

What will her heart say? *I love you* is all she can think of. *I love you, I love you, I love you.* Will it be enough?

The time comes to meet him and Tania walks over the causeway, through the path of cordgrass and there on the beach, he waits.

He turns to look at her and in his eyes she can see the possibility that everything might be okay.

She takes the final steps over the sand and closes the gap between them.

After Labor Day, they dismantle the screen house and store it in the garage for the winter. Otherwise, the salty air will grind it down to nothing but a pile of rust.

"I hate to see it go every year," says Millie.

"It's the symbol of it," says Anne.

"It means summer is over," says Millie.

"I like winter," says Tania. "I like the cold on my face. I like the way the sun looks at sunset—the sky all purple. I think winter sunsets are prettier than summer sunsets."

"I really love fall," says Vivian.

"But it's sad to watch it get all packed up," says Guin.

They sit on the porch and watch Pickle and Frank laugh and talk as they take the screen house apart like a puzzle. Tania imagines the possibility of Shea being here helping next year. She tugs her hair twice, knocks on the wooded side of the porch. She crosses her fingers.

Guin and Tania will be moving to their new homes this week.

The men move the parts of the screen house to the garage. The women gaze out at the ocean and one by one, their gaze moves to the place where the screen house was. A giant ring imprinted in the sand containing hundreds of footfalls. The imprints of their feet.

The screen house gone—the giant ring remains.

THE MOSQUITO HOURS

ABOUT THE AUTHOR

Melissa Corliss DeLorenzo earned a Bachelor of Arts degree in English Literature from the University of Massachusetts and a Masters of Fine Arts in Creative Writing from Naropa University in Boulder, Colorado. She served as Senior Editor for Her Circle Ezine, an online journal of women's arts, literature and activism. She writes, unschools her kids, blogs, practices yoga, reads too many parenting books—mostly in her kitchen. Melissa drinks matcha green tea lattés. She loves them so dearly that she plans her day around drinking them, which is ideally between 2:30 and 3:00 in the afternoon. She lives in Massachusetts with her husband, son and twin daughters and is currently at work on several novels. *The Mosquito Hours* is her first published novel. Visit her at www.melissacorlissdelorenzo.com and follow her on Twitter @melcdelorenzo.

Made in the USA
Charleston, SC
01 May 2014